ECHO
THROUGH THE
STARS

JESSICA LYNN MEDINA

ECHO THROUGH THE STARS

THE ECHO SERIES BOOK ONE

Printed in the United States of America

First Printing, 2019

ISBN 978-1-7336145-4-2 (*paperback*)
ISBN 978-1-7336145-2-8 (*ebook*)

Library of Congress Control Number 2019931675

Rising Moon Creatives
St. Louis, MO

www.RisingMoonCreatives.com
www.JessicaLynnMedina.com

Editing by Marinda Valenti
Cover Illustration by Allie Preswick

For my parents, who always told me I should write.
I should have believed them sooner.

And for my love, for helping me to see the horizon.

CHAPTER ONE

The earth's ground level stunk of some horrid combination of rotting biofuel and stale mold. Avery ignored the temptation to let air in her nose, breathing instead through her mouth. The smell was unavoidable if you wanted to shop in the ground markets.

She only visited the surface once a month. And if she could afford to purchase more than a meager amount of supplies during those trips, she would go even less than that. Ground level wasn't exactly the safest sector in New San Fran. But if she looked people straight in the eye and stayed on the main street, nobody would bother her. Despite Gran's reluctance, Avery didn't need a chaperone.

Megan, on the other hand, probably needed ten.

"Oh, come on, Avery," Megan whined. "What's so bad

about trying to find the Underground?"

Avery rolled her eyes at the question.

"Don't be ridiculous," Avery replied, laughing as she focused on the rows of ancient herbs and oils lined up on the shelf in front of her. "You know the routine down here. Besides, I have to get the supplies Gran sent me out for. I told you that when we left Level 5."

"Yeah, but I didn't think you meant go to one shop and then leave." Megan pouted, reaching out to pick up a pack of herbs. Her petite nose wrinkled as she smelled it before placing it back on the shelf. She nervously glanced over her shoulder toward the back of the stall where the owner, a balding man with a large snake tattoo covering half of his face, watched them closely. "And it smells weird in here."

"It smells like that everywhere," Avery replied dryly, sinking to her haunches to peruse the lower shelves. The little apothecary was pretty average for businesses on the ground level of the city. It was rudimentary, sure, but so was everything down there.

In the ground markets, owners could do business without the worry of government interference, which meant they didn't bother adhering to Federation regulations. The products they supplied were rare, high quality, and probably illegal. They were also the best in the city.

"If I have to spend my break carting you around the lower levels," Megan said as she dropped beside Avery, "then you owe me. I want to go to the Underground."

"You wish," Avery murmured, grabbing a bottle and stuffing it into the bag that rested low on her hip as she stood.

Doing her best to ignore a sulking Megan, Avery smiled politely at the snake-tattoo man as she approached him. He held out a clear tablet and jerked his head toward the screen in what Avery could only assume was an indication for her to pay. Deftly touching her wristport to the screen, Avery withdrew the credits from her account.

With Megan trailing behind, Avery ducked under the stall flap and into the street, looking to the sky above. No matter how many times she ventured to the ground level, she still marveled at how far below they were. The city rose above them for miles, lanes of cruisers on each level zooming over their heads at speeds that shouldn't be safe for such close proximity.

"Are you just going to ignore me?" Megan said, planting her hands firmly on her hips. A few people eyed them, her white miniskirt not exactly blending in with the usual custom of dirt and grime. Not for the first time that day, Avery was happy that she had worn sensible, soft pants and a tank.

"I'm not ignoring you," Avery said, moving past her to walk down the road lined with merchant stalls. They still had to grab the custom order from the hardware shop.

She wouldn't have to visit the markets at all if the pharm tech stores weren't so blazing expensive. It was ridiculous how many credits the government charged for healing supplies. Gran had been smart to open her own apothecary in one of the upper districts.

"Come on, Avie," Megan pleaded, following Avery into another shop. "It can't be that bad. Everybody at university has been. They say you can find the best Echo food in the city down there."

"Is that supposed to tempt me?" Avery asked with a skeptical look. "If you think this place smells bad, the Underground is going to be ten times worse."

"How would you know?" Megan scoffed, following Avery

to the back of the shop. "I can't go back without at least seeing it. Don't be such a white dwarf."

Avery ignored her, touching her port to a control panel by a lockbox built into the wall. She heard some shuffling from the back before it opened. A small box sat there, Gran's name printed across the top. Avery grabbed it, taking her time stuffing it in her bag along with the other supplies.

In truth, Avery wouldn't know anything about university, considering she hadn't been accepted. Connections were the only way to secure advanced education beyond what the government provided. Either that or loads of credits to grease the wheels. And Avery had neither.

Megan's family, on the other hand, had both. The Federation's requirement for public schooling had thrown her and Avery together as kids, and they had been inseparable ever since Megan punched Linden Cramer when they were six for calling Avery's freckles an ugly star system. Megan's family had already pulled strings to get Avery into the same school for secondary grades. There was no way they could get her into university, too.

But even without her family's money, Megan would have been able to secure a sponsorship. She had a habit of using her looks to hide her intelligence, but Avery knew how smart Megan really was. Living in the shadows of two older, incredibly successful brothers had driven her to act out in unconventional ways.

Like wanting to spontaneously venture to the Underground.

Avery had lived her whole life on Level 5. Just her and Gran for as long as she could remember. She had never been off world. Never been out of the city. Moon above, she hadn't even been above Level 13. Her life was one big lump of disappointment, mostly in herself for not being able to do anything about it—the way Megan could.

Avery's wrist suddenly vibrated, and a notification in her ear announced an incoming message. She flipped her wrist over, the internally planted screen illuminating her skin as text flashed across in faint blue lettering. It was from Gran.

Where are you? Come home—I just got a call and need those supplies asap.

Avery tilted her wrist back down to deactivate the port, neglecting to respond. She wanted to stay out just a bit longer. Gran wouldn't try a vid comm for at least another half hour.

Gran had raised Avery from a little girl, all by herself, and it hadn't been easy. They weren't scrounging around eating slop handouts at the kitchens on the ground level, but there had been times when they had scraped by. They had enough to keep them happy and healthy, however, and Gran was always quick to remind Avery of that.

Dreaming about university or living on an upper level was just a waste of time. In this world, you were born into the level where you would die. So in the spirit of practicality, Gran had been training Avery to take over her practice. Not that Avery was doing a very good job of it so far. She was probably the worst chemist this side of the Pacific.

Maybe trying something a little out of her comfort zone would be fun.

"How can you even eat that off-world stuff?" Avery asked as they made their way back outside. Just the thought of the traditional foods from the sister planet across the Gate made her stomach cramp.

"Does that mean you're considering it?" Megan grinned,

her blue eyes flashing.

"Look, Miss Level 10, you do know that it's not safe down here, right? And you're not exactly blending in with the locals," Avery added, eyeing Megan's pristine outfit and white platform boots.

"But that's what I have you for!" Megan was nearly bouncing on her toes as she reached out to grab Avery's hand, starting to drag her toward the back of the market street.

Avery looked around, ignoring the stares from a few people browsing the outdoor vendors. "How do you even know where you're going?" she asked, anxiety tickling her chest. She had never been this deep into the market stalls. "Maybe this isn't such a great idea."

"You know my dad has a big story to cover on Echo in a few days. My parents are turning it into a family vacation. You should come," Megan said cheerfully, pretending not to hear Avery and looking around at shop signs. "Maybe it would help you get over your complex about New Earth stuff."

"This is about getting robbed, not my aversion to Echo," Avery replied, keeping an eye on the few people milling about. Still, she didn't like the idea of being small-minded. Sometimes it felt like Megan intentionally tried to point out the differences between their lives. "It just weirds me out. The whole jumping through the Gate thing . . . they say you get time sick like nothing else. It's even worse than hyperspeed."

"And what would you know about hyperspeed?" Megan laughed. She turned to look at Avery, adding in a gentler tone, "I thought you wanted to get out of here."

"I do," Avery admitted with a short laugh, pulling Megan along this time. Anything to distract her from this awkward sincerity. "But . . . I mean that I want to get to the top level or see another continent or something. Not—" Megan yanked on her hand, pulling them to a stop. "What?" Avery asked.

"This is it," Megan said reverently, staring at a door half-hidden in shadows behind a front market stall. A blue neon sign stuck out above it that read *Akhaten Cantina,* a small icon of a star pulsing beneath. The entrance was in some old bar?

As many trips as she had made to ground level, Avery never had the guts to venture to the Underground areas. The Federation didn't have much presence on the ground level, and beneath the surface they were practically nonexistent. But they did conduct the occasional raid. And getting caught in an illegal sector was . . . better not to think about.

"Let's go," Megan said quickly, dragging them forward and opening the door, blonde hair spilling over her white jacket. Avery stared at Megan's hair with a pang of longing. Her own hair was flat and brown with just an offensive tinge of frizz. And then there were the freckles.

And not freckles in a cute way. Freckles in a "Hey, what's that on your face?" way.

Adjusting to the darkness, Avery gasped as she realized it wasn't a bar at all. They stood on a grated walkway that circled the edge of a wide chasm. Stairs spiraled downward, disappearing into the blackness below. The door slammed shut behind them with a heavy thud, and Avery jumped, reaching out to grip the grimy railing. It was ironic that a girl who dreamed of living on the upper levels was afraid of heights. One of the many ways fate had decided to screw with her.

"I don't think this is such a good—"

"Stop saying that," Megan said with a roll of her eyes. "Besides, it's too late now." She grabbed Avery's hand, hauling her across the metal and down the stairs, deeper into darkness. "Torch on," Megan's voice echoed around them, her wrist lighting internally to cast a dim glow on the stairs.

Avery swallowed her fear, refusing to admit they were in over their heads.

It didn't take long before they reached the bottom. A warm yellow light beckoned them toward a wide-open doorway. Megan turned her wristport off, grinning at Avery as her feet carried her faster toward the sounds of the Underground ahead.

The doorway opened into a cavernous space with a high-domed ceiling, lit by three artificial suns floating above the crowds. People bustled around them as vendors yelled out their prices to passersby, customers haggling just as loudly for the best prices. Avery's craned her neck, trying to take it all in. There were so many people.

She realized too late that she had breathed through her nose. But it was the savory smell of a meat stall that drifted deliciously through the air, contrasting with the sweetness of a nearby bakery that promised fresh breads and pastries.

Megan gasped, her face excited as she took it all in. Avery couldn't keep the smile from spreading across her own. The energy there was palpable.

"Told you." Megan grinned, reaching out to grab Avery's hand again. "Let's go get one of those meat pies."

They moved throughout the market, the concrete streets weaving in an impossible maze between the many shops and stalls. There were more options available there than even the ground markets could provide. And the vendors were much more willing to negotiate, as Avery found when Megan haggled for a piece of Plutarian jewelry. They could easily make a good profit if they began to purchase supplies in the Underground.

But Gran would never allow it. If she knew Avery had ventured this far below, Gran wouldn't let her leave Level 5 for months. But it seemed to be even safer than the ground level. They'd even seen a few other people who were clearly high-level dwellers, if their clean clothing was any indication. Maybe Gran just didn't know what it was really like down there.

"Moon above, did you see that?" Megan squeaked, her eyes fixed on a tall girl who passed with hair shimmering pink even in the dim light. No one on Earth wore anything but natural enhancements. Strange-colored hair, eyes, or skin markings— that was only seen on Echo. She was a Native.

Megan darted off, her boots bouncing delicately across the cracked pavement as she followed the girl through the crowds.

"Megan!" Avery called, trying to give chase. She pushed frantically past people, her eyes searching for a glimpse of platinum hair. It might have seemed safe, but Avery knew Megan shouldn't go off alone. Neither of them should.

Suddenly, someone collided with her shoulder, swinging Avery around hard as she fought to regain her balance. Large hands grabbed ahold of her arms, keeping her from falling ass-first to the ground.

"Sorry." The murmured apology drew her gaze upward, and Avery was caught off-guard by the blue-gray of his eyes, like clouds on the verge of an acid storm. Full lips pulled into a grin as he added, "Maybe watch where you're going next time."

Avery blushed, eyes widening as she jerked away from his grip. He shrugged, winking at her as he turned to keep running and disappeared into the crowd.

"Maybe *you* watch it!" she called after him, but he was gone.

"Avery!" Megan clutched her arm, startling her.

"Where the blazar did you disappear to?" Avery frowned, pulling her arm away. "You can't just run off like that. You scared me!"

"Do you know who that was?" Megan breathed, looking as though she was about to tear off into the crowd after him. "I heard he was in town for some press thing, but what was he doing down here?"

"What?"

Megan's head swung back around to look at Avery. "What did he say to you?"

"Who?"

"Finn Lunitia!" Megan nearly shrieked.

"Who?" Avery asked incredulously.

Megan rolled her eyes. "Seriously, what *do* you do with your free time? He's like, famous." At Avery's blank expression, she continued with a sigh. "His family is the face of the Armistice or whatever. Not only that, but he's rich, politically connected, and did you check out that body?" She smirked, looking back the way Finn had left.

"Okay, I've heard enough," Avery said, laughing.

Before Megan could reply, the crowd rapidly thinned out. The two girls looked around as vendors closed their shops, locking their wares and disappearing from sight. They shared a confused look, and Megan clung to Avery as they were pushed along with the crowd.

Already there were few people left in the square around them. The market had all but cleared.

"Megan," Avery said warily, her voice shaking. Something was off.

Suddenly, a group of Federation soldiers barreled past, the blue of their uniforms striking against the muted tones of their dirty surroundings. Avery cowered back, fear causing a sickening drop in her stomach. But they ran on, barely sparing the girls a glance.

"Time to go," Megan said, and they broke into a sprint, hastily retracing their steps to the entrance and the safety above ground.

Shit. Shit, shit, shit.

Finn tried not to panic as he ran through the abandoned streets of the lower levels, sprinting to his ship. He had thought he would have more time before the Federation noticed he was missing. At least before they could track him down.

He rounded a corner, nearly doubling back as he tore up the open platform into the ship's main cargo hold. His feet clanged across the metal grates, his breath coming in short pants from the exertion. Taking a last look behind him, Finn paused to initiate the ramp closure with a tap on his wristport before resuming his climb.

The blow to his face came swiftly and without warning. His head swung around from the force, the tang of warm copper invading his senses as his mouth filled with blood. It was only quick reflexes that allowed him to stay on his feet. Bracing himself for the imminent onset of pain, Finn whipped his head around to confront his assaulter with a glare. His fist clenched.

"I wouldn't if I were you," a calm voice delivered the warning from somewhere in the sea of Federation soldiers lining the open hull of his vessel. They had been waiting for him.

The one who had punched him stood close, presumably waiting for him to try something. His eyes scanned the ship, roving the stairs leading up to the dark corridors of the second level. Except for the dozen or so soldiers in front of him, it was empty. They couldn't have been there long.

At least he had gotten the droids out. Even if he couldn't complete the mission, their directive was clear. The information would get back to the others on Echo. To Nick. He would know what to do with it.

An officer stepped forward, his chest decorated in the ribbons of a long military career. Finn's pulse jumped. A captain with battle experience was too high-profile for a routine patrol squadron. This was no ordinary Underground raid—they knew his identity.

Well, at least that explained the blow to his face.

"You have probably guessed why we're here." The captain paused, typing on his wristport as he spoke, his fingertips flying across the skin. "That's good. I wouldn't want there to be any conflicts in the paperwork." He looked up at Finn with a placating smile. "Politics. I'm sure you understand."

Finn didn't respond. His mind was too busy calculating the distance to the nearest escape pod. They weren't intended for terrain use, but he could make it work. His whole mission on Earth was at stake if they took him into custody. He didn't have the necessary papers to grant him amnesty, and he was fairly certain Nick wouldn't be able to talk him out of this one.

"Now, what I want to know," the captain continued calmly, "is what you were doing with those droids?"

Finn's stomach lurched. He needed to change the subject, and fast.

"Do you have a permit to search my vessel, Captain?" With gusto, Finn spit out a mouthful of blood near the officer's feet. He could bluff his way out. Wiping his chin on a tailored sleeve, he added, "I'm sure Minister Klein would love to hear that you've mistreated one of the faces of the Armistice."

The captain let out a bark of laughter. "Armistice? As though your pathetic little excuse for a rebellion on Echo could negotiate a treaty for peace. The Federation does as it pleases."

Finn's blood boiled, his clenched fists shaking. He wanted nothing more than to ram them into the man's smug face. Finn wasn't used to curbing his temper. His brother was the politician. Not him.

"So no," the captain taunted, "I don't think the minister will mind overly much. Particularly since she is the one who sent me here to fetch her little rogue celebrity. But then, I think you knew that, didn't you, Ambassador?"

Finn met the captain's stern gaze. Yes, he knew. As Minister of the High Council, she effectively controlled the entire Federation. And she kept everyone under her command on a tight leash.

"If I know your family," the captain drawled, "you weren't exactly acting in the interest of the government today, were you?"

So they knew Finn had sent out droids, but they clearly didn't know why. He was cornered, but not defeated. Not yet.

It was now or never.

He reached for the blaster strapped to his leg, shooting out the illuminations above them and making a dive for an open hatch in the flooring. Finn's shoulder slammed against the panels of the lower cargo area with a loud crash and a grunt of pain as he rolled into the momentum.

Pushing to his knees, Finn managed a few more blasts through the grates of the floor above, the loud fires echoing off the metal. He jumped to his feet, tearing down the corridor in a mad scramble.

"Activate pod twelve!" he shouted at the ship computer, his boots clanging. It was stifling in the lower compartment near the engines, his hairline coating quickly with sweat. He didn't have much time.

"Pod twelve activated," the computer echoed back to his mind, its system in tune with the frequency of his port. "Can I be of any other assistance? Your vitals are elevated."

"No shit," Finn bit out, rounding a corner and nearly slamming straight into the wall, the sound of a blaster close on his heels. There was no way he would make it to a pod in time to outrun them in in the city. Even if he made it out of atmosphere, there was nowhere to go.

He was going to fail.

Finn had risked everything for this idea. An idea that Nick had vehemently opposed. In fact, he had ordered Finn to forget about it. To attend his duties for the High Council on Earth, show his face to the media, and come home. And Nick had been right. As always.

But even if they killed him, Finn knew the data would still transmit. The droids would find the right gene sequence. That market had been full of refugees, running from the war-torn planet that had once been their home. With so many, one had to match. He just had to give the droids a little more time.

Now *that* he could do.

Finn stopped abruptly, turning to rest against a wall, the metal plating hot against his back as he focused on controlling his frenzied breathing. He braced himself, his blaster ready to fire at his shoulder, one finger hovering over the trigger.

If he was going down, he'd damn well take a few Feds with him.

CHAPTER TWO

By the time Avery and Megan climbed the stairs and ran back to the docking bay on Level 1, they were both shrieking with the exhilarating fear of being caught. Collapsing in a fit of winded laughter against Megan's silver-plated cruiser, they struggled to catch their breath.

"What is that?" Megan said suddenly, her voice still tinged with humor. Avery looked to where she pointed in the air behind them. A circular, white droid hovered, the blue ray of its sensor scanning the area. "Is that a Fed droid? Did it follow us?" Megan screeched as it turned the blue light toward her, moving closer.

"Get away from it!" Avery ordered, her voice rising quickly. It got a full body scan of Megan before she was able to jump back and run to cower behind Avery.

The droid zipped toward them with surprising speed. The way it moved almost seemed like Echo tech. There was no way the Federation would let this thing run free in an Old Earth city. Avery backed away slowly, Megan gripping onto her shoulders from behind as if Avery could protect her.

"What the blazar does it want?" Megan whispered in her ear.

No sooner had Megan asked the question than the droid scanned Avery, its sensors running down her in a fluid motion. The droid let out a few disconcerting beeps before launching itself out of the dock, into the open air beyond.

Avery ran after it, leaning over the edge of the walkway barrier to look up into the air traffic above. But the droid disappeared, too fast to follow. It was probably just a routine Fed scan. They were just searching for undocumented people running from the market.

Gran wouldn't be happy. She detested government observation. And as much as Avery believed it was some ancient ideal from the twenty-first century, Gran's paranoia wasn't entirely misplaced. The Federation controlled everything, and they certainly wanted everyone to know that. Going below ground had been a mistake.

"I told you coming down here was crazy!" Megan exclaimed, bringing Avery's attention back to the loading dock.

Avery raised her eyebrows, shooting Megan a look of disbelief. Like the Underground had been *her* idea. Right.

"What?" Megan asked, cocking her head as she ducked into the already open doors of her cruiser. "Let's just get out of here, okay?"

Avery's wrist vibrated. Gran was messaging her again. A wave of unease rolled through her gut as she gave one last look toward the exit.

"Are you coming or not?" Megan's voice carried up from the lifted door.

Shrugging off the feeling, Avery jogged back and slid into the passenger seat. "I am never going anywhere with you again," she said sullenly.

They eyed each other before breaking into another fit of loud giggles. They both knew that couldn't be farther from the truth.

"Where have you been?"

Avery was startled when Gran greeted her at the door. A worried look wrinkled her face that, for her age, was surprisingly devoid of many permanent lines. Tiptoeing around her, Avery gently dropped the bag from her shoulders.

"I was out with Megan. I told you she was back home for break." Avery did her best to keep her defenses from rising. Moving into the small living room, she set her bag down on the little table in front of their faded green sofa.

"Why did you ignore my comms?" Gran followed her, settling her hands on her hips in a stance Avery recognized from childhood. Avery's anger was quick to respond.

"We went for some food before she dropped me off," Avery replied cryptically, a frown creasing her face. Gran had never been suspicious of her activities before. She had never needed to be. "Why are you questioning me all of a sudden?" Avery asked, careful to keep any attitude out of her tone, but her temper was paper thin.

"I just needed those supplies I sent you out for. It was a rush request." Gran's gaze faltered. A small twitch, but Avery noticed. "Can you bring them in here, please?" Gran asked, moving to the small kitchen that doubled as her lab. Kitchen was a generous term for the room. It was more like a large closet with appliances and a sink.

Avery watched her grandmother disappear around the corner, one long, gray braid swaying softly against her back. Disappointing Gran was a constant fear. An inevitability, after today. Avery grabbed the bottles and headed after her.

Together they unpacked the supplies, securing them in vials and tucking things into the storage drawers lining the counter. The place was meticulously arranged, always in an ongoing experiment. Gran never stopped her work.

"So where did you girls go today, besides the apothecary?" Gran asked lightly. Avery didn't miss the thread of tension laced within her question. "Did you run into any Federals? I saw plenty of them out today."

Avery's breath caught in her throat. Gran couldn't know . . . but that was ridiculous. Of course she didn't.

"Nothing. I mean, nowhere," Avery corrected herself, leaning against the counter in an attempt to look casual. "We just floated around the levels to try out Megan's new cruiser."

"Are you sure?" Gran asked, peeking at Avery from of the corner of her eye, keeping her hands busy. "You didn't see any bots or anything?"

Avery was quiet. There wasn't any way Gran knew what had happened unless . . . no. There was no way Gran would track her. "Why are you asking?" Avery countered, her heart rate climbing.

"I have a right to know where you've been."

"Did you . . ." Avery started, pausing as she looked away. "Did you put a tracker on my port?" She asked, her voice tight.

"Calm down. It's not what you think." Gran's face proved her guilt as she took Avery's shoulders in her hands.

Avery felt her lip curl. "I can't believe *you*, of all people . . . ." She wasn't even allowed this anymore. Her own privacy.

"I just wanted to make sure you—"

"Make sure I what? When have I ever given you reason to doubt my actions?" Avery let out a little scoff and shrugged off Gran's touch. "This is blazing ridiculous. How long have you been tracking me?"

Gran ignored her question, reaching for her once more. "Avery, we have to make certain—"

"Make certain of what?" Avery spat, moving away. "The government isn't out to get us, Gran. The people who play nice with them? They do just fine. They get cruisers and go to university and have normal lives! I'm so sick of living like this!" She heard the hysterical shriek in her voice but couldn't bring herself to care.

"Don't speak to me with that tone, Avery Vey." Gran placed her hands back on her hips, straightening to her full height as her features solidified into stone. "You have to trust my judgment."

"Oh, because you seem to trust me so well?" Avery stomped off, heading for the sanctuary of her bedroom. Perhaps it was the stress of what she and Megan had been through, but Avery refused to acknowledge that. She held on to the anger, encouraging it to take over. "I'm nineteen! Well old enough to not be monitored! This is blazing ridiculous."

"Stop right there, young lady." Gran raised her own voice as she followed Avery out into the living room. "You haven't given me a chance to explain."

"Explain what?" Avery threw her hands out at her sides and turned to face her grandmother. "After all your lectures about privacy and maintaining your rights as an individual citizen, you turn out to be the one I should be worried about. What the blazar do you expect to find?" Gran didn't respond and Avery continued, too worked up to care about the consequences. "Yes, we ran into a droid today. Yes, it scanned me. Are you happy now? We also snuck into the Underground market and ate some food and then this guy ran into me and—"

"What did you just say?" Gran interrupted her, a horrified look on her face.

"I— I thought you knew we went—"

"Not that." In a moment, Gran was across the living room, her hands shooting to Avery's arms, gripping her so hard that she knew it would leave bruises tomorrow. "A droid scanned you? What did it look like?"

Gran's irritation deflated so suddenly that it took a great deal of wind out of her own sails. She responded hesitantly, "I— It was a model I didn't recognize."

Gran pulled away, a hand coming up to cover her own mouth as she let out a strained sigh. Avery's frustration was quickly melting into fear.

"Gran?" she asked. "What's going on?"

Her gray eyes moved to Avery, as though realizing she was still in the room.

"We have to get you out of here," she said quietly. Her hands balled into fists at her sides as she added, "Damn it, I thought we'd have more time. I should have come to get you as soon as I read your feed."

"What? Why are you acting like a paranoid loon?" Avery

asked with a slight laugh. "It was just a new Fed droid, I'm sure of it. Nothing is going to—" her words were cut off as a boom sounded at the door. The control panel exploded into an electric fire, the door sliding open violently. In the next second, dozens of Federation soldiers burst into the tiny space of their apartment, blasters raised and ready.

Avery barely had time to process, the shock so real that it felt like someone had reached inside her chest and forcibly stopped her heart from beating. She backed away from the soldiers toward the wall of windows that looked out onto the skyway. Gran moved in front, pulling a blaster of her own from the back waist of her pants. How had Avery not seen it tucked there underneath her shirt? Did Gran even know how to use a gun?

"Put your hands up where we can see them," one of the helmeted figures said, his voice automated from his protective mouthpiece. "Don't try anything, Dr. Vey," he warned.

"Avery, listen to me," Gran said under her breath as she backed nearer toward Avery, moving them both closer to the glass behind. "Take this." She frantically thrust out her hand, drawing Avery's attention to the small of her back. There was a data chip grasped between Gran's fingers.

Avery couldn't think, much less do as Gran asked. Her eyes flicked back to the soldiers, panic lancing her chest.

"Avery!" Gran said fiercely, drawing her granddaughter's attention back with a choked exhale. "Get away from here as fast as you can. Don't trust anyone," she whispered without facing Avery. The soldier began to press in closer. "I love you," she added desperately.

"Gran, wha—" Avery's words were stolen from her throat as her grandmother turned, the long, gray braid whipping around her in a wide arc. She heard the blastfire, followed by a waterfall of shattering glass behind her as Gran's fist slammed violently into her chest.

And just like that, her grandmother pushed her out the window.

CHAPTER THREE

A very plummeted through the air, her stomach lurching as the wind sharply whipped her hair around, stinging her face. Her arms flailed as she fell, any scream silenced by panic. She hit a soft surface and then bounced harmlessly until she landed on her back.

Avery let out a cry of surprise, adrenaline catching up with her brain. The hazard barriers had activated and caught her. Thank the galaxy! Blood pulsed in her ears as she lay there in a daze looking up toward the apartment, a gaping hole of broken glass where the main window had just been. She heard shouting. Blastfire followed, a rapid staccato in the night.

Shaking, Avery jerked her hands to grasp the barrier beneath her. She was lying on a safety bubble about five feet from the edge of the Level 4 sidewalk. She had to move. She had to hide from those Feds somehow.

Wobbling precariously on the edge of a drop that would send her straight down to ground level, Avery swallowed hard. She rolled to her hands and knees, clawing her way to the edge of the platform. Grabbing on to the sidewalk railing, Avery pulled herself up and over, feet landing firmly on the metal surface. Several people watched her with wide eyes. It wasn't like they saw a girl come flying out of a window every day.

Ignoring them, Avery quickly made her way toward one of the inner hallways. She trotted down the dimly lit corridor past a few shops, stopping at a public washroom. Ducking inside, she was thankful to find it empty as she barreled into a stall, the door sliding shut behind her with a soft swoosh. The door light turned red as it locked behind her, and she felt marginally more secure.

Avery rested her back against the wall, leaning her head against the cool, white metal as her ponytail dug into the back of her skull. She struggled to steady her breathing. Something sat heavily on her chest as she sucked in breath, tears threatening to escape. She let out a helpless whimper and squeezed her eyes shut in protest.

But the only thing behind her eyelids were horrible images conjured by her imagination. Gran being shot. Gran lying on the floor of their apartment, blood pooling around her. Gran gasping for breath. Gran dying.

So many shots had been fired when Avery had fallen. Even more as she lay there looking up at the sky on that hazard barrier. How could Gran be all right? Moon above, what was happening?

Avery covered her face with shaking hands, beginning to sob. She moved her hands to her chest, clawing with her fingers to try and settle the rapid beat of her own heart. She felt something hard there, digging into her skin. Wildly, she pulled at the neckline of the shirt, reaching under the edge of her bra.

The data chip. Gran must have slipped it in her shirt when she shoved her.

Scrambling, Avery turned her forearm over, brushing the chip against the reader embedded under the skin of her inner wrist. A message appeared, glowing blue in the darker lighting of the stall.

If you're reading this, we've been separated and there is no other way—you must get to Echo. I'm so sorry I couldn't protect you. Find a woman named Lissande Brinstal—she has connections in the capital and can help from there. I don't dare trust more information on this chip, but know that I love you. Be brave. Trust no one.

Avery's eyes devoured the message again and again. Her breath stopped, moisture beading on her eyelashes until her wrist was a messy blur of light in her vision.

Go to Echo? Impossible. She couldn't even fathom going to the upper levels, let alone another planet.

Avery gasped as her wrist began to heat up, pain searing as her veins filled with liquid fire. She gripped her hand, nails biting into her skin, willing the pain to recede. Her port lit up brightly before glitching with a jarring shock, leaving nothing but the unilluminated skin of her wrist in its wake, muscles spasming softly as the discomfort eased.

Horrified, Avery pawed the inside of her forearm, flipping her arm over in a panicked investigation. No matter what she tried, nothing could make the screen light up again. What the blazer had that chip done to her tech? She was completely cut off. Entirely alone.

Her mind raced out of her control. How could she figure out something like getting off planet when she didn't even know where to begin? She couldn't just travel to a hostile world. Avery didn't have any knowledge of what life was like there, beside the fact that it was dangerous.

Earth citizens regularly traveled through the worm gate connecting the two galaxies, but the political state was still shaky. Smaller towns on Echo were in turmoil, the Federation still fighting Rebellion forces that wanted humans out of their world.

And there was something else. The government didn't teach it in school, but there were rumors—and the occasional viral—that showed what the Natives could do. Their powers. Avery shuddered.

You didn't go to Echo unless you had enough money to visit the capital and stay out of the local areas. Like Megan's family.

Megan! Didn't she just mention they were headed to Echo? It was risky, hoping that Megan's parents would be willing to help. They would probably just as soon hand Avery over to the Feds than have a fugitive in the house.

But Megan's dad was a high-profile media caster. . . . Maybe he could help point Avery in the right direction to find this Brinstal person. At the very least, maybe Megan could help her get her port up and running again.

Voices approached in the hallway outside and Avery jerked her head up, her heart leaping straight out of her body. The sounds drifted out as the footsteps passed. Avery let out an audible choke of relief.

She didn't have the luxury of debating this now. She either trusted Gran or she didn't, and right now she would do exactly as she was told. She had to go to Echo.

Unlocking the stall door, Avery quietly made her way to one of the washbasins, staring at her reflection in the mirror that ran along the wall. She looked ragged, her hair flying about in disarray around her face and refusing to stay in her tie. With a small frown, Avery tried to straighten up her appearance.

Wiping her sweaty palms on her pants, Avery slipped into the hallway, navigating through the maze of shops. A few minutes passed before heavy footfalls fell into step behind her. The Feds. She increased her stride. Maybe she could outrun them without drawing attention to herself.

"Citizen! Come to a stop!"

Avery ignored the command, picking up her pace into a sprint. Maybe she could do it. She could get away. She knew these halls better than they did, and she wasn't weighed down by all that gear. She turned on a dime and took the next corner, nearly running into the wall from her momentum.

The chorus of footfalls picked up behind her as they gave chase, the female soldier's voice reaching her ears once more. "Avery Vey, stop now or we will be forced to shoot!"

No, she couldn't stop now. Avery ignored the burning in her lungs as she pushed herself faster. If she kept rounding corners, they wouldn't be able to get a clean shot. She could make it out. She had to try.

She ran, knocking a few people out of her way and throwing a hasty apology over her shoulder. She was actually gaining a lead.

Pulling into a long hallway, her pulse raced, thudding in her ears as she willed her muscles to drag faster. A line of elevators beckoned her to safety not two hundred feet away. She was so close. If she could jump into one fast enough, Avery could head to Level 10 and get the blazar out of there.

She hazarded a glance behind her, a stab of panic surging through her heart. One soldier was still hot on her trail, and gaining. The woman pulled out a blaster, slowing to a stop to take better aim.

Avery whipped her head back around, concentrating on the burn of her legs. Just a few more steps. That's all she needed.

She felt the sting before she heard any shot at all.

A small jolt in her shoulder, tendrils of warmth curling through the muscles of her back, tickling down her spine. It actually felt nice, before the pain set in.

Avery's body jerked, throwing her out of the run and sprawling to the floor in a heap. The momentum sent her sliding into the adjoining wall, her head slamming against the concrete with a sickening crack. Groaning, Avery registered the tangy smell of iron, her cheek resting in a pool of her blood. And then she couldn't think. Her body convulsed, jerking in a manic reaction to pain unlike anything she'd ever felt before.

"Hurts like a bitch, doesn't it?" The soldier lowered her blaster and approached Avery. "The electrodart is frying your system. I would recommend you don't try and fight it," she added, turning away to type on her wristport.

Avery tried to scream, but it came out as a mewl. The painful shocks of the dart coursed through her body, causing her nerve endings to fire out of control. She had the passing thought that she probably looked like a fish out of water, flopping around and struggling for air, and how Megan would have found it funny—if not for the cause.

Just as she felt her muscles begin to unravel from her bones, the whole world went black.

The headache slammed into Avery's consciousness like a direct blow to the face. She squinted in confusion against harsh lighting, piecing together that she wasn't at home in her own bed. She parted the dry tightness of her lips, her tongue a thick, rough thing moving awkwardly against the roof of her mouth.

Attempting to move her arms as she cracked open her eyelids, Avery found her hands cinched at her sides. Panic making her movements frenzied, the skin at her wrists tore as she tried to wriggle her hands free.

"I wouldn't do that if I were you." A voice startled her, the speaker hidden somewhere in the room. The walls were covered floor to ceiling with mirrors, her reflection glaring back at her. She was wild-eyed. Desperate. Someone had dressed her in a white jumpsuit, and her feet were bare.

"Who said that?" Avery croaked at the empty room, her voice grinding against the dryness in her throat. She'd bet her entire credit bank that there was someone on the other side of the mirrors. Watching her.

"My name is Captain Harding," the voice responded with frustrating calm. "And you're currently under Federation arrest."

"Where am I?" Avery cleared her throat. "What do you want? I— I haven't done anything wrong!"

"Now, Miss Vey, we both know you were evading Federation pursuit."

"They broke into our home!" Avery shrieked, memories flooding back to her. "What have you done with my grandmother?" she demanded, her voice breaking. The headache worsened. She was probably concussed.

"I believe I'll be the one asking the questions, Miss Vey, if you don't mind. You don't happen to be holding any cards at the moment."

As Captain Harding's voice filled the room, Avery was overwhelmed by some unnamable emotion. Anxiety, hopelessness, anger . . . they all mixed within her, burning a trail through her system. It poured through her, flooding her brain and pulsing heavily behind her eyelids until her headache was a roar in her ears.

Avery lost her focus, an image flooding her mind as if of her body's own volition. Gran, lying on a cot similar to her own. Avery looked down at her, as though she were standing in the same room. Gran's eyes opened, their familiar gray depths filled with determination and strength. But it faltered, showing Avery a glimpse of something she'd never before seen there. Fear.

Gasping, Avery pulled herself out of her own mind and blinked away stinging tears. What the blazar was that?

She was in shock. She had to be. Had that electrodart completely fried her brain along with her body? Her head dropped back to the cot as she stared blankly at the ceiling.

"None of that now, Miss Vey," the captain warned, his eerie laugh distorting the speakers around her. "We don't want you showing off until we're ready for a full demonstration. There'll be plenty of time for that later."

"Showing off?" Avery barely got the question out through trembling lips. Her already massive headache amplified, and she closed her eyes to seek the refuge of cool darkness. "I want out of here!" she screamed.

"Behaving like a child will get you nowhere, my dear." His

tone was annoyed. "I'm sure you just need a bit of time to adjust to your surroundings. You should be thankful you were brought to us unharmed."

"Unharmed?" Avery yelled, pulling her hands forcefully against their restraints as anger reared. "I want to know what happened to my grandmother, and I deserve my rights! You can't just do this to a citizen of Earth!"

"Oh, Miss Vey," responded Harding with gentle chiding. "Let's not pretend, here. You are no more a citizen than the moon is a planet."

Avery shrieked in frustration, kicking her bare feet and struggling against the cot in earnest. She didn't care if she looked like a child throwing a tantrum, she couldn't just sit there and let this happen. The injustice of her situation was entirely ludicrous. Wrong, even. The Federation couldn't just abduct people. Could they?

She would be missed by someone back home. . . . Someone would ask questions. Be concerned for her and Gran. Megan! Megan would come looking for her. She couldn't disappear unnoticed. It wasn't possible.

"I can see you're too emotional to act sensibly at the moment," Harding said calmly. Avery stopped struggling, her chest heaving. "There will be plenty of time for us to get to know one another. And if you're still unwilling . . . Well. I'm sure we can figure out something to incentivize your cooperation," he added, his tone darkening into something unnatural.

When his voice did not return, Avery picked her head up, peering around the room in distress. "Hello?" Silence greeted her. She wondered if there was still someone watching her from the other side of the glass.

Avery ran her dry tongue over her lips. She was so thirsty

she would have sold her wristport for some water. If she still had a port that worked, that is.

Lying there for what could have been hours, Avery nearly jumped out of her skin when the mirror in front of her feet slid open. A soldier walked in from the white hallway beyond, guiding a hover tray. Avery got a good look at her petite stature and features, the cropped black hair . . . Avery gasped. "You're—"

"Yeah." The girl grimaced.

It was the same soldier that she hadn't been able to lose on Level 4. The same one that had shot her with that electrodart and gotten her into this mess.

"What the blazar is going on here? Why am I being held like a prisoner?" Avery hated the way her voice wavered.

Their eyes met briefly before the girl's shifted away. She had a blaster secured to her back with a strap over her shoulders, another holstered to her thigh over her blue uniform. Avery's headache continued to grow, blossoming anew in the back of her skull. She shut her eyes against the sensation.

"I brought you some food," the girl said curtly, ignoring Avery's questions. "You came around from that electrodart pretty quickly."

"You mean considering you tried to kill me with it?" Avery couldn't keep the acid out of her tone. And why should she? Just because this girl was playing good cop to Captain Harding's bad one didn't mean that Avery would fall for it.

"Fair enough," the soldier replied. "But I didn't know you were—" she cut herself off, her eyes shifting briefly to the mirrors behind them. "You need to eat something," she bit out roughly, moving the hover tray closer. The girl entered a code into the cot's control panel, and it lifted to angle her up. Even her cot was hover tech? This facility was state of the art.

"Where are we?" Avery asked, trying to ignore the rapid increase of her heart rate. Or the fact that her brain was beginning to boil from the inside out. She struggled to normalize her breathing.

"Have you heard of the Port Station?" the soldier responded, pulling the domed lid off a bowl that sat on the tray. The delicious scent of broth filled Avery's nostrils even as her eyes focused on the glass of water perched beside it. Her thirst contrasted sharply with the feeling of her mind splitting in two.

"We—we're off planet?" Avery asked, her voice far away. She must have been out for longer than she imagined. Things had completely spiraled out of her control. Alarm carried her up and far away, her breath degrading into stilted pants. Up and up it took her, her mind flying away and out of her grasp.

And suddenly she felt nothing. She was a fly on the wall, floating in the corner of her own mind. Her headache had vanished.

"Yes."

It took Avery a moment to realize the soldier was responding to her question. Avery fixed her gaze toward her. The girl's vibrant green eyes had glazed over, as though she had suddenly been pulled into a daydream.

It was an odd thought, but Avery had the sensation that she was looking into a mirror. As though she was staring at herself.

"I thought it was strange," the girl continued, "that they wanted us to pursue some citizen on the surface, but I have to keep up my end. It's not like I'd argue, getting to shoot someone down there."

Avery flinched at her response, wondering why she was offering up such personal information. She had been so terse before. Avery tried to lick her lips, but her tongue stuck in her throat as she swallowed, causing her to erupt into a coughing fit.

"I'm sorry," the soldier apologized, picking up the glass and holding it to Avery's lips. She nearly wept as the cool liquid invaded her mouth, her tongue absorbing the water like a sponge. A good bit trickled down her chin, but Avery ignored it, drinking greedily.

"Would you like to eat?" the girl asked.

Avery pulled away, wiping her chin on the shoulder of her jumpsuit. She jangled the restraints on her arms, asking, "How am I supposed to do that with my hands tied to—"

"Moons above," the girl replied with distress, quickly setting down the glass and bending to the floor. She returned, a knife in hand. It must have been secured in her boot. "Here, let me help you," she said, setting to work on the restraints.

Avery flushed with relief as her hands were released. She brought them together as she sat up, gently touching the welts on her wrists. They had gone numb, and Avery shook them out to recirculate the blood flow. Lifting her eyes upward, she stared skeptically at the girl. She didn't even know her name.

"Petra," she said, as though reading Avery's thoughts. "I'm so sorry about all of this," she continued, glimpsing at Avery's wrists. "Would you like to eat now?" Petra reached for the bowl of broth, holding it out to her.

Avery looked down at the bowl, wondering why Petra's demeanor changed so suddenly. This was something beyond interrogation tactics.

Petra smiled, pushing the bowl toward her, and Avery carefully took it. She couldn't help slurping the broth and grabbing the bread from the tray right next to where Petra had left her knife unattended. As she picked apart the slice, shoving pieces into her mouth, Avery slowly stood from the cot. Her feet touched the cool, white floor, tingling painfully as blood rushed in.

She had to find Gran and head somewhere safe for their next steps. They could escape, find some normal clothes, get a ship . . . Echo truly was their best bet at avoiding the Feds now, until they could sort this out.

Savoring every last crumb of the bread, Avery walked to the other side of the tray as stealthily as possible. She reached out for the knife . . . but it was gone.

She wrenched back around, eyes widening as she stared at the weapon in Petra's hand, the hilt presented to Avery. As though Petra wanted her to take it.

"Here," Petra said flatly. Short, black hair framed her heart-shaped face, flattering her features. She was quite beautiful. "Didn't you want it?"

Avery staggered backward, disbelief spearing her stomach. Could that girl read her mind? What kind of stuff were they doing on this space station, anyway?

"I know where they have your grandmother," Petra added, taking a few steps toward Avery. "If she's still alive, that is, I know where they would hold her. I can take you to her. I can get you out of here."

"What?" Avery asked, certain the girl was crazy.

"I can get you—"

"Yeah, I heard what you said," Avery responded, still skeptical. "If you wanted to help me, then you shouldn't have shot me back on Level 4."

Petra's face fell. "I'm sorry." Her dark brows came together, as though she was fighting to remember something. "We have to get you—"

"I don't have time for this," Avery cut her off. "Where is Gran?" If there was even a small chance that Petra was telling her the truth, then Avery would take it.

"If we're going to get out of here, it's going to be difficult," Petra responded, pulling her blaster from around her shoulders. "I should go ahead to the bay and secure us a vessel. Here," she said, handing Avery a small tablet. "There's a layout of the base on there. You collect your grandmother, and we'll get out of here as fast as possible. The lunar colonies are probably our best shot at getting through the Gate."

"How do you know I'm looking to go to Echo?" Avery asked.

"Aren't you?"

"Yeah, but—"

"Listen," Petra interrupted, her eyes flashing to the mirror behind them, "if we want to make this happen, it has to happen now." She reached down to the holster at her thigh and pulled out a small pistol. Holding it out to Avery handle first, she waited for her decision.

Avery nodded shortly, grabbing it. "What do I have to do?"

CHAPTER FOUR

F inn banged his head in a steady rhythm against the wall behind him. He had given up on trying to figure out how he was going to escape. If Nick hadn't sent some kind of emissary to free him yet, it probably wasn't going to happen. Pressing fingers gingerly to his swollen cheek, he sucked in a quick breath as pain shot up into his eye socket.

What were they telling the officials back on Echo? Surely, they couldn't explain his disappearance to the media so easily. He had done his damnedest the past few years to make a public spectacle of himself. There was no way his absence was going unnoticed. Then again, Nick certainly wouldn't risk letting the Federation know that they had something on them. Their family had to maintain appearances.

Finn's father hadn't believed in blindly following the Federation's wishes, even when their family had lived on Earth. As a member of the council, his father had moved his family to Milderion, Echo's capital, when Finn was a toddler. Finn could still remember the first time he met a Native. How frightened he had been.

The propaganda circulating on Earth was created by the Federation, meant to scare Old Earth citizens into compliance with the genocide that was happening a galaxy away.

But the Rebellion was failing. Even the people themselves were starting to lose hope in the fight against the Federation. If they weren't able to ignite the fire in the cause, to inspire some real hope, all of Echo would fall into Federation hands. For good.

Finn could only hope that the encryption on those droids would hold against the Federation hackers. He wondered briefly if they would kill him for it.

No. He was too much of a public figure for that. They wouldn't put a scratch on him if they could help it. He ran his tongue across his busted lip. Well. Maybe a few scratches.

They had roughed him up, but nothing enough to do serious damage. And Finn hated his position for that. He wasn't treated as a true Rebel despite his obvious involvement.

Blastfire sounded from the other side of the door, sending Finn flying to his feet as muffled shouting bled through the walls. Had Nick actually sent a rescue party? Finn's hand went to his hip holster, only to touch empty air. Blazing Federation soldiers had confiscated his gear when they arrived. And he had really loved that gun.

Before he could think of a plan beyond breaking down the door, it slid open to reveal a girl in a white, sleeveless jumpsuit, weapon waving wildly in the air. She leaned away from him, stepping backward as she took him in.

He lifted a brow, returning her perusal, from the top of her light brown hair pulled into a messy ponytail, to the small bare feet poking out of her jumpsuit's too-long pants. He stifled a confused smile as his eyes returned to her face. Why did she look familiar?

Her forehead creased, a little line appearing between her eyes as she lifted her blaster and aimed it directly at him. "Who are you?" she demanded.

Finn put up his hands to pacify her. She held the gun like it was contagious, clearly scared to handle it. Fate had just delivered him exactly what he needed.

"Don't shoot. I'm rather attached to myself," he quipped, walking slowly to one side as he spoke.

"I'm not going to ask you again," she responded, her voice wavering. He had to admire her spirit. Despite the fact that she was clearly terrified, the girl had a lot of guts to keep that blaster pointed at him.

"Finnegan Lunitia," he responded, not missing the way her breath caught. "But my friends call me Finn. Now, are you going to tell me who you are, or do I get to guess?"

She faltered, and Finn saw his opportunity. He took it, one hand coming up to bat the front of her blaster toward the wall. He brought his other hand down on her elbow, detaching the weapon from her grip and launching it into the air. He twisted, bringing one arm around her neck while the other pinned her to his torso, securing her arms against her sides.

"Well, that was fun," he whispered into her ear, smiling. "Care to go for round two?"

She let out a frustrated screech, struggling against him. He tightened his grip. She brought her foot down on his boot, but without any shoes her efforts brought little result. Finn grinned. This would be entertaining if he weren't being held hostage on a Federation space station.

"Let me go!" she yelled at him. He wasn't stupid. He could hear the rashness in her voice. She was in serious trouble, this one.

"Not a chance, sweetheart," he replied coolly, situating his grip. "How about you tell me what it is you're doing and then we come to a solution from there? I've got a need to get off this heap of metal, and it looks like you've had a bit more success than me in going about it."

"I don't have to tell you anything," she ground out, turning her head away from his face.

"That's true," he admitted with a little nod. "But I can guarantee you that you don't have much of a chance getting out of here without my help. No matter what kind of gun you've got, it doesn't do you much good if you don't know how to use it."

"That guy doesn't seem to agree with you," she said then, gesturing to the soldier slumped in the hallway.

Finn laughed, noting the dozen or so blast scars on the wall behind. "Lucky shots don't count." She tensed beneath him, and he knew his hunch was correct. She didn't know how to handle a weapon after all.

Which begged the question: What was she doing as a prisoner on the Port Station? She could be an important bargaining chip. He couldn't just leave her.

When she refused to speak, Finn sighed. "Listen, I get the feeling you're in a bit of a hurry to get out of here. Considering you probably just activated about a million sensors when you blasted your way into my cell, it might be a good idea if you tell me what the blazar is going on." Still, he was met with silence.

He clenched his jaw. Moons above, but she was stubborn. "The clock's ticking, sweethea—"

"Fine!" she said through clenched teeth.

"What did you say?"

"Fine!" she yelled. "Let me go, and I'll help you get out of here."

He nodded, glad she agreed so quickly, and released his grip.

Surprise reeled through his system then as she lunged at the discarded blaster by their feet. Throwing his body toward hers, Finn let his weight carry them both down hard against the floor. He straddled her legs, trapping her beneath him and pinning her arms to her sides.

"Do you have a death wish?" he asked sharply. "What is wrong with you? I'm trying to help, you idiot."

For the first time, Finn faced the girl at close range and was able to get a good look at her eyes. They were such a pale brown, they nearly appeared golden in the light. It shocked him enough to wipe the frown from his face. "Then again, maybe you're right," he said with a wink, his gaze falling to her lips. "This position is a little better."

"Get off me, you—"

"Not until you promise to let me help you," he said in all seriousness, his eyes returning to meet hers. "You seem like a reasonably intelligent girl. Haven't you ever heard that two heads are better than one?"

She stared up at him silently, the two of them refusing to move. They both jumped as an alarm began to whine loudly from the door, lights flashing around them.

"If that sound is any indication, you haven't got much time to decide," he said, genuine urgency siphoning his humor. "Either way, I'm getting out of here. But whether or not I leave you locked in this cell is your choice."

"I suppose this can't get any worse," she mumbled as she closed her eyes, fine lashes brushing against freckled cheeks. When she opened them again, they were clear and direct. "I'll help you. But if you call me sweetheart one more time, I *will* figure out how to use that gun on you."

He grinned. "Is that a promise?"

Avery sighed, relieved, as Finn lifted his body off hers. She hopped quickly to her feet, scrambling away from him as he picked up the blaster. She watched him warily, wondering what she had gotten herself into. What kind of person made jokes when they were obviously so close to being caught?

She remembered him clearly from the Underground. Even if Megan hadn't made such a big deal about it, Avery doubted she'd be able to forget the intensity of his eyes. Had the Feds come after her because of him? At least he hadn't recognized her.

"What do I call you?" he asked, moving quickly to the doorway to look around the corner. Avery could tell he had some sort of military training. Maybe he had a point about teaming up.

She still hadn't found Gran. That was her number one priority, and this little detour had cost her precious minutes.

"My name's Avery," she replied shortly, moving to stand behind him. "My grandmother's here somewhere. We have to find her."

"I hate to break it to you, Avery, but getting your grand-mother out of here isn't looking good." He kept his eyes trained on the hallway. "We don't have much time to save our own skin, let alone hers."

"I can't leave her here." She shook her head madly. "I am not going anywhere without her."

"And I'm not going to waste my freedom hunting for little old ladies in this place," he replied, shooting her a look. "We have limited time, do you understand? Not to mention that in about two minutes there are going to be soldiers swarming this place, and I can't remember my way around the Station well enough to get us to the docking bay without making a few wrong turns." He turned back to the hallway, adding defini-tively, "It's not gonna happen."

"You can do whatever you want, but I'm going to find her!" Avery raised her voice, nearly yelling. She had never encoun-tered such an ass in her life. She had never wished so vehement-ly that she knew how to throw a punch more than she did in that moment. Or better yet, how to handle a blaster.

He turned back to face her, the muscle in his cheek twitch-ing as he stared her down. His jawline was striking beneath the stubble shadowing his chin. Avery wondered if he had been wrongfully incarcerated, or if that was just wishful thinking. So far his attitude seemed more like that of a convict than any-thing else. She didn't have much faith in celebrities to begin with.

Blastfire erupted across the hall and they both ducked for cover. Avery yelped as Finn pushed her behind him, raising the blaster to shoulder level to take aim. "Looks like our time just ran out," Finn said darkly.

He shot down the five soldiers running at them, not wasting more than a single blast on each. His aim was impeccable. He barked a terse, "Follow me," as he pressed forward, crouching to maneuver behind an arched metal pillar.

Avery watched him go, unable to move. Finn was starting to look like her only hope of escaping, but he refused to help Gran. There was no way she could leave her grandmother unprotected to face the wrath of Captain Harding, whoever he was.

"Avery!" Finn's voice called, and she caught his eye. "Get your ass over here!" He frowned, nodding to the space beside him.

What a jackass. Before she could tell him to kick rocks, blastfire rained down on them again. Avery jumped back from the doorway, catching a glimpse of the three soldiers that had just arrived. Finn huddled against the pillar for cover, his tall frame barely able to find sanctuary.

Avery took a steadying breath. She would have to keep moving without him. If there was a chance to save Gran, she would take it. As Finn distracted the soldiers, Avery made a break down the hall in the opposite direction from the fight.

She hadn't gone twenty feet before five more soldiers appeared, coming straight at her, blasters raised to shoot. Her heart clogging her throat, Avery screamed as they fired. Her pulse accelerated into a heavy throbbing, her head exploding with a pain centered behind her eyes. She saw white and black, squeezing them closed in shock. Tucking her head away from the source, Avery threw her hands up instinctively to protect herself from the blasts.

And then nothing.

Gasping, she forced her eyes open. Finn ran up behind her in hot pursuit, his own eyes wide in wonder. She had barely a second to think about his reaction before her attention was back on the soldiers in front of her. They had frozen in their tracks, staring at her in much the same way.

Had she grown horns or something?

Before she could ask as much, Finn was grabbing her arm and pulling her to the side of yet another pillar. He got off a few more blasts around the corner, barely even aiming this time. The soldiers came to their senses, resuming their attack.

"Shit, there's too many of them," he snapped, sneaking a look around the corner one last time. There was blaster residue smeared across his face, a black mark marring the side of his forehead. "Even if your grandmother is down there, there's no way we can get through."

Avery looked away from him, concentrating on the floor. Her feet were dirty and freezing. She flinched with each shot that echoed around them.

"Make a choice, sweet—" He caught himself before finishing the endearment. "Avery," he corrected. "You know we have to go the other way if we want a chance at getting out of here."

She had no choice. They had to leave Gran. Avery uttered a choked sob as she nodded. "Okay." She brought her eyes to his. "Okay," she repeated, "get us out of here."

With a crooked smile, Finn spun back around and crouched low. "Move to the next pillar," he told her, standing and heading backward as he fired at their attackers. He followed her, his aim so good that he was able to keep the soldiers from advancing down the hallway any farther.

"All right," he said between shots, "I'm going to stop shooting, and we're gonna run like hell down that corridor. I think the next left should lead us—"

"I have a map," she told him. She had actually forgotten, in the stress. Pulling out the small tablet from her jumpsuit, she held it up for him.

"And you chose *now* to tell me?" he asked, his attention still on the soldiers he was keeping at bay. "Okay, then, you be scout leader."

She ignored his sarcasm, studying the map and correlating it with the information that Petra had told her. She could get them to the docking bay. Maybe if she could figure out what was happening, she could find some way to come back and save Gran. Finn had to know something useful. If he really was some famous ambassador, maybe he could help.

"Ready?" he asked, shooting her a glance.

"When you are," she replied.

"Lead on, Captain."

Avery broke into a run, zipping out from behind the pillar and gaining enough momentum to hop over the bodies of the soldiers that Finn had felled earlier. They were dodging the shots now, and Avery prayed that they were real rounds this time. She couldn't handle another electrodart. She would rather die.

She focused on her destination, rounding the corners of the halls with ease, as if she knew where she wanted to go without the map. Avery soon saw the docking bay ahead, a wide corridor opening into what looked like a large hangar full of military-grade spaceships. As they ran, the floor transitioned to a metal grate, causing Avery to cry out harshly as her feet dug into the sharp teeth.

"Why the blazar don't you have any shoes?" Finn asked. His gaze swiped to the bay before them, back to the hallways from where they came, and finally landed on Avery. "You're going to have to hop on my back," he said. He shook his head at her hesitation. "We don't have time for second-guessing."

"Okay," she said, relenting, her eyes flying to the hallway as a soldier made her way around a corner toward them.

Finn lifted his hand and fired a shot from a pistol, the ear-numbing blast making Avery flinch violently in surprise as the soldier crumpled to the ground. Where had he picked *that* up? He grabbed her hand, settling the weapon in her palm.

"If anybody comes at you, point and squeeze the trigger," he advised. Then he turned around and kneeled in front of her. She delicately wrapped her own arms around his shoulders and hopped up, her legs gripping the side of his waist as he hooked her knees. "Just try not to shoot my ear off while you're at it," he added, breaking into a sprint with Avery on his back.

They made it to the bay as a group of soldiers rounded the corner after them. Avery twisted her torso, trying not to flinch as she sent off a few shots in their direction.

"Did you hit anything?" Finn asked sarcastically, his breathing ragged.

"Keep running!" she yelled at him. "There!" she exclaimed, pointing with the gun at his eye level toward a large ship that had its engine roaring. Avery saw Petra waving frantically at the side lift gate before she disappeared into the hull of the ship.

"I hope that's our ride," Finn said, picking up his pace now that he had a destination.

"I hope so, too," Avery responded, looking behind them as a new hail of blastfire followed. Thankfully, their long-distance accuracy seemed dubious, at best. She shot two more rounds before the pistol clicked uselessly. Blazing prehistoric things. She couldn't fathom why they still used them. She threw the heavy weapon toward the soldiers with a grunt.

"Oh yeah," Finn said, "that'll show 'em." He faltered, stumbling to the side, and Avery nearly slipped off his back. He'd taken a shot to the leg, blood already soaking his tan pants. But he recovered quickly and kept running, his breathing increasingly labored. They were only ten yards away now. Almost there.

"Let me down, Finn," Avery cried in his ear, soldiers advancing behind them. The faster ones among them were gaining significantly. Finn ignored her, and she struggled against him. "You can't make it with me on your back like this."

"Moons above, girl, shut the blazar up and let me—"

Another shot tore through his arm, and he dropped one of her legs, causing them both to stumble and fall to the ground in a painful heap. Avery jumped up, ignoring the bite of the metal grates as they dug into her feet. Moving to Finn's side, she grabbed his arm and dragged him up with her, pulling him toward the ship.

They began to run, Avery limping as the pads of her feet were sliced with each stride. She pushed the pain to the back of her mind, focusing her energy on that open lift gate, beckoning to them like a finish line of safety.

"Stop!" a soldier shouted behind them, closer now than ever. Before Avery could turn to look, one of the mounted guns on the front of the ship turned toward them with a quick swivel and opened fire. Avery covered her ears against the screams, still concentrating on the last couple yards between her and safety.

And then her feet were on the solid surface of the ramp, and it was Finn who was pulling her up as the hatch began to close, bringing them at last into the protection of the blast-proof hull of the ship.

CHAPTER FIVE

They collapsed to the floor of the loading bay, losing their balance as the ship lifted from the hangar. Avery hoped Petra knew what she was doing, and where the blazar to go next. For that matter, she prayed Petra's allegiance would last.

Finn let out a painful curse beside her, grabbing his upper arm with a shaking hand. Despite the effort, blood oozed steadily from between his clenched fingers. It traced a wet path down his side, darkening his shirt.

"Are you guys secure?" Petra's voice sounded over the ship's PA system.

"We're good," Avery responded, looking up at the ceiling, hoping Petra could hear her. "Just get us out of here!"

"We're good?" Finn demanded, bringing Avery's attention back to him sitting on the ground. "I've been shot, damn it!"

The ship lurched, sending Avery rolling into the engine core taking up the center of the cargo area.

"What are you doing to my ship?" Finn yelled, looking up at the lights in the same way Avery had moments before.

"We have some Feds hot on our tail," Petra responded. "I'm going to have to put her into hyperspeed to outrun them."

"Oh, no, you don't!" Finn raised his voice, using his momentum to stand while clutching his wound. He swayed on his feet, stumbling toward one of the staircases leading up to the upper level.

"Stop!" Avery called out, pulling herself up with one of the grips on the side of the engine core container. "You need to treat that wound!"

"We don't have time for that," he grunted out, limping his way up the steps, his boots clanging on the metal.

Avery tottered behind, dragging her wounded feet underneath her. When she reached the stairs, she swallowed the lump in her throat. More grates. At least these didn't have little jagged teeth.

Gripping the railings on either side, Avery pulled her way after Finn. He had disappeared, but she could easily follow his trail. A red smear of blood painted the floor in front of her, curving down the hallway toward the front of the ship. Besides that, she could just follow the sounds of their arguing.

"You can't just jump into hyperspeed!" Finn yelled.

"It's our only choice to outrun those soldiers back there," Petra insisted harshly. "Why do you think I chose this vessel? None of those Federation attack ships have the capability."

Avery turned the corner to the bridge, its doorway opening wide before her. Petra sat at the main control panel, with Finn hovering over her, a fierce scowl on his face.

An explosion rocked the ship, throwing Avery into the wall, and she slid to the floor as her feet gave out beneath her. She gripped the arch of the doorway to keep from completely collapsing, looking frantically between the two of them. Alarms started screaming and the lights reduced to red and white flashes.

"That's not good, is it?" Avery asked, voice shaking.

"No, no, no!" Finn whined, running to a side panel, flipping switches and buttons like a mad man with his one good arm.

"We have to go! Now!" Petra yelled at him, her hands flying over the command touch screen as she sat down in the captain's chair.

"At least let me get the—"

"There's no time!"

And then Avery couldn't think at all, because her brain was ten feet behind her. Her organs pressed against the back of her ribcage, her bones fighting to keep her muscles and skin from completely ripping apart. She snapped her eyes shut and counted internally, reaching five before the feeling gradually receded, her innards returning to their normal arrangement within her body.

"Moons above, are you trying to kill us?" Finn shouted from somewhere in front of her. She wondered if he felt as strange as she did. Was that hyperspeed?

"We're safe, aren't we?" Petra retorted, the sound of hazard alarms still wailing around them. "Now we just have to pray they can't track us."

"Don't ever touch my ship, Fed," Finn snapped.

Avery peeled her eyes open. Petra had risen from her chair and now leaned over the large command screen as Finn tried to push her out of the way.

"I wouldn't have had to touch it if you had been able to keep it," Petra countered through clenched teeth.

"Why you ungrateful . . . ." He trailed off. "I ought to throw you right out the vac seal."

"I'd like to see you try."

Avery tuned out their bickering, gasping at the sight before her as she pulled herself to her feet. The entire dome of the bridge was encompassed in clear blast glass, allowing them a half-spherical view outside the ship. Even the floor was glass, farther out into the domed nose.

And there in front of them, floating bigger than anything she had ever seen in her life, was Saturn. Its rings glowed eerily in the light from the sun, the beige colors of its main formation swirling together as the outer gasses moved in a rhythmic dance. Avery's chest tightened, her eyes prickling.

"Are you all right?" Avery heard Petra ask, a light hand touching her shoulder.

"I'm fine," Avery said. "I just . . . ." She couldn't continue, her eyes blurring until the planet was a mass of watery gold.

She was millions of miles away from Earth. From her home. From Gran. Her gut twisted, shooting a wave of nausea up her throat. Her breath strained, the air weighing down her stomach. "I've just never been off planet before."

And then, much to her mortification, Avery bent over and emptied the entire contents of her stomach onto the glass floor. Heat filled her face instantly as she clenched her knees with her hands, breathing heavily in the shocked silence of her companions.

"I'm not cleaning that up," Finn remarked dryly.

Petra was quick to pull back Avery's hair, rubbing her back

in small circles as she dry-heaved a few more times. Wiping the side of her mouth with the back of her hand, Avery shot Finn what she hoped was a withering glare.

He raised a dark brow. "I told her hyperspeed would be too much for you." Swaying on his feet, he hissed through his teeth, cradling his injured arm. "Now," he added, looking down at his hand as fresh blood seeped through his fingers, his arm coated in a film of dark red, "does anybody have a Band-Aid?"

Avery barely remembered making it to the medical bay. She guessed that Petra half-carried her the entire way there. Petra shoved a small paper pill into Avery's mouth, which dissolved pleasantly on her tongue, and her sickness dissipated. She blinked, amazed at the sudden relief.

"Pain reliever," Petra said, as though reading her mind again. The soldier continued her examination of Avery's feet as she lay on the metal table in the center of the room. Avery stared at the bright white lights above, trying not to think about the ribbons of cut flesh that must be her feet. Finn snored gently from the bed to her right.

From necessity, Petra had treated Finn first, giving him a heavy dose of some narcotic to help numb the pain from the soldering she'd had to do on his injuries. The melting foam had brought the skin together on his arm, and they'd only had to use a little bit on the wound in his leg. In a matter of minutes, he'd be practically good as new. He'd just have to take it easy for a few days.

Avery jerked as Petra applied a cool antibiotic spray to the soles of her feet, apologizing for being ticklish. Petra smiled, following it with a thin layer of the melting foam. Avery was thankful she couldn't feel it.

"Why didn't you just give Finn that pain reliever stuff?" Avery asked with a confused frown. "It seems strong enough, even for his injuries."

"I was sick of hearing him complain," Petra replied quickly, concentrating on her task.

Avery laughed, for the first time since . . . how long ago had her life fallen apart?

"Two days," Petra said, wrapping her feet in a light gauze.

"What?" Avery asked.

"It's been two days since they took you," Petra added, cutting the ends of the gauze with small scissors and securing them.

Avery looked away nervously. *Could* she read minds? So far, Petra had been helpful, but what were her motives? She was a full-on Federation soldier one minute, and a fellow escapee the next.

But she couldn't trust Petra, or even Finn. *Trust no one.*

Gran, a voice inside of Avery cried out, and she fought against the hard knot in her throat. She would go back for her. Somehow, Avery knew she was still alive. It was as though she could feel the connection between them, strong and unbreakable even across the distance that separated them.

She had to honor Gran's instructions and get to Echo. Find this Brinstal person. Beg for a way out of this. Then she could make plans to get Gran back.

With a sigh, Avery closed her eyes and let go of the urgent stress that had taken over her body ever since she had woken on that cot at the Port Station. Finally, there weren't any immediate threats. She wasn't running for her life or being shot at or—

The sound of a gun cocking forced Avery's eyes open and she jerked upright. Her body froze as she stared down the barrel of a pistol that Petra pointed directly at her face.

"What the blazar am I doing here?" Petra asked, her green eyes narrowing in accusation, a lock of black hair falling over her forehead.

"What?" Avery asked, her hands gripping the sides of the bed.

"What did you do to me?" she yelled, demanding.

"I—" Avery faltered. "I didn't do anything to you! What are you talking about, Petra? You just—"

"Shut up!" Petra interrupted her, screaming now. Her eyes filled with moisture as she looked around savagely. She was distracted. Maybe if Avery could launch herself off the table, she could find a way to knock Petra out. Unlikely, given her wounded feet. If only Finn weren't snoring like a . . . but there wasn't any noise coming from the bunk where he had been sleeping.

"It doesn't matter how you did it," Petra said forcefully, her voice wavering with emotion. "But I'll be damned if I'm going to—"

Petra fell to the ground as a heavy metal tray slammed into the side of her head, and she crumpled into an ungraceful heap on the floor. Finn stood above her, a sly grin pulling at the corner of his mouth as he looked up at Avery. "I've been wanting to do that for hours."

CHAPTER SIX

A fter Avery had helped Finn hoist Petra up on his good shoulder, they secured her in one of the rooms that Finn had already decked out to serve as a brig. Avery didn't want to know why he should have use for something like that. She realized that she still knew relatively nothing about him and tried to shrug off the feeling that she was alone on a spaceship with a stranger. Not to mention an incredibly unpredictable Federation soldier that wanted to kill her. And they were millions of miles away from anything she'd ever known.

Why had she decided it was a good idea to go with them again?

Finn had shown her to a room in the living quarters, thrown some clothes at her, and indicated a shower she could use. She was grateful for the time to collect herself. She still didn't know how to confront him about the Underground and what he had been doing there.

She had come so close to being killed. More than once. How had her life turned into this so quickly? It seemed like just yesterday she had been goofing off with Megan. But now she was so far away from everything. So utterly alone.

What would Megan do when Avery didn't respond to her comms? She looked down at her wrist longingly, wishing she could message her best friend. Avery felt disconnected without the familiarity of the port, as though a piece of her was missing. That info chip Gran had given her had completely fried it, and Avery couldn't get it to cycle back on.

A wave of emotion passed through her, welling up in her heart and making its way up into her throat to choke her. She wanted to go home. She wanted her boring little world again, where she was safe and Gran was with her. And if she wanted that to happen, she had to keep moving forward.

After showering, she changed into the clothes Finn had provided. The tan cargo pants were a size too big and the green shirt a size too small, but it worked. He even scrounged up some boots for her, and the extra room in those let her wounded feet breathe.

She left her room, heading down the hallway that cut centrally through the ship and led directly up to the bridge through a set of blast doors. The gray metal door slid open as she approached, and she found herself once again overwhelmed by the beauty of the gigantic ringed planet before them. It looked so peaceful and quiet. Who would be able to guess what awaited them back on Earth? Or on Echo, an entire galaxy away?

"Don't tell me you're going to vomit again." Finn's voice brought Avery's attention to the captain's command on her right, where he was sitting with his feet propped up on the console and leaning back in his chair as if he owned the universe.

"Don't start," she warned, moving to take one of the seats behind a large panel of transparent monitors. She supposed it was intended for navigation command.

Now that they were out of danger, she felt supremely awkward trying to speak to him. During the past few hours, everything they had said to one another had been out of necessity. Now the air was strained with unfamiliarity.

"You and I need to talk," she said stiffly, glancing in his direction.

"That would be an understatement," he replied, bringing his feet down firmly in front of him. He leaned forward, resting his elbows on his knees as he met her gaze directly. "You need to tell me what the blazar is going on. Why were you on the Station?"

Her defenses rose sharply, and she came to her feet again. "You're the one who needs to explain yourself. What were you doing there? And while you're at it, why were you on Earth at all? You were the one they were chasing in the Underground in the first—"

"What did you say?" he asked, genuinely surprised.

"I know who you are," she said, her eyes unable to stay on his. Moon above, he cleaned up nicely. He'd found a laser somewhere and his jaw was now clean-shaven and smooth, allowing her to see that he had a well-defined dimple in his right cheek when he smirked. "You're famous, right?" she continued. "Why the blazar were you in that market? Is that why they took me, too?"

"I knew I recognized you from somewhere," he drawled, the dimple deepening as he laughed. "Fate has one hell of a sense of humor."

She glowered at him. "Is everything a joke to you?"

"Only when my life's in danger," he replied, sobering to a grin.

"That's not funny."

"Fine. You want to be serious?" Avery took a step back as Finn came to his feet, leaning his hip against the console. "I saw what you did to that blastfire, Avery. It would be more reasonable for me to be asking you the questions."

"What?" she asked. Had those blasts fried his brain as well as his arm?

His jaw clenched before he replied, his voice rising. "Let's not play games. I know you're a Native. Just come off the excuses, okay? I'm on your side."

Avery's heart raced, the air tightening around her as she digested his words. "What the blazar are you talking about?" A headache blossomed as an unfamiliar emotion took hold of her senses.

"I'm talking about how you stopped those shots about an inch before they hit you," he said, crossing his arms over his broad chest.

"No, I didn't!" she protested, knowing that she sounded slightly hysterical. "Are you blazing psycho? How could I be a Native? I was born on Earth. I've spent my whole life there. Don't you think I would know if I'd ever been off planet?" It was impossible. She refused to even entertain the idea.

Turning away, Avery focused on Saturn sitting before them, huge and quiet and eerily beautiful.

How could he even suggest such a thing? Her mind shifted back to the moment Gran had realized she'd been scanned. She had known the Feds were coming, moments before they burst into their apartment. There had to be something more. . . .

Avery stopped herself. Was she actually considering the possibility that she might be an alien? The idea was so absurd, she nearly choked on it.

Blood careened through her veins in an overwhelming sensation. It was familiar now, this intense pain behind her eyes. The quickening of her heartbeat. Her hands began to shake, and she swiftly brought them to her chest, clutching them together in an attempt to prevent the inevitable.

The control panels in the bridge started vibrating, the navigation terminal cracking with a loud shatter as Avery's vision clouded. Fear dominated her instincts, making the situation worse, the entire room beginning to shake as though it would be torn from the ship.

"Whoa, whoa, whoa," Finn said, alarm in his voice.

Avery stared at the floor, blackness threatening to take over her vision entirely. She could practically taste adrenaline surging through her system as the force of whatever she was doing flowed through her and around the room. The harder she tried to control it, the worse it became. The entire ship was shaking in a violent tremor.

"Hey!" Finn yelled at her. "Get a hold of yourself!"

"I—" she began, looking frantically around her. "I can't control it." Her eyes flew to his, and she saw his own panic, which drove hers to new heights. The pain started again, concentrated and pure behind her eyes, and she squeezed them shut in protest.

Was this how it was going to end? She was going to kill them both because she couldn't control whatever this thing was that raged inside of her.

"Look at me." Finn's voice brushed her ears, so close he

must have been standing right in front of her. His hands moved to her shoulders, grounding her to reality. "Open your eyes," he implored, his voice heavy.

She did as he said, her vision flicking immediately to the domed glass above their heads that looked ready to burst into a thousand pieces at any moment. They'd be pulled out into the vacuum of space, dead in a matter of seconds.

"Don't look at that, look at me," Finn said, drawing her focus to him.

Avery shifted her gaze, peering into the calm blue of his eyes. How could he seem so steady when whatever she was doing was about to tear the ship apart? She couldn't stop it. She couldn't even begin to know how.

"Breathe," he said, his eyes forming a composed plea. He was offering his support. "Focus on your breathing," he repeated. "You can control it."

She mimicked his breaths in and out, concentrating on the way her chest rose and fell in a steady rhythm. As she focused on them, she remembered that his eyes weren't just blue. There were flecks of gray all throughout them. This was how they had looked when he ran into her. When they had first met.

Avery's eyes fluttered shut, and she pictured the flow of oxygen as it chilled her nostrils and filled her body, breathing out through her mouth in the steady pattern Finn had established. The overwhelming panic was ebbing. It was working.

Slowly, the ship stopped rattling, her shaking reducing to only a slight tremor. Even her heart began to settle, returning to its regular rhythm in her chest. She sent up a prayer, thanking the stars that she had been able to calm herself. Or had that been Finn?

"Moons above." He sighed. "I thought I was gonna have to

knock you out like Peeta down there."

"Petra," she corrected, opening her eyes as she sagged against the navigation command.

"Yeah, whatever." He ran a hand through his dark brown hair and let out a relieved breath, flopping into the captain's chair. "The next time you don't agree with me, can you please just slap me or something? I've had girls mad at me, but that"— he gestured in her direction— "was certainly a first."

"What is wrong with you?" Avery frowned, clenching her fists at her sides. The room was suddenly stifling, the air like warm cryo-gel. She tried to ignore the beads of sweat beneath her hair. "I just want to go home! I just want my grandmother safe and to go home." To her embarrassment, a few tears escaped down her cheeks. God, would she ever stop it with the ridiculous waterworks?

"Listen, sweetheart." Finn's brows drew together as his tone became serious. "I don't know what kind of game you're playing, but there are things happening out there. Things that are bigger than you and your grandmother. You have an obligation to play your part. We all do."

Avery didn't respond, her gaze dropping to her feet.

"You want to know what I was doing in the Underground?" he asked sharply. "I was looking for people like you. I risked everything to find survivors I could bring back to the Rebellion. You want to shrug off what happened with those soldiers? Fine. But you just about tore my ship apart with your mind, so I think your 'Oh look at me, I'm a normal human' argument is getting pretty old."

Heat crawled up Avery's neck, her mind sifting through the missing connections in her life. She had never so much as seen a picture of her parents, and Gran had never wanted to talk about them. Avery had always assumed it was grief. But what if it was something more? Her throat was unbearably tight.

And after what had just happened, it's not like Avery could deny Finn's reasoning. She wasn't normal, and that thought frightened her more than anything that she had been through so far. But even if it was true, how could she have any responsibility to Echo? It wasn't her place. She was human. Her whole life was on Earth.

All she had ever heard about Natives—or learned in school—was that they were dangerous and wild. They lived by a different set of morals, their societies governed by oppressive leaders. That's why the Federation was implementing rule there: to bring order to Echo. It was the entire reason the war started in the first place. Avery couldn't fathom why Finn thought she'd want to join their side.

"I don't care," Avery said tightly. She didn't know what he was going on about, and she didn't even want to begin thinking about those questions. She wished she had paid more attention to Megan's gossiping or even the media streams. Perhaps if she knew more about Finn, she'd have some kind of leverage.

"You don't care?" Finn scoffed. "There are hundreds of thousands of people on Echo suffering under the oppression of the Federation. If you are what I think you are, you could make a real change in their chances of fighting back. Why do you think the Feds were holding you there at the Port Station? What do you think they do to Elites?"

"Elites?" she repeated, shaking her head. "I don't understand anything you're saying. Anything you've been saying. I don't want to be part of a war or a rebellion or any fight. All I want is to get my grandmother back and go home. Why can't you understand that?"

Finn looked at the girl and saw her focus scattering. She couldn't meet his eyes. Even if she'd never realized what she was, there couldn't be any doubt in her mind now. She was refusing to come with him, even knowing the truth.

But if she had been raised on Earth, perhaps she didn't understand what was happening on Echo. The propaganda released to the citizens on Earth was heavily censored, manipulated to suit the Federation's needs. In reality, the war was just a front. An excuse for the mass genocide of an entire race. Faces flashed before Finn's eyes. Friends he had lost. Families that had been torn apart. This girl held the power to change that. And she didn't even know it.

Taking a steadying breath, Finn backed up to give her some space. He briefly looked out the bridge windows at the rings of Saturn, wishing that this responsibility wasn't resting on his shoulders. Nick would be so much better at handling something so delicate. Something so important. Finn was good at either entertaining people or roughing them up, not manipulating them.

Finn had heard stories of the power of the Elites his entire life, but he had never seen it for himself. They were all but extinct on Echo. A part of him had never believed it possible. But seeing her struggle to control it, Finn realized that this gift was as dangerous as it was beautiful.

He couldn't believe his plan had actually worked. And to think, if she hadn't been in that market the same day, he might never have found her. He couldn't wait to see the look on Nick's face when he waltzed into camp with Avery in tow.

"Listen, if you can't help me,"—her sharp words brought Finn out of his thoughts—"then just get me to the lunar cities. I can find my own way once I get there." She was pretty tall for a girl, just a few inches short of his height at six feet. As much as her quick temper annoyed the blazar out of him, he admired her tenacity. She wasn't easily intimidated.

"Do you really think things can go back to the way they were?" Finn asked impatiently. "That you'll go back to San Jose and settle down and get a job selling turnips or whatever and live out your life in peace?"

"San Fran," she corrected.

"What?"

"I'm from New San Fran, not San—"

"You know what I mean," he interrupted her. "The Feds will never stop hunting you. You'll never be able to live a normal life. Not like the one you had."

"Then what do you suggest?" Her voice shook, and he swore the color of her eyes shifted, lightening until they were nearly golden. "I am *not* going to join a rebellion or fight in a war. This is all a huge misunderstanding, I'm sure of it. I just have to—"

"Look," he said, a plan forming. She wasn't going to be easy to convince, and he sure as blazar wasn't going to be able to do it on his own. "You're not going to get anywhere from the lunar cities on your own. I'm your best bet at getting to Echo."

"You?" She raised an eyebrow. "You're not my best bet at anything."

Guilt speared him, and Finn knew he had made his choice. Avery was too important to let go. Whether she wanted it or not.

"I'm probably your only chance at getting through the

Gate undetected, and I think you know it. Without your port, you don't even have any credits to pay your way." He nodded to her wrist, and she self-consciously covered the area with her other hand. "But if you'd rather sell yourself to the miners, be my guest," he added flippantly. "I'm sure they'd pay a pretty good price for a little piece of—"

"All right, fine," she interrupted him, her voice snapping. "I'll go with you. But only through the Gate. Once we reach Echo, I'm going my own way."

"I'm sorry, what was that?" he asked, touching a finger to his ear. "Did you just ask for my help? I didn't want to miss it."

"Over my dead body will I ever ask you for anything." She turned to leave, stopping at the door. "But thank you," she added, and then she was gone.

The guilt hit his gut harder, pure and striking, cutting him clean through. He was doing what was best for the Rebellion. What was best for the family he'd come to love. She would see it was the right choice once she had a chance to understand. She had to.

He couldn't believe that she was as unfeeling as she professed. Everything about her indicated otherwise. And as for what she was, no one could be in that much denial. The people of Echo needed hope. And that was more important than anyone's grandmother.

Movement on one of the log screens captured his attention, and he grabbed the video with his fingers, enlarging the feed so he could see it properly on the clear screen before him. The Fed chick was awake. Finn wasn't surprised; Avery had rattled the ship like a toy.

He squinted at the screen, trying to make out what she was doing on the floor with a . . . was she pulling back the floor panels?

Finn was out of his seat in a flash, descending the stairs two at a time into the living quarters. He trotted to the room on the far end, touching a few selections on his wristport to turn the entire outer wall into clear glass.

Petra's head shot up, glaring at Finn through the barrier. She dropped her tool—a pipe from the bathing area—and stood. She rubbed her grimy hands on the blue pants of her uniform.

"Do you have any idea how long it's going to take to fix that?" he asked, nodding to the water running freely at the little sink where she had ripped the pipe from the wall.

"Where am I?" she asked, eyes narrowing.

"Look, Petra." He paused, adjusting to lean his shoulder against the glass. "It *is* Petra, isn't it?" She didn't respond. "That's what I thought. I know you remember what happened. And I also think you know what Avery is by now."

She stared at him with immovable green eyes, her jaw clenching.

"I'm pretty sure that from your training, you've probably learned that an Elite can only control Natives. Am I right?"

Again, a stare.

"So let's cut the crap. I've had enough Natives pretending not to know what they are already today. You're not a Fed, which means we're on the same team. And more importantly, you're not getting out of there until I let you out." He leveled her with a stare of his own. "No matter how many pipes you pull out of the wall."

Petra shifted, turning away from him before asking, "Where is Avery?"

"Why? Do you want to point a gun at her face again?"

She turned, her face a mask of anger as she stalked toward him. "You don't know anything, you ridiculous buffoon."

"Buffoon. Now that's one I haven't been called before." He was mildly impressed.

"I know who you are," she bit out, her emerald eyes flashing with contempt. "Unlike you, I was trying to make a real difference. Not sitting on my ass and playing politics until the Federation wipes out our entire race! What could you, a *human*,"—she said the word with hatred dripping from her lips—"ever do to help us?"

Finn felt the sting as her attack hit its mark. Her words mirrored his exact sentiment about his family's position. He wanted to do more. To be more for the Rebellion.

"So I take it you've never seen an Elite, either?" he surmised. Her face reddened, and she quickly tilted it away from him. "Weren't exactly familiar with being hijacked, were you?" She didn't respond. "That *is* what happened, right? It's why you were helping us at all."

"Why I do anything is none of your business," she replied, seething. "Where is Avery? I want to speak with her."

"Oh no. You don't get to see her until I have some guarantee that you aren't going to attack her again." She let out a sound that reminded him of an angry space rat. "Neither of you are very good at controlling your tempers, are you? Must be a genetic trait."

"Don't you dare insinuate that I would lay a hand on her—"

"You see?" He let out a small laugh. "Am I the only one who remembers the gun-in-the-face thing?"

"I—I was disoriented," Petra stammered. "It won't happen again. The merge is not something that should be done without consent. It leads to . . . confusion."

"The merge?" he asked, pushing off from the glass and facing her with interest. "Is that what you call it?"

"I won't discuss it with you." She lifted her chin. "If you insist on keeping me in here, at least bring Avery to me. She will let me out once I explain."

"I wouldn't be so sure about that," Finn mumbled. "Your fearless leader is roaming around the ship right now, debating how she's going to get back to the Port Station and rescue her little old grandmother. She doesn't have much interest in helping the Rebellion."

"What?" Petra asked, seething. "What did you say to her? You weren't meant to explain things to her. I was going to—" She cut herself off, shaking her head as she looked at the floor.

"Regardless of what you were or weren't going to do, I intend to take her back to Nos Valuta with me." He watched her carefully for a reaction. "Whether or not she consents to it."

She remained silent, assessing. "Then," she added quietly, "we are in agreement."

A grin tugged at his mouth. "I was hoping you'd say that." With a flick of his wrist, Finn unlocked the door, the glass sliding into the floor. "That just earned you your—"

He was cut off as Petra strode forward, connecting her fist in a solid blow to his face. Finn stumbled back and collapsed on the ground across the hall. He blinked as the pain began to spread throughout his jaw, up into the roots of his teeth.

Petra stepped out of the room, walking past him as she called out, "That was for the med tray."

"What the blazar is she doing here?" The words were out of Avery's mouth before she could stop them as she entered the bridge. Petra was standing beside Finn, looking over some kind of schematics on the control screens.

"Was that moping session all you thought it would be?" Finn commented, not bothering to so much as glance in her direction.

Avery frowned, moving in a wide arc around Petra to take her seat at the navigation command. She swiveled the chair to face them. At least she seemed docile enough now. "Isn't she supposed to be locked up in the brig?" Avery tried to sound unconcerned.

Petra's face quickly flooded red as she tucked hair behind an ear, avoiding eye contact. No one spoke for some moments.

"What Petra means to say"—Finn turned toward Avery while putting a hand on Petra's shoulder—"is that she's very sorry for her med-bay meltdown. She's back on board now. One big happy family, right?" He turned his head toward Petra, jerking his chin back to Avery.

"He's right," Petra said, her green eyes raised to meet Avery's. "I'm sorry about earlier. . . . I just wasn't ready for—"

"Yeah, yeah," Finn interrupted, returning to his position behind Petra's seat. "We can get to all that touchy-feely crap later. As I was saying"—Finn pointed at the map in front of them, and Petra reluctantly returned her attention to the screen—"I think we can hop in with that crowd of miners from Mars. The Federation is paid off by the companies that run the digs, so we wouldn't have to worry about any type of inspection."

"But to move into another group's hyperspeed? That's risky, at best," Petra countered, typing figures into the computer. "It would be difficult, even for me. With you at the helm, we're more likely to be broken apart by the gravity clash than caught by Federation soldiers."

"Excuse me," Finn replied in a tone that was fairly close to a whine, "but you've never even seen me in action."

Petra let out a snort. "It's not like I need to. You've got a reputation that precedes you. This type of jump requires pinpoint accuracy, and you know it."

"Fine," Finn said grudgingly. "By all means," he added, gesturing to the captain's seat as he stood, grabbing a rectangular chrome case that had been resting on the console. "Let's just get going."

Opening its lid, Finn pulled out a syringe capped by a long needle. He popped the top off and shook the tube. The clear liquid inside clouded to a bright shade of green.

"What's that for?" Avery braced herself as he made his way toward her.

"Now don't go getting all panicky on me again," he said, gesturing to the needle. "It's a prep shot for the hyperspeed. It will keep you from getting sick."

"I don't like needles," Avery said, staring at the thing. The thought of it poking a hole in her skin made her squirm. "Isn't that a bit primitive? Don't you have a med strip or something I can use instead?"

"Don't be such a baby." He came over to her side, crouched beside her seat, and positioned the needle above her shoulder. "This one doesn't even hurt."

He plunged the needle into her skin. She jolted at the sharp sting, feeling the liquid spread immediately from the source like electricity blazing through a circuit underneath her skin. "Ow!" she exclaimed, grabbing her arm as he pulled away, trying to ignore the ache that reached her bones. "You said it wouldn't hurt!"

"Yeah, I lied," he said with a grin, throwing the syringe down a waste chute in the wall. "That one hurts like a bitch. But at least you won't blow chunks all over my bridge again."

Avery scowled at him. "Are you always such an ass?" she asked sullenly, still rubbing her sore arm.

"Only with the pretty girls." He winked at her, and she looked away, catching Petra staring at them.

Averting her gaze, Petra cleared her throat as she typed in some commands. "The blastfire we took during our escape damaged a partial engine, but I think I can counteract using the reserve hyperfuel. Strap in."

Avery pressed the button on the side of her seat, safety restraints extending automatically up and around her body. Finn took a seat beside her and strapped in, too.

Petra took the hologram controls, the computer recognizing her hand movements and translating them into commands for the ship. With a slight twist of her wrist, the ship began to shudder as the hyper engines fired up.

"Here we go," Petra said with a slight smile, rotating her hands in a half circle as the engines increased speed.

Avery looked out the windows in front of them, getting one last view of Saturn before it blurred with the surrounding stars, and the three of them sped through space, faster than light.

CHAPTER SEVEN

"You *what?*" Harding nearly yelled, rage itself overcoming any desire to control it.

"We . . . ." The soldier reporting to him focused intently on the control panel in front of them as he continued. "We lost the asset, sir."

Harding jerked away, taking in a swift breath as he made his way to the front of the Port Station bridge. Looking out at the Gate, he counted deliberately down from five in his mind. It was a good tactic, suggested by his therapist, to gain control of his anger.

Five . . . four . . . . How had that little slip of a girl managed to get away? He cracked the fingers on his left hand, meticulously and in succession. *Three . . . two . . . .* His eye twitched.

"Explain to me how an Earthen girl managed to escape one

of the most protected facilities in the galaxy!" he burst out, spit flying from his mouth.

"Well, sir, there's a full brief in your por—"

"I don't want the brief," Harding interrupted, raising his hand to gesture toward the wall of blast glass looking out into open space. "I want to know how you let her get away."

The soldier took a shaky breath, glancing around at the other tech specialists in the room. But they stealthily avoided eye contact. "She had help," he said tentatively.

Harding felt his gut twist. "What do you mean?"

"The ambassador," he added, swallowing hard, "escaped with her."

Harding heard the growl of frustration before realizing it came from his own throat. He whipped around, unholstering his sidearm and shooting off six blasts at the glass wall in front of them.

White flashes illuminated the room, the blasts ricocheting and littering the bridge around them in a chorus of exploding tech. Personnel scrambled, diving to the floor to avoid being hit.

Harding stood silently, staring at his reflection in the glass. Steam hissed from one of the consoles behind him, mingling with his harsh breaths. In and out, over and over.

His entire reputation was riding on this. Minister Klein expected results from the Vey girl. Harding had already contacted one of the best minds from the Lares Project to begin her experimentation. Just when things were finally lining up for him. . . .

Finn Lunitia. That bastard had slipped from his grasp. And taken the most important Federation find in decades right along with him. He should have killed him when he had the chance, High Council orders be damned. Harding abhorred the entire Lunitia family. Even their father had been a privileged waste of space.

"Captain Harding, sir," one of the techs interrupted his thoughts.

"Not now," he growled through clenched teeth.

"But sir," she pressed, "Minister Klein is requesting to be patched through to your comm."

The blood quickly drained from his face. Harding closed his eyes, unable to keep his lip from curling in disgusted frustration. "Go ahead," he ground out.

His audio piece beeped the incoming comm before Klein's vid pulled up on the glass in front of him. Harding forced himself not to flinch.

"Captain," Klein said, her firm chin rising as one elegant blonde brow lifted.

"Minister," he answered, dipping his head quickly in a show of deference. "We seem to hav—"

"I'm not interested in your excuses this time, Harding," she interrupted. Harding swallowed the irritation clawing up his throat. "It seems you cannot accomplish a simple task set out for you, even when I deliver what you need right to your hands. Things should have been simple when Lunitia practically threw the girl into our lap."

Harding was keenly aware of the room behind him. It was filled with people, all under his command. All watching his moment of weakness.

"Ma'am, if I may—"

"It has become clear to me that you need more direct assistance, Captain," she continued calmly, as though he hadn't even been talking. "My source will help you reacquire the asset, and you would do well not to waste his collaboration this time," she warned, her tone darkening. "You are forcing me to use a card I'd rather keep hidden. I do not appreciate the inconvenience."

"Ma'am," he replied with a slight nod. Harding knew better than to speak further. Klein was in a rare temper, and he refused to give her more whip with which to flay him.

The acquiescence seemed to placate her. She relaxed, wiping the frown from her face as her sharp features brightened. "Chin up, Captain," she added. "We may be able to fix your mess without much loss in the end."

Harding clenched his teeth so tightly that his jaw ached in pain. As he listened to Klein explain their next steps, he focused on showing no emotion at all.

It was only later, in the privacy of his own quarters, that he rammed his fist into a wall. After repeated hits, his knuckles were a bloody mess, the white wall smeared with bright red. And as the aching discomfort flooded his arm, throbbing through his veins with each heartbeat, Harding was able to forget about Lunitia . . . the incompetency of his team . . . his anger.

There was only pain.

They reached the moon with little difficulty. Petra had been right about her calculations. They cruised right into the moon's airspace without anyone the wiser, least of all the Federation. Even Finn couldn't complain.

Since they couldn't travel through the Gate in a small vessel, they had to secure passage on a larger cruise ship to make the jump. Avery was amazed at how quickly Finn found them space simply by making a few comms to the right people. Maybe he really was an ambassador.

Avery looked at Finn warily out of the corner of her eye while he administered the bio supplements she needed to avoid the time sickness of the Gate jump. He told her it would be about a hundred times worse than hyperspeed, so she couldn't shrug off the twenty-minute treatment.

But Avery still couldn't shake the feeling that she was out of her element. That Finn and Petra were hiding something. Perhaps it was just Gran's warning, making her paranoid.

Despite trying to convince herself Finn was crazy, Avery couldn't deny what had happened to her the past few days. The things she had done. There was something happening to her. Something big.

Avery's only lead was to find this Brinstal person. Maybe then things would start to make sense.

The capital city of Milderion was a mecca that could provide her with a few leads, and she was used to chasing them on all those errands she ran for Gran on the ground level back home. If Finn had connections, perhaps she could convince him to point her in the right direction, even if he wouldn't help her himself.

Maybe she wasn't a Native. Maybe Finn was wrong. The Federation could have done some weird experiment on her while she was on the Station to change her. She had been there for days before she awoke. Who knows what they had time to do to her?

But Gran had known those Feds were coming, and it was the bioscan that tipped her off. Avery felt sick, knowing if Gran was here, she could explain everything.

As her mind stormed, Avery perched on the med bay table as Finn prepped the med patch dispensary. He was actually pretty good with his hands. She leaned back on the table trying to relax, while stealthily stealing glimpses of his profile.

"Where are you from?" she asked, unable to squelch her curiosity. Maybe if she knew more about him, she could find a way to convince him to help her.

He barely looked at her as he continued working. "Why does it matter? You're going your way when we get to Echo anyway, right?"

She averted her eyes, focusing on the inside of her arm where he attached the med patch. Her face grew hot. Avery realized she was ashamed of the choice she had made to not follow him.

"I was born on Earth," Finn answered her question, anyway. "But my father moved us all to Echo when I was a kid."

"So you're human," she said, almost to herself. "Then why are you fighting for the Rebellion?"

Finn let out a sound that was something between a laugh and a grunt, securing the last of the supplies in the cabinet beside Avery before turning to lean against the white counter. "Why the sudden interest?"

"Don't tell me it's because of a girl," she countered, hoping to prod him into opening up. When he didn't respond, she continued, "Or maybe because of a boy?"

"If you are expecting to get a rise out of me," he said with a slow smile that dimpled his cheek, "I think I have to warn you that it doesn't work that way."

"What way?"

"I get the rises out of people," he explained. "Not the other way around."

She rolled her eyes, wishing she could come up with something smart to throw in his face. As if his irritating humor wasn't enough, the guy had to be full of arrogance, too. She wondered if he got anywhere with that kind of attitude.

"And no," he continued. "It isn't because of anyone. Of any sexual orientation."

Avery narrowed her eyes, challenging him to answer seriously. She ignored the peculiar sensation that tickled her stomach as she stared into his eyes. It was probably the meds making her lightheaded.

But he wouldn't break, neither of them backing down. After a moment, he folded his arms over his chest, settling farther against the cabinet as he crossed his legs with a loud sigh.

Avery was the first to break, a grin forming on her lips as she looked away. She couldn't make him talk if he didn't want to. And perhaps that was best. If she learned his reasons for joining the Rebellion, it might make it more difficult for her to stay her course.

But he was the one who had asked her to come with him. Surely, he couldn't have thought that she would consider it without learning his own motivations to fight.

Clearing her throat, she asked, "So how's this going to work?"

"How's what going to work?" he replied.

"When we get to Echo,"—Avery gestured above her head with a wave of her hand in reference—"are you going to give me a clue where I should start to find some help in the city, or am I just going in blind?"

"Well, I figured we'd just push you out the cargo door with a parachute and a smile," he quipped.

"I'm serious."

"So am I."

"Why are you so—" she began.

"Charming?"

"I was gonna go with frustrating," she retorted. "Is this thing done yet?" She nodded toward her arm.

He walked to her side, and she refused to look up at him, focusing instead on the dark brown leather of his boots against the white sterile floor. His hand gripped her arm gently, and she ignored the warmth of his skin against hers. She wanted out of this situation altogether.

"Just about finished," he said, pulling the med patch from her arm. It tingled where it pulled her skin, leaving a small, round red mark on the inside of her elbow. "Don't get up for about five minutes," he advised. "I'm gonna get back to the bridge. No telling what Petra's doing to my ship alone up there."

And then he was gone, leaving nothing but silence behind him. Avery shivered as she felt a slight boom from somewhere far away, wondering if it was the engines of the main cruise ship pushing them through the Gate. She hadn't thought to ask Finn if they would feel anything, though she supposed not. Her treatment was supposed to alleviate any reaction to the jump.

After waiting what she hoped was five minutes, Avery hopped down from the med table and made her way after him. She climbed one of the two staircases in the cargo hold, walking down the curved hallway that led to the bridge.

Finn and Petra were speaking, and remarkably, it didn't sound like an argument. Their conversation halted as she approached, both of them concentrating on the screen in front of them. The ship lifted, and Petra guided them out toward the rear of the cruise hold. A smaller hull door opened, allowing them to fly into open space.

Except the stars were no constellations that Avery had ever seen. They *had* gone through the Gate without her feeling it. This was a whole new galaxy spread out around her.

And then Petra turned the ship around, bringing the planet of Echo into full view. Avery's breath caught. She walked forward between the captain and navigation commands to enter the glass nose of the ship.

The planet was so blue. It was bluer than Earth, even, with swirls of white smeared all over its surface. Like someone had rolled a sapphire marble through white paint. The vibrant colors of the oceans that dominated the globe seemed to glow against the blackness of the space around it, like some magical force. Her eyes flickered to the white objects hovering around the outer edge of the planet, and Avery realized she was looking at Echo's moons. It had three of them, but she could only see two, half shadowed by the sunlight of this solar system.

"It's something, isn't it?" Finn asked, coming up beside Avery as they both observed the planet in the distance. He loved this world, Avery could tell, even if it wasn't his birthplace. But Earth would always be her home. Not this foreign place.

Avery turned, making her way back to the commands as she said with as much flippancy as she could muster, "I guess it's okay." She didn't miss the way Petra tensed.

Finn laughed, taking the seat at the navigation command without responding to her barb. "Take us in, Petra," he said, glancing at her as she leaned forward, increasing the speed of the ship. "You might want to sit down," he added to Avery.

She did as he said, focusing on the blue mass of a planet before them. What would it look like once they were on the ground? Her mind filtered through the pictures she'd seen of the place in games and movies.

Beautiful and lush and tropical and full of natural life. They said it was like what Earth used to be, thousands of years ago. Before humans had taken over the natural habitats on their planet. On Earth, you could only find vegetation in the cultured habitats within the city walls. And even then, only the rich had access to the forests and parks. An average person could go their whole life never seeing a single tree.

Avery had been to the park on Level 13 once, on a field trip with her class. She remembered the way grass had felt beneath her bare feet and the fresh smell of the leaves on the bushes that grew around the water features. That was the only time she had ever been to a natural park. The fees to visit them or, galaxy forbid, become a member were just too high for Gran and her to afford.

Now Avery descended through the atmosphere, and she stifled a gasp as the main continent came into view, green and bright against the blue of the ocean that surrounded it. They moved in quickly, the landmarks becoming more visible as they approached.

Avery saw the huge mountain that sat against the background of Milderion, Echo's capital. The tall, elegant buildings blended seamlessly with the mountainous region in a way that effortlessly combined the structures with nature. Milderion was a tourist destination, and even Avery could recognize its features. This was where they would leave her. In a matter of minutes, she would be walking its streets. Free to find her own way to save her grandmother.

Avery prayed she could hold her own amongst the Natives. The Federation controlled most of the city, but there were areas where Earth tourists were warned not to venture. Hopefully she could keep herself out of trouble. She had gotten through a few scrapes on the ground level before. This couldn't be much different.

She had to come up with a plan. Maybe there were common trade areas like on Earth where she could poke around. Ask a few questions, do a quick search. If only she still had her wristport, she could at least look up Brinstal. Or she could message Megan to ask for—

Avery's heart leapt as she realized Megan's family would be in the city soon, if they weren't already. She could easily find a public comm board and send her a message to meet up. Megan's father was one of the more popular media reporters covering the Federation war, so there was a good chance he already had some connections. Things were looking better already, and Avery let the optimism tug a small grin from her lips.

But as she looked at the city contemplating her next moves, their ship continued past the capital center, moving up and gaining altitude quickly. The smile wiped from her face as she realized that they were leaving Milderion behind them, heading toward the mountains beyond.

"Wait, what's going on?" she asked, nearly coming to her feet. "That was Milderion back there, wasn't it? That's where I wanted to go." She tugged the side of Finn's sleeve. "Does she know what she's doing?"

Finn's jaw clenched, his face hardening in an unfamiliar way before he said with a slight nod, "We're not going to Milderion."

Avery felt her stomach drop. She laughed nervously. "I'm sorry, I thought I heard you say we're not going there."

"I did." He nodded again.

"Then where are we going?" she asked, aware that her voice was sliding perilously close to shrill. When Finn didn't respond, she leaned back to level her gaze at Petra, deliberately focusing her energy. "Where are we going?" she asked harshly this time, feeling something primal reach out from herself in connection.

"To Nos Valuta," Petra replied, her tone flat as it had been back on the Station. "The Rebel camp."

Finn closed his eyes in annoyance as he heard Petra respond in that calm voice she hadn't used since their escape. Avery must have been tapping into her mind again. He could only hope that Petra's willpower would hold out long enough for them to get safely to the ground at Valuta. He wondered if Avery could make Petra do something that she completely didn't want to do, like turn the ship around.

He'd just have to distract her long enough for that not to be an issue.

Standing, Finn faced Avery where she stood from her seat. Her light brown eyes were fiery again, swirling with emotion as she narrowed them. Her hot temper might just help him in this situation.

With a grin, he held out his hands and said with a trace of humor, "Now, let's stay calm. No need to try and blow up my ship again or anything. I know I told you how important you are, sweetheart."

"I swear to all that's holy," she spat at him, "if you call me sweetheart one more blazing time, I'm going to do more than blow up your ship."

"Fine," he conceded, walking toward her as she backed away. The engines picked up speed, hopefully an indication that Petra had some control again. "Although it's not like you can control it. Your powers, I mean." He saw her face redden and kept pushing her. "You *could* learn to control them, Avery. We have Elders here, ones that could help you figure out how to use them the way you were meant to."

"I don't want to control them!" she yelled, emotion cracking her voice. "I trusted you, damn it! I knew I wasn't supposed to, but apparently I did, and I can't believe I was so blazing stupid!"

"You aren't stupid," Finn replied quickly, keeping her gaze on him. He tamped down the guilt that was clawing up his belly at the sight of her face, which was full of heavy emotion. He didn't owe her anything. She had a responsibility from her birth, just like everybody in this damn fight. "So I was a little less than honest—"

"Less than honest?" she scoffed. "You're a liar, Finn. You promised to take me to the city, and you deliberately went back on your word." Her eyes lit with something new. Hate, he thought. But he felt the ship settle down onto the ground, and it didn't matter. "I don't know why I expected a Rebel to be honest."

He gritted his teeth, telling himself that it didn't matter what she thought about him. The lives of the hundreds of people hiding here in the mountains mattered. The thousands more that were at risk at the hands of the Federation all over the world. This was the right thing.

"Listen to what they have to say. Please." Petra saved him from having to respond, and he was thankful. He couldn't face Avery another second. He shrugged, turning his back on her as he looked out at the Rebels already walking toward the ship.

"Why should I trust you any more than him?" Avery's voice was lined with disgust. "You two aren't any better than the Federation. You can't just take people against their will."

"You have the freedom to walk away," Petra told her. "But you owe it to yourself and your people to—"

"My people?" Avery cried, and Finn swore he could hear the tears in her eyes. "I only have *one* person, and she's up there! Locked away in a Federation cell where they're doing God knows what to her. I just want to help her! *Only* her. Don't you get it?"

Finn peeked up at the frame of the ship, expecting it to begin rattling again as it had during Avery's last outburst. With a tap to his wristport, he activated the cargo door on the side of the ship to allow the Rebels entry.

"Avery, please," Petra implored, and Finn turned back. Avery stood against the far wall, her back as straight as a circuit board. "If you learn from us, you will have the tools to rescue your grandmother yourself. I promise you."

Finn could tell the moment it dawned on Avery that Petra was a Native, shock written plainly on her face. What was going through that head of hers? Then her eyes connected with his, a thrill shooting through his veins. Perhaps his reaction to her was a result of her powers. He hoped this strange feeling around her would recede as she learned to control herself.

Or better yet, perhaps Nick would finally let him rejoin the frontlines. He yearned for the feel of a blaster in his hands again. The thrill of hand-to-hand combat. He prayed that the risk he took in leaving without Nick's permission would pay off once Nick learned that Finn had found and brought home an Elite. A So'Reange.

Maybe he'd finally be able to make a difference again.

CHAPTER EIGHT

A very had briefly forgotten that it was popular on Echo to in-
dulge in genetic modifications for fun. She blanched when
the soldiers entered the bridge. One of them had vibrant orange eyes that set her on edge. The other sported hair so bright
and blue that it was nearly neon.

The Federation had put a stop to that on Earth years earlier,
claiming that such modifications went against the very fabric
of what made them human. It was one of the largest forms of
propaganda for the war. If citizens of Earth wanted to show
support, they would reject such unnatural forms of expression.

It was more prevalent, among the rich at least, to merely
modify their traits. They wouldn't condone anything unnatural, but claimed it didn't hurt to do a little enhancement. The
entire thing was completely hypocritical.

Still, Avery followed them off the ship, refusing to look at Finn, even as he gave them orders. She wondered just how involved he was in this thing. It didn't matter, though. If she couldn't get it through his thick head that she didn't want to be here, perhaps these Elders would listen.

Avery barely caught a glimpse of the sky and terrain before she was back inside, passing through a door hidden in the side of the mountain. Expecting to find a cave, Avery was surprised when they entered what looked like a modern facility.

The technology was foreign, and the writing on all the signage was Native. The entire camp must have been built by them. It was obviously hidden in the mountains, but just outside the city. How had they been able to remain unseen by the Federation?

She glanced behind her as they walked swiftly through the rounded corridors, Finn and Petra close on their heels. However much she distrusted them, at least they were something familiar.

Her escorts stopped in front of an arched doorway, each standing on either side of the entrance. As they gestured for her to continue, Avery took a small breath, bracing her shoulders.

The room was filled with a small crowd, all eyes fixated on her. It was relatively silent as they stared, making her uncomfortable.

From what she could tell, this group wasn't really all that old. To be called Elders, that is. There were eight in total, all dressed in the draped robes of traditional Native culture, a modern take on an ancient style that had always appealed to her. It contrasted strangely with the brightly colored gen mods she saw on a few.

"Welcome, Avery," a younger man spoke first, approaching

her with a smile. His eyes were warm, his voice gravelly and kind in a way that made her think he would certainly understand. Perhaps she could appeal to him. "We've been waiting for you," he added gently.

Avery returned his smile hesitantly, following as he took her arm and led her toward a large white hover table centered in the room.

"That's the thing," Avery began delicately, taking the seat he offered. "I don't think you quite understand, but I didn't exactly choose to come here."

"What do you mean by that?" one of the women asked with a touch of caution. Her eyes were a vibrant blue.

"Well I—" she began but was interrupted by the man who had greeted her.

"I'm sure there will be plenty of time for all of that." He turned to address the others. "We should take it slowly with her, for reasons that you all are aware. She's been through quite the ordeal, if Finnegan's log is any indication."

Avery kept quiet for the moment, her gaze flickering between them as they began to talk amongst themselves, moving to their various places around the table. She had been given a seat at the head, feeling conspicuously as though she was on display. Who knew what Finn had told them?

"I'm sorry, I haven't introduced myself," the man said, taking the open seat beside her. He wore a closely cut white shirt with intricate folds running over the shoulders. It was an obvious Native design but more familiar than the long, flowing robes of the others. "I'm Nick," he said with a slight inclination of his head and a grin. "Don't worry. We don't bite."

Avery nodded awkwardly, insecurity making her palms sweat. She rubbed them against the fabric of her too-big pants, shifting her feet. She so clearly didn't belong there.

"Listen," she began, looking at Nick and trying to give him her best attempt at a damsel in distress. Hadn't she seen Megan do it hundreds of times? "I really don't think—"

He put a finger to his lips and gestured toward the other end of the table where an older woman began to speak. It was in the Native tongue, and Avery didn't understand a word as the others joined in. She focused instead on the woman's graying pink hair, clenching her hands together in her lap.

She peeped back at the door, hoping to catch sight of Finn—or even Petra—and quickly chastised herself. She didn't need either of them. She could deal with this on her own. Play their games until she had a chance to make her argument. Maybe this was the perfect place to start her search for Brinstal.

These were the leaders that represented the people of Echo, or what was left of it. How long could a little protocol take?

It only took a few hours for Avery to realize that she wasn't going anywhere anytime soon. She was out of her depth, having let the opportunity to voice her opinion pass her by, and now she was stuck in a perpetual state of awkward silence.

Avery sighed quietly, leaning against the smooth table and relishing in the cool surface against her forearms. She was firmly situated in their camp, and each minute she spent there took her further away from her goal of getting back to Gran.

But she couldn't see any way to get out of it, if the Elders wouldn't let her speak. They were obviously operating under the misunderstanding that she was some Echo Native from

Earth, thanks to Finn and his big mouth.

Bitterness filled her at the thought of him. She had actually begun to think he was a decent human being, which made the betrayal all the worse. Not to mention Petra. They couldn't expect her to stay here when they had tricked her in such a way.

As far as she was concerned, she had been abducted first by the Federation, and now the Rebellion. All for some far-fetched theory that couldn't be real.

But was it so unbelievable? Avery couldn't deny what she had done in that ship. Or what had happened with Petra. There was absolutely some kind of . . . connection between them. And then there were the visions and the headaches. A strange awareness had settled around her, particularly in this place.

But even if she was . . . a Native . . . there seemed to be plenty of them there. They could just use their own powers to help.

What had Finn called her? An Elite. She had no idea what that meant. Avery clenched her fists on the table. It was enough.

She pushed back her chair, standing in a fluid motion as the discussion at the table tapered off, all eyes on her. "I . . ." Avery began, suddenly unsure of what she was going to say.

"Go ahead." Nick's voice was a gentle nudge beside her. "If you have something to say, I am sure we are all eager to hear it."

She took a small breath. "I can't stay here," she started shakily. "I'm not who you think I am. Who Finn thinks I am, that is. There was a big misunderstanding, and yeah, I was at the Port Station, but I really think he's just blowing this out of proportion. I mean, even if I was, you know, a Native, it's not like you need me here." Her fingers gripped the table. She was rambling. "It's just really important that I make it back to Milderion because I have to find this Brinstal person to help my grandmother who is still—"

"What did you say?" The older pink-haired woman half stood from her seat, the hover table adjusting as she leaned more heavily against it.

"Uh." Avery's eyes shifted to Nick and back. "My grandmother . . . she's still in danger on the—"

"No," the woman said, stopping her again. "Brinstal. You mentioned you were looking for a Brinstal."

Avery's mouth went dry as she realized perhaps she had revealed too much. "Yes." She nodded quickly. "It's a name my grandmother gave to me. I'm supposed to find her. . . . Do you know her? Can you help me find her?"

The pink-haired woman appeared alarmed, the rest of the Elders exchanging looks with one another that Avery couldn't identify.

"Please," Avery said, embarrassed that her voice cracked ever so slightly. "It's the only chance I have to save her."

"Who is your grandmother, child?" she asked in a gentler tone.

Avery's chin rose. "Nestra Vey."

A murmur went through the room, the woman dropping into her seat with a look of surprise on her face. An Elder with feline pupils said something sharply in Native tongue, and Pink Hair replied calmly before the table erupted into a babble of animated arguments.

Avery observed Nick, who remained silent. He stared at the group intently before catching her gaze, the look evaporating from his face. Instead, he smiled gently, nearly apologetically.

"Enough!" Pink Hair silenced the chatter, laying her long arms out across the table for effect. "Nicholas, I think you had best show our guest to her quarters. Things have become infinitely more complicated."

Avery panicked, moving to protest, but Nick's hand was on her arm and urging her into silence. He clearly held power but wasn't fully participating with the others. Perhaps he wasn't one of them after all.

"It's hard to shut them up once they get started, anyway," Nick said in a low voice as they entered the white hallway.

She ignored him, too irritated to placate his good temper. "What are they talking about? Do they know my grandmother?"

"I am sorry about all of this," Nick replied. "You have every right to be angry, of course. It's a frustrating situation, and not one that has an easy solution. Now," he said, withdrawing his hand from her arm, "let's see if we can't get you settled. Once you eat and rest, we'll be able to sort this out, I'm sure."

She followed him, if only for the excuse to have something to do other than feel overwhelmed. Perhaps he was right. If she had some time alone, she might figure a way out of this mess.

They passed a few people as they walked, who mostly smiled politely and kept their heads down. Avery wondered if they were Native as well. Surely Finn was an indication that the Rebellion had human sympathizers. She wondered what his role was in all of this.

"What has Finn told you about our life here?" Nick asked, as though reading her thoughts.

"Nothing," she replied bitterly. "I've been trying to tell you, he dragged me here against my will."

Nick stopped, turning to face her. She came up short, her head tilting up to meet his eyes. They were gray, like Finn's. But there was a seriousness there, swirling delicately with his friendliness. He was stable, as though he was used to supporting others.

"Did Finnegan not tell you the importance of your position?" His voice was soft.

"He mentioned some nonsense about Elites." Avery shrugged. "But what the blazar that is, I couldn't tell you."

He cursed, reaching out to take her hands, his warmth seeping into her cold fingers. "I am so sorry," he apologized. "He should have had more tact. We have a lot to discuss, you and I." Releasing her, he turned to continue down the maze of hallways, indicating for her to follow. It would be difficult trying to find her way out of there on her own.

"Quarters have been prepared for you," he said, slowing as they approached a large rounded door at the end of a single hall. "The Elders do hope you'll be comfortable here."

Avery's eyes widened as they entered, every surface gleaming a perfect white. The entire wall of the living quarters was curved glass, looking out into an open chasm that dropped into the mountains beneath. Other windows peeked back at her from across the space, wrapping around as though lining the inside of a cylinder. She peered down the chasm that extended hundreds of stories beneath them.

Just how big was this base?

Her attention turned back to the room where a glittering crystal chandelier hung from the ceiling in an intricate, organic arrangement, sparkling light on every available surface. Taking up the living area was a plush gray rug that invited her to a circle of ivory sofas. There was also a long hover table in the dining area beyond, featuring foods of all colors and varieties. And nearest to her, a small set of stairs led to what looked like a bedroom suite.

She turned slowly to face Nick. "What the blazar is all this?"

"Your rooms," he said, gesturing to the opulent surroundings. "Don't you like them?"

"Who wouldn't?" she said suddenly, a small laugh bubbling up to her lips. "Aren't the Natives supposed to be in hiding? Like, in a war zone or something?"

"Avery," Nick said in a calm voice with a slight smile coloring his words, "despite what the Federation would have you believe, the Natives aren't heathens hiding away in a hole in the ground. This is a sanctuary beneath their holy mountains. Not all enjoy the luxuries you will come to know, but you will learn the culture," he explained, gliding to the dining area. "And your place in it."

"And if I don't want a place in it?" she asked. "Please listen. I don't belong here. My grandmother is—"

"I'm sure she is safe," he said, his gray eyes warm. "The Federation values you nearly as much as we do. They would not harm her knowing that she is significant to you."

"Why do they value me? Nobody is explaining anything." She clenched her fists at her sides as she continued. "I'm not some child. I deserve to know what's going on."

"I agree," he said, motioning his head toward the food. "Come and eat, and we can talk."

If she wanted answers, she supposed she had no other choice. As they sat, a servant appeared from somewhere, discreetly filling their glasses. Avery looked at the peculiar fruits on her plate and her heart faltered. She had last eaten Echo food with Megan, back home.

"When the human explorers first landed here hundreds of years ago," Nick began, taking a swig of wine from his glass, "they never expected to find intelligent life, let alone one that so closely resembled their own. It defied logic, to have found a civilization across the universe that was effectively the same species as humans."

Avery nodded, recognizing the story from her science classes in school. She took a tentative bite of some chopped yellow fruit and suddenly found herself ravenous, devouring the rest at an alarming speed, even for her.

"As the first settlers interacted with them, they soon realized that the Natives—or the Reanges, as they called themselves—had a vastly superior intelligence. They could manipulate matter and substance, and some even had the ability to alter their own DNA, stemming from a higher function of their brain capacity." Avery tamped down surprise. This version of history certainly wasn't in the Federation textbooks. "However, these abilities were a unique trait, inherited only through genetic anomalies. Therefore, the Reanges who possessed these powers were made leaders, given the honorific of So'. They were a royal line, if you will." He paused, taking another sip. "The humans called them Elites."

Avery choked on the fruit, grabbing a glass of wine to wash it down painfully.

"By the time the settlers were finally able to build the Gate to connect this galaxy with our own, hundreds of years had passed. Humans had integrated with the society here on Echo. The two cultures assimilated, living peacefully together, as the Reanges were never, and have never been, violent. They never had any need for it. Being able to communicate telepathically alleviates any kind of—"

"Wait a minute," Avery interrupted. "Are you telling me that they can read one another's minds?"

"Absolutely," he replied with a small smile. "Honestly, what do they teach you in the Earth schools these days?"

"Then why talk at all?" she asked, genuinely interested.

"Unfortunately, the connection of mind is only established with the unique powers of a So'. We are incredibly lucky that Finnegan came across you. When I think about what the Federation would have done to you in that base . . . ."

"And I'm so much better off here?" she asked resentfully.

"Well, for one thing, you aren't going to be tortured. Or experimented upon. Or dissected," he added darkly.

"What does that mean?" Avery asked frantically.

"When the Gate was first initiated and the Federation came through from Earth, they were surprised to find the Natives, to say the least. The settlers had a mission to find a planet that was good for expansion of humankind, but Echo was filled with an intelligent species already. One that could pose a serious threat to humanity, if it chose."

"But you said there wasn't an issue with cultural integration," Avery pointed out.

"And at first there wasn't. The Federation promoted immigration and the Gate was left relatively unchecked. But soon tensions rose, as no one could agree on why our two species were so similar. You can imagine how this discovery shook the very foundation of both cultures. And after the terrorist attacks at the start of the century were blamed on Reange immigrants . . . there was no turning back to peace."

Avery nodded, finally familiar with something. The terrorist bombings nearly fifty years earlier were the main reason the Federation dealt with Echo so harshly. Natives—or Reanges, she supposed—were trying to intimidate humans into staying out of their affairs. At least that was the spin the Federation had put on it.

"The Federation soon locked down the Gate and began an

aggressive campaign here on Echo. There were orders to kill every Reange found on sight. That initial wave was devastating. The Natives could hide amongst the human population, of course, but if their DNA was scanned . . . ." He trailed off, insinuating the worst. "This happened within months of the Federation realizing what the Reanges, and specifically the So's, were capable of. It is our belief that the early propaganda pitting us against one another, even the terrorist attacks themselves, were driven by the Federation. But even with evidence, once fear takes root . . . it is nearly impossible to weed it out."

Avery gripped the table. Could the Federation truly have gone to such lengths? She was afraid she already knew the answer.

"The Elites, however," Nick continued, "weren't lucky enough to merely die. Because of their gifts, they had extreme value for experimentation. As you can imagine, skills like that would be an asset to acquire for the Federation." He paused for a few seconds before adding, "We haven't been able to find an Elite for going on thirty years. Some people have given up hope that they even still exist."

Fear paralyzed her. If she really was an Elite, as they all believed, her life was a ticking time bomb. The Federation didn't care about who they hurt in the process to discover what she was. They wanted to use her. What would have happened if she hadn't escaped the Port Station? A chill ran up her spine.

"Are you beginning to understand now?" Nick asked quietly.

"But why is my presence so important? Even if I am . . . ." She couldn't bring herself to finish the sentence. "Where is the good in that when it comes to facing an entire army of Federation soldiers?"

Nick smiled, leaning back in his chair. "Finnegan mentioned that you had some experience with the merge?" She frowned, not understanding. "That you influenced the mind of the girl who saved you?"

Avery flushed, unsure of how to answer. She could barely face it herself, if that's what had truly happened.

"That is where you become a real threat," he explained. "You have the ability to unify the minds of the Reanges. If you train, you can harness the ability to influence the thoughts of thousands at once. It would make a fight nearly unbeatable, with the right motivation, weapons, and circumstances."

"And you want me to do this?" Avery replied skeptically. "I've never led anything in my entire life. I can barely tell you when I'm even using this power, or whatever it is. I nearly blew up Finn's ship on the way here." She paused, trying to slow herself down. "There's no way I can do what you want me to do. I'm not what you think I am."

"You should have more faith in yourself, Avery." He brought the glass to his lips once more, taking a deep drink of the purple liquid. He studied her for a moment before rising, placing his discarded napkin on the table.

"I'll make you a deal." He leveled her with a clear and honest gaze. "If you give this a chance and some real effort"—the corner of his lip turned up in a hint of a smile—"then I can guarantee that we will do everything in our power to negotiate your grandmother's release." Avery felt her pulse skip at his words, real hope blossoming in her chest for the first time in days. "But you will have to cooperate. You won't be of any use to either us or your grandmother if you can't control your gift."

She was quiet, weighing her options before speaking. "How can I know that you'll keep your word?"

"I suppose you'll have to trust me."

"Why does everyone keep telling me that?" She looked away from him and focused on her plate of half-eaten food. Heat crept up her neck beneath his silent stare.

"I think I should leave you to rest for a while," Nick said, making his way toward the door. "I'll send someone for you in the morning."

As he left, the door solidified behind him. Such strange technology set her on edge. She was in a completely different world now.

Rising from the table, Avery moved to the curved windows, looking down into the circular pit that rose up from deep in the mountains. She could make out rows and rows of windows, as far down as her eye could see. There was a whole world of survivors down here that nobody knew about.

Nick had said that she could control thousands? How was such a thing even possible? The weight of what was happening began to sink into her, heavy and full of purpose.

Had Gran always known? Learning how to use this thing could be the best way to truly save her. At the very least, she finally had a bargaining chip.

Suddenly exhausted, Avery stumbled up the few stairs into the bedroom. Falling onto the bed, she curled into the plush covers. She could think more clearly in the morning. Maybe something would make sense by then.

And then she had no thoughts at all, falling into a sleep as deep and thoughtless as the infinite darkness of a starless sky.

CHAPTER NINE

"You can't be serious." Finn struggled not to raise his voice as he stared at his brother in bafflement. "I just saved your ass, and you're assigning me to guard duty?"

"You deliberately went out of your way to disobey me, Finnegan," Nick replied with authority. His face was stern. Immovable. "There were specific reasons I told you not to proceed with your idiotic plan."

"And none of them made any sense!" Finn paced across the living room of their shared quarters. He could never control himself when Nick resorted to ordering him around like he was still the little kid brother he had once been. "Why can't you just admit that I finally did something worth a little recognition?"

"You got lucky," Nick replied calmly.

"Lucky?" Finn laughed. "If it had been you stuck on the

Station with her, there's no way in hell you would have gotten out. My training is what got us out of there. Nothing else."

"And it was also your actions that got you both *in* there, or have you forgotten?" Nick leaned forward in his chair, rubbing his forehead. "I really don't have the time to argue about this. The Elders made their decision, and preparations need to be made."

"Yeah," Finn scoffed, "and instead of a real position back on the frontlines like I deserve, I get to be her glorified babysitter."

"You should be grateful I don't send you back to Milderion to attend to our duties with the Armistice Council. The treaty is on shaky ground as it is. You made a spectacle of yourself on Earth, and your absence was not unnoticed to the public."

"Yeah? Then why aren't you there, smoothing feathers?" Finn asked, ignoring the petulant sound of his own voice.

"Because someone had to come here to deal with the mess you made!" Nick's voice raised this time. "We do not have the luxury of doing as we want, Finn. Because of Father, we have an obligation to—"

"Yeah, I know the story, okay?" Finn interrupted him. "You made it clear when you dragged me out of my life here when he died. I play the part of village idiot to the media and pretend like we have nothing to do with the Resistance. It's a real party, living large in the city while people are out here dying."

Silence fell between them.

"Listen, Finn," Nick said quietly, standing. He was always so damned calm. "I know it's not the frontlines again, but this is a position of honor. You should know, more than any human, the reverence the Reanges give to their So'. And for all intents and purposes, Avery is the only one left."

Finn looked away to the dark stone floor. He couldn't hold

his brother's assessing gaze now any more than he could when they were children. And just like always, he was at Nick's mercy, doing as he was told.

"Despite the fact that you brought her back here," Nick continued with his lecture, "you did so with as little delicacy as ever. To be known for flaunting your many paramours to the media, one would think you'd have learned a little finesse when it comes to political maneuvering."

"It's not my fault the girl is a psychopath half of the time!" Finn protested. "If she was like any other normal female, then I *would* have been able to get her here just fine."

"Well, thankfully, I was able to smooth it over. With a little bargaining."

"What did you tell her?" Finn asked, worrying that Nick had offered something he wouldn't be able to provide. Their name had weight here, but not enough to override the Elders. For some reason, the thought of lying to her again bothered Finn.

"Politics, Finnegan, have never been your strong suit." Nick stood with a sigh, walking past him toward the main entrance. "Just do your job and watch her."

"And what am I supposed to do with her?" Finn asked incredulously. "She can't stand the sight of me."

"I'm sure you'll figure something out," Nick replied, the door dissolving open. "You are right that we'll have to return to the capital soon. There's a function with the minister that I'd like for you to attend. Just make sure she stays secure until then." Finn watched the door solidify to white, enclosing him in the room alone.

This wasn't the way things were supposed to go. The risk he had taken on Earth had been worth it. His scheme to find an Elite had worked, and he deserved to rejoin the soldiers he had trained with. He was never as useful as he had been there, in his element.

Finn had only been five when their parents brought them to Echo nearly eighteen years ago. But Nick had been fifteen, practically an adult. He would never understand what it was like to be denied the right to serve beside his friends. Finn had lived, learned, and grown up alongside Reanges.

When anti-human laws prevented him from joining the militia, Finn had forged his paperwork and operated under the guise of a Reange for a good three months before anyone found out. By then, it was too late for them to protest, and he was too good at his job. Finn was given his own command a year later. It was the only place he had ever felt truly useful.

It was law on Echo that every able-bodied Reange serve in the military against the Federation. You couldn't live amongst the Rebellion forces and on the Nos Valuta base unless you contributed your sweat and blood. The fact that Finn wasn't able to stand alongside them, when all of his closest friends were out there risking their lives, made him feel ill. It was a double-standard that he felt, harshly. If only he had been born the oldest, he would be the one making the decisions for their family.

Their parents had always supported the way he chose to help the Rebellion, encouraging Finn to follow his own path. His father had been ambassador in those days, struggling to negotiate the Armistice that was barely in place now. But when he died, things changed. Their mother followed soon after, heartbroken.

Without him, political tensions grew unchecked, and Nick took over their father's position as Ambassador to Echo, soon deciding it would be best to have both of the Lunitia offspring taking up their father's mantle. A little over a year had passed since Nick pulled him from the battlefield. Now Finn's life was spent mostly in Milderion, attending soirees and functions to bring sympathy to the cause instead of actively doing something about it. And it wasn't even like he had a real title. His ambassadorship was purely ornamental, where Nick was the respected politician. It was unbearable.

Because he was human, Finn couldn't petition the Elders for reconsideration of his position. His entire life was in Nick's hands. If his brother said that Finn belonged in the capital with Federation leaders and obnoxiously rich Old Earth tourists, then that was where he'd have to go.

Rising to his feet, he let out a harsh breath, running a hand through his hair. At least by protecting Avery, he would be allowed to stay in Nos Valuta a little while longer. Going to the capital again so soon would kill him.

She hadn't painted him in the best light, if Nick's reaction was any indication. What his brother didn't know was that Avery was wired to be stubborn. Her ridiculous attitude was costing him the only thing he had ever worked for in his entire life. It was blazing unbelievable.

But of what he'd seen so far, the key to unlocking her power was connected to those fiery emotions that she let slip so easily. And it just so happened that he knew exactly how to activate her circuits.

A vengeful grin settled onto his face. If they wanted him to watch over her day and night, then so be it. No one ever said he had to be nice about it.

They wanted to test her limits, and he was just the man for the job.

"Are you going to wake up anytime soon, or do I just get to sit here and watch you sleep all day? Like that's not weird."

Avery cracked open an eye at the sound of the masculine voice. Her circumstances came flooding back to her in a rush, and she burrowed deeper into the covers.

"Hey." He nudged the side of the bed, and Avery felt it begin to sway, realizing that it must be a hover tech, too. This place was much too extravagant.

"Go away," she mumbled, opening her eyes to glare at Finn standing above her. He had shed his practical military gear for a deep charcoal sweater, the soft fabric folding over his shoulder in a modern fashion, hugging his strong form elegantly. "How long have I been asleep?"

"Too long," he said, placing his hands on his hips caustically. "But it was the soonest your little slave would let me in."

"What?" she asked, annoyed as she sat up.

"Petra," he said, as though she should know what he was talking about. Avery gave him a blank look, not bothering to cover her mouth as she yawned. "She's been out there standing guard at your door. I thought maybe you were . . . you know . . . ." He gestured to the side of his temple, wiggling his finger. "Manning the helm."

She frowned, genuinely offended at his insinuation. "I don't even know how to do that," she barked out, throwing the covers off and sliding to the bed's edge. With another yawn, she rubbed her eyes and tried to run a hand through her hair. Her fingers tangled immediately in the mess. Great. Bedhead had always been a really good look on her.

"Could've fooled me," he murmured, peering off toward the door of the bedroom.

"What?"

"Nothing. I'll wait out there." He pointed at the dining area. "There should be some clothes for you in your closet, but hurry up. We're already late."

"What are you even doing here, Finn?" Avery asked, raising her voice so he could hear her across the way. "I thought I was supposed to be meeting with the Elders again."

"Change of plans," he responded flippantly. "I'm taking you to some training thing. They already decided on keeping you. Big shocker."

Avery grimaced, heading toward the bathroom she had found last night. She had no idea that it would start so soon. Whatever *it* was.

Nick had said that she would have to commit to learning how to use her gift. The air constricted in her chest.

She showered and dressed quickly, amazed at the buttery-soft texture of all the clothes she found. The black pants she chose fit snug on her legs, wrapping around her form as though they were a second skin. The gray shirt covered her arms in intricate swaths, meeting in a gathering of extra fabric at the neck that exposed her collar bone.

If she could only get her hair to behave, she might look the part she was expected to play. With no other option, she sat on the edge of the bed to braid her hair down the back of her head. She thought wistfully that a little makeup wouldn't hurt either. The bags under her eyes weren't likely to go away on their own.

Avery avoided eye contact with Finn as she left her room, striding toward the main door. When it didn't open as she approached, she reached out to push at the surface, looking around the frame for an activation port.

Finn laughed, suddenly beside her, and she fought against the urge to pull away. How had he gotten so close to her without a sound? The hairs on her arm stood.

"Don't know how to open it, huh?" he mocked, his voice smiling.

"Shut up." Heat bloomed in her cheeks.

And then the door melted away, opening the hallway in front of her. She refused to ask him how he did it.

In the hall, Petra jumped to her feet, looking refreshed with her black hair shiny and shockingly blue in the artificial light. Perhaps it had been blue all along.

"You're up," Petra said, smiling. She caught sight of Finn and scowled. "Come on, we're late already."

"Told you," Finn breathed. She ignored him.

The pink-haired Elder was waiting for them when they entered what appeared to be a medical lab of some sort, along with a middle-aged woman with fair blonde hair and animated eyes. Both women watched her as they approached, and Avery struggled to hold her ground. She could do this.

"Avery," Pink Hair said, taking her hand in a warm grasp. "I'm so sorry about how brisk we were with things yesterday. I wanted to take the time to personally apologize, but I'm afraid you dropped quite a bombshell on us, as humans might say."

"Oh," Avery said, nodding even though she didn't understand.

"We didn't even have the time for proper introductions." She smiled. The pink hair really did complement her skin tone. "My name is Milupe. I am head of the Elder Council here at Nos Valuta. May I officially welcome you to the Resistance?"

"Uh,"—Avery's eyes shifted to Petra and back again—"sure,

I guess. I'd like to know what my grandmother has to do with any of this. Nick still hasn't answered that."

"Direct, I see." Milupe smiled again, sharing a look with Petra. "You'll do well here. As you wish, we'll get straight to it, then." She gestured for the blonde woman to step forward. "This is Lissande Brinstal."

Avery couldn't disguise her shock. "Brinstal?" she repeated, nearly in a daze.

The woman nodded before replying, "I heard you've been looking for me."

"Yes!" Avery exclaimed, taking a step forward, although she hadn't the slightest idea what to say.

"Avery," Milupe said gently, laying hand on her shoulder and leading her farther into the room. "What you're about to hear may come as a shock. But I think Healer Brinstal will be able to answer your questions."

"What do you mean?" Avery asked, looking between the two women.

Brinstal took a breath before answering, "Your grandmother and I . . ." she started, stumbling before continuing. "We worked together. For the Federation."

"What?" Avery gasped, faltering. Gran had worked for the Federation? No. That couldn't be right.

"It's true," Brinstal said slowly. "It's not something either of us were proud of, but the Federation can be . . . persuasive." There was something unsaid in her tone. "We were part of a project called Lares. An initiative to experiment on So's and learn the source of their powers."

"So you're . . . ."

"Human? No," she replied with a strange frown. "I was sent to work on the project as an undercover agent of a radical

Reange group called the Origin. I was to gather information on the project and find a way to sabotage their efforts. Your grandmother . . . " She looked away, breath shaking, before her smile returned. "I had never seen kindness in a human before her." Brinstal's voice softened. Petra tensed slightly at the words.

"Gran worked on this . . . this Lares project?" Avery asked uncertainly.

"Yes." Brinstal nodded. "Your grandmother was the best bioengineer in both galaxies. She was recruited early by the Federation, although she never had the stomach for the kind of cruelty the position required. Experimentation without ethics is not for the faint of heart."

No. Gran wouldn't have been able to use science in that way. She never would.

"So . . ." Avery said delicately. "You're a doctor, too?"

She nodded. "Strictly trained in research, mind you, but I had a lot to learn from Nestra. She . . . " Brinstal paused, as though searching for words. "She changed me. How I thought about the war . . . about humans. But we were both stuck there. Bound by duty and tied to our people."

Avery couldn't believe it. Gran working for the Federation? The people she despised most in the universe?

"But then they found one. A So'. A little girl, showing signs of power even as a toddler. Something unheard of." Her eyes brightened. "Nestra was assigned as her keeper, the Federation wanting to keep the child under constant supervision as we studied her. But your grandmother . . . she couldn't."

Avery's heart sank, knowing what was coming.

"She told me she was making plans to run. To take the girl with her. She wanted me to join her, but . . . I had my own obligations. To the Origin. To my family. But I did have connections that could help her. I knew that if she took the child to Earth and raised her as a human, it would be the best chance for survival. Echo was too dangerous, too volatile."

"No," Avery whispered, shaking her head, unable to hide from the truth she was hearing. Her throat was tight, her chest heavy.

"So I gave her my real name, told her my truth. That if she should ever need me, I would be there to help them, if I could. I told her to send the girl to us, when it was time. When she was ready."

Avery took a step backward, nearly stumbling. Petra steadied her, keeping her hand lightly on her arm. It was reassuring, somehow.

"Avery," Milupe said, her face gentle. "You were that little girl."

"This is truly amazing," Brinstal muttered a few hours later. Her eyes roved over data projected on her port's hologram feature, floating in the air in front of her. If Brinstal's confession wasn't enough, preliminary testing gave irrefutable proof that Avery was a Native. A Reange. She couldn't deny it now. The validation was staring her in the face in the form of her own DNA strands.

There was no going back.

"Your genes are mutating." Brinstal sounded fascinated.

"What?" Avery asked, puzzled.

"Exactly," Brinstal replied, typing in commands to her wristport as she looked at the results that floated just above her wrist. "Although the rate is actively slowing. Even since you first stepped into the lab. It's like they're settling after being disrupted."

Avery hopped off the exam table. "What does that mean?"

"Unless I'm mistaken," she said carefully, "Nestra has been altering your genetic makeup. From the reaction of your cells, I'm going to guess it's been going on for quite a while."

"She changed her DNA?" Petra asked the question before Avery could get it out. Finn stood at the edge of the room, shockingly quiet since they had arrived.

"Yes, and it's remarkable. Genius, even, though I'm not surprised." Her voice was tinged with pride. She pointed at a hologram that looked like clumped-together goop. "See this formation here? The alterations are temporary. Created with the specific intention to wear off after a certain period of time."

"Is that weird?" Avery asked.

"It's incredibly difficult to engineer. Unprecedented. How did she ever. . . ." Her light-blonde brows lifted. Brinstal caught the others' blank stares. "Most gene tampering is permanent, for the plain reason that we don't fully understand how to create a temporary alteration."

"Gran could . . . could do all of that?" Avery was bewildered.

Brinstal paused before replying, "She had one of the greatest minds of our generation. I'm not surprised she found a way to protect you, even as—"

"Protect me?" Avery scoffed. "She lied to me. All these years, and she lied to me about who I—about *what* I was."

"I know it's difficult, Avery," Brinstal said cooly. "But you must face the facts. This is why your gift hasn't surfaced until now. Why you've been safe."

Avery clenched her teeth. She sounded just like Gran.

"But that doesn't make any sense," Avery countered. "How would I not know it was happening? Wouldn't she have had to use something like a med patch?"

"Not necessarily," Brinstal answered, closing the hologram and leaning against the metal work table behind her. "I've heard of new tech being developed that allows you to make alterations without a therapy session. All it would take would be a micro pill, slipped into your food or drink. You'd never even know it was there."

Avery felt a tickle in her throat and turned away, trying not to think of the pang of deceit. Even Gran had hidden things from her.

Avery looked up, locking eyes with Finn from across the room. He leaned against the wall, arms folded over his chest as he observed. Just as he had been doing all day. She focused on the floor, swallowing the wide ball of emotion that threatened to choke her.

"Maybe we should take a break," Petra suggested brusquely.

"Yeah, that might be a good idea," Avery replied, taking a small breath.

"Absolutely," Brinstal clipped. "Where are my manners? I'm sure you'd like a tour. Perhaps to the dining hall? You need to get your mind off things for a while." A timer beeped from her wristport then and she jumped, running to a waiting test tube. "Go relax," she urged, distracted.

Petra led her away from the lab, and they walked together in silence for a few minutes. Avery was glad she didn't try to force conversation. In fact, the silence was comfortable, even. She was surprised Petra seemed to understand her so well. It was strange, considering their rocky start, but Petra was the kind of person Avery could easily become friends with. They were similar, in many ways. They were both good at being alone.

"Well," Finn's voice made Avery flinch. "Was anyone else as bored as I was back there?"

"Moon above, would you stop doing that?" Avery chided, glaring over her shoulder.

"Does the human never shut up?" Petra rolled her eyes.

"Well, you guys weren't talking. It was weird."

"I guess it was too much to hope that you would have stayed back there with the other experiments," Avery said, eyes set straight ahead.

"Oh, she's making jokes now," he replied. "As much as I'd love to let you guys bond or whatever, I hate to tell you I'm your guard dog for the time being. Or did you forget that you're a precious commodity around here?"

"So everyone takes such great pleasure in reminding me," Avery said under her breath.

"It's an insult that a human should be given such a role," Petra commented, acid lacing her words. "I would have been a much better choice."

"Yeah, why *are* you here, now that you mention it?" Finn asked.

Avery glimpsed at her from the corner of her eye and saw Petra's face go red. "I volunteered to help with Avery's training. They'll need someone—a Reange," she stumbled over her words, "to practice on."

"Are you telling me you *want* to be hijacked?" Finn asked incredulously. "After the way you reacted last time? Do you really think—"

"I told you that was an accident." Petra raised her voice,

whipping her head around to berate him.

"Can you two stop arguing for five minutes?" Avery asked, bringing a hand to the side of her head. "I think I'm starting to get a headache. What is that noise?"

"The dining hall is around the corner," Finn said, as if that was explanation enough for the loud humming that was vibrating through the walls.

Avery winced, the small ache turning into a heavy throbbing as they rounded the final corner. A wide opening featured a large dining hall beyond, revealing lines of tables filled with people, and a vaulted ceiling stretching up above their heads. Reanges began casting looks toward them, curiosity staring at her from the sea of unfamiliar faces.

"Why is it so blazing loud?" Avery asked, raising her voice loudly. Petra only blinked at her, clearly confused.

But the vibrations weren't coming from the people sitting at the tables. Most of them weren't even speaking as they caught sight of her standing there with Petra and Finn. It felt as though her very skin oscillated with the hum of a thousand conversations.

What was happening?

The tiny movements traveled up her skin, seeping into her brain as shooting pain stabbed her eyes. The edges of her vision blackened.

Shaking her head to try and clear it, Avery widened her eyes when Finn came up beside her. His mouth was moving, but no sound emerged. Peculiar, when it felt like her brain was on fire with conversation.

Finn looked past her to shout something, the ringing in her ears drowning out his voice. It was too much. She brought her hands to cover her ears, but it did nothing. She began to collapse on her feet, and Finn's arms swooped around her to keep her from falling. But the blackness dominated her vision, blocking out all thought, ushering her into the bliss of unconsciousness.

CHAPTER TEN

A very opened her eyes and looked up at the brightly lit ceiling of the med lab, squinting as her head throbbed in a quiet rhythm. The cold metal of the table chilled her skin through her new clothes.

"What happened?" she asked, bringing a palm to her forehead to try to dull the ache. Through her squinted vision she managed to see Brinstal, Nick, and Milupe hovering close by.

"Do you feel all right?" Brinstal asked, coming around the table and lifting Avery's wrist, checking her pulse.

"I have a blazing headache," Avery said, closing her eyes again. "How did I get here?"

"Finn carried you," she replied, and Avery peeked over toward the corner where he stood at his regular post, a frown on his normally blasé face. An image flooded her mind—her body being supported by his arms—and she balked at the sudden dip in her stomach. "Do you have any dizziness? Any blackness in your vision?" Brinstal asked, activating her port and running a quick bioscan as she spoke.

"No," Avery replied, her voice weary. "Can somebody please tell me what happened?"

"You passed out," Nick said then, taking a step closer to the table.

"I think that's a little obvious," Avery replied. She pushed down a wave of nausea as she sat up fully, swinging her legs over the side of the table.

"It seems your gifts are progressing quicker than we anticipated. You're already beginning to feel the telepathic connection," Brinstal explained, studying the results from the bioscan on the charts projected from her wristport.

Avery gripped the edge of the table. "Are you saying that I was hearing voices? In my head? Other people's thoughts?"

"Well, they're not precisely voices," Brinstal said, looking up at Avery. Her eyes were bright, like she was excited about the idea. "It's more of a mental impression created through a mixture of chemical react—"

"But why haven't I heard anything like it before?" Avery interrupted her, the uncomfortable confusion outweighing her concern for polite behavior. "I'm sitting here with you all right now, aren't I? Why isn't it happening now?"

"Your body is just now learning and adapting past your genetic modifications. The sudden influx of telepathic activity must have jump-started your system somehow. The increased brain activity is probably the reason for your headaches," she concluded, eyes drifting as though she was running mental calculations.

"Most So'Reanges learn to control this part of their gift more slowly," Milupe added with a nod beside Brinstal. "As their gift develops, they have time to adjust. Unfortunately, you don't have the luxury of a gentle introduction to your new senses."

Avery was overwhelmed. She tried to wrap her head around the idea that what she had experienced was a natural part of her sensory abilities. Could you control something that you didn't know you were doing? How was that even possible?

And then something changed. A lightness entered her mind, as though she was floating above her body, her head a cavern waiting to be filled. An acute cloud of worry swept upwards, filling in the cracks of her own thoughts.

Moons above, I hope she can handle a strain on her system like this.

"What strain?" Avery asked, unease coloring her voice before realizing that Brinstal hadn't actually said anything. Milupe's eyes grew, and Avery stopped breathing. Brinstal's worry slowly sifted out of the forefront of her head, leaving behind a strange mixture of confusion and awe. There was little comfort knowing that those feelings, at least, were her own.

"Avery isn't at risk, is she?" Milupe asked, her head tilting in the healer's direction. "You know her importance."

"She can't be put in any danger," Nick added harshly.

She is our last hope to fight back. She is the only way we stand a chance against the Federation.

The voice melded into her mind in a seamless transition, a cloud of sorrow billowing inside her this time. At first Avery thought it was Nick, but she met Milupe's gaze, deep blue eyes connecting with her own, and she knew. It was the Elder woman.

Milupe's feelings ran over and through her, like fog floating thickly throughout her mind. The sorrow and pain Milupe felt. Every day. Every moment. It never faded or went away. It was constant—a regular way of life now for this woman and so many others. The fear of her culture, her entire species, being wiped away from their planet sunk into the very cells of Avery's blood in an instant.

Tears filled her eyes rapidly, spilling out and down Avery's cheeks as she lost her breath. Wrenching her eyes away, she bent over to let out a mournful gasp as she clutched her hands to her chest. Was this what they felt? Was this their reality? It was unbearable.

Avery retreated from the sensation, swiftly pushing out the clouds of thought and feeling until she was alone in her mind. But it was still there . . . a part of her. The pain. The loss. The desperation.

Avery realized what she meant to these people, at last. And it would never go away, she knew. This feeling. She was their last hope.

The next few days passed with little to no excitement for Avery, at least compared with what she had been through so far. She was escorted to and from the lab every day to spend it with Lissande, who had insisted on her first name when Avery had tried to call her Brinstal.

Although Avery yearned to ask Lissande more about Gran and her life, she couldn't bring herself to do so. It was still too fresh. Gran had lied to her, for her entire life. She feared that if she examined herself too closely now, she might break. Better to keep pushing on the task at hand. Once Avery mastered her powers, she could get Gran back and ask her all the questions she wanted.

She hadn't seen Finn since that first day, but she told herself that it was a relief he was gone. Finn set her on edge in a way she didn't want to think about. When he was around, she felt aware of everything. Like he was a live wire that charged the air. It was good that he wasn't there to distract her.

But Petra was always there. She was constantly helpful and calm, despite being bristly with everyone else. And Petra seemed to have endless patience as Avery tried to develop her new gift. It actually felt like someone was on her side in all of this. She was a source of strength and support that Avery would sorely need moving forward.

She was beginning to understand her telepathy, as her gift flourished. If the feelings were strong, there was little Avery could do to keep them from invading her senses. Their intensity bubbled over and into her, unbidden. Like they were reaching out to her.

And that wasn't always a bad thing. Knowing everyone's secrets left little to the imagination, and it certainly prevented anyone from scheming behind her back. That was invaluable to her after all she had been through.

But it was exhaustive, and she wasn't allowed to interact with others yet. They didn't know for certain how much her system could handle as she adjusted.

Most nights she spent curled up in her favorite chair overlooking the chasm from her quarters. It was lit from solar reflectors high above them, giving the illusion of sunlight during the day. But now, as the sun set outside of the mountain, so did the daylight.

There were so many survivors, and more arriving each week. The Rebel soldiers went out to clean up the mess when the Federation attacked smaller cities and villages. They would help what survivors they could, and recruit those who were willing and able. Living underground in Nos Valuta was still better than being put in a Federation work camp or forced to see your home destroyed.

Avery put her head in her hands, letting out a sigh. How could she go back to Earth, knowing what she did now? The Rebels barely held on during fights. They had never learned combat techniques . . . had never needed it in their society. Yet Earth had studied and perfected it over thousands of years.

Reanges relied on their So's to lead and connect them, when needed. When a So' merged an entire army, the best fighter's skills became available to the worst. They relied heavily on their shared knowledge, and the Federation had unknowingly done the one thing that would utterly cripple them. The So's had been their only chance at fighting back.

She had to hope that Nick would keep his agreement to negotiate Gran's release. It was her best chance, short of forcing the Rebels to storm the Station herself. And seeing as how she could barely have a conversation without accidentally losing control, that scenario wasn't bound to happen anytime soon.

There was a gentle double-beep from the door behind Avery. She turned her head as Petra entered, carrying her nightly tray of dinner. Her short hair was remarkably blue against the white lights. Perhaps she had been dyeing it black to fit in when she was undercover with the Federation.

She followed Petra to the dining table. "Thanks for doing this," Avery said, breaking the silence as she reached for a small plate. "I feel bad that everybody has to keep bringing me stuff. I'm not completely useless, I swear," she added with a smile.

"You'll get there," Petra replied, loading her own plate with a few fruits.

"I'm getting better. I really don't think it will ever be as bad as that first day again," she added, taking a bite of a sweet green fruit that had purple skin and a delicate fuzz of yellow hairs. The pulp was delicious, but the furry bits got stuck in her teeth. Avery ran her tongue across them, making a face at the bitter flavor.

Petra laughed. "You didn't eat the skin, did you?" When Avery nodded, she scrunched her nose in a little grimace. "Nobody eats the skin. It's too bitter."

Avery swallowed the lump of fruit, frowning at the rest of her plate. "Well, how am I supposed to know how to eat it?"

"You really don't know anything about our culture, do you?" Petra asked, bewildered.

Avery's face flushed, picking up another piece of the fruit and only biting the green fleshy part this time. "That's what I'm here to learn, right?" she asked, juice running down her chin. She wiped her mouth with the side of her hand, sucking on the pulp until all of the sweet juice was gone.

"This," Petra said, picking up a piece of the fruit on her own plate, "is called a pletch."

"A pletch?" Avery repeated, sneering again at the fruit. "What a horrible name."

Petra smiled, peeling back the skin until the rounded half of the fruit was inverted, pushing the green pulp out. "This is how you eat it," she demonstrated, taking a bite of the green that was now easy to access after she had popped it out.

"Ah," Avery said with a nod, letting out a laugh. "That was

much more refined than my attempt."

Petra sobered, her face concentrating as she looked down and poked at the food on her plate. "Doesn't it bother you?" she asked.

"Doesn't what bother me?"

"The fact that you were taken from us," she stated forcefully, the power of her feeling rushing forward to brush briefly against Avery. She felt a tinge of Petra's anger. Her need for vengeance. It frightened her.

Avery quickly pushed Petra's feelings away, letting out a breath she didn't know she was holding. Maybe she really *was* getting the hang of it.

"I haven't really given that part a lot of thought yet," Avery said candidly. "All I've ever known is back on Earth. That's the life I grew up with, the one that I had planned for. Thinking about what I used to be before all that . . . ." She looked out the windows. "I think it's safer not to dwell on it right now. Not until . . . not until I get Gran back."

Petra averted her eyes, peering down at her own plate again as she picked up another piece of fruit to munch on. Their connection was stronger than with most other Reanges she had encountered. Perhaps their friendship made things easier between them. Still, Avery could feel Petra's disappointment.

"I know what the Elders said," Avery said finally, suddenly stifled by the room and yearning to change the subject. "But can we get out of here? Go for a walk or something? I'm going crazy being cooped up in here and the lab day in and day out."

Petra hesitated, her feelings clouded.

"Please?" Avery added, willing to use a little old-fashioned begging. "Don't you know somewhere we can go where there won't be many people, or something?"

Petra met Avery's gaze, her gen mod eyes too brightly green to be natural. Petra looked away, measuring her options.

"You just said you wanted me to learn more about our culture." A wave of pleasure surged through Petra in response. "Isn't showing me some more of Valuta a step in the right direction?"

Petra let out a mix of laughter and a sigh, and Avery knew she had won.

"You're right," Petra agreed, grabbing Avery's hand. "I think I have an idea."

They always kept the training room at a near sweltering temperature. Finn dragged his hand across his forehead, trying to wipe away some of the sweat. After a lifetime here, he still didn't understand why they kept it so blazing hot. Something about cleansing the body as it worked. But it was a horrible way to learn new techniques, if you asked him.

Walking past mats filled with trainees, Finn grimaced as his thoughts turned to Avery. He couldn't seem to help it lately. He had felt something dangerously close to fear when she blacked out, and he didn't like it. There were reasons it wasn't smart to get attached.

Yeah, maybe he was attracted to her, but he knew better than anyone how to compartmentalize emotion. He would be stupid, in his line of work, to do otherwise. She would never be allowed to be with anyone other than a Reange, anyway. And then there was that whole pain-in-the-ass thing.

Which was why he didn't protest when Nick had sent him

to the capital for a couple of days. Getting back into his routine, however useless he might consider it, did a lot to assuage the unsettled feeling that had been plaguing him.

Milderion had been much the same as always. Cam bots in his face constantly, and tourists falling all over themselves to get to him. Hypocrites, the entire lot of them. He had never been comfortable in that world. But now it seemed he wasn't entirely comfortable at Nos Valuta, either.

"Ah, the prodigal human returns," a familiar feminine voice chided, bringing him out of his thoughts.

"Is that what they're calling me nowadays?" he asked skeptically. Nova barely had a drop of sweat on her. But in all the years they'd been friends, Finn had admittedly never seen her look anything other than put together. "How are you not sweating? It's hotter than blazar in here."

She laughed, her long blonde hair bouncing in the ponytail behind her head. "It's just your human blood. Can't take it the way we can, I guess."

"Don't mess with him, Nova." Finn cringed inwardly, recognizing Grigg's voice and knowing what was coming. His closest friend had yet to find a level to which he wouldn't stoop to get a laugh. "It's not his fault that humans are castrated at birth."

"That has to be it," Nova responded, a grin lacing her tone. "His body just can't regulate his hormones."

Finn gritted his teeth. The surest way to get them to shut up would be to ignore them.

"Moons above, I thought he'd be over it by now," Grigg said caustically.

"Thought I'd be over what?" Finn crossed his arms over his chest.

"Getting shit-listed again," Nova said with a laugh.

Finn raised a brow.

"Oh no, he's starting to make faces . . . ." Nova's eyes widened, glancing at Grigg.

Finn frowned, unamused.

"I can't tell, Grigg, is that a pout he's giving us?" Nova jeered with a grin.

"I think it may be," Grigg said with a chuckle. "It's just his hormone imbalance making him cranky." Finn's gaze darkened, and his friends both collapsed into a fit of laughter. Some of the other instructors looked in their direction. Finn rolled his eyes, intending to wait out their moment of hilarity.

It was all well and good for Grigg and Nova to laugh at his sour mood. They had active posts in the field. The only reason they were here now was to get their required instructing quota for the year.

Finn, on the other hand, was forbidden to leave the sanctuary of Nos Valuta, except on official political business. He hated his family's status for the restrictions it placed on him. A pit of shame rotted in the depths of his stomach.

"Come on." Nova put a hand on his shoulder. "You can't be that pissed that your plan didn't work out."

"I refuse to acknowledge that statement with a response—and my plan did, in fact, work out," he said, shrugging her off.

"What did you think was going to happen? They were going to finally let you do what you want?" Grigg asked. "You're worth more to the Rebellion now as a representative of Earth, no matter how good you were as a commander," he pointed out, all traces of humor gone.

"It doesn't matter," Finn bit out, clenching his jaw.

"Well, how long are you going to mope around? It's not

like you didn't get rewarded. You're in charge of the So's security detail," Nova said, placing her hands on her hips. "Do you know how many of us would kill for that opportunity?"

"Yeah, well, you haven't met her," Finn mumbled under his breath.

"Speaking of," Grigg elbowed his side, "why aren't you standing guard over her yourself right now? Rumor has it, you haven't been on her detail since you got back from the capital yesterday. How are we supposed to get an introduction if you're hiding down here with all the recruits?"

"I barely feel like I'm doing anything stuck in this damn mountain as it is. Following her around like a little lapdog?" he scoffed. "Thanks, but no thanks."

"A lot of the soldiers think you're finally showing your humanity," Nova pointed out. "Like you're scared of her or something."

"Moons above," Finn cursed, turning to face both of them. "I'm not scared of the girl, all right?"

"They say she's not too bad to look at, either," Grigg pointed out, waggling his eyebrows.

Nova rolled her eyes and laughed. "As if they'd ever let a human get anywhere with our only So'Reange."

"How are the recruits shaping up?" Finn asked, trying to change the subject. He gestured to Nova's group grappling on the mat in front of them. There was a gangly boy going up against an older girl. They looked about as coordinated as two newborn pups, fumbling through their moves with just as little grace.

"Horrible," they both said simultaneously.

"Well, maybe that's because you're spending too much time running your mouths and not enough time instructing," Finn goaded, finally grinning.

"Oh, and you'd do such a better job?" Nova asked.

"As a matter of fact, yeah."

"I smell a wager." Grigg chortled. "What do you say, Ambassador?"

Finn grinned, narrowing his eyes. "The stakes?" he asked.

"Oh, I should think lady's choice." Grigg motioned to Nova.

Nova's eyes filled with suspicious glee as she took a moment to think. "You have to fight a recruit of my choosing."

Finn laughed loudly. "Now, you know that's just not fair. They won't last more than five minutes."

"Done," Grigg interceded, drawing Finn's attention. "Finn fights a recruit. If the kid lasts more than five minutes, he loses. Winner chooses the spoils."

"All right, then," Finn said, real anticipation bubbling in his chest for the first time in days. "Who do you have in mind?"

"Listen up!" Nova yelled loudly to the fighters around them, the grapplers on the mats going still. "Who wants a chance to go up against the human?"

Finn let out a low breath, shaking his head. She played dirty.

Backing away as Nova handled the oncoming challengers, Finn tried to ignore how many young recruits were chomping at the bit to take a swing at him.

"Why does this feel like a supremely ludicrous idea?" he asked Grigg, beginning to stretch out his muscles to warm up.

"Probably because our ideas usually are," Grigg replied before adding with a smirk, "but that's what makes them so much fun." Turning toward the spectators, Grigg raised his wristport into the air. "Anybody care to place a bet?"

Finn smiled, shaking his head as he jumped up and down on his toes to get his blood moving. The tan shirt he wore was drenched in sweat already, clinging uncomfortably to his back. Feeling as though it would impede him, he pulled the thing up over his head, throwing it to the ground beside the mat. It landed with a wet slap on the stone.

Nova spoke loudly to her recruit of choice, trying to be heard over the murmurs of the increasing crowd. Finn smirked, the idea of an audience spurring him on. Maybe this day wouldn't be so bad after all.

"What is this place?" Avery asked Petra, her voice echoing off the white walls in the large empty room. She had brought her through a maze of hallways and a long ride down a spherical elevator to get there. Avery could only imagine how deep they were within the mountain.

"You'll see," Petra replied cryptically.

Giving her a little push, Avery stumbled to the center of the room as it transformed around her. Suddenly she was standing in a field, a gentle breeze caressing her face as she whipped around to see that Petra had vanished. Bewildered, she squinted up at the sky above and the strange, overly white color of the sun. Milderion's skyline spread out against the horizon in the distance, far beyond an endless ocean of golden grass.

"Do you like it?" Petra's voice called out, but Avery couldn't see her anywhere.

Avery laughed, turning a little circle in the field around her as she replied, "What is it?"

Petra materialized, as though walking through an invisible wall and straight into Avery's line of sight. "It's a simulation hologram," she answered. "It's used mainly for educational purposes. There's an entire map of Echo in the databank. You can see anything you want."

Avery turned away, looking up at the puffy purple clouds that floated in the blue-tinged sky. She took a deep breath, filling her lungs with the warm air and taking in everything around her. She could even feel the sun's warmth kissing her face. Smell the sweetness of the dry grass rising on the waves of hills surrounding them.

She had never been outside of a city before . . . not that there was much natural terrain on Earth anymore. Nearly all of the habitable areas were either heavily developed, owned by the government, or virtually destroyed by the Final World War. Humans no longer spread out across the land, but up into the sky.

"That's Milderion, right?" Avery asked, pointing to the city in the distance. It was extraordinary, to be out under an open sky. Even if it was in a sim. "This is fabulous!" She laughed, raising her arms and twirling around in the sunlight. It looked like old pictures of Earth. Reaching down, Avery tried to touch the yellow grass that rose to her knees, but her fingers passed through the image.

"Take us to the coast," Petra commanded, squinting up at the sky around them that seemed to go on for miles.

And then they were flying, or at least it felt that way. Everything around them blurred into a long smear, wind blowing Avery's hair from her shoulders as they surged across the ground and over the rolling hills away from the city. Instead of following up the side of the mountain range that bordered the plains, they soared down into the valley below, slowing as the ocean came into view.

They were standing on a thickly pebbled beach where a shift in the wind swept a saltiness onto Avery's tongue. She looked at Petra and shared a grin before shifting her gaze down the bluffs of the coastline. Waves crashed on the shore, the water rushing against the rocks of the beach in a soothing rhythm. She could swear there was even a fine mist floating on the breeze.

A small town sat a few hundred yards away, nestled in a cove where the water had dug a hole into the side of the land. There were no skyscrapers; no buildings that were over five or six stories tall. Avery couldn't even make out any cruisers buzzing around in the sky.

"What's that city?" she asked Petra, raising her voice above the waves.

"It's called Dru-udi." Petra moved to stand beside Avery. "It's a fishing village," she explained, her voice tight.

"It's lovely," Avery said. "I don't think I've ever seen anything so quaint before." Petra didn't respond, but her emotions spoke when she could not. She felt the longing. The sweet pain of that place.

It's my home.

Avery took a breath and paused, looking down at the sand under her feet that wasn't really there. The water didn't shift underneath her weight, but rather flowed along the beach as though she wasn't standing there at all.

"Do you miss it?" Avery asked to break the silence. Taking a deep breath and releasing it, she pushed Petra's essence from her mind as easily as though it was the air leaving her lungs. The control over her gift was beginning to come more easily.

"Every day." Petra's tone turned bitter, and Avery couldn't

bring herself to look up. "Now it's full of human tourists. Wasting our resources and polluting our land. While the Reanges cater to their every whim. Like slaves."

Avery fought to keep her face from heating, her mind immediately thinking of Megan and her family who were probably here on Echo right now. Vacationing from Earth and enjoying the natural beauties of a planet that hadn't been ruined by its inhabitants. She was embarrassed. Embarrassed for the action of a species that wasn't even her own.

"They came to our home when I was fourteen. Nobody thought the Federation would care about the outer villages. Back then they thought the oppression would stay localized to Milderion. Fools," Petra spat out angrily. "My mother forced my little brother and me to hide beneath the docks when the soldiers came. I think she knew—" Her voice chipped, and she cleared her throat. "She knew what would happen to them. When she tried to keep them from forcing us out, they killed her. Right there. My father, too." She continued tightly, "We got out, though. There are ways to survive, even if we can't stop them."

Avery's throat went dry. An awkward blanket of silence settled back over them as she fought vigorously to keep Petra's feelings from touching her. If they did, she would break. The faint taste of her tormented grief teased Avery, scratching against her mind.

"But with you here now . . . ." Petra's sorrow shifted to hope that radiated from her like a supernova as their eyes locked. She added in barely more than a whisper, "For the first time, we have a real chance."

Avery's eyes flickered away as words tumbled out of her mouth. "I'm so sorry, Petra. I can't imagine what you . . . I . .

. ." She trailed off, not knowing what to say. "I'm sorry," she finished lamely.

"Why?" Petra replied, hair blowing across her face. "It's not your doing."

Avery couldn't respond, knowing Petra wouldn't value the right words, even if she could find them. Actions would soothe her, and nothing else. They stood silently together, looking out across the open ocean beyond the cliffs.

"What else can we see?" Avery asked, hoping to change the subject. Petra's feelings had calmed, making it easier to focus.

Petra paused before answering, "This program is normally used to educate children about stuff like ceremonies, historical events . . . famous people. You can pretty much see anything you'd like if it has to do with Echo."

"Why do you even call it Echo?" Avery was relieved to have something to lighten the mood. "Isn't that what the humans named it as a code for New Earth? November Echo. Even if you've used our language since the humans settled here, why isn't there a name for the planet itself?"

"We don't name things that are sacred," Petra replied, a gentle smile crossing her features as Avery became even more confused. "You know how powerful your mind is. When you truly harness your gift, it will allow us all to merge as one. The ancients were all blessed with this gift and once, long ago, our language was entirely silent. Although we've developed speech out of necessity as our species evolved, there are some terms that we prefer to leave unsaid."

"But if that's true,"—Avery frowned, a chill running over her skin as the breeze surged—"then how do you continue that tradition without someone to connect you? Won't the thoughts be lost if you can't share them telepathically?"

Petra nodded, looking toward the town once more. "There are a few left who do still hold the original thoughts."

"But not you?" Avery asked.

"I was too young to ever remember a true merge." Petra met Avery's eyes again as her face softened. "But all that can change now."

Avery looked away, the weight of the responsibility settling heavily on her shoulders. She alone would be responsible for carrying on an entire planet's traditions. Their history—the really important parts—would disappear without her.

Swallowing around the lump in her throat, Avery let out a sigh. "You know, I think I've had enough of simulation rooms for today. How do you turn this thing off?" Even as the words left her mouth, the images faded away, leaving them alone in the open, white room.

"You'll get the hang of the tech soon enough," Petra added with smile.

Seeing a door on the opposite side of the room from where they entered, Avery asked where it led.

Petra turned to look before replying, "Oh, that's an entrance to the training observation deck. Want to check it out? It might actually be a good place to try out your sensitivity."

"Sure," Avery said, already following Petra. The room was really just a long hall, lined with windows on one side. An arrangement of gray seats sat on a raised platform that stretched along the entire length of the opposite wall.

She turned her attention beyond the glass, marveling at the sheer size of the room below. The observation deck was set up high to see the entire area, very much resembling a hangar of sorts. All along the ground, there were large blue mats with walkways between, soldiers sparring on every available surface.

"Are they training or something?" Avery asked, her eyes running across each soldier as they grappled and fought.

"Or something," Petra replied sardonically. "Any reaction with the proximity?"

"I don't think so," Avery responded. There was a slight pull, almost like a gentle tugging in the back of her mind, but nothing she couldn't handle. "How many are down there?"

Petra came closer, her arm brushing against Avery's as her eyes roved over the soldiers beneath. "Probably a few hundred. Looks like this group is all new recruits. That's my brother," Petra said with a grin, pointing toward one of the center mats. "He just got cleared for duty last month."

Avery saw a young boy talking with his instructors, his hair the same blue as Petra's. "What's his name?"

"Taisto," Petra replied quickly, focused on the mat. "But we call him Tai. He's really pretty good with . . . ." She distractedly tried to finish the thought, "With hand-to-hand."

There was a crowd gathering around Tai's mat, a bigger guy stripping his shirt as he moved to stand in front of the boy. "What's going on?" Avery asked, concerned.

"Son of a bitch," Petra ground out harshly.

"What?" Avery asked, suddenly nervous. "What is it?"

"That bastard is going to fight him," Petra said, turning on her heel and bolting toward the doorway on the opposite end of the hall. It opened when she approached, a set of stairs twisting downward on the other side.

"Wait! Petra!" Avery called, running after her quickly before the door solidified. But Petra was already disappearing down the stairs. Avery had no choice but to follow.

CHAPTER ELEVEN

A wall of heat hit Avery in the face as the stairs brought her straight into the training dome. She started to sweat almost immediately. Surely no one could do physical activity in these conditions. She saw Petra tearing across the mats at a full run, paying no heed to the walkways between them as she sped toward a mass of jeering people.

Avery looked uneasily at the crowd. Thoughts and emotions pulled on her even as she quickened her pace to a light jog. Excitement teased her, someone's delight making its way into her mind. She pushed it away, determined to find Petra. She had been practicing. She could handle it.

The crowd grew louder as she approached, nearly everyone in the facility swarming around the fighters. Avery dove into the assembly, the loud smack of a skin-to-skin hit making her cringe.

A slow yearning tugged at her, demanding attention. As she threaded through the crowd, it grew stronger, more insistent. Hundreds of thoughts clawed her brain, begging to be heard. She paused to focus her breathing, her body jostled by those around her as she fought for control.

Suddenly she felt Petra, her presence clear and strong. And her rage, so pure and violent that it shocked Avery. But it was the strength of Petra's emotion that allowed Avery to follow it, like a pulsating lifeline through the others around her.

A jolt of pain slammed into her jaw, and she shrieked in surprise, clutching her chin.

Now alert, Avery broke through to the center, looking toward the two fighters on the mat. But Petra stood there, ready to do battle on the far side of the blue square. She regained her footing from a blow, a large gash bleeding profusely from her lip and leaving a thick trail of red down her chin.

Avery gasped, her eyes flickering over the others around them. She spotted Petra's brother crouched on the ground near the edge of the crowd. He was angry, his scowl hostile. She quickly returned her attention to Petra's opponent, who faced away from her.

The fighter had discarded his shirt, bouncing lightly on his feet. He was well-built, with a strong frame that handled itself with the practiced grace of a fighter. Tan pants slung low on his hips, accentuating the sleek movement of muscle beneath skin.

Petra moved quickly, advancing in a run to grab her opponent's waist with both arms. Shifting her weight, she flipped the man over her shoulder, his body slamming on the ground with a heavy slap of skin against mat. The crowd exploded with excitement, the smell of sweat and heat overwhelming.

Petra went down with him, maneuvering to lock his neck

with one arm, the other pounding a few blows to his side. Avery finally saw his face as he fought against the hold.

It was Finn.

Finn, who was struggling to untangle himself. No wonder Petra's hatred had been so vibrant. The shock of seeing him there pushed Avery out of her own mind long enough for Petra's feelings to make a firm claim on her priorities. Her mind was no longer her own.

Tai was being abused by that brute of a human. He shouldn't even be here, and yet he had the audacity to train our soldiers.

Her veins erupted with fire.

No. It wasn't her anger. It was Petra's. Avery couldn't tell where her mind ended and Petra's began. She was dizzy, the mixture of panic and violence curdling in her stomach.

Finn gained enough momentum to tip Petra over, lifting her body along with his back. In a hard slam, he threw them both to the mat, crushing Petra. Avery lost her breath, pain surging up her own back as she half collapsed.

Petra lost her lock on him, allowing Finn to land a swift blow to her face. Avery's own head rocked to the side, eyes watering from the pressure and sharp pain. She flashed her eyes back to the fight where Petra scrambled out of harm's way, ready to attack again.

"Stop it!" Avery screamed, trying to force Petra out of her mind. This was more than mere emotional connection. She could feel Petra's pain. "Stop!" she yelled again, but Petra's emotion was too powerful to counter.

Avery's heart throbbed against her ribs, her head pulsing painfully. It was stifling, surrounded by the crowd. The air was thick and malleable, as though every molecule called out to her.

Finn and Petra continued to circle one another.

Her head pounded and her skin itched, as though it was scraping against rough concrete. She clenched her eyes shut. The powerlessness was too much. It swirled within her, coiling into a tight ball of energy centered somewhere within her chest.

"I said *stop!*" Avery cried. Something snapped as the energy exploded, bursting from her body in a rush. The relief was immediate as her power finally found its outlet. The air vibrated around her in soft waves, charged with her power and within her control.

The room fell into hushed silence, murmurs humming around her like a whisper in the air, making the heat tremble with tension. Avery let out a breath, finally removing Petra's emotion. It seemed almost easy, her thoughts slipping smoothly away.

Avery opened her eyes. But Finn and Petra were nowhere to be seen, the mat empty.

Slowly, she followed the gaze of the others. Up. She stifled the gasp that rose to her lips.

Finn and Petra floated in the air above, nearly ten feet from the ground. The slightest movements rotated them slowly, as though they were suspended in a weightless environment. The itchy tingles ran over Avery's skin, tiny threads of energy flowing like a tether to the air around them.

She clenched her hands in surprise, and they wobbled precariously in the air. She was controlling it.

Finn gained his composure first, scanning wildly through the crowd beneath him. His sharp gaze zeroed in on her.

"What the blazar are you doing, Avery?" Her stomach dropped when his eyes connected with hers, and she stepped back reflexively, looking away.

The crowd around them lit up with animated conversation,

many people pulling out the capture devices on their wristports to record what was happening. A blush crept up Avery's neck as she lost her connection with whatever energy she had tapped. The peculiar sensation swept away, evaporating into the hot air.

Finn and Petra both yelped as they dropped to the ground with loud thumps, rolling away from each other instinctively.

Finn groaned loudly, slow to rise. "That was a little less graceful than I imagined."

Avery stared at them, disbelieving. Had that truly been her power? Pain stabbed behind her eyes, and she winced, placing a hand on her temple.

"Avery?" Petra questioned, walking toward her with a slight limp. Tai trailed behind. "I'm so sorry, I don't know what—"

"You damn well better be sorry," Finn interrupted from his spot on the mat, looking up at the three of them.

"He's right," Tai burst out, surprising them all. "You shouldn't have interfered. I had it under control."

A bark of laughter escaped from Finn.

"Excuse me?" Petra balked. "I saved your ass from a beating, little brother."

"No," he protested, nervous eyes flickering to Avery and back again. "I can handle myself."

"Moons above, he's your brother?" Finn muttered as he rose to his feet, rubbing his hip. "No wonder you came at me like a rabid dog." He caught Avery's gaze, immediately frowning. "You got a little something there."

"What?" Avery asked. Tai grimaced, and he gestured to his nose. Avery brushed her fingers across her upper lip, a spark of anxiety unfurling in her stomach as her fingers came away red and sticky with blood. She quickly tried to rub the rest away with the back of her hand.

"What is going on here?" an authoritative voice sounded loudly across the space, the crowd hastily dispersing. As though they hadn't just been huddled around screaming at a fight like a pack of wild animals. Avery turned as Nick approached with Milupe in tow, concern on both their faces as they eyed the scrambling soldiers.

"Are you all right?" Milupe came to Avery, grasping her elbow firmly.

Nick shot a glare in Finn's direction. "Why do I get the feeling this is somehow your fault?"

"Me?" Finn responded indignantly, pointing to his own chest. "I just got back from the city! How could this be—"

"Of course it's your fault!" Petra's voice interrupted now as she walked up to Finn to roughly push his shoulder. Tai stood awkwardly behind both of them. "You can't just come in here and make a game of this, you dumb son of a—"

"Watch it with the name calling, all right? You have a real problem with—"

"Enough!" Nick yelled, cutting them both off with a dark look. "I don't care about your excuses. You were both given strict instructions not to bring her to any populated areas until Healer Brinstal gives her approval. Who brought her down here?"

Avery sagged against Milupe, sweat breaking out in earnest on her forehead. Petra stepped forward.

"It was my fault," Avery burst out before Petra could speak. Tai looked to her, surprised. "I asked to get out of my quarters."

"It was your idea?" Nick sounded dubious, clearly not buying it.

"I thought that I was ready to test my—myself." She faltered as she wobbled on her feet. How could one little trick have drained her strength so quickly?

Little trick? She lifted two people in the air. With her mind.

"Nicholas, she needs to see Brinstal," Milupe interjected, placing her hand on Avery's back for support. "We can leave the questioning for later."

Nick paused before agreeing. "I suppose you're right." Turning his gaze back to Finn and Petra, he added, "But I want to talk to both of you as soon as I see Avery to the labs. Together. And you"—he turned to Tai—"get back to your duties."

"Sir." Tai obeyed the command, and Avery wanted earnestly to follow him as he jogged away. Residual emotion from Petra. Avery hoped they wouldn't get into too much trouble on her account.

But Finn could rot for all she cared. She glanced at him, still shirtless, his torso glistening with a sheen of sweat. She closed her eyes, blaming her headache.

It didn't matter how well formed his muscles were. He could still rot.

"I want an explanation for what happened down there, and I want it now."

Finn's mouth twist at his brother's tone. Petra met Nick's gaze stubbornly, holding a cooling gel pad against her split lip. She was pretty tough, Finn had to admit. When he saw her come flying out of the crowd and push that kid out of the way, he was already spoiling for a fight. And surprisingly, she had some real skill. She nearly beat him, despite being half his weight and lacking his muscle.

For the first time, Finn gave some serious thought as to what Petra had been doing working undercover for the Federation. Nick had never fully debriefed him concerning the details of what had happened at the Port Station, not that he was owed explanation. But Petra had advanced training, and not the kind someone could just pick up on their own in their free time.

"I'll not ask you again, Petra," Nick said ominously, gaze darkening at her.

She lifted her chin, the cropped blue hair falling away from her face as she replied, "I don't answer to you."

"Under any other circumstances, I would agree with you," Nick conceded. "But it seems that your little escapade has now been broadcast across Valuta." With a few touches to his wrist-port, a hologram filled the space between them. Finn fought back a grin as he saw the image of himself circling Petra, their bodies unceremoniously lifted into the air by an unseen force. "We no longer have the luxury of introducing the existence of a So' gradually to the people."

"And whose idea was that to begin with?" Petra asked harshly. "You have no right to suggest such measures to the Elders. What we choose to do with her is our business. Not that of a *human* with some meaningless title."

Even Finn was surprised at the sheer hostility radiating off Petra. The way she was treating Nick made her regular personality seem cordial.

"And what if this leaks to the Federation? To the capital? To Earth?" Nick chastised, shutting off the holo with a flick of his hand and leaning against the desk behind him. "Regardless, the Elders have decided you're too much of a risk for Avery. Your privileges have been revoked."

"What?" Petra yelled, stepping forward. She cast a hateful

scowl at Finn. "This is all that pig's fault, anyway! If he hadn't beaten a boy like some senseless mongrel, none of—"

"Now, wait just a second," Finn interrupted her, holding up his hands in defense. "Pig?" he added wryly. "That's just hurtful."

Petra screeched, balling her hands into fists at her sides.

"Finn," Nick censured, pinching the bridge of his nose with his fingers.

"What?" Finn asked innocently, trying to keep the grin out of his voice.

"You're not helping."

"This is a disgrace," Petra snapped out, turning on her heel and making for the door.

"Where are you going?" Nick called out after her as she left. She didn't reply, muttering obscenities without looking back. Nick turned to Finn as the door closed, a question in his eyes.

"Don't look at me." Finn shrugged. "She's always been like that." Rubbing his palms together, he jerked a thumb at the door. "So am I free to go then?"

"We haven't even discussed your behavior," Nick said sternly.

Finn was quick to think of excuses. "It was just a bit of fun. Ask anyone in the training dome. Sometimes they just need to let off a little—"

"I don't care about the fight, Finnegan."

"Then what the blazar do we have to talk about?" he asked, suddenly weary on his feet. Petra had bruised a couple ribs when she got those jabs into his side. Breathing was becoming a bit of an issue.

"You were supposed to report to Avery as soon as you arrived back from Milderion."

"I put a post at her door!" Finn argued, trying not to wheeze. "Some of the best soldiers that we ha—"

"Some of the best soldiers aren't you," Nick countered, a lecture brewing. "I don't trust anyone else with her. I thought you would take your responsibility seriously."

"If that's the truth, then why send me to Milderion at all? You know I hate those damn public appearances. Nothing could make me feel more useless than kissing the asses of those rich—"

"Useless?" Nick scoffed. "You say that you want to help the Rebellion, but you're throwing away your best chance to do so. Finding a So'Reange is the most influential thing to happen to these people since before humans landed on Echo."

"And who the blazar brought her to Nos Valuta, I'd like to know?" Finn raised his voice. "I don't see you thanking me for that. You do remember that she wanted to walk right back into the Federation's hands, don't you?"

"And the Elders have thanked you for that by bestowing you the honor of guarding their most precious asset!" Nick's voice met his volume.

Finn looked away stubbornly, refusing to meet his brother's eyes as they settled into a stalemate of silence. It was a battle of authority that he would never win.

Nick cleared his throat. "Listen, I know this isn't what you want. You were never made for politicking. I know that. But the Elders have agreed—"

"Don't give me that," Finn countered with disdain. "I'm not an idiot, big brother. We both know you hold more sway with them than ever before. If I've been assigned as her guard dog, it's because you requested it."

Nick's eyes shifted warily. "We are blood. There is no one

that I trust more to act as I would than you." His words hung in the air, weighing it down with something unsaid. "She is to become their leader, Finn. Avery will be the key, for all of us."

Finn knew that. But despite understanding her importance, he had never really thought of her as some all-powerful leader that could change his fate. And she was. At least, she would be one day.

If Finn needed to convince the Elders to let him fight, then perhaps Avery was the way to do that. He supposed he could handle getting on her good side. Her powers were obviously spiraling into the realm of the physical. If she was going to become a viable aid to the Rebellion, then she was going to need some battle training.

Finn's gaze flickered back to Nick, and their eyes locked. He nodded curtly. It was as good of an agreement as his brother was going to get.

"You have a bad habit of fainting when things get tough, you know."

Avery refused to open her eyes in response to Finn's baiting, enjoying the darkness behind her lids. They were alone in the room together. Sometime during the past few days, Avery had learned she could feel when Reanges were close. Like some internal homing device.

She cracked her eyes open to find him lounging in a chair beside the exam table.

Avery pushed herself into a sitting position, smoothing down the hair that was pulled back in a braid. As she swung her legs to the side of the table, only the slightest pulse of a headache plagued her. At least she was improving somewhere.

"I didn't faint," she grumbled, suddenly awkward.

"Oh yeah?" She heard the grin on his face. "Then what would you call it, your majesty?"

"I was sleeping. And don't call me that," she ordered, hopping down from the table. She did her best to frown. "How long have I been here?"

"A few hours," he replied with a shrug. "The last half hour or so has been fascinating. I never knew girls could snore like that."

Avery tamped down the bubbling embarrassment, making a show of stretching out her muscles instead. She pulled one of her arms across her chest, asking, "Where is Petra? I'm pretty sure you don't need to hang around."

"Actually, I do," he said, coming to his feet to tower over her. "Looks like you can get into a little more trouble than I gave you credit for, So'Reange."

"Don't call me that, either," she snapped.

"All right." He raised his hands. "But we're going to be stuck together for a while."

"Why? Did you run out of kids to beat up?"

"I knew you missed me." He winked, that dimple forming in his cheek.

Avery rolled her eyes. "Cut the crap, Finn. Where is she?"

"Probably hiding in a corner crying somewhere." Avery didn't respond, waiting for further explanation. "She was banned from seeing you," he added.

"What?"

"Yeah, I think she's a little over-attached, too. I wouldn't be surprised if—"

"Why would they do that?" Avery asked, her hackles rising. Her only friend was being taken from her. Just when the isolation had begun to ebb.

"It probably had something to do with sneaking you out of your room, exposing you without clearance from the Elders, leading you to go all full-nose-bleed and black out again," he said casually.

"I didn't black out!" she cried, furious. Petra was the one person she had finally begun to trust. The one person who didn't hide anything from her. "Besides, you're the one who's been MIA recently! You should be the one they punish, not her," Avery clipped.

"Keep talking like that, and I'll start to think you don't like having me around," Finn said, placing a hand to his chest.

"This is ridiculous," Avery mumbled, her head shaking slowly, ignoring the tightness in her throat.

"Be that as it may," Finn said in a gentler tone, "when the Elders issue an edict, it's incredibly difficult to get them to change their tune."

"But I never would have even—"

"You're clearly exhausted," he interrupted. "I would have carried you to your room, but how many times can a guy do that before it starts to look desperate?"

She ignored him. "I really think I should try to talk to someone about this," she said, not bothering to conceal her distress. "It's my fault."

"Listen, you know as well as I do that Petra can handle herself," he reassured, heading for the door and gesturing for her to follow. "Try not to worry too much about it."

She leaned away skeptically. "Why are you being nice to me?" she asked, approaching slowly.

"I'm always nice to you," he replied, genuinely surprised.

"Since when?"

"You think I'm not nice to you?" Avery saw him tilt his chin, a lock of hair falling over his forehead. She stared, the sincerity making her uncomfortable.

"Forget it," she mumbled, moving forward to lead him into the hallway toward her quarters.

For once, he didn't force conversation between them as they walked. Avery concentrated on the sounds their boots made against the crisp floor of the hallways. It was strange, having him back after so many days acclimating on her own.

She wondered if anyone had bothered to wash the dried blood off her lip from earlier. Her hair was probably a wreck, too. But what did she care what Finn thought, anyway? It wasn't as though he mattered.

She kept walking, discreetly wiping her upper lip with her sleeve.

CHAPTER TWELVE

On the third day of having Finn as her only companion, Avery was beginning to question his sanity. The guy was a walking contradiction. He clearly had difficulty taking anything seriously, and his sarcasm was grating.

But then there were moments when he was utterly sincere. And those were sometimes more difficult to deal with than anything else. Avery could see how much the people here meant to Finn. In many ways, his passion for the Rebellion even rivaled Petra's.

Things had been much simpler with Petra. Avery hadn't needed to guess her intentions or thoughts, as they were an open book to her. It was comfortable. Familiar, even.

But with Finn, Avery was always alert. She couldn't relax. Her mind worked double time whenever he was near, straining to track his every movement. Trying to understand how his mind worked as they spent so much time together.

He always beat her soundly in Noring, a traditional Reange board game that he insisted she had to learn. She had been horrible, of course, and he had laughed at her the whole time. He goaded her for losing, and even though it made her want to stab him in the eye with his game piece, she still went to bed feeling lighter than she had in weeks.

Lissande had begun to track the connection between Avery's DNA irregularities and her emotions. Apparently, the key to controlling her powers was in the way she controlled herself. Not a huge surprise, if she considered it, but at least they had some quantifiable data.

Still, Avery left each day of training feeling like a failure. She was wasting time, without a clear idea of where she was headed. They were floating around chasing theories. Perhaps the only way to make any progress was to take bigger risks.

Not that the Elders would ever agree to risk-taking. They visited frequently to dine with their So', hosting formal dinners in her quarters, as they had that very evening. Avery felt like some prized lost treasure instead of the leader they professed they wanted. To them, she was just this abstract concept.

None of them saw her. Not really. But how could they? She wasn't even sure she saw herself anymore.

Poking what remained of the food around her plate with disinterest, Avery resolutely ignored Finn across the table. Ignored the way he was watching her. He was the only constant, even if he confused the blazar out of her. Her face began to flush beneath his gaze.

"What?" she snapped at him, looking up. His blue-gray eyes clashed with her own in silence. "What?" she asked again.

"What's wrong?" he said, his voice gravelly and deep. So he was sincere tonight.

"Nothing." She averted her gaze quickly, a real blush climbing up her neck to stain her cheeks as she stood. Wanting to keep her hands busy, she began to stack plates for the servant who would come by soon to collect them. It was still strange, having people wait on her. But they wouldn't let her do things herself.

"Avery, I think you should know that I know by now," Finn drawled, leaning back in his seat.

"Know what?" she asked, trying unsuccessfully to appear occupied.

"That you're a horrible liar."

She forced a laugh, the sound artificial even to her own ears.

"And a horrible fake laugher," he added as he picked up his glass of wine and drained it.

Avery ignored him, not having the strength to argue this evening.

She was beginning to feel buried down here, so far beneath the surface without any hope for escape. The hope of saving Gran was slipping through her fingers, and she was unable to stop it.

It didn't help that the traditions of the So' were passed down through the mind only. Since it was sacred, nothing had ever been written down. And because she was the last, no one here knew how to train her. Trying to master her gift was like running without gravity—her movements were a waste of energy, taking her nowhere.

She started scraping at the dishes with so much gusto, Finn thought Avery might break them in half. Something was bothering her, in a big way.

She was as easy to read as an open book. Every nuance of feeling was written across her freckled face, like groupings of stars mapped into constellations.

It was refreshing, her candid honesty. Finn couldn't deny that.

She had been retreating into herself over the past few days, and he felt like he was the only one who could see it. Didn't anyone realize she was near her breaking point? Her deepening depression was palpable as she withered away under the pressure. He couldn't just sit there and watch it happen. He refused to.

He hadn't missed the blush blooming on her face before she had begun to frantically scrape and pile dishes. He made her nervous. Finn stifled a grin.

Before he knew what he was doing, Finn was on his feet, reaching for her hand across the table. Her fingers were a flash of cold before she jerked away, amber eyes staring him down.

"What are you doing?" she asked with a frown.

Blazar if he knew.

"Do you want to get out of here?" What was he saying? Nick would kill him, not to mention the Elders. He didn't need to end up like Petra.

"What?" she asked, looking at the hand he still held out to her.

"I know a place." He gestured with his head toward the

door and added, "We can go above ground." Her eyes brightened, and Finn knew that it was worth it.

"But—" she began to protest, the weight of reality settling in as she began to overthink. A bad habit of hers.

"C'mon," he said, moving around the table and grabbing her hand again. Her fingers felt small and frozen in his.

He really couldn't give two shits about what they were going to do to him when they found out. Once he had seen the real fire lighting her eyes again, there was no power in all the stars that would deter him.

The Elders could kiss his ass.

"Where are we going?" Avery asked breathlessly as Finn tugged her out into the hallway, his stride long and purposeful. She pulled her hand from his, unable to stand the way her pulse sped when he touched her. "I can walk without holding your hand, thanks," she said abrasively.

"All right." He smirked at her. "No need to bite my head off."

She blushed, grateful he couldn't see, and focused on keeping up with his pace. They rushed through the hallways, but she didn't miss the way he cautiously approached each corner. They definitely weren't supposed to be doing this.

Could he really take her above ground? Avery's breath caught as she thought about it. It was after dark, so she wouldn't be able to see much. But just the thought of breathing in fresh air was hypnotic.

They came to the little round elevator that Petra had once

taken her through, and Avery stepped into the small space with him. They fell into silence, and she refused to break it. If she said anything now, it would feel forced and artificial. She chewed on the inside of her lip.

Once they reached the level he had entered in the keypad, the door opened, and they proceeded down another long hall. Finn stopped her with a hand in front of her chest, pressing her against the wall beside him as people passed around the corner.

Avery's heart pounded, but she felt exhilarated. They hadn't been seen, she could tell from their thoughts. Her powers were finally useful for something.

Starting forward again, Finn cut a hard right at the end of one of the halls, coming to a smaller door that led to a tiny upward-spiraling staircase. He started up, and she followed. Thankfully, they didn't climb long before Finn was pushing open an old-fashioned hinge door at the top and guiding her through.

Cool air caressed her skin, chilling her lungs as she took her first breath. She stepped through the doorway, her eyes devouring the area illuminated by the lights of the stairwell.

They were on top of a mountain, perched on a little lookout that had been carved into the edge of a cliff. There was no railing, and fear immediately clawed up her throat as she realized they were no more than five or six feet away from a straight drop down.

"Something wrong?" Finn asked, still waiting for her to move away so he could shut the door behind them.

"No," she murmured, taking a few cautious steps to the side as she reached for the stability of the rocks behind her. Finn closed the door, letting it click shut behind him as he turned to peer out at the view beyond.

Avery followed his gaze, her eyes adjusting to the darkness as she looked beyond the ledge. They were on a cliff face that faced toward the main capital. Milderion glittered brightly in the not-so-far distance, the lights of the city dancing in the deep black of the night.

She gazed up to see the three moons settled heavily in the night sky, letting out a small gasp. Their glow lit up the ledge, making Finn clearly visible in the moonlight. His dark hair blew wildly in the breeze that whipped around them.

He walked closer to peer over the edge of the cliff, and Avery's stomach lurched. She leaned back, resting fully against the wall. Sliding down, her hands grasped the rough surface behind as she sat.

She rested her head against the cool rock and closed her eyes, taking in a lungful of the sweetly chilled air. She could smell the ocean. It couldn't be far. Just beyond the city.

Avery opened her eyes as Finn took a seat next to her. Long legs stretched out beside her, his hand on the space beside her own. It was strangely intimate.

She cleared her throat, nodding toward the city. "What's Milderion like?"

"A black hole," he responded quickly with a gentle laugh, and she turned to look at him quizzically. "Nah, it's okay," he acknowledged. "Just my position there that's unbearable." He pushed a hand through his ruffled hair, and continued, "The tech is pretty advanced, and the buildings are phenomenal. A unique mix of human and Reange ingenuity. It's a pretty amazing example of what we can do if we put our heads together, you know?"

Finn was an idealist? She never would have guessed. "What exactly do you do there?" she asked.

"I'm a puppet," he said with derision. "Another shiny object to distract the ignorant masses as the Rebellion does real work with their other hand."

She was shocked, unable to say anything as his words struck a familiar chord within her heart. It was too similar to her own feelings. She focused up at the stars and took in another deep breath. There was one thing to be said about heights. It felt pretty marvelous on top of the world.

She focused on the moons hovering heavily in the night sky, their foreign beauty practically removing her power for speech.

She could make out the deep craters in their barren surface. There were no colonies or winking lights blinking back at her. The people of Echo had yet to destroy their natural beauty.

"Moons above." She giggled with awe. "I just realized that's why you say moons instead of moon. Because you have three." Her giggles turned into a laugh which quickly became hysterical as she struggled to control it. But her despondency was finally surfacing, and she couldn't stop. Embarrassment clawed at her as the laugh tapered off into quiet tears. She refused to wipe them as they fell down her cheeks.

To his credit, Finn didn't say a word. They just sat together, watching the lights of the city twinkle in the distance. Some long minutes passed, silence the only thing between them as Avery calmed, regaining control.

The heat from his body radiated amid the cold beside her. She shivered.

"Feel better?" Finn asked, his voice as rough as moon dust. She nodded, unable to look in his direction.

"I feel that way too, sometimes," he said softly.

Her throat tightened, her pulse quickening in her veins.

Gathering some courage, she turned her head toward him. His eyes met hers, pure silver in the moonlight as they shifted back and forth between her own. She couldn't breathe.

"Thank you," she whispered, her voice nearly carrying away on the wind.

His gaze dropped to her lips, and her heart plummeted into her stomach.

Looking away, she stood up swiftly, still keeping a hand planted firmly on the rock behind her. "How far up are we?" she asked, hazarding a glance farther out to the edge.

"A few thousand feet, maybe. Why?" His voice was rough, scraping against her and making her toes curl. She heard him stand, too, and walk out closer to the ledge again.

"Oh, God," she shuddered, closing her eyes.

She felt his grin in the darkness, even if she couldn't see him.

"Don't laugh at me," she warned, familiar annoyance finally surfacing. This was how she should feel around him. This was normal.

"Are you afraid of heights?" he asked, his regular humor tainting his voice as he spoke. If he made fun of her right now, so help her, she'd push him right off the edge.

"Mildly," she acknowledged, swallowing as she peeked at him. She saw his grin, warning him before he spoke again, "Don't you dare start, damn it. I was just starting to like you."

Her face burned, her eyes shooting to the ground in front of her as she processed what just came out of her mouth. But he finally listened to her, making his way to her side without a word. Together, they watched the stars pass across the night sky.

CHAPTER THIRTEEN

Another week and Lissande was so impressed by Avery's progress that by lunch time she suggested they should take her skills out for a test run. The idea of actually interacting with a large group of Reanges again scared Avery, but she was excited to finally be moving forward. A change of pace was just what she had been asking for.

Avery missed Petra, and Finn wasn't any help on that front. Every time she brought it up, he'd just conveniently change the subject. But she was beginning to seriously miss civilization. Now that Lissande felt comfortable enough to let her try out some new territory, perhaps Avery could find Petra herself.

As they made their way down the halls to the cafeteria, Finn reminded her, "You're kind of a celebrity around here, so don't freak out on me if people start to recognize you."

"Since when do I freak out?" she asked skeptically.

"Just stay under the radar, all right?" Finn said, looking straight ahead. His jaw sported a bit of stubble, accentuating the firm line of his chin. "I don't want to have to drag your ass back to the labs again when you pass out. My pride really takes a beating when I get chewed out over it."

"Well, the thought of you getting yelled at almost makes the idea worth it," she replied pleasantly, giving him a charming smile.

"Watch it, or I might just let your pretty head slam into the ground the next time you go down during one of your fainting spells." He ended his warning with a grin.

"How many times do I have to tell you?" she asked, gritting her teeth against his prodding.

"Yeah, yeah, you don't faint," he replied with a wave of his hand. "Shit." He stopped suddenly and turned to face her.

"What?" she asked, attempting to look around him at whatever he had seen ahead. They had to be just around the corner from the cafeteria.

"Listen, maybe we ought to go check out the armory," he said quickly, a hand running through his dark hair and pushing it into disarray. He took her arm, trying to turn her back the way they came.

"What? Why?" she asked. "I'm hungry—"

"We'll pick up something from your rooms on the way." He brightened his face, adding an upbeat little nod as he began to push her gently. "C'mon, it's a much better idea. Nobody wants to see the cafeteria. It's just full of boring crap like . . . food."

"Finn!" a cheerful voice rang out, and Finn grimaced. "Are you headed to chow? Join us!"

"Who is that?" Avery asked, turning her head and rising on the tip of her toes to try to get a look. If Finn was on edge about something, she damn well wanted to see what it was.

"Where the blazar are you going?" a girl's voice called this time. "Get your big-shot ass back here—you still owe me a drink! A bet's a bet!"

"Ignore it," he said, nudging her again and jerking his head in the opposite direction.

"I don't think so, 'big shot,'" she mocked, pulling her arm from his grip. One thing was certain. If Finn was trying to avoid them, they were most definitely people she wanted to meet.

Finn stifled a groan, turning to follow Avery as she darted around him. Nova and Grigg were the last people he wanted her to meet, if he was going to make a good impression. In fact, it might do a lot to confirm her low opinion of him if she got to know his friends.

"Really," he protested, trailing after her, "you sure you don't want to check out the armory? Or maybe go see Petra?" he added in a frenzy of words. He'd even deal with that nutjob if it meant avoiding this.

She stopped in her tracks, turning to look up at him with those golden eyes of hers. "We could do that?"

"Yeah," he said, pushing aside the feeling in his gut as her face lit up. He cast a glance down the hallway where Grigg was making his way toward them with a mischievous grin.

"You better not be trying to run off with our So', Finn!"

Grigg called out, picking up his pace to a jog, and Finn scowled. There was no avoiding it now.

Avery grinned suspiciously before turning away from him again, angling toward Grigg and Nova as they approached. Finn shot Grigg a warning glare as he trotted up, with Nova following at a slower pace behind.

"Aren't you going to introduce us, Finn?" Grigg grinned.

Nova made it to Grigg's side with a smirk of her own, adding, "You know he'll never give up until you do. You might as well give in."

Finn threw his eyes to the ceiling and let out a sigh as he waved his hand at Avery. "This is Avery." Waving his hand in his friends' direction, he added, "Grigg and Nova."

"Eloquent as always, Finn," Grigg commented dryly, holding his hand out to Avery. Finn tamped down annoyance as Avery gave him her own. Grigg brought it to his lips for a kiss. "It's an honor, my So'."

Avery smiled, her face all amused surprise as she giggled. She actually giggled. Finn had to stop himself from gagging.

"Were you heading to get food?" Nova asked curiously.

Finn didn't reply immediately, feeling Avery's demeanor change as she looked at Nova. Her eyes shifted in color as she sobered from Grigg's attention. She was using her powers. His own eyes narrowed, wondering what she was hearing in Nova's mind. Thank the moons she couldn't read his.

Last week had been a mistake. Not that he regretted taking her to the lookout, but sitting there and listening to her cry had nearly undone him. Moons above, he had almost kissed her.

Thank the galaxy she seemed in better spirits lately. Sure, Finn wanted to get on her good side, but he certainly couldn't have a tryst with the almighty So'. He would be flayed alive.

Much good that would do for his plea to the Elders. So why did he have to keep reminding himself to stay away from her?

"Yeah," Finn answered Nova's question, giving Avery a nudge with his elbow. "Her majesty here worked up quite the appetite using up all those fancy powers of hers this morning."

"I told you not to call me that," Avery hissed, sending him an angry sidelong look.

"Right, it must have slipped my mind." He smiled sweetly at her.

"Stop harassing her, Finn." Grigg came to her side, taking her elbow in his grasp and leading her toward the dining hall. "Just stick with me, Avery. Finn's been getting his ass kissed in Milderion too long to realize what an idiot he can be sometimes."

Finn followed close behind with Nova, attempting to defend himself. "I've never had any complaints before."

"That's because you never stick around long enough the morning after to hear what they're going to say," Nova quipped, jabbing him in the side with her elbow and sending Grigg into a fit of laughter.

Avery looked curiously at Grigg, and he quieted himself long enough to explain. "You see, my So', our boy here is quite the lady killer."

"Finn?" Avery scoffed, humor in her voice. "Now why do I find that hard to believe?"

Strange. Finn realized he had never really heard her joke around. He liked her like this. The way her mood lifted as though a weight left her shoulders. It seemed to lighten the burden from his own.

"I know, I know . . . ." Grigg sighed. "You wouldn't believe it to look at his face, but—" Finn punched Grigg from behind, satisfied when Grigg tripped forward and nearly fell on his face.

"Speaking of, I haven't heard much chatter on the vid streams from your recent sojourn to the capital," Nova commented. "Not up to your usual antics lately?"

"See, this is why I didn't want to introduce you," Finn said with exasperation. "You make me look bad."

"Oh, trust me," Avery replied over her shoulder, "you do that all on your own."

Grigg and Nova exchanged a look before letting out barks of laughter so loud they caused others to take note from their tables as they entered the dining hall. Avery stiffened, causing Finn to tense as well. He didn't like the idea of her passing out again, no matter how he might have teased her about it.

As they walked through the rows of tables, the noise of conversation dropped to low murmurs. She couldn't go unrecognized. She would be watched all of the time, even here. Finn got a small taste of it when he was forced into the city, but nothing like the constant eyes on her in this place. It wasn't going to be easy. He wondered if it would be this way for the rest of her life.

Grigg leaned over and whispered something in her ear that made Avery throw her head back and laugh openly. Finn kept himself from clenching his fist.

"Did you get any word on when you can rejoin your command?" Nova asked from beside him, distracting him from Avery and Grigg. "I suppose Nick had a few choice words for you about it, after that stunt in the training room."

"Don't remind me." Finn sighed heavily, rubbing his neck as he continued, "Same old tune I've been hearing for two blazing years."

"What tune?" Avery asked, craning her head to look at him

as Grigg grabbed her a plate from the assembly line. He hadn't realized she'd been listening.

Grigg offered, "Finn's been downgraded since the ambassador died."

"But aren't you and Nick both ambassadors?" she asked.

"Not until their father passed away two years ago, passing on the torch," Nova replied, grabbing her own plate and handing one to Finn. "Then Nick took over the position, and Finn hasn't been allowed back in combat since. Spends his time high-rolling with the fancies in the city, right Finn?"

"Wait,"—Avery looked at Finn with surprise—"Nick is your brother?"

"You're just realizing this now?" His response came out amused.

"I guess I never thought . . ." she trailed off, turning pensive. The freckles on her face scrunched together when she was thinking. "You *do* have the same hair color," she conceded.

"Ha!" Grigg cackled as he piled their plates with food. Avery would never eat all of that. Her appetite for traditional Echo dishes was limited. "That's where the similarities end, trust me," Grigg added.

"Yeah, yeah, so I come from a home with a less-than-perfect compatibility rate. Who doesn't?" Finn said, taking his plate from Nova. "I turned out just fine, thank you."

"That's a matter of opinion," Avery said, turning her attention to the food that Grigg was still piling.

"You know something?" Grigg smiled at Finn over Avery's head. "I like her."

Finn rolled his eyes, knowing what Grigg was trying to do.

Finn had done it himself hundreds of times. Why should he even care if Grigg was trying to charm Avery? It's not like he could have anything with her, anyway.

She wasn't even that beautiful, when it came down to it. He must be out of his mind. So she had eyes the color of a fading sunset, changing from warm amber to honeyed cinnamon. And when she smiled, it lit up her whole face, like watching a star crest around the horizon of a planet. Big deal.

Nova was right. It had been too long since he'd had any female attention if he was beginning to think about Avery that way.

Reaching out and dumping a large helping of pletch pudding onto his plate, he resolutely decided to ignore her for the rest of the meal. Let Grigg flirt all he wanted with her. At least if she was preoccupied with some Reange, then she would be less of a hassle for him to win over.

He was still telling himself that a half hour later as he laughed right alongside his friends at her jokes throughout their meal. She continued to surprise him in a number of ways.

Their eyes met across the table. A blush crept up her neck as she looked away, focusing keenly on what Grigg was saying.

A flash of movement caught his eye, distracting him. Rebels were filing into the cafeteria in subtle formation. They carried their blasters strapped to the front of their bodies, ready for action. And he didn't recognize a single person.

Finn's instincts took over, adrenaline spiking harshly in his veins.

Grigg's loud antics grew quiet, sensing the change in Finn's demeanor. Nova followed his gaze, her head jerking sharply. None of the other diners seemed to notice, but then most there at that early hour were trade workers, not fighters.

Finn clenched his jaw.

"Get her out of here," Nova said under her breath, her

hand finding the pistol strapped at her thigh.

And that was all the time they had before the room erupted into chaos.

Blastfire echoed through the chamber, so suddenly that Avery half jumped out of her seat. Her heart lurched violently as Finn grabbed her arm, yanking her up and behind his body. He backed up, and she had no choice but to stumble until he pressed her against the wall. His gun was out and up, ready to shoot before she even registered what was happening.

The food hall was full of people, falling into mayhem as the attacking soldiers blocked the only exit. They were spreading throughout the aisles, systematically taking out anyone in their path. Avery turned her face away as she saw bodies drop heavily, agonized screams clawing at her temples.

"We're blocked in," Finn yelled, pulling her attention back to her companions.

Finn held one arm out, blocking Avery from moving forward, and his blaster was outstretched in his other. Grigg and Nova acknowledged him with quick motions as they made their way across the room. They expertly fired at the invaders, overturning tables for cover. The few others trained in combat followed suit, setting up a kind of small barrier to protect them. But even Avery could tell they wouldn't be able to do so for long.

"What's happening?" Avery got out, her body shaking as a Reange spasmed on the ground across the aisle from them. His limbs convulsed, like he was seizing violently. Electrodarts. She had never felt anything like the pain of being shot by one. A small whimper escaped her lips.

"Avery, I need you to listen to me," Finn snapped. His eyes flitted around the room, as though he was calculating a way to magically get them out of there. "I need to clear out a path for us, which means I'm going to have to go out there. As soon as I yell at you, get the hell out of here and head for your quarters. You got that?"

She shook her head. No. She couldn't do that. She couldn't even move. He turned his head violently toward her, blue eyes searing.

Tremors began to rack her body, the screams around them getting louder until they blocked out all other sound. The fear in the room swelled around her, emotions slamming against the wall she had built against them. It was too much for her to bear. There was no way she could hold out against the onslaught. Her limbs softened beneath her suddenly unbearable weight, vision blurring the room into a mess.

"Avery!" Finn yelled at her, bringing her halfway back from the void. "Did you hear me, or not? We've got one chance at this!"

"I—" she stammered, heat raging through her veins as a violent pull ignited within her. There was a pressure behind her eyes, not necessarily pain, but a growing need that called for her to let down her barrier. How could she keep a hold of herself if they all wanted a part of her?

"Damn it!" Finn cursed, turning his focus away from her and back to the room. "Stay here and stay low, do you hear me?" And then he was gone, moving away from her.

She crumbled beneath the weight of the voices, her barrier fracturing beneath the pressure. One curling tendril of thought entered her mind, teasing at her control.

And one tiny crack was all it took. The entire wall crashed down in a disastrous torrent of emotion. Feelings rushed in, hitting Avery like a mighty wave until she lost sight of the surface, drowning.

Fear. Anxiety. Confusion. Pain. Hundreds of thoughts coursed through her and in her, becoming a part of her. Only this time, she wasn't gifted with unconsciousness. She was forced to endure it, her heart pounding furiously within her chest and filling her ears with its rhythm as she connected to every Reange in the room.

But it was nothing compared to the physical pain that followed, slamming into her like a force to the chest. She had forgotten about the electrodarts.

The excruciating agony pulsed through her system, as real and tangible as if she was the one being shot. But not just one. She could feel each dart hitting its target, the pain multiplying over and over in her body.

Avery clawed at her temples, squeezing her eyes shut, tears trailing down her cheeks. She heard the scream before realizing it came from her own throat. She curled in on herself, huddling on the ground.

The endless cycle of torment froze her in place, the physical pain and mental onslaught ripping her apart.

And then suddenly, there was a small tinge of relief. She followed the solace desperately, her mind pushing out against the fog of thoughts that consumed her and seemed to grab hold. She could control them, these emotions, one by one. It seemed to keep the pain at bay, so she continued on.

With each new connection, control returned slowly. Her body no longer shook. She could breathe again. She grasped each mind, holding them firmly within her consciousness. They were connected but not allowed free reign of her.

Slowly she opened her eyes, able to take in the scene around her, even though her breathing was labored to the point of exhaustion. Sweat trickled down her lower back, and she felt moisture on her lips. She wiped the back of her hand against her nose, her fingers glistening with fresh blood.

Jerking her head up, Avery was finally in control. For the first time since she arrived in this galaxy, she knew her power. What it was meant for, and what it could do. She looked around the room, seeing it with more than her eyes. Her perception was on another level; she saw with the eyes of every Reange connected to her. As though her mind could understand what was going on in every location.

And nothing was happening. Everything was still.

There were no screams. No movements. No chaos. Every Reange had stilled and quieted, as though in a trance. Even the soldiers had stopped shooting, so shocked by what they were seeing.

Avery's eyes zipped to movement at the center of the room, where Finn was engaged in hand-to-hand combat. He took humans down easily, moving one by one with practiced skill. But he was slowing. He wouldn't be able to keep it up much longer.

She had to help him before they shot him. She couldn't just let him die, no matter his order to stay put. Avery took two steps in his direction, gasping when the room moved with her.

All the Reanges who had gone catatonic suddenly focused their attention on Finn as well, moving with purpose toward him.

Avery's focus on him intensified as she observed his fight from all angles throughout the room. The sensation was foreign and strange, yet her body acclimated quickly. She had the knowledge to help, she realized, or someone in her control did. Channeling it through the tethers that held their minds together, Avery moved everyone toward him. The room came alive, everyone fighting back simultaneously.

And slowly their tides seemed to change. They were advancing, beating back the invaders with the practiced skill of a well-trained group.

People who had cowered in fear before now seemed to have the capacity to fight back, and with extreme skill. Avery saw them and felt their assurance in their abilities, knowing even in her own mind—or was it someone else's?—that they could actually win this.

With renewed vigor, she poured her concentration into weaving the mind tethers together. Her head throbbed, but she couldn't let go. They were very nearly to the breaking point. She had to focus on all of them. This was what her power could do. They finally had—

She didn't see the soldier until he was right in front of her, a silver blaster pointed directly at her face. Fear paralyzed her as she stared at him. A bead of sweat trickled down the side of his face. He looked just as scared as she felt.

"Avery!" Finn yelled from somewhere across the room, as though he could somehow get to her in time before the man fired.

There was no way out of this one. She squeezed her eyes shut.

A shot rang out, deafening in the small cafeteria as the sound reverberated off the vaulted ceiling.

Avery's eyes widened, echoing the face of the soldier in front of her as his gaze slid down to watch the rapidly growing stain of red exuding from his chest. In the space of a few heart-beats, he crumpled lifelessly at her feet.

Horrified, Avery's adrenaline peaked as she threw her gaze up. Nick stood at the entry to the room, a small pistol in his hand.

Moon above, he had gotten there just in time. Relief poured through her system, her breaths coming in lurching gasps. Acting quickly, Avery ran to him for safety, her way clear as the Reanges around them finally took the upper hand.

"Are you hurt?" Nick asked, laying a heavy hand on her shoulder. Avery shook her head, focused on Finn once more. He had formed a group with Grigg and Nova, battling their way through the team of invaders. "Good," he replied, nodding to the people behind him in the hallway.

Avery followed his nod and saw more soldiers moving in to surround her, barely registering their familiar blue and black uniforms.

"What is going—" She barely began the question before comprehension dawned on her. One of the Feds grabbed her hands, shoving them roughly behind her back into restraints. "Nick?" Avery asked in confusion, her eyes roving wildly to the man who she thought was a friend.

Her gaze flew across the room to Finn, panic surging through her as her confidence faltered. If Nick was part of the Federation, did that mean . . . ?

Almost immediately, she began losing her firm grip on the Reanges' minds. A few slipped away, the rest then unravelling with alarming speed. She saw Grigg and Nova yelling out her name even as their faces contorted with discomfort.

Avery fought against it, trying to gather the threads back together as best she could, but they slipped through her grasp.

It was useless to try.

In a flash, the agony was back on top of her, and the shock sent her over the edge. She screamed, pulling her hands against her restraints as she jerked her body.

"Don't let her hurt herself," Nick bit out sharply. "I didn't think she'd have the ability to control them like this yet. She's pushed herself too far."

Even in her haze, Avery could hear the resistance she had tied together beginning to fall apart in the room beyond. Screams faded to whimpers and cries as their fight died. She heard a guttural cry, and her eyes flew to Finn, watching as a soldier took down both Grigg and Nova with electrodarts to the chest.

Finn was still holding his own, perhaps because he hadn't been fazed by the merge that Avery had forced on everyone else. But they took him easily enough, two Feds grabbing his arms and hauling him across the room.

They threw him at Nick's feet, and fresh terror hit Avery when she saw blood pouring out of a wound on his head.

"What the fuck is this, Nick?" Finn demanded savagely, his blue eyes flying to meet Avery's before returning to his brother's. He tried to stand, but Nick motioned to the soldiers who then grabbed his shoulders and slammed his knees back to the ground.

"What does it look like?" Nick replied balefully.

Finn's brow furrowed in confusion. "I don't understand what—"

"Don't be simple, Finnegan," Nick interrupted. "I'm delivering her to the Federation, as promised. It's a straightforward enough concept. I would go as far to say that everyone else here has figured it out by now."

"What?" Finn spat out, his breathing coming in labored gasps.

"It's all right, brother," he said with a knowing smile. "I just need you to trust me. I told you that I needed you here protecting her for a reason, didn't I?"

"You—you've been working for the Federation?"

"She'll need someone she trusts if the minister is going to get anywhere with her. You finally brought me the piece I needed to barter for our security in the capital. We'll be heroes, Finn. To our own people."

Despite the pain, disbelief coursed through Avery. Others in the room heard it, too. They had all been betrayed. Sold out to the Federation by a human. Nick had brought them here to take Avery back.

"You're insane." Finn's voice was deathly calm as his features settled in understanding. "We've fought our whole lives for this," he reasoned. "The Federation is corrupt, Nick. They're cruel. You are the one who taught me that!"

"You're wrong!" Nick yelled, losing his composure for just a moment. "Father taught you that. Taught *us* that. And look where it got him. He abandoned his family for his ideals a long time ago, dragging us out here to live amongst aliens." His eyes flickered to the room full of Reanges. "There's so much you don't know about what he—" Nick stopped himself. "I refuse to follow his path."

"So what?" Finn studied Avery hastily, his eyes calculating. "Are you going to just run off with her? You won't get farther than the nearest lock. They've got to be sending in troops even now. You're trapped."

"Oh brother . . . do you know me so little?" Nick smiled, pulling up his wristport to type in something with deft taps of his fingers. "I have all the codes to Nos Valuta. We're locked down." He pulled up a message, and Avery struggled to focus enough to read it from her hunched position, without any luck. "But it looks as if our ride is here already. I didn't really plan on it taking so long to convince you." He frowned.

Finn let out a bark of disbelief, realization dawning. "You think I'm going to side with you?"

Nick looked at him, his jaw set and eyes narrowed. "Your petulance is tiring. You know that I need you, Finn. We're blood," he said simply.

"That doesn't mean I'm going to follow you blindly, Nick. These people"—Finn gestured behind him—"are our family."

Nick's eyes hardened. "Our family is dead."

They stared at one another, discord thickening until Avery couldn't watch them any longer. She turned her face away.

Nick let out a loud sigh. "I really don't have time for this." He reached into his jacket and pulled out a blaster. "You made your choice," he said, firing straight into Finn's chest.

CHAPTER FOURTEEN

Finn could hear Avery screaming as they dragged her away, helpless to stop it.

Nick had shot him. Point blank.

Nick had shot him, and he wasn't dead. Why wasn't he dead? He couldn't move, but he certainly was still alive.

"The Minister wants a handful for specimens. Kill the rest," he heard Nick hiss to the other soldiers as he lay paralyzed on the floor. Finn concentrated on the cold surface beneath his cheek, willing the pain to recede. He had always been good at enduring pain.

Avery was gone. Every instinct in him cried out to get up. To follow her. To do something other than lay there in a useless stupor.

His eyes moved wildly, searching rapidly for Grigg and

Nova. Where the blazar were they? Surely, they could power through those electrodarts soon.

For a moment there, the whole room had fought as expertly as his friends. It was incredible. He had let himself believe for half a moment that they would win.

Finn watched as the Feds filed out, some in the tan regs of the Rebellion, and others in the blue colors of the Federation. Each carried an unconscious body. Grigg passed him, hanging limply from a shoulder. Then Nova.

Blastfire rang loudly as boots passed in front of his line of vision, Feds shouting in response. A brief scuffle and a few more shots, then nothing.

The boots returned, stopping directly in front of him. Petra kneeled, her face tight as she hauled him to a sitting position. Pain surged through his body, and he fought against passing out.

"Where is she?" Petra screamed, shaking him. "Damn it! You were supposed to protect her!" She dropped him, his head slamming to the floor. He couldn't move. What the blazar had Nick shot him with?

He could hear Petra's ragged breathing as she paced. She knelt in front of him again, rummaging through the pack strapped to her side. Pulling out a nasty-looking syringe, she gave him a glance. "This is going to hurt."

And that was all the warning she gave before plunging it into his chest.

She pressed down on the plunger, liquid fire running a swift blaze throughout his veins. He wanted to rip them out as the fluid surged through his body, spreading like roots branching out from his chest. His heart skipped three solid beats.

He shot up, as though there was a string attached to his collarbone pulling him skyward. Senses on high alert, he quickly took in his surroundings. Some were dead, others missing. Grigg and Nova were gone.

Moving into action, he crossed the room to grab a blaster and pistol off a Fed Petra had killed. He tucked the pistol into his holster, holding the blaster ready as he took off down the hallway. Petra was hot on his trail.

They had to get Avery back. A fresh surge of adrenaline flooded his heart. He wouldn't let them take her. He wouldn't let her become some test subject. She was more than that.

Picking up his pace, Finn sprinted after them. If Nick was waiting for a ride, they had to be heading for the upper landing platform. It was the only place to get out, unless they were going on foot.

"Finn," Petra panted beside him, struggling to keep up, "how many do they have? We need a plan. Neither of us will be any good dead."

"Not enough time," Finn got out as he pushed harder, leaving Petra behind him. The hallways began to slope upward in the large spiral that led to the landing.

The sound of Avery's screams echoed down the central column, and his eyes flickered upward. Her fear cut him straight through. Sweat poured down his face as he forced himself harder, syncing his steps with the beating of his heart. He wouldn't let them have her.

Finn neared the top as an engine roared to life, readying for takeoff. It came into view as he rounded the final corner, the sloped spiral leveling out to a flat landing pad.

"Finn!" Petra yelled from behind, too far to do any good. He couldn't wait for her.

He focused every ounce of will he possessed on pulling his

legs up in front of him to gain more speed. The ship, the sleek gray model of the Federation, was lifting off the ground ahead.

Swinging the blaster over his shoulder, Finn concentrated on the burn of his muscles, his heart slamming rapidly. He gained on the ship as it pulled away, his speed climbing until it was nearly superhuman.

Perhaps it was good that Petra had drugged him. If he had been sober, there was no way in two galaxies Finn would have tried what he did then.

Springing from the ground, Finn stretched his body fully in the air, reaching out toward the vessel.

His hand caught the landing gear, the weight of his body jerking him violently as he struggled to hang on. Flinging another arm up to secure his grip, Finn pulled upward to straddle the metal. It quickly folded into the underbelly of the ship, Finn along with it.

Finn barely avoided being crushed as the gear stored itself snugly against the hull of the ship. The outer doors to the compartment closed, and he dropped his weight to the surface. He found the panel to the undercarriage easily enough, slamming it open with his feet.

He moved into the ship as stealthily as possible, not easy when his blood pumped a heavy rhythm through his brain. His combat experience kept him from exploding into a thousand pieces. Instead, he harnessed the adrenaline for his own use.

Carefully, he followed the sounds of Avery's cries, maneuvering to the upper deck. She must have been trying her damnedest to fight them.

Finn rounded a corner as Nick exited a room, Avery's anguished screams echoing loudly from behind him. She quieted suddenly, which couldn't mean anything good. His fist clenched painfully at his side. A group of soldiers trailed after Nick as the door slid closed behind them.

They weren't on alert. No one knew he was there. More importantly, they had left Avery unguarded. Idiots.

He moved forward, pulling out his blaster to shoot out the control panel in a burst of electricity and smoke. Finn braced his hands on the door itself, sliding it open with a little effort.

Avery huddled in the corner with wide eyes, half standing upon seeing him. A heavy red welt spread across her cheek.

Her eyes darted pointedly to his right, and he dodged to avoid a fist thrown by the remaining guard. Finn threw his shoulder into the body, using his momentum to carry the soldier across the room and slam her into the wall. The woman crumpled into unconsciousness.

"Didn't see that one coming," he said, his words unnaturally quick.

Avery was on her feet, cheeks wet as she stumbled across the room toward him. Finn grabbed her hand, pulling her quickly out of the room. Escape pods had to be somewhere near the back of the ship. That was their only chance at getting out of this.

Hearing a group of voices ahead, Finn slowed, releasing Avery's hand to pull the blaster from his back. Finn motioned for her to stay put as he indicated the sounds around the corner.

The air thickened, the molecules closing in around his body. Wall panels vibrated with energy, rattling softly in the silence of the hallway. He jerked his head back toward Avery. Shit, he'd have to move fast. She wouldn't be able to keep it together for much longer.

He crept toward the corner, his back firmly against the panels behind. The voices were discernible now, and Finn risked a glimpse around the edge. Avery's anxiety radiated around him, like the heated rays of a star. It was only a matter of time before they felt it, too.

"What took you so long?" Nick stood a few feet away, reprimanding two Feds. Finn's jaw clenched painfully. "The girl's gift has advanced so far that she was nearly able to overpower us."

"With all due respect, sir," the Fed with his back to Finn replied, "we answer to the minister, not you. We came when there was an appropriate avenue to do so, per her orders."

"Well, don't blame me if you have more trouble holding her now," Nick replied, his voice acid. "I trust that her condition won't affect my arrangement."

"On the contrary," the soldier countered. "Minister Klein is eager to begin testing with such advanced progress. We have high hopes that this will allow for better results."

"Excellent." Nick turned to walk farther down the hallway, away from Finn and Avery. "I've transferred the information on Nos Valuta to your database. Your forces should have everything you need."

Disbelief ripped through Finn's core. Nick was giving away the Rebellion's last defense.

"The Federation is grateful, Ambassador," the soldier continued. "Once the Gate falls, I know that Minister Klein will be happy to have you to help deal with . . . ." Their voices faded as they rounded a corner down the hall.

Finn's body swayed toward them, everything inside of him calling out to charge down that hallway and demand answers. Finn thought of Valuta and everything they had built, his brother's betrayal quickly burning a hole through his heart. His knuckles turned white around the blaster in his hands.

He took a step before a hand gripped his arm, fingers digging into his jacket.

Turning back to Avery, Finn met her frightened eyes and schooled his features immediately. Now wasn't the time to leave her, no matter how valuable the information. He had to secure Avery—get her somewhere safe. Then he would go after Nick.

Finn grabbed her hand again, moving as fast as he could drag her. As soon as Nick reached the flight deck, he'd realize Avery wasn't where she was supposed to be. Well, at least they had the element of surprise.

He tore down a flight of steps, coming to a small hall lined with orange lights indicating the emergency escape. There were four pods, two on each side of the walkway. Their small, round hatches were all open, ready and waiting.

"What are we doing?" Avery asked, voice shaking.

"Getting you the blazar out of here." He dropped her hand, hopping into the nearest pod and activating the autopilot launch with deft movements. If he could set off the other three as a diversion, it might slow their pursuit down.

"We—" She choked on the words. "We can't leave them."

He met her eyes. She meant the hostages. Grigg's and Nova's faces flashed through his mind. His gut twisted.

She rubbed the back of her hands against her face, wiping away the traces of tears that lingered. Half-dried blood covered her chin and most of her shirt. Even now, it dripped lightly from her nose. He was amazed she was still conscious.

"Look," he said, grabbing her by the shoulders, "any of them would give their life for you." Whether he was trying to assure her or himself, he couldn't tell. "I know you don't want to hear it, but right now, you're more important."

Her eyes glistened like wet amber as she raised her chin.

"No," she said fiercely.

He scoffed, jerking away from her. If he had to force her into the damn pod, that's what he was going to do.

Fighting a wave of dizziness, Finn ducked into the second and third pods to send them off as decoys. His vision blurred. If he didn't get them out of there soon, he wasn't going to be much good to anyone. His body was on the verge of crashing.

Pulling himself back into the hallway, he caught Avery's eye. She wouldn't look away, stubborn as ever, even as boots ran quickly across the floors above their heads.

"We don't have the time for this, sweetheart," Finn pointed out tightly, struggling to stay on his feet.

"What's wrong with you?" Her voice was panicked as she moved to steady him, an arm wrapping his waist.

"Jus' get in the damned pod," he slurred, using the weight of his body to push her toward it. Together, they tumbled in, and he shoved her into one of the six seats that circled the controls.

"But Finn, we can't just—"

"Strap in and shut up, damn it!" he snapped at her.

She looked like she wanted to argue. But for once, she did as he told her.

Finn had just enough time to drunkenly type in coordinates and initiate a launch before darkness closed in around him, ushering him into oblivion.

"Finn?" Avery strangled out as he slumped against the controls. She craned her neck to peer out the hatch window as they careened on a course that he had failed to disclose to her.

She thought of the hostages the Feds had taken, choking back a ragged sob. Even Grigg and Nova had been there. How could Finn just leave them? Avery hadn't been able to save them. That was the whole purpose of this damn thing, and she couldn't even do that.

She turned back to Finn, tapping the little button on her chest to release the restraints and moved to crouch in front of him. She used what little strength she had left to pull him back into his seat.

His eyes were closed, his breathing shallow. The pallid tone of his skin was a sad semblance of its normal healthy tan. Nick had shot him. She had seen it with her own eyes. Frantically, she ran her hands over his chest, searching for any signs of blood. There was a singed hole in his shirt, but he seemed unharmed.

The little pod hitched, and Avery was thrown to the floor, her shoulder slamming painfully into the side of the main console. Avery scrambled to secure Finn before finding her own seat.

"Autopilot disengaging," the feminine voice of the computer rang out in the pod.

"What?" Avery squeaked in disbelief.

"Autopilot disengaging," it repeated.

"What? Why?" Avery balked. There was no way she could fly this thing. One look at the controls told her that its operating system was vastly different than any craft she'd ever handled.

"This A.I. is not licensed to land in locations with an active population. Autopilot will disengage in ten seconds. Please have the pilot take control."

"But I'm not licensed to fly it, either!" she yelled, reaching over to grab Finn's shoulder with an urgent shake. "Finn! Finn, wake up!"

"Five . . . four . . ." the computer began a countdown.

"Really?" Avery squinted up at the ceiling.

"Three . . . two . . . ."

She leaned past Finn, placing her hand on the console's directional ball. One peek at the view window told her Milderion was coming up fast. They were practically on top of the city already, sleek silver buildings rapidly rising beneath them as the pod flew through the air.

"Autopilot disengaged."

The craft was fully in her control. Sweat beaded in the center of her back, her muscles tensing when the pod bounced in response to the uncertainty of her hand. Moon above, she had to do something.

"Give me the coordinates pathway," she said firmly, hoping the tech was similar enough to Earth systems to work. Avery let out a little whimper of thanks as a green line appeared on the window in front of her, along with an arrow indicating the current trajectory. If she could just keep aligned with the green path, it should work out fine.

Soon they were surrounded by buildings, the pod flying high down the streets as cruisers popped up in her path. Warnings blared as drivers attempted to avoid them.

"Approaching destination," the computer informed her.

"How do you slow this blazing thing down?" Avery asked, and the computer complied, beginning to decrease its speed. Avery hazarded a glance at Finn beside her, still unconscious.

If his coordinates were any indication, the path they were on came to a dead end at the base of a large building. It looked like a store, the front wall completely encased in glass reaching at least three levels up.

Avery's pulse quickened. They weren't slowing down enough to make a safe landing.

"Slower, damn it!" she screeched, but the computer didn't respond.

Avery's eyes roved the console, searching blindly for some kind of manual break. There wasn't enough time. Hunkering low in her seat, Avery activated her restraints, the belts unfolding up and over her chest.

Squeezing her eyes shut, she envisioned the pod swerving out of control toward the building and exploding on impact. She let her anxiety build, the familiar sensation of warmth spreading until she was ready to combust. A pounding sensation echoed in her head, sparks igniting behind her eyelids as the painful pressure built.

But this time she was ready. She had the ability to harness the wild energy building inside of her.

In a single moment, Avery felt everything around her. The pod came alive, every angle and component opening up to her senses. Following instinct, Avery focused the energy until it built in front of the vessel, pushing against its momentum. The pod began to slow. It was working!

She opened her eyes, panic surging as they still approached the building much too fast. Fear broke her concentration, and her control slipped entirely. They careened straight into the wall of glass.

Avery supposed she should have been grateful for the belt that kept her from breaking every bone in her body. The waterfall of shattering glass was deafening as they hit the building. The centrifugal force of the pod's roll compressed her brain until her vision was a shaky blur of images.

At last, they came to a stop some distance from the gaping hole they had ripped in the glass. Avery hung suspended from her restraints, the pod on its side. Finn was in a similar position, hanging limp and looking paler than ever. Avery swallowed hard. Whatever time Finn had bought them, it wouldn't be long before the Federation was hot on their trail.

She hit the button at her chest, releasing the restraints and catching herself clumsily when she fell from her seat. She noted her dead wristport wistfully. She had no resources to find her way in the capital at all. And Finn's would be of no use, since he was unconscious.

Megan was there in Milderion somewhere, but she seemed so far removed from all of this. Avery wasn't even certain she wanted to drag her into it. It was far too dangerous. Too real.

Voices echoed down from outside the pod. Avery's head jerked toward one of the windows that had broken open in their crash, her mind on high alert. Moon above, she thought they would have more time.

Avery warily released Finn, catching his body as he slumped to the side and fell, half draped across her. She whimpered trying to lift him. He was heavy. Too heavy for her to move.

She couldn't leave him. He may have been a pain in the ass, but he had risked his life to save her. More than once. And more than that, in some strange way he was a part of what she was becoming.

The voices grew louder, and she looked around in distress, searching for a solution. Gritting her teeth, Avery let out a cry of resignation.

She leaned in close to Finn, gripping the collar of his blood-stained shirt as she promised, "I'll get you out of this. Just hang on."

She turned to the window, kicking out fragments of glass, and pulled herself through the small opening. She let out a harsh gasp when her hand caught, her palm slicing open on the jagged ledge.

Glass crunched beneath her boots as she pushed off, scouring for a place to hide. Maybe if there weren't many of them, she could hold them off long enough to find a way to get Finn out of there.

But it wasn't Federation soldiers, as Avery had assumed. In fact, they looked like ordinary civilians. She huddled behind a pillar in the dark beyond the pod, trying to assess the situation.

There were only three, two men and a woman. They approached the wreck cautiously. Avery bit the inside of her cheek.

"Is it Federation?" the older man asked, his voice rumbling through the empty offices around them.

The woman kneeled in front of the pod to study the markings, strikingly red hair falling across her forehead. "Definitely," she confirmed, looking up at him.

"We've got a survivor," the other man called out as he investigated closer. "He's unconscious."

Avery's heart stopped. She shouldn't have left him in there. Finn was helpless. She couldn't just sit there and—

"Holy blazar, it's Finn Lunitia." The older man sounded surprised.

"What's he doing here, Mylan?" the woman asked darkly.

The man's gaze shot up, peering into the darkness as Avery sunk down farther. There was no way he could see her.

"Something's wrong," Mylan stated, finally abandoning his stare to look out the windows into the open sky of the city.

"We've got to get below ground before the Federation shows. If he's discovered here . . . ." He shook his head. "Get him out of there." He gestured to the other man, a larger guy with muscles his jacket could barely contain.

"How could something have happened so quickly?" the woman asked Mylan anxiously, her voice so quiet that Avery struggled to hear.

Avery nearly gasped aloud as she tuned into her senses. Why hadn't she noticed the feeling before? The familiar tug on her mind. The need for connection. They were Reanges. But could they be trusted?

She reached out toward them, tentatively touching the mind of the woman. With a talent she didn't know she had, Avery coaxed feelings from her. Adrenaline. Fear. Determination. Avery felt the little tether of the woman's thoughts settle firmly into her grasp. She let out a soft breath of air. That wasn't so hard.

Reaching out toward Mylan with firmer resolve, she was pleased when his feelings floated toward her eagerly. Compassion. Trust. They settled her nerves even as she sought to wrap her control around his will.

Avery.

A voice sounded in her mind. Avery jerked her head toward them, her eyes narrowing intently.

Do not be afraid, he urged. Mylan. *We are here to help.*

He was speaking to her. Somehow, he knew she was poking around in his head. Too frightened to respond, she stayed silent.

He looked out into the darkness toward her again. He knew. He knew she was there. She lost her grip, dropping the connection.

Her eyes shifted as the other two dragged Finn out of the wreckage. Avery's heart squeezed painfully. She took in a slow, deep breath.

"Can I trust you?" she called out, her voice echoing around them.

The other two dropped Finn in surprise. They moved in immediately to flank Mylan, pulling out their weapons, ready to fight.

Mylan pushed the others behind him as he stepped toward her. "We would never harm you, my So'."

It was her only option. If she wanted to save Finn, she had no other choice. Their eyes settled on her as she rose, stepping into the light.

"You know who I am." It wasn't a question.

Mylan nodded slowly, bowing his head in a quiet salute. The other two barely hesitated before quickly echoing the gesture. Avery's eyes were pulled to Finn, his breathing shallower than ever.

"My friend needs help," she choked out. Avery had made the choice to trust them. She could only hope that it wouldn't be the wrong one.

CHAPTER FIFTEEN

They had been walking for hours, through some kind of system of underground tunnels. She had heard of similar ones on Earth, leftover from ancient transportation systems, but nobody had traveled underground in hundreds of years. Not since the first independent cruisers had gone commercial.

They walked in strenuous silence, the only sounds coming from the echo of their footsteps on the curved walls entombing them in the city's underbelly. But since they moved at a swift pace, she was grateful for the lack of conversation.

Surely her instincts weren't wrong about Mylan. His sincerity had been stark and straightforward, but how much of that could she really trust? There was still so little she knew of it. So little she knew of herself.

Avery struggled to make him out in the near darkness. The

only light came from the glow torch he held to light their way. His face was heavy with lines and sun damage, gray hair blending into white at the temple. He may have been even older than Gran.

His eyes slid to hers, and she quickly stared back down at the cement beneath her feet. "You still haven't told me where we're going," Avery bit out. Her voice came out loudly, bouncing harshly against the silence.

"Somewhere safe," Mylan replied cryptically, his attention not straying from the path. "You'll be told everything soon, Avery. Trust us for now."

A groan echoed softly through the darkness, and Avery jerked her head around, slowing to a stop. Finn stirred from his position draped over the other man's back. Krez. And the woman was Fiora. They both were methodical, clearly trained and used to action of this kind. Despite the obvious strain, Krez didn't complain.

"He needs a healer," Avery stated worriedly. Finn's breathing was more labored than ever before, his face drenched in sweat. Whatever was wrong with him, it was getting worse.

"She's right," Fiora agreed. Mylan looked back at them uneasily. "We won't make it there tonight anyway, at this pace. Perhaps we should make camp for a few hours."

"I could use a rest," Krez conceded, shifting Finn's weight on his back.

Mylan shone the light on Finn. His pale face was positively green beneath the glow torch, and dark blue circles had formed beneath his eyes. Avery bit the inside of her lip to keep from trembling.

"All right," Mylan said. He nodded in the direction they had been heading. "There's a platform not too far ahead. We'll stay there for the night."

Tucked into a carved-out section of wall, the platform sheltered them from the open expanse of the tunnel. A cold draft moved over them, the air thick with a heavy wetness. Avery shivered.

Krez pulled out a white circular disc and set it on the ground, touching his wristport to its edge. The circle lit up with a brilliant light, heat radiating around them until it was comfortably warm. The glow of the disc illuminated the area, casting soft shadows against the walls.

Fiora took the first watch, standing at the edge of the raised landing on which they camped. Her eyes roved the darkness of the tunnels beyond, her body relaxed yet alert. Mylan leaned against the wall, his eyes closed in what Avery assumed was sleep, while Krez stretched out close to the warmth of the heat disc. His soft snores were the only sounds in the quiet.

Avery settled on the other side of the disc with Finn, tucking the pack Fiora had been carrying more securely beneath his head for a makeshift pillow. For the hundredth time she pressed her hand to his forehead. It was on fire. She had helped Gran often enough to know that without medicine, a fever of this height could have serious consequences.

She scooted closer, tucking her knees up to her chin as she studied him. Dark hair fell across his forehead, the lock drenched in the sweat of his fever. She reached out, pushing the hair off his brow as pain shot through the gash on her palm. They had bound it as best they could, but the cut was deep. She winced, trying to isolate it.

If only she could actually do something to help his fever. The thought of sitting here as he slowly slipped away was unbearable. If she lost Finn, she would truly be alone.

She had come to trust him. She relied on his steady presence by her side. For all his faults, he had never left her behind. He was always there for her when she needed him. Avery knew Finn would never let anything happen to her if it was in his power to stop it. Even if he only did so out of duty.

That night on the mountain lookout, his eyes had burned as they sat beneath the moonlight. Silver and piercing and immovable. His gaze always confident. A constant anchor.

It was so quiet, she could hear a soft dripping sound echoing off the walls of the tunnel in the distance. If anyone pursued them, at least they'd hear them coming from a mile away.

Her own eyes began to droop, and Avery stretched out beside Finn. Using her arm to cushion her head, she studied his profile against the soft glow behind.

"You're gonna be okay," she said in a low whisper, for him alone. And perhaps for herself.

After a few fretful hours of sleep, they continued on the next morning. Or Avery could only assume it was morning. There was no telling the time when there was no light. She kept tripping over her own feet as they walked, seemingly for miles. They had to be traveling well out of the city boundaries.

At last they reached a door, hidden in a crevice of the wall itself. The opening was so small even Avery had to fold herself over to get through. Fiora and Krez passed Finn through sideways.

His fever had worsened. He was so hot that her hand burned when she touched him. This was the real danger. A fever so intense could most certainly cause permanent brain damage. A heavy knot of dread had settled securely in her gut.

She could barely focus as they made their way down a spiraling metal staircase that seemed to go on forever. Just when she thought she could feel the pressure weighing down on them, they reached the bottom that led to another path. Unlike the larger tunnels, these halls were tight with a roughhewed surface. Krez's head grazed the ceiling as they walked.

Finally, Avery saw an opening ahead of them, beckoning with the glow of warm light. The small tunnel opened into an enormous cavern that stretched on for thousands of feet into the dark.

Row after row of meticulously lined tents filled the space. Artificial lights hung from poles along the walkways in between, their yellow glow fighting off the darkness. Avery's eyes traveled up, losing sight of the ceiling in the dark. The cavern had to be more than three levels high. She had never seen anything like it, outside of history vids.

And it wasn't empty. People busily moved throughout the paths, a functional city hidden beneath the surface. Right under the Federation's nose. As their little group moved down the stone stairs onto the floor level, a few people stopped to stare curiously at the newcomers. A group of children gasped and pointed, running off into the darkness.

Avery wasn't stupid. She knew they were Reanges. Even without her gift, she could have guessed that these were more survivors. And their presence was all around her, in the very air. Their interest teased her mind, the unique feelings calling to invade her defenses. She kept her wall secure, refusing to allow a single thought through.

"Mylan," Krez's voice called out warily. Avery turned quickly to see him drop Finn, his face wary. Finn convulsed on the dirt floor, foam trickling from the corner of his mouth. Panic clawed furiously up Avery's chest and into her throat.

"What's happening to him?" she got out frantically, running to drop to her knees beside him. She grabbed Finn's shoulders to try and steady his body, wishing she could do something—anything—to help. "He needs a healer, damn it! You promised me he'd get a healer!"

Mylan called out to someone beyond her vision, and Avery's fear crescendoed, eclipsing everything. She couldn't focus on anything beyond Finn's sickness.

The panic welled up and flowed out of her in waves, crashing over everyone in the vicinity. She could feel her impact on the others, powerless to stop it. They were confused and panicked, absorbing the energy she pressed upon them. A few children began to wail loudly.

But he was dying.

"He needs help!" Avery screeched, anguished tears filling her eyes as she fought against her powers. The surrounding hysteria did nothing to help her control.

"A healer is coming, Avery," Mylan spoke near her ear, kneeling beside her. She turned her head, their eyes locking as she saw her own frenzied despair reflected back at her. He was doing an admirable job at controlling it. He spoke to her tightly. "You need to govern your feelings. Bring them back into yourself, or you will cause mass panic."

Avery returned her gaze to Finn, focusing on the air moving in and out of her lungs. Breathe in. Breathe out. The only way she knew to steady herself. The sounds around her quieted, the cries petering out to silence. Her panic began to ebb. Someone was coming. Someone who could help.

And then a woman was there, pushing Avery's hands out of the way and pulling a bag with supplies up beside her. Surely, she couldn't be old enough to be a healer of any experience. She barely looked older than Avery, with pure blonde hair the color of wheat piled into a messy bun on top of her head.

The healer pulled up Finn's eyelids, flashing a little hand-held light into his eyes and frowning as he continued to drool foam. "How long has the fever had him?" she asked, concentrating on her task.

"About a full twenty-four hours, I think," Avery replied, watching the woman work. In a strange way, she reminded her of Gran.

"And the onset? What were his symptoms?" she asked succinctly, rummaging through her bag and pulling out a bottle filled with thick liquid.

"Um." Avery thought, knowing what sort of information Gran would want. "Dizziness, slurred speech. He was shot by something that knocked him out. I thought he was dead. That's the burn mark on his chest."

The woman quickly inspected his chest, sucking in a sharp breath.

"What?" Avery asked sharply, her eyes flicking back and forth between the healer and Finn. "What is it? Can you help him?"

The healer pulled out a syringe from her overly large brown coat and filled it with the liquid. Avery cringed, not used to needles. It was such a primitive way to distribute medicine.

"Hold him." She gestured to Finn's shoulders, and Avery complied, glad to do something helpful. The woman pulled his arm out and used her teeth to rip his shirt at the elbow, pulling the sleeve off to expose the vein of his inner arm. She inserted the needle deftly and pushed the plunger down, emptying its contents into his bloodstream.

His spasms stopped almost immediately. Avery released a breath she didn't know she had been holding. Her eyes flickered to the woman who had saved him, encountering a bold, blue-eyed stare. It was unnerving. Avery averted her gaze, focusing on Finn to distract her.

"We have to get him to the clinic." The healer addressed Mylan, who was still standing above them. "Gently, though." She came to her own feet and added, "He shouldn't be moved more than necessary."

Mylan nodded, gesturing to the edge of the path where two older boys moved forward to help. Avery stood as they picked up Finn from each end, taking care to handle him gently.

"Do you know what happened to him?" The question came from Mylan.

Avery tried to ignore the growing crowd around them. Many pairs of eyes focused on her, and more uncertain feelings than she cared to acknowledge threatened to break down the wall surrounding her mind. The effort of it began to strain her system, giving rise to a headache.

"There was a puncture wound on his chest," the healer replied to Mylan. "I have a feeling someone gave him a dose of Telcum." Avery felt the anger radiating from her, mingling strangely with Mylan's shock.

"What the blazar is Telcum?" Avery asked.

"A stimulant," the woman answered, following the boys as they carried Finn down a pathway branching off from the main walkway. "Meant only for Reange. When given to humans, it has a very short efficacy period and a high mortality rate."

"What?" Avery struggled to keep up, craning her head to

keep Finn in her direct line of vision.

"Considering the burn marks on his chest, he was probably hit with a stun blaster. The Telcum would have been used to jumpstart his system," she answered gravely.

They entered a much larger tent than any of the others in the camp, passing through a flap pinned open to the side. It was a sort of primitive hospital, with beds lining either side of a central walkway. There were quite a few beds with occupants as they passed, staring at her with wide eyes.

Avery put a firm lock on her mind. She didn't want to know what they were thinking.

They settled Finn on the bed farthest from the entrance, Avery taking a seat at his side. The healer, Nevril, treated the wound on Avery's hand, although they couldn't fully close it. Apparently, they had limited supplies, preferring to use them only out of necessity.

Mylan tried to convince her to get some rest in quarters that had been prepared for her, but she couldn't leave Finn's side. Not until she was sure he was all right. But after Nevril set up a drip patch to counteract the Telcum effects, his fever soon broke. Even his breathing had regained its steady rhythm.

They put up a sort of makeshift screen, offering a little privacy from the prying eyes. Even if she couldn't keep the minds from pressing in on her.

At least they were out of immediate danger. But who knew where they had ended up.

"Avery." A voice woke her, and Avery jumped in her chair,

wiping a bit of drool from her mouth. "Sorry to wake you," Mylan said from the foot of Finn's bed. "But I thought you might like to get cleaned up."

She glanced down at her clothes. Her white shirt was nearly brown with filth and crusted with dried blood. The idea of a shower was incredibly tempting. Guiltily, she raised her eyes to Finn sleeping peacefully in front of her.

"He'll be fine," Mylan said quietly, gesturing toward the exit with a slight nod of his head. "Come, we have quarters set up for you."

She stood tentatively, eyeing Finn a final time before following Mylan out of the small clinic. She hoped it wouldn't be long before he awoke. They needed to find a way out of there. To warn the others back at Nos Valuta.

They walked quietly beside one another down the pathways, the floor beneath their feet a hard-packed dirt. The lights were drawn so low, they could barely see in front of them.

Mylan was a man of few words, which suited Avery fine. Given her level of exhaustion, she doubted she could keep up a coherent conversation, anyway.

She was walking through a hazy dream, nothing quite real or solid before her. Maybe this *was* all a dream. And tomorrow she would wake up in her room beside Gran's. They would laugh about how silly it was over breakfast. Tears pricked the corners of her eyes.

Mylan knew she was on the verge of breaking. He tactfully moved ahead, increasing their pace to a tent close to the med clinic. He pulled back the flap for her, gesturing inside.

A desk sat against one wall with a small chair, and a little sitting area featured two chairs with a table between. Across the tent, a single bed with clean sheets beckoned her with unassuming comfort.

"You'll find the washrooms just down the path to the right. It will lead you straight to them," Mylan said, as though reading her thoughts. Had he? She was too tired to have noticed, even if he did.

"Thank you," she said quietly as he started to leave.

"Someone will be here to escort you in the morning. Rest up." He smiled. "You're safe now."

She couldn't prevent a sarcastic curl of her lip as he left her there on her own. Where had she heard that before?

A quick rummage through a chest by the bed revealed a change of clothes that seemed they would fit, along with a clean towel. Perhaps the tent belonged to someone.

The showers were little more than another large tent with several stalls separated by hanging tan cloth. She ignored thoughts of privacy and stripped off her clothing. The scalding water collected around her feet on the concrete floor, running in a river to disappear into a drain.

In all her time at Valuta, no one had ever told her of another Resistance in the city. And what of the many Reanges living here? It was clearly a functioning society, and they operated with even more secrecy than the Elders back at Nos Valuta. They called it the Origin. It sounded familiar.

She finished cleaning, donning her new clothes—a simple outfit of gray pants and a green shirt with sleeves capped just below her shoulders. She had forgotten to grab shoes and so she walked barefoot back to her tent, wet hair hanging down her back.

She couldn't prevent the sigh of contentment as her head sunk into the crisp, cool pillow on the bed. Tomorrow. Tomorrow she would sort it all out. Right now, she would sleep.

Captain Harding waited in the ambassador's sitting room, his knee bouncing up and down as he counted down the long minutes. He had been shown to the large living area overlooking the Milderion skyline nearly half an hour before. These apartments were certainly extravagant, but then, it was no secret that the Lunitia family never lacked funds. Not many knew where it came from. But he did.

Making him sit here alone was all part of Nick Lunitia's game. Just like his father, the older son was just as conniving. But Harding didn't have the patience to play.

Standing in a swift movement, he turned just in time to see Lunitia himself walk into the room from the back living quarters.

"Captain," Lunitia said, wiping his hands with a towel as though he had just washed them. "To what do I owe the honor?" He stopped, keeping his distance on the other side of the room.

"You know damn well why I'm here," Harding spat. "You won't answer your comms or respond to any inquiries. You made me come to this Godforsaken planet just to get in touch with you."

"I've been busy," Lunitia responded, gesturing around him.

Harding strode toward him. "It has been weeks since you promised the delivery of the Elite girl, and yet I've seen nothing. Nothing!"

"I did deliver her," Lunitia said calmly, walking over to the kitchen area that looked across the open living space. Setting the towel aside, he grabbed a pitcher of water and poured a long stream of liquid into a clear glass. "It isn't my fault if your soldiers can't keep hold of her," he added, taking a swig of the water.

"It was your brother who freed her," Harding said bitterly, rage rising in his throat. "You said he wouldn't be a problem. Against my advice, I might add."

"Yes, well . . ."—Lunitia looked away briefly before returning his gaze—"I overestimated him. Regardless, it is not my responsibility anymore. I held up my end of the bargain. Although I have yet to be paid."

Harding let out a bark of disbelief. "And you're not going to see one blazing credit until we have that girl secured in Federation control. I'll see to it that you never—"

"Captain, I think I should warn you not to issue threats on which you can't follow through. Minister Klein is a particular . . . friend of mine. She wouldn't like to hear that you've soiled our relationship. I'm rather valuable to the Federation, as a public figurehead of the Armistice. You might want to remember that."

Harding couldn't speak. Couldn't process the insolence of such a response. Rage boiled in his veins until the edges of his vision darkened as he fought to control himself. Turning away, he surveyed the tall glistening buildings of the city beyond the wide windows. He started counting his breaths. *One . . . two . . . .* Klein wouldn't forgive him if he killed Lunitia.

"Now," Lunitia started again, and Harding used all of his willpower to block out the sound. "If you wouldn't mind, I was just—"

"I absolutely do mind!" Harding snapped, turning back to face the ambassador. He clung to the reason he had come here, distracting himself with purpose. "You may be a friend of the minister, but you are not a friend of mine. And you are deluding yourself if you think Klein will grant you one bit of slack once she finds out it was your brother who snatched the Elite girl from us, not once, but twice. You should have kept him on a tighter leash."

Nick was silent for several beats before saying quietly, "What do you suggest, then, Captain? It's not as though I can make her appear from thin air."

"You are a man of many connections, just as your father before you," Harding replied, his anger subsiding as he realized Lunitia was actually considering cooperating. "We have intel that the Origin got a hold of her. They were seen descending into the tunnels under the city shortly after you lost them."

"*I* lost them?" Nick frowned as Harding said nothing. He scoffed, shaking his head before adding, "Why didn't you just follow them down there, then?"

"Earth tech doesn't work beneath the surface. Surely, even you must know that. It's the same reason we haven't been able to find Nos Valuta before you gave us exact coordinates. Blazing heathen planet," Harding shot back, frustration returning. "We've sent in teams to try and find the Origin, but they never come back. Why worry about a few radicals living in the ground? They'll die out soon enough."

Nick said nothing, merely looking out toward the city scape as though he was thinking through something. The man was too cryptic, and Harding loathed that fact. Full of flowery words one minute and silent the next. If only people were more straightforward, the universe would be a much more peaceful place.

But Lunitia needed this to work just as much as he did.

"We have reason to believe your brother was in contact

with the Origin himself," Harding said, laying his cards on the table. "Which means you must have some idea how to get word to them."

"And if I do?" Lunitia asked, setting his glass down on the counter. "They'll know by now I betrayed them."

"Oh." Harding felt a grin spread across his face for the first time in months. "I'm counting on it."

CHAPTER SIXTEEN

"Avery Vey. I've waited a long time to meet you, young lady," an elderly woman croaked out as Avery walked into a large tent that served as some sort of council room. A few others sat in a circle of chairs around her, observing. Avery met the old woman's eyes, the wrinkles on her face suggesting she was nearing somewhere to a century in age.

Avery masked her emotions. Everyone already knew who she was. What she was. Mylan caught her eyes from his seat in the circle. He inclined his head, and she returned the small gesture.

She wanted to ask about Finn but knew she had to figure out their position there first. Avery hadn't missed Nick's words on that ship that had ignited Finn's wrath. The Federation was planning an attack on Nos Valuta, and soon. They didn't have time to waste.

"Come, girl, don't stand there like a fish out of water. Move forward—I'd like to get a good look at you." The old woman spoke sharply, and Avery glowered even as she obeyed the command. She was tired of this constant assessment.

"Yes, you have the look of a So' about you." She clucked her tongue appreciatively, a gleam lighting her eyes from within. Despite her age, this woman was not to be underestimated. Compelled by pure curiosity, Avery opened her mind, searching for that familiar thread that would bring the woman's thoughts into her own.

She met a firm wall as soon as she tried.

"Now, now." The woman waggled a bony finger at Avery. "None of that. Not until we've been properly introduced. You don't want to start off making rude advances on people, now do you?"

"You—" Avery clamped her own mind shut, her eyes widening in surprise. "You could feel me?"

The woman laughed. Some of the others in the room joined her with softer chuckles. "Child, you do not know a thing about us, do you?"

Avery blushed, lowering her gaze to the floor as she felt her indignation stir. It wasn't long ago that Petra had asked her the exact same question. She clamped her jaw shut and tried to ignore isolation pooling within her heart.

"My name is Leviathan," the woman said with a gentler tone, bowing her head slightly. "I am the presiding council leader here in the Origin. Normally, we operate with a system of joint democracy, of a sort. But since I am quite possibly the oldest still living amongst our people . . . I have a bit more say in matters."

Avery's gaze swept across the many faces surrounding her. "I—" Her voice broke. "I wasn't told there were any more Rebels left in the cities on Echo."

"We are not part of the Rebellion," Leviathan said haughtily. "Unlike our brethren at Nos Valuta, we do not believe a peace is possible between our people and the humans. Those fools are going to lose more of our kind than do any good in reclaiming our home." She looked away, as though remembering something of importance. "But fate, it seems, has placed you right in our lap."

Avery remained quiet as Leviathan continued to stare, her gen mod eyes a bright violet. The Origin. No wonder it was familiar to her. Lissande had worked for them when she met Gran. They were extremists who blamed all humans for the sins of the Federation.

But perhaps there was a certain truth to it. If the humans were gone, everything would be restored. Echo would be free.

No. She didn't feel that way. Did she?

It was difficult to sort out her feelings from the others there. Avery couldn't quite tell where their minds ended and hers began.

But she knew humans. Had been raised by them and beside them. Earth was still her home. Avery conjured images of Gran's kind face, of Megan's laughing smile. Finn's calm blue eyes as he reached for her hand, beckoning her to follow him. His laughing expression when he teased her.

Avery mustered her courage. "What do you plan to do with me? And Finn?"

"Ah, yes." Leviathan brought a thin hand to her chin. "The infamous young ambassador. It seems that we owe him for leading you in our direction."

"You didn't answer my question," she pressed.

Leviathan's features hardened, her hands coming to rest on the arms of her chair. "Humans are not allowed in the Origin. They never should have brought him."

"But you can't mean to just throw him out," Avery argued, looking to Mylan for help. "He's sick."

"What he is or isn't is none of our concern," Leviathan answered, her voice strict. Avery could see others nodding in agreement. Mylan was stoic. "Humans are not wanted, nor do they belong here. He will be deposited on the surface at the first available opportunity, which you should be thankful for. It would have been better to have let him die."

Avery clenched her fists, fingernails digging into her palms. "You can't be serious."

"I assure you, I am."

Avery couldn't respond. After a moment, she found her voice again. "And what are your plans for me?"

"For you?" Leviathan smiled, as though finding the question vastly amusing. "Why, we're going to help you, my dear. And in return, you are going to help us. To help us all." She gestured to the room.

So many eyes pinned her to the ground. More politics. More people using her for their own ends. Would she never be free of it?

All she had ever desired was to live a better life than what she had been given. To have nice clothes and take fancy cruises and go to university. But for all she wanted, her life had at least been her own. Now, it belonged to others.

They couldn't honestly mean to let Finn die.

She returned her eyes to meet Leviathan's purple gaze. Avery lifted her chin. "And if I refuse?"

Leviathan exchanged a look with Mylan before speaking. "You speak cavalierly of things that will affect more than yourself, girl."

Shame coursed through her veins. Finn had said something similar to her once. An idea surfaced, and she grasped onto it like a life tether to a spaceship. She had something they wanted.

"I will help you," Avery said delicately. "But only on the condition that Finn is allowed to stay."

Leviathan's eyes narrowed. She obviously did not like being challenged.

"I will do everything you ask of me," Avery continued, "be everything you need me to be, if you promise me that he will be taken care of. And that he will be allowed to leave, freely, once he heals."

Leviathan's lip curled, argumentative murmurs erupting around the circle.

"You have an unnatural attachment to the human," Leviathan said darkly. "Mylan did warn me as much." Avery tried not to read too much into her words, pushing past the blush that crept up her neck. "But it is impossible. As I said, you should be thankful we haven't killed him outright."

Avery's fists tightened, fear cutting through her. "If you touch him, I'll—"

"You'll what?" Leviathan countered with a small smile. "You can barely control your gift. Do you think we will bend to your will? You are not a So' yet, girl."

Silence settled around them, anxiety curling in Avery's belly.

"Perhaps we should consider it," Mylan spoke from his seat, drawing both their gazes.

"Are you mad?" Leviathan snapped. "You know the law."

Mylan nodded before continuing, "I do. But this is a small price to pay for her cooperation. Sometimes concessions must be made. And Lunitia has been a valuable ally in the past."

"You would vouch for him?" Leviathan asked.

"Yes," Mylan confirmed.

Leviathan was silent as she considered, her eyes moving to the others. Avery held her breath, thankful that at least someone saw sense in this strange place.

"So be it." Leviathan was curt as she agreed, her eyes snapping to Mylan once more. "But I hold you entirely responsible for him, Mylan. Make no mistake. And he will be moved to a holding area, not housed in the clinic. We have too few resources to waste them on parasites."

Avery viewed Mylan as she prepared to argue, but he lifted a hand, signaling her to silence. She bit the inside of her lip, trusting he would explain later.

There was no backing out. Real fear threaded through her veins at the thought of failing again. Of bringing ruin down on these people, as she had for those at Nos Valuta. What would the Federation do if they found this place? Who would they take this time?

Leviathan rose to her feet. She reached for a cane beside her chair as Mylan rushed forward to help. She brushed away his support with a half growl. "Come." She made her way to Avery's side. "Walk with me."

The camp was coming alive with people, all discreetly throwing glances as they walked. Avery focused on keeping her mind securely blocked, ignoring any feelings that threatened to seep their way past her defenses.

Leviathan progressed slowly, and Avery matched her steps to the older woman's speed. Avery took the opportunity to really take a look at the camp as the people meandered around with different tasks. She had read a book once about people who lived underground. They stayed there for a hundred years, waiting for the earth to rejuvenate itself after a nuclear fallout. This place reminded her of that. A city beneath the ground, shrouded in orange light and quiet shadows.

"I'll not coddle you," Leviathan said brusquely, breaking the silence. Avery said nothing. "I've lost more people than you've probably known in your short time in this universe. Good people. People that deserved to live."

Avery was quiet. Her thoughts shifted to Gran. How long ago was it that she had left her on that space station? Who knew what the Federation was doing to her? Or if she was even still alive. Her throat tightened.

"I don't, however, wish to see any more of it." They rounded a corner and started down a different path. Avery was already turned around, unable to keep track of the maze. "I don't have much time left, but I have a responsibility, and I intend to see it through. Now what about you?"

"I don't think you—"

"Let's not play games, girl," Leviathan interrupted her. "I know what you've gone through. I've felt it in you. I felt it the moment you got close to our camp. The moment you merged with that group back at Valuta."

Back at Valuta? What was Leviathan saying? She could read Avery's thoughts? That could only mean . . . . Her eyes jerked sharply to the elderly woman leaning heavily on her cane.

"There it is," Leviathan said with a smile, her thin skin wrinkling into a hundred lines across her face. "No, you're not the last surviving So'Reange. Perhaps the last useful one. But not the last."

"But I thought—I mean, I was told that there were no others," Avery got out.

"That's because those good for nothing know-it-alls who had the nerve to try and train you don't really know anything except how to wipe their own asses." She huffed, and Avery fought to stifle a surprised laugh. "As if a So' could be trained with science alone. It's absurd."

She knew from her vague history lessons back at Nos Valuta that to be a So' had once meant to be near royalty. Leviathan certainly exuded that kind of confidence.

"But then if you're a So', why am I even needed?" Avery asked hopefully.

"If it was that simple," Leviathan countered, "I would have done it by now." She continued walking, and Avery followed, waiting for further explanation. "As we age, So's lose the ability to control our gifts. Much in the same way as other senses fade for the elderly, so does this. As much as I may wish it, I cannot help our people now."

Avery heard the words, her heart sinking into her belly. Any hope she had of freedom was definitively extinguished.

"I know your feelings, girl. Do not think I don't understand the pressures of those in our position. None of the others—no one—will ever know what you go through. Perhaps once it was not such a burden, when there were more of us, but now . . . ." She trailed off, waving her free hand for emphasis. "Now we are relied upon by too many."

They walked on in silence.

"As much as you may wish to run from it, you have that responsibility as well," Leviathan said resolutely. "But it does not have to be as lonely as you imagine."

Avery bit back a response. Nothing would ever be able to

make her feel less alone. She was stuck between two worlds. It was an impassable gap that she would never be able to cross.

"Think on what I've told you," Leviathan said. Avery felt genuine concern from her, but could she trust it? How did she navigate through a world where people could force her to feel things that weren't real? "Don't worry, child. In a few weeks, you'll wonder why you hesitated at all."

Avery dropped her eyes, nodding. She didn't really have any other choice. Not if she wanted to save Finn. Not if she wanted to master her powers.

"This will not be easy," Leviathan stated severely.

"I'll be ready," Avery replied.

She would conquer this, like everything else that had been thrown at her. If Gran was here, she'd tell her to keep going. Whatever the Origin leaders wanted from her, no matter how insane their opinions seemed, these people were suffering, too. If Avery had any chance of helping, she couldn't give up on that.

Her mind drifted to Gran. And the people Nick had taken with his Federation soldiers. Grigg and Nova. So many others. Their lives were on her head, too. Avery's heart wrenched painfully in her chest.

Now, more than ever, she couldn't turn back.

That first day, they moved Finn from the clinic to a small tent near the outskirts of the camp. It brushed against the edge of the cavernous darkness, almost entirely blanketed in shadows. Avery knew that it served as some kind of holding area.

A guard stood post at the small entrance. She did her best to ignore the bloodstains on the stone floor.

There were no beds, and Finn was laid out on a pallet of blankets on the ground. The small comfort was Mylan's doing. He and Nevril had made sure Finn at least had the basic medical necessities. A med patch on Finn's arm still tracked his vitals, the monitor beside him beeping softly in the stillness.

But he looked so alone. So vulnerable. They didn't let her stay with him long.

Being there frightened Avery. In many ways, more than anything else had so far. The people were violent, clinging to their laws and extremism as though it would be the very thing to save them. Staying there and learning from them was almost nonsensical. Little better than blindly following the Federation itself.

Avery couldn't miss the whispers as she walked through camp the next morning. They saw her as some kind of savior, a secret weapon that would finally turn the tides.

She had made a bargain with them for Finn's life. If she had to play their game to harness her gift, then she would. But it would be on her terms.

She didn't want to fight it any longer.

Avery opened herself to Leviathan as she walked. The strong band of willpower emanating from the woman wrapped securely around Avery, guiding her through the paths like a beacon. It was a peculiar sensation, to be connected so instinctively. As though they weren't merely establishing a link, but sharing themselves entirely. Perhaps it had once been that way between all So's.

Your questions will be answered in due time, Leviathan answered Avery's thoughts.

When will we begin? Avery asked.

Now. Do not be so hasty with your feelings. That is the first lesson you must learn. A thousand faces flashed through her mind, and she wasn't certain if they were her own memories or Leviathan's. Avery wasn't even sure it mattered. *You will not be able to connect them if you cannot distance yourself from the waves of your emotions.*

Avery stopped when she reached a tall tent at the end of one of the paths near the back of the camp. Larger than any of the others, the tent reached nearly a full level in height. Leviathan waited inside, along with others. Hesitation curled, thick and dense in the pit of her belly. With a steadying breath, she set off purposefully toward the entrance.

She craned her neck as she entered, realizing the tent served as a gym. A running track wrapped along the edge, with a rudimentary obstacle course made from salvaged cruiser parts sitting in its center. The air smelled thickly of metal and sweat.

"Finally, you join us," Leviathan's strong voice greeted her. "I didn't realize that you would sleep for so long. Perhaps your time with the humans has affected you in ways we will have to rectify."

Avery's mouth twisted, attempting to ignore the barb. Fiora stood beside Leviathan, a small smile on her face.

"What is this?" Avery asked, moving beside them as her gaze roved over the track. The entire place was empty. "I thought you were going to teach me how to use my gift. Why are we here?"

"Again, humanity falls off you like a stench you cannot wash out," Leviathan responded, narrowing her eyes. "Thousands of years, and they still think that mental clarity is separate from the physical." She pressed her mind forcefully into Avery's. *The first step to mastering your mind is to master your body.*

Avery's eyes shut tightly in response to the invasion—to the way Leviathan dominated her so completely—as she backed away a few steps. In vain, she tried to push Leviathan out and bring back her shields.

Leviathan laughed softly. "You'll be spending your mornings here with Fiora as she teaches you control of the physical. The afternoons will be with me, working on your mental clarity. Time is essential. We do not have as much as one would like."

The old woman pulled her mind away, leaving Avery blissfully to herself in her own head. She bit her lip to prevent an audible sigh of relief. "I'll leave you to Fiora's care," Leviathan said, leaning heavily on her cane as she made her way toward the exit.

"Well. I'm glad that's out of the way," Fiora said in a cheerful voice, clapping her hands together and rubbing her palms. She took Avery's arm in a firm grip, leading her toward what looked to be makeshift locker rooms near the edge of the tent. "You'll need to change. We've got a lot of ground to cover."

Avery frowned. "I'd like to check on Finn first."

Fiora scoffed, derision falling off her in waves. "You'll be notified of any change in his condition. It's best to focus on other things, for now."

Avery nodded hesitantly. At least she could tell when others were lying. She would just have to keep moving forward.

"Now tell me"—Fiora started to ask, grinning wide—"how are you with sprints?"

CHAPTER SEVENTEEN

In the days that followed, Fiora was always there. Always pointing out what she could be doing better. Always pushing her harder. It had been nearly two weeks, and nothing had changed. Her routine in the Origin was fast becoming an exhausting habit. She trained. She ate. She learned. She slept.

Her mornings were for Fiora and the Tent. Not that it was the only tent, but the gym was where most of her torture took place, so it was the only one worth naming. This was usually followed by lunch with the others where they tried their best not to stare at her. And later she met Leviathan where they would go over history lessons and etiquette, often carrying out entire sessions without voicing a word.

Avery failed to see how learning the proper way to greet someone would come in handy with winning a war. Far be it from Avery to question Leviathan, though. Every time she even thought of voicing her own opinion, the old woman was there, reading her thoughts and cutting off any protests before they had a chance to touch her lips.

And if it wasn't the mental fatigue, it was the physical. Avery could feel her stamina improving, but that was the only thing changing. Fiora made her run laps and sprints for hours, lacing in strength training in small bursts. She would push her body until she either heaved up her breakfast or collapsed, always to the edge of her limits.

At least there was a certain comfort in the regularity of her pain. It helped distract her from the fact that Finn had yet to wake up.

Nevril initially thought his coma would last a day, two at most. The fear that the fever had taken a toll on his brain was a constant worry, choking Avery's heart until she felt it pulsate rapidly in her chest. But she didn't have time for worry.

So she ran. She continued to run, just as Fiora ordered. She worked on etiquette and manners and proper control of her mind, just as Leviathan mandated. It kept the loneliness at bay, pushing emotion to the back of her mind.

Fiora was insistent that they first build her endurance before moving on to anything else. They hadn't tried combat techniques at all. And what did Avery know about it? She had no place to argue their methods. If this was the only way to master her powers, then she would push herself into the ground.

Although discouraged by Leviathan, Avery found time to sneak away every so often to check on Finn. And it wasn't just the old woman. Others judged her, too.

These Reanges hated humans, in a way that was difficult for Avery to understand. She didn't like the bias that hovered in the subconscious of the camp, always simmering beneath the surface. She did her best to avoid their emotions.

Fiora explained that survivors here had no interest in peace with Earth. No interest in sharing their planet or their resources. They wanted the humans gone, and they didn't care how that happened.

Their beliefs didn't sit well with Avery, but Leviathan was a means to an end. Everyone here had been through something that changed them irrevocably, whether for good or bad. She couldn't fault the emotion that had driven them to such ideals, but Avery would never be convinced it was right.

She was beginning to recognize faces around camp. There couldn't have been more than a couple hundred living there, and she could count the number of children on one hand. They were people who had lost their homes, friends, and families. Some had nowhere else to go. Others still had loved ones in the capital, or elsewhere. But they were all there to fight. The Origin offered a path forward to do so.

And they warmed to her quickly, even if remaining aloof. This was merely politeness on their part. In a society where everyone had once been interconnected, they learned to value independence of mind. Emotional distance was a mark of respect, precious to everyone.

It was the highest form of rudeness to invade someone's thoughts without having permission. Like barging into someone's home unannounced. Having endured the sensation herself, Avery could certainly understand this rule. It wasn't pleasant to have thoughts plucked out of your head. Especially without your knowledge of it happening.

Although some people *could* tell when it was happening.

Some Reanges, like Mylan, were blessed with the ability

to feel their own mind being touched. This was unique, a trait passed down from an immediate line of So'. When a child was born without the full gift, often they would show this quirk.

"You're distracted." Fiora's accusation pulled Avery out of her head long enough to realize that she had slowed her running down to a jog. She braced herself for a verbal lashing as Fiora trotted up beside her.

"Sorry," Avery mumbled, picking up her pace.

"You haven't been focusing for hours," Fiora said, her cadence quickening to push Avery faster. It may have been rude to eavesdrop into people's minds, but sometimes Avery couldn't help it. Fiora's frustration poured off her like a heavy fog. The woman was worried. She wanted Avery to push herself harder, desperate for further progress.

Avery didn't respond, her eyes narrowing on the black track in front of her. She moved her arms to pull into a sprint, forcing air in and out of her lungs in time with her gait. The burning in her legs was a satisfying pain.

Fiora kept pace beside her, barely breaking a sweat.

"Maybe we should switch gears," Fiora said, nodding her head in the direction of the center of the track and slowing her speed. "Come on," she said over her shoulder as she took off toward the group training there.

Avery slowed, her breathing heavy as she wiped sweat from her forehead with the back of her hand. She stifled a grimace as blood rushed into her toes. She had blisters all over her feet from her stupid boots. What she wouldn't give for a good pair of running shoes.

Although the gym had been empty that first day, it had been an exception for her benefit. It was the one place constantly in use, as able-bodied survivors worked on their own training.

There was an anxious energy that lingered in the Origin, floating on the air like dust mites that tickled her throat. As though the survivors were constantly awaiting some cataclysmic event. She couldn't blame them for putting that energy to good use in the gym.

She followed Fiora, the fighters on the mat quieting as she approached. There were about ten of them, along with the two boys on the mat. She felt one of the girls' excitement overload her own senses as she approached, the giddiness filling her chest as though it was her own. Avery had to push away a grin.

Why would they be excited? What did they expect from her?

Krez appeared from the other side of the mat, tall and overbearing as he moved forward to greet Fiora. Although the information had never been offered, Avery had accidentally discovered they were married. There was love in Fiora's eyes that Avery could have identified, even without the ability to read her mind.

Krez was curt, on a good day, and barely spoke at all. While Fiora was the lead trainer in the Origin, Krez was her silent supporter. His size would have intimidated anyone, even if they weren't aware of his fighting skills.

"I thought we might show Avery something different today," Fiora said, moving to stand beside him on the edge of the mat.

"Is she ready?" he asked cautiously. Unable to resist, Avery tugged on the thread of his mind. *Did Leviathan give her approval to start so soon? I hope Fiora knows what she's doing.*

Avery slammed her barriers down, blocking any more of his thoughts. So Leviathan was still in command, even here.

It shouldn't come as a surprise. The woman was a borderline tyrant.

Had So'Reanges always commanded others as though they were superior, or was that just an effect of Leviathan being the last?

"Am I ready for what?" Avery asked, sweat beading down the sides of her temples. Her dark green shirt stuck wetly to her back, bunching as she moved. As her sweat cooled, the sensation bothered her.

"Just get on the mat."

Avery stepped forward onto the soft surface.

"Not sure this is such a good idea, Fi," Krez said darkly, gesturing for a girl to join her.

"Nah. She's bored," Fiora said with a little smile. Avery tentatively reached out to her, her head tilting as she realized she couldn't get in. Fiora's thoughts were somehow blocked from her. Avery should have walked away right then and there. She should have called it quits.

Krez shot her a sympathetic glance from his side of the mat. If nothing else, Fiora's next words should definitely have sent her running.

"Let's give her a little bit of fun."

"That certainly looks painful," Leviathan said dryly as Avery hobbled into her tent later that afternoon.

Avery winced as she moved to take her regular seat on the couch, ignoring the old woman's comment and sinking into the plush cushions as her muscles gave out. Her eye was rapidly swelling shut, and a dark bruise blossomed along the line of her chin.

Although she was normally ravenous after training, today Avery hadn't even had the stomach to eat lunch. Fiora had made certain that she wouldn't have an appetite. Possibly ever again.

"If you weren't ready for more intense training, then perhaps you should have been more attentive to your exercises," Leviathan reprimanded.

Avery shot a scowl at the old crone. "As if you didn't know. You were firmly blocking everyone's minds in there from me."

A small smile tugged at Leviathan's lips. "We can't have you at an unfair advantage, now can we? You must learn. As any normal Reange would."

"I thought the point of this was to help me learn to use my powers." Avery closed her eyes, resting her head on the cushions behind her. "How is beating me to a pulp like a *normal Reange* going to help?"

"The better you learn combat and controlling your body under stress, the better you can control those things for others. You mustn't forget what it was like for you in that cafeteria back at Nos Valuta." Leviathan slammed her cane forcefully against the packed dirt floor. "This is how you will avoid such pitfalls in the future."

Avery opened her eyes and took a steadying breath as she met Leviathan's gaze. "But can't I just harness other people's knowledge for my own? Why is there a need to learn combat if I can borrow from someone else's mind?"

"The day may come when you don't have someone to leech off of. Your responsibility as So' is to be the best. At everything," Leviathan replied, her face solid as stone. It wasn't merely her opinion. It was fact. A necessity for the So' in her place of power.

"Okay. So I need to learn to fight," Avery said with a whoosh of breath. "What else? Or does everything get to be a delightful surprise like today?"

I understand your impatience, girl, but it will not do to get ahead of yourself.

"I don't feel quite up to that today," Avery replied, exhausted. "Can we just talk like normal human beings for once?"

"You are *not* a human being!" Leviathan snapped fiercely. Her sudden burst of anger slammed through Avery like a wave, soaking her through. She sat up in surprise, watching Leviathan warily.

The tables on either side of the couch rolled across the floor of the tent. A large chair against the far wall lifted to slam into the dresser, breaking the mirror perched above it in a cacophony of shattering glass. Lights flickered once . . . twice . . . accentuating the painful silence that followed the outburst. Outside of the tent, the normal sounds of the active camp had gone still.

Avery looked down at her feet, cursing herself for her slip of the tongue. She didn't speak in the wake of that anger but merely clenched her jaw and quietly erected a barrier to shield her mind. She could feel the frustration oozing off Leviathan as they sat there, two immovable objects in uneasy quiet.

Leviathan probed her mind, but Avery resolutely held onto her control. She would rather die than let the overbearing woman into her head. A small smile tugged at the corner of Leviathan's mouth.

Before she could ask what was so amusing, someone burst into the tent, blaster at the ready. Avery caught the flash of blue hair. The vibrant green eyes. It couldn't be . . . .

"Petra?" Avery found herself exclaiming in surprise, even as she came to her feet. Her friend's familiar face sent a pang of eagerness through her as she smiled broadly.

They had come! Reinforcements had made it from Valuta to free them! She was halfway to Petra's side before she realized that something was off.

Petra's eyes flashed to her quickly before addressing Leviathan. "Nothing's wrong?"

Avery stilled, her stomach turning cold.

"No, girl, just a little disagreement." Leviathan waved her away with a clipped sigh. "You were supposed to wait another week. What are you doing here so early?"

"The lines were dropped," Petra responded curtly, avoiding Avery's wide eyes. "When I didn't receive any communication from you, I grew worried."

"Wait." Avery found her voice, holding her hands out as though to physically stop what was happening. "You know each other?" She gestured between the two.

Petra's eyes met Avery's, immediately shifting away. Avery's mind shot out in a surge of disbelief, forcing her way into Petra's consciousness.

Dread. Fear. But more than anything, guilt. It was there in her feelings more clearly than Petra could ever explain to Avery with words.

Petra wasn't there to help her. She felt a stab somewhere beneath her ribs.

Avery probed further, seeking the truth. Images and feelings flashed through her mind in waves. Leviathan. Tai. Her parents. The Feds killing her mother. The Origin taking them in. The Feds hunting them, keeping them constantly on the run. Leviathan sending Petra to Nos Valuta. To train, to infiltrate. All the while working for the Origin.

It was all there. Laid out for Avery to read, like a book of pictures and feelings. Petra was a mole, spying on the Rebellion, and ultimately posing as a human Fed to go one level deeper. Never with the intention to help the Rebellion. Only the Origin.

Petra had wanted all along to sway Avery to their cause. It was in everything she ever said or did. She would have forced Avery to come here regardless of what had happened back at Valuta. Eventually she would have found a way to secure Avery for the Origin, too.

And there was hate. So much of it. Threaded through the core of each memory, Petra's revulsion for humanity drove her every action. The truth of her heart had finally been laid out before Avery in all its stark reality. How had she hidden it, all this time?

As if by instinct, Avery threw her own feelings out wildly. The disgust, the betrayal . . . everything that had been forced to the surface. Petra gasped, physically recoiling when it reached her. Good. She should know how it felt. This loss.

"That is not the way, Avery," Leviathan chastised her with a lift of her chin. "Such actions are beneath the So'."

"As you always take so much pleasure in reminding me," Avery ground out, "I'm little better than a human, anyway."

Overwhelming emotion billowed out and around them, the pulse throbbing behind her eyelids as she closed them, focusing on her breathing. Empty space compressed around her in that familiar way before she usually lost control. The air vibrated in response to her overload.

"Do not let it control you," she heard Leviathan say in an

unusually tranquil tone. "You have the ability to master this. It is natural to make matter bend to your will. Do not be afraid of it. Face it head-on."

Taking a deep breath and letting the air out harshly, Avery grabbed onto the force around her that connected directly to her power. It slipped easily through her grasp, beginning to take shape as she gentled her approach.

"That's it," Leviathan praised. "You cannot force it, but guide it to your bidding."

Avery swirled the forces until they moved in various directions, responding to her gift. Untapped energy radiated around them, begging to be controlled. By her. She had a direct link to the very atoms of the air.

Avery grabbed hold of the molecules around her, moving her hands outward to help her concentrate. She seized the bright energy, gesturing as it lifted her body off the ground. Her hands balled into fists, nails digging into her palms.

The open air beneath her feet gave her a sense of release. Using her gift had finally set something free within herself.

Concentrating on maintaining control of the elements around her, Avery slowly opened her eyes and looked down to see that she was indeed nearly a foot off the ground. She was floating in midair, and it felt as natural as breathing. It was calming, even. More cathartic than anything she had ever experienced.

She raised her eyes to meet Petra's who quickly dropped to a knee in subservience. Avery looked to Leviathan, the woman's stare a piercing violet.

With measured awareness, Avery returned herself to the ground. The heaviness of her body settled back into her bones as the energy left her. A surge of fuzzy euphoria tingled her skin in the aftermath.

"Petra, my dear," Leviathan said, breaking the silence in the tent. "I do believe we should have brought you onto the scene a bit sooner. That's more progress than we've had all week."

"You're unbelievable," Avery spat. "Get up," she said to Petra's kneeling form. She complied, standing before Avery, eyes still downcast. "Leave. Now," she ground out harshly. Avery ignored the way Petra fractured in response to her words as she obeyed. It didn't matter anymore.

Turning back to Leviathan, Avery narrowed her eyes. There was little this woman wouldn't stoop to for the cause. She was beginning to realize that.

"Don't be so naive," Leviathan said coarsely. "Things will not be easy for you, or any of us, ever again. That is not my fault, nor is it Petra's."

Avery's eyes faltered, hearing the truth. A stab of pain shot up her arm, and she winced. The gash on her hand had re-opened, still unhealed from their pod crash. She tilted her palm toward her, studying the way the flesh had separated, blood oozing from the cut.

"There will come a time," Leviathan said softly as she made her way to Avery's side, reaching for her wounded hand, "when your only limits will be your own imagination."

Cupping Avery's hand in her own, Leviathan looked down, concentrating. Avery felt the room thicken and come alive with the woman's own power. She claimed the lingering energy, swirling around Avery's hand and compressing until the very skin began to tingle with fire.

The open edges of flesh came together, sealing the cut completely until only healed skin remained. Avery stopped breathing, her mouth open in shock. Leviathan relinquished her hold on the power that surrounded them, leaving only cold silence. Her palm itched.

"You must learn to control yourself before that time comes," Leviathan warned, her voice faded. "Now leave me. I must rest." She dropped Avery's hand, pressing thin fingers to her forehead.

Avery stood there for a moment, staring at her palm where the gash had plagued her for nearly two weeks. How was such a thing possible? Was there no end to what her power could do? The intensity frightened her.

Word spread fast throughout the Origin. Or perhaps it was Leviathan herself who shared the image of Avery levitating in the tent. But by the time she was on the outskirts of the camp, the Reanges were a mass of excited reverence. She was proving to be exactly what they had hoped.

Avery impulsively headed to the holding tent, unable to face being alone. She didn't speak to the guard, pushing straight past and into Finn's small cell. Her heart lurched painfully as the hanging glow torch above him cast his features into harsh shadows. He was still as ever.

His color was back to normal, although he had lost notable weight in his face. The line of his jaw was sharper now. Nevril was forcing nutrition tablets down his throat when she could, but he needed to eat a real meal. Leviathan refused to spare supplies to truly help him. If he didn't wake up soon . . . .

She moved to sit on the floor beside him, wrapping her arms around her knees.

What would Finn have done, in this situation? She felt a dry grin tug at the corner of her lips. He would have probably tried to beat Petra to a pulp before anything else. It made sense now, at least. Petra's hatred for Finn. With a sigh, she stared at his profile.

His strong nose ran a straight line from his forehead. His eyebrows were dark, nearly black as they spread out across his skin, and if his heavy stubble was any indication, his beard would be a similar shade. He had full lips. Though not feminine, they held a pleasant curve to their shape. She was not used to seeing them still and closed. Finn hardly ever kept his mouth shut for more than two minutes at a time.

But he was loyal. He had saved Avery, more than once, and at the risk of his own life. He believed in her value to the Rebellion so much that he would die for her, if it meant helping the people he called family.

Avery wished she could be that honorable. To have that much faith in each and every choice she made.

There were lives that depended on her. Her life was no longer small enough to remain her own. It may not have been her choice, but it was her birthright. If she had the power to help, then Avery would give it her all. It was the only way forward.

Despite their radical beliefs, no one else could educate her the way these people had done so far. She had come farther in two weeks than in all her time at Nos Valuta. Perhaps she had a real chance at this.

Avery grinned, her gaze finding Finn's face again as she studied the pattern of his steady breathing.

She had made herself levitate. In thin air! Just like she had done to him in the training room at Valuta. But this time she had known what she was doing. She had controlled it as easily as wiggling her toes.

Avery braced her hands together, resting her chin on top. If Finn could fight so bravely for what he believed in, then she could, too. Her grandmother wasn't the only one to consider anymore. In her heart, Avery knew that Gran would want her to help the Reanges. Even if it meant a sacrifice.

If Avery could help these people reclaim a home that had been stolen from them, and stop the Federation's senseless genocide, then how could she stand by? Inaction could be just as much a crime as active violence, if you had the ability to stop it.

Avery knew that she would keep on this path she was traveling. She would save Gran if she could, but there were things of greater importance than just her life or her grandmother's alone.

There was a sense of peace in her decision. Avery's eyes prickled at the thought of never seeing Gran again. But she had to let go in order to move forward. Tears slid slowly down her cheeks, wetting her arms beneath her chin.

If they wanted a leader, then by the galaxy, she would give them one.

CHAPTER EIGHTEEN

"In fifteen days, Milderion will host its annual Petralias celebration and festival." Mylan addressed the tent full of council members, seated in a wide circle.

At first, Avery resisted attending, unable to see how listening to a group of extremists would help her. But she soon realized it could be an excellent way to gain valuable information.

That, and Leviathan wouldn't take no for an answer.

Although she accepted her responsibility, Avery grew increasingly anxious about the knowledge that the Federation could attack Nos Valuta at any moment. They could have done so already.

Despite her requests, Leviathan and the others refused to compromise their position in order to notify Valuta. With Avery's presence, the Origin had gone on a complete lockdown until they were sure she had a firm grasp of her skills. Leviathan would not take any chances.

"We have gathered intelligence that the Federation is hosting a gala in honor of the occasion," Mylan continued. "In conjunction with the ambassador and in the name of the Armistice. We have confirmation that Klein herself will be there."

The room erupted in a chorus of hisses, a sure Reange sign of intense disapproval. Hatred billowed around her in a thick cloud.

"As much as we disapprove of the concept of humans exploiting a sacred holiday, it does offer the perfect opportunity for us to send a message once and for all," Mylan said intensely, meeting pairs of eyes one after the other. "A message that this is our planet, and we will no longer tolerate the unnatural presence of humans."

Avery scowled, her jaw clenching. She felt the energy pulsating around her. The anticipation. She knew what was coming next.

"As we speak, a team is being created to infiltrate the event. This is what we've been waiting for. A perfect opportunity to launch the Origin's new assault on the human invasion. Fiora, if you would." Mylan gestured to her, sitting beside him. She normally didn't attend these meetings, but Avery guessed she was there in an official capacity as leader of their militia.

Standing as Mylan sat, Fiora met Avery's eyes briefly before speaking. "We have a team of six. This won't be the most complicated mission, but it will require stealth and experience. We've gathered enough supplies to get us into Milderion, and Krez has been able to engineer pulsar detonators. Enough to level the entire building, if we need."

Avery's breath caught. Level the entire building? They

would kill everyone. Even the innocents. Leviathan glanced at her, always observant. Always judging her reactions. Avery concealed her emotions.

"And the ultimate objective?" a woman asked. "Why not just destroy it to begin with? Why bother infiltrating the event at all?"

"Don't be simple, Elesta," Leviathan snapped at her. "We cannot act until we are certain Klein is in attendance. It would be a waste of our resources."

"But surely taking out the ambassador is reason enough."

"If that was true, then we might as well string up the human we have here," she countered, sending Avery's pulse into a frenzy. "He is an ambassador as well, is he not?"

"And why don't we?" someone else voiced. Tightening her fists, Avery fought to control her reactions.

The room filled with quiet mumbles of consideration. They were thinking about it. The council was actually mulling it over. Their eagerness at the thought of harming Finn floated up and around her, an irritation rubbing against her brain.

"All respect to our young So'," Elesta continued, drawing Avery's eyes to her, "but the idea does have merit."

"That is true," a man's voice agreed. "Mylan, isn't he a major figure in the Earthen media? It could certainly have the effect we want with the least amount of risk."

"Although your words do hold merit," Mylan responded, "we have made a promise to Avery that no harm will come to him. And I would stand by it. Finn has been an informant to us in the past, and the moons would not favor us if we did wrong by his actions."

"But surely—"

"No," Avery bit out, her voice rising. Elestra went silent

at the single word, and Avery wasn't sure if it was because of her powers or merely her tone. "He said no," Avery repeated, standing as well. "Finn is absolutely off limits to anyone here."

She was pleased by the hush that followed, forcing her absolute will out on everyone in the circle. When she encountered Leviathan, she met resistance but also a grudging satisfaction.

You are making excellent progress, Leviathan acknowledged silently. *We will not harm your human. I gave you my word, and I will keep it.*

Avery nodded, looking back to Fiora, who was still on her feet. "Am I going on this mission as well?" Avery wasn't sure what answer she wanted to hear.

"No, my So'," Fiora replied, casting her eyes toward the floor. Avery didn't relish in the submissiveness. It was unlike her to be so yielding.

"The danger is too great," Mylan added, as calm as ever.

"Then surely my influence could only help," Avery reasoned.

"Avery, perhaps you do not fully understand. It is . . . ." Mylan paused, as though searching for words. A strange tension rose in the room around her. *She doesn't know. . . Why would she . . . .* "It is unlikely that they will return."

"What?" Avery couldn't prevent her shock from bursting out, falling over the council members in a rushing wave of surprise. "You can't be serious. You're saying this is a suicide mission?"

"We are prepared to make that—"

"Well, I'm not," Avery said forcefully, turning to Leviathan. "It's bad enough you are planning on killing innocent people, but to kill yourselves in the process? There is absolutely no point."

"On the contrary," Leviathan spoke firmly. "Sometimes a symbol is more powerful than reason."

There was no way they intended to go through with this. Fiora was committed to the cause, but even she couldn't mean to actually die in some misguided attempt to send a sign to the Federation. And Mylan? One of the few people Avery had come to trust as an ally?

"You can't mean it," Avery pressed. "This will merely cause more anger and suffering for both sides." *This is not the way.*

And what would you know of it? Leviathan opened her words to the minds of the entire room. Connecting them all as one as she spoke to Avery. *Your reluctance is a result of your upbringing, but this is the necessity of our cause. Sacrifices must be made.*

Agreement sounded all around in her mind, and Avery backed away, shaking her head. Leviathan was leading them down a dangerous path. One with no outcome that she would be able to live with.

While she understood their motivation, Avery would never agree with this. But the more time she spent with them, perhaps the more chance she had to change their minds. Avery couldn't believe they would be blind to reason.

Her position gave her the power to change their course, even there. And she would not take that for granted.

"You can't just suspend your opponents in the air when they're beginning to best you, Avery," Fiora rebuked in a loud voice from across the sparring mat.

"I don't see why not," Avery said with a smile as she dropped

Krez from her control. He fell to the mat with a heavy thud, immediately followed by an ill-tempered groan. "If I get angry, I should harness my emotions to work for me."

"How many times is she going to do that?" Krez asked painfully as he rolled to his feet. Avery stifled a grin.

"You will never get better at fighting if you keep avoiding contact altogether," Fiora explained, ignoring her husband. "I know you are beginning to master your more advanced skills, but you can't ignore this part of your training."

Avery rolled her eyes, turning away to lightly jog in place to keep her muscles from cooling down. It had been a month since they arrived here. A month and two days since Finn had gone into a coma, and he had yet to wake up. Five days since she realized what the Origin was capable of. The lengths to which they would go.

And no amount of pleading would change anyone's mind. Avery knew better than to press Leviathan about their suicidal mission, and Fiora refused to discuss it. It was hard to reconcile those she had come to know with what they were planning to do. Their measures were radical, absolutely, but the Reanges were just people. Just trying to do what they thought would bring them peace.

Avery was convinced it was Leviathan's leadership. The others followed her because they had no other choice. No other hope. Until now.

If anything, it only strengthened Avery's resolve to make a difference. She committed to her lessons as fervently as though she was a native-born Reange. She ate their food, listened to their music, learned their history, fully immersing herself to gather enough knowledge to stop this somehow. Or to gain enough trust to change their minds.

As a result, her powers had flourished. She communicated effortlessly with the others, having little to no need to exert any barrier. She accepted the connection between each of them and welcomed the sharing of feelings. She had even merged twice with Fiora, completely taking over her free will in an open act of trust as Avery practiced her control.

Leviathan explained to her that this was a sacred rite, one that should only be done in times of great stress or need. It was extremely difficult for a Reange to accept the merge. Losing sight of yourself and your own mind was not something to take lightly.

At least it explained why Petra had freaked out after Avery unwittingly merged with her on the Port Station.

She hadn't spoken to Petra since she had appeared in the Origin earlier that week. She didn't know why Petra was fine with leaving Tai back at Valuta, considering the risk of a Federation attack, but her curiosity didn't outweigh her lingering anger. Avery did her best to avoid her, closing her mind against her completely. And Petra had given her a wide berth. Thank the galaxy for that, at least.

"Maybe I'm just not a violent person," Avery replied to Fiora, shifting to lengthen her arms toward the floor. Hugging her legs and leaning into the movement, she added, "Did you ever think of that?"

Fiora scoffed. "Or we haven't found you a sparring partner that you want to hit badly enough."

"Maybe I can help with that." Avery stiffened at the feminine voice carrying across the gym from the entrance. Petra walked confidently toward them, dressed in her usual black outfit, blue hair gleaming in the glow of the lights.

Avery turned her back, catching Fiora's gaze as she spoke to her mind, *I don't want her here.*

Fiora glanced back and forth between the two girls, her expression turning quizzical. Avery knew immediately she had said the wrong thing.

"I think this is exactly what we need to take your game to the next level," Fiora said, excitement floating happily over to cloud Avery's own feelings.

With relish, she pushed back into Fiora's thoughts with the image of an obscene hand gesture, and her trainer immediately threw back her head with a full-throated laugh.

Avery ignored her, stretching her arms across her chest, focusing on Petra as she approached the mat. The girl's small features were set in concentration as she gave Avery a quick nod. They circled one another, each waiting for the first move.

Petra gathered the courage to speak first. "You can't stay mad at me forever."

Avery lunged, using her momentum to drive a front kick aimed at Petra's side. Petra took the hit with a grunt of pain, holding Avery's gaze a scant second before throwing her leg away. She was taking it easy on her, which only pissed her off more.

Avery moved forward quickly, throwing a swift uppercut at Petra's face. The girl dodged it, blocking Avery's other fist as she tried to deliver a blow from the opposite side. Petra pushed her away, moving back to dance lightly on her feet.

"Stop playing with me," Avery growled, throwing all her weight into a lunge to Petra's middle, dragging her a few feet with the impact. Petra resisted the move, wrapping her own arms around Avery's head in a tight hold to keep from succumbing to the momentum.

"Only if you'll stop freezing me out," Petra said quietly so that only the two of them could hear.

Avery brought a knee up and caught a solid blow to Petra's ribs, forcing the other girl to release and back away with a wheeze. Avery wiped the sweat from her brow as they circled each other once more.

"Are you saying you don't deserve it?" Avery asked, her breath coming in spurts. "You *used* me. Moon above, you made me believe we were friends!" With the last comment Avery twisted in the motion of a kick Fiora had her working on, using the fire of her anger to control the air surrounding her body.

Her feet flew off the ground as she whipped her head around, her entire body suspended for an unnatural moment before her leg followed the arc, coming down to catch Petra solidly in the side of the neck.

Petra was too shocked to block it, catching the full weight of the attack and going down in a heap of groaning limbs. Avery allowed the girl's pain to infiltrate her mind, relishing in it. Despite what anyone thought, she could hold her own when need be.

Avery stepped back and hopped from toe to toe as she allowed Petra to haul herself dazedly to her feet. Petra twisted her neck, rubbing the point of contact. She eyed Avery with something that wasn't quite annoyance.

"Excellent, Avery," Fiora praised, and Avery glanced her direction. Even Krez looked on admirably. Good. Let them take this back to Leviathan. Perhaps it would finally prove that she was ready to move forward with—

A blow hit Avery just below her left ribs, and she doubled over in shock as Petra moved into position to lock around her neck. "Never let yourself become distracted," Petra hissed in Avery's ear as they grappled, spinning in a circle before Avery swung Petra around, dragging them both to the floor.

Petra maneuvered over Avery, wrapping her legs across her torso as she pried herself out of Avery's arm. Her legs held Avery to the ground as she pulled on the arm, overextending the joint. The pain was nearly unbearable, Avery's face stretching into a grimace as she fought to keep from crying out.

Avery collected her pain, forcing it directly into Petra's mind. Her hold faltered. The relief was short-lived but enough for Avery to find the escape she needed from Petra. Turning into the move and twisting her arm as she pulled Petra's weight with her, Avery scrambled out of the hold.

She locked onto Petra from behind, bringing her elbow up under her chin in a strong chokehold. Petra clawed briefly at Avery's arms before standing, Avery still latched onto her back. Petra slammed Avery toward the ground, intending to shock her into letting go.

But Avery had no intention of letting that happen.

She called on the energy around her, filling the space beneath as Petra dropped them. They hit a soft cushion of air before rising, floating in their locked position.

But Petra refused to submit. There was no way, hovering in the air as they were, that she could hope to get out of the hold. So why didn't she give up? She was rapidly losing oxygen. Perhaps she was stubborn enough to pass out before acknowledging defeat.

Avery reached into Petra's mind, immediately recoiling. She felt the anguish there, the need to be forgiven surging through Petra's entire consciousness. Even as blackness closed in around the girl's vision, she had one thought. One desire. That Avery would forgive her.

Avery pulled back, dropping Petra unceremoniously to the

mat as she brought herself gracefully to her feet. Petra choked and spat on the ground, trying to clear her throat from the hold. Avery ignored her, bending to catch her own breath.

"Fabulous attempt, I have to admit," Fiora said, clapping softly from where she and Krez watched. "Not exactly fair, but it's much better than you've been doing so far." She nodded toward her, adding, "Petra stays."

"What?" Avery practically screeched, throwing a sulking look back at Petra. She was lying on her back on the mat. Grinning.

"You can't deny that's the best you've ever fought, Avery," Fiora said, walking toward the bench at the edge of the training circle. She threw a towel her way.

Avery caught it, wiping sweat from her face. "I can't work with her."

"Why not? If she brings out the best in your skills, then she is well worth the inconvenience," Fiora countered, and they both turned to view Krez helping Petra to her feet. "A poor show of effort is just as bad as none at all."

Avery clenched her jaw, averting her gaze. She refused to acknowledge it, but Fiora was right. If Petra could help advance her skill, then she would do well to use the opportunity.

No matter how much she still hated her.

"Good," Fiora said, sensing Avery's acquiescence. "I'm glad we agree."

Avery ignored her, used to her bossy sarcasm by this point. She brought the towel around her neck and worked to control her breathing.

"You are coming to the Petralias thing tonight, right?" Fiora asked expectantly. "It's a tradition that you really shouldn't miss. A chance to experience what it's like to really be a Reange."

"I'm not really certain why we're doing this. Not with what the real night next week will mean," Avery said, sobering. Their mission was just around the corner, weighing heavily in everyone's minds. "You can't really mean to go through with this ridiculous plan to—"

"We've been through this, Avery," Fiora replied, sighing and looking away. "I don't want to discuss it."

"But it just doesn't make sense—"

"Drop it, okay?" Fiora snapped, cutting her a hard glare before softening. The gym became eerily quiet as they stood there awkwardly.

Avery bit the inside of her cheek. How was she going to convince them that this wasn't the answer? There had to be another way. She refused to give up. She would just have to think harder. If only there was more time.

"Well?" Fiora smiled, her bright spirits returning. She was eager to let it go.

"Well what?" Avery replied, irritated.

"Are you coming tonight?"

"Of course," Avery said, surprised she would even ask. Hadn't she made every effort to fully assimilate into the culture there? She couldn't afford to miss a single opportunity to influence them. Not if she wanted to save them from themselves.

"You know what we're celebrating, right?" Fiora asked with a grin, back to her usual self. Avery was amazed she could move on so quickly from anger.

"It's one of the biggest holidays of the year," Avery replied, mimicking Leviathan's ancient voice as she recited her lessons nearly word for word. "A time to remember the sacrifice of our forefathers and those before them. The Originals—the first So's—were given their gifts on this day millennia ago to join the people together as one. And so we celebrate our commitments to one another and the unity of all."

Fiora laughed, shaking her head as she reached down to pack up the supplies they had been using that day. "That's about the gist of it," she said. "At least it gets you out of lessons with Leviathan today, right?"

"Yeah, I guess there is that," Avery acknowledged.

"It's actually my favorite holiday," Fiora said as she observed Avery. "Food and drink and laughter. People need those things in times like these, you know? Especially now."

Avery returned her smile somberly. The cloud that had settled over the camp the past week was palpable. Everyone was on edge. Readying.

"Besides, tonight we celebrate the ties between our people. If anything, the humans have shown us how rare a gift that is." She smiled, hefting her training bag over her shoulder.

"Not to mention, a night to celebrate our sacred bonds," Krez added quietly as he approached. He reached for Fiora's hand, bringing it to his lips for a kiss, and giving her a look that made even Avery blush. Had she thought him a man of few words? Perhaps he only said them when it counted.

Fiora flushed in response to her husband's unusual show of affection, her skin turning nearly as red as the hair secured in a knot on her head. Pulling her hand back to herself, she met Avery's gaze and laughed as she explained, "Couples will renew their vows tonight, and the new bonds will be formed."

Avery's eyebrows lifted, a small smile grabbing the corner of her own lips. "People only marry one night out of the year?"

"Yes," Fiora replied. "On the sacred night meant to remind us of the bond we all share."

"Well, that's terribly romantic." Avery didn't miss Petra

eavesdropping from her place on the mat. She smiled at Fiora and Krez. "I guess I'll see you guys tonight, then." But they were in their own world, ignoring her goodbye as she made her way toward the exit.

Her mind suddenly shifted to Finn. She had hoped that she would be able to spend the evening watching over him in peaceful solitude, but yesterday Leviathan had crushed that dream. Avery would be expected to participate in a ceremony of some kind for the festivities. And she couldn't afford to miss any opportunity.

But not visiting him made her feel empty and unsettled. She would just have to deal with the strange pit in her stomach.

If only she could convince them to listen to her. To consider other ways to make an impact. But as it was, she would have to develop a plan for her people alone.

She showered fast, returning to her tent to find two girls waiting for her. Cristane, a younger mute girl who often sat with Avery during meals, stood at the foot of her bed, a small smile on her round face. She held the hand of an older girl—Avery remembered her name was Kistralia. She had hair of pure gold with a sweet feminine face and soft blue eyes, reminding Avery of Megan.

"My So'," Kistralia said with a respectful bow of her head, and Cristane followed suit. "We're to help you dress for this evening."

Avery laughed. "I don't need help getting ready." She walked over to her chest to put down her dirty clothes, effectively dismissing the ridiculous notion. "Have you seen my wardrobe selection?" Avery added. "I have like two shirts and one pair of pants."

"But my So'—" Kistralia began before Avery cut her off.

"I appreciate it, but I really don't—" She stopped when Cristane came at once to her side, grabbing her hand. The girl pulled her along toward the bed and gestured at the fabrics lying there. Dozens of dresses laid out on her normally barren gray bed.

"They're from my own collection," Kistralia said enthusiastically. At Cristane's hurried gestures, the girl smiled and added, "Cristane helped me pick them out for you."

"I really appreciate the thought, but I couldn't possibly take one," Avery replied.

"You can't intend to go tonight in your regular clothes," Kistralia said, Cristane shaking her head in horror. "It's a formal affair."

"What?" Avery groaned. "Why does nobody tell me these things?"

"Well, thank the moons Cristane thought to get my help. Don't worry about a thing, my So', we'll handle it. Now just pick out a dress that catches your eye. Cristane will work on adjustments while I deal with the rest of you."

"The rest of me?" Avery let out a nervous laugh, making her way to the bed to begin pawing through the gowns. "I'm scared to ask what that means."

"We may not have gen mods down here anymore, but I can do some serious work with some old-fashioned makeup and a few hair accessories," Kistralia promised ardently.

Avery's first inclination was to refuse, because who had the time to worry about crap like this anymore? But after a moment's hesitation, she nodded gently.

"Yes?" Kistralia squealed in excitement.

"Yes." The girl's mood was infectious, pulling a grin from her lips. Even the demure Cristane was jumping enthusiastically as they all began to giggle.

Avery could definitely use a bit of normalcy. She used to love sleepovers with Megan when she'd get all dolled up just for the blazar of it. They would pretend they were famous and rich, living on the top level in some fancy penthouse with a Gate view. But that life was so far away now. Still, it was nice to remember what normal had been for her once.

Avery could use a bit more normal these days, if just for a few hours. Pushing aside thoughts of politics and responsibilities, she turned her attention to picking a shade of green that would best bring out the color of her eyes.

CHAPTER NINETEEN

He was falling.

That was the first conscious thought that stabbed Finn's mind. He shot up in his bed, gripping the blankets and holding on for dear life.

It was dark wherever he was, the barest glow from a torch above him lighting the small circular area. People spoke in hushed tones somewhere beyond the walls.

Despite his raging headache, Finn fought the painful throbbing to recover his memories. Flashes surfaced. The attack in the cafeteria . . . confronting Nick . . . trying furiously to save Avery.

Avery. Where was she?

A new urgency surged through his veins, causing the wireless monitor lying on the floor beside him to chirp loudly. Finn frowned, grabbing the med patch on his arm. It ripped away from his skin with a loud suctioning.

He pushed the covers back and came to his knees, bracing against his thighs as a wave of nausea erupted. He was dressed in tan medical pants and a soft green shirt, neither of which were his.

Panic set in, his heart rate rising. *Avery.*

He had found her on that ship and gotten her to the escape pod before . . . damn it, he couldn't remember anything past that. Nick. That son of a bitch had caused this. If anything had happened to Avery, he would kill the bastard, brother or not.

They planned to attack Nos Valuta. Nick had given the Federation everything they needed to wipe out the entire base. Finn choked back a fierce shout as he realized it could already be too late. All of those people. All of those innocent lives. His fists clenched rigidly at his knees.

There was a low table to the right of his pallet, against the canvas wall. A small glass of water sat there, and he lurched for it, experience teaching him to sip slowly.

The cool liquid slid down his throat, wetting the thick fuzz that was the inside of his mouth. Despite his caution, he drained the cup quickly. It did little to settle his unruly stomach.

Finn realized he was in some kind of tent. He struggled to hear the voices from the other side of the thin walls. There was giggling, but he couldn't make out much else.

He stood slowly, his bare feet touching the solid rock floor. It was cool and slightly moist against his skin. The air was damp, like he was underground. There was no place in Nos Valuta like this. His only other thought was . . . .

It couldn't be. Could Avery have found her way to the Origin without his help?

If they had taken her, she would have no hope standing up to their council without his help. She didn't know what she was getting herself into. These people were, in many ways, more dangerous than the Federation itself.

For that matter, why was he still alive? The Origin didn't take prisoners of war. They killed humans without a second thought. As easily as you would kill a mosquito that landed on your arm.

Finn abandoned the guesses, moving carefully to the partially open flap of the tent's entrance. He was weak. His limbs protested his movements, wanting nothing more than to lie back down. He squinted through the small sliver of open canvas. Two girls spoke quietly outside, dressed in evening attire. One was strikingly blonde, the other older with dark hair and an animated face.

". . . so amazing in that pale green gown," the blonde one was saying. "You know, the one I wore to Petralias two years ago? Except she's going to look even more spectacular than I did. I bet she'll get all kinds of offers tonight!"

"I wouldn't be surprised if she bonds already," the dark-haired one giggled in response. "If I wasn't already taken, you know I'd make a move."

"Liar, you wouldn't have the guts." They broke into a fit of laughter.

Finn's breath caught. Petralias?

He rapidly did the math in his head, running through dates as he calculated. Four weeks. Moons above, what had Petra put in that cocktail she injected into his chest?

Squeezing his eyes shut, Finn pressed his fingers against his sockets until they ached painfully. If the Federation was making a move on Nos Valuta, they could be dead and gone now. Everyone he ever knew and loved could be— No. He couldn't think about that. He wouldn't.

Steps. Next steps.

No one knew he was awake. He could use that to his advantage. There was still a chance he could do something. Anything.

Quickly, he returned to the bed, searching for some sort of weapon. With no other option, he grabbed the drinking glass and tucked it beneath the pillow. Finn pressed down to crush it into usable shards, the pillow muffling the sound.

He grabbed the largest piece, wrapping its base in a small bit of sheet to act as a rudimentary handle. Reaching for the discarded med patch, he peeled off the outer layer, exposing the microchip underneath. He folded it in half, breaking the tiny green square to shatter the concentrated laser within.

Finn pressed this against the flat side of the glass shard, leftover adhesive securing it tightly. The raw laser would follow the lines of the glass, making its edges as lethal as a laser knife. Carefully, he used the leftover outer layer of the med patch to wrap the handle, rendering it safe to his grip.

Turning the weapon over in his hands, he inspected the now-glowing red edges of the shard. Lowering it to the metal leg of the bed, the steel hissed and began to smoke as soon as the shard came into contact. It would do.

Moving fast, Finn cut a small hole in the canvas of the rear wall. He crawled out, hands scraping against the rocky ground as blood rushed painfully to his head.

He kept the glass shard ready as he moved throughout what appeared to be a large camp. Looking up, the cavern stretched high above into the darkness. The small tent was situated on the one spot of higher ground, so he could see the general lay-out of the place fairly easily. The space beyond was well lit, warm lights dotting the pathways throughout.

He could hear the din of a crowd toward the outer edge of the main tent area. There was a larger glow of light there, on the edge of the darkness, where he could only assume Petralias was taking place. It made sense that the camp was empty. On Petralias, everyone celebrated.

He had never been allowed to take part in the traditional bonding ceremony, always watching in awe. But he celebrated with friends in the raucous parties afterward. The food . . . the dancing . . . the love making. The holiday was a favorite among many. Especially during these times.

Keeping to the outer edges, Finn made his way forward to investigate just what he was up against. And how the hell he was going to get out of there alive.

Avery glanced up as a third person asked to secure her hand for a dance after the ceremony. What could she do but say yes?

And what was this, the twentieth century or something? People didn't ask for dances anymore. At least not back on Earth.

She blushed what she hoped was prettily—although she was fairly convinced her blushes looked like some sort of rash—and accepted. The woman bowed and thanked her for the honor before moving away.

Avery had been slightly dismayed to realize that she and Leviathan would be seated on a pedestal in garish, overly large chairs. As though they were on display for the crowd to fawn all over. It was strikingly reminiscent of the kinds of royal assemblies they held in vid stories back home, and it made Avery uneasy. More and more, she realized that So's were treated as sovereigns, despite how many people said otherwise.

She didn't like it. Traditions be damned.

The dress she had settled on was truly gorgeous. A stunning seafoam green creation with yards of effervescent fabric that clung to her hips before wrapping around the bodice, cupping the low neckline in a deep V. It draped heavily just over either shoulder to meet in a complex knot low on her back. There must have been nano tech in the threads, because as she walked the skirts let off a soft iridescent glow.

Even if she was a tad overdressed, Avery couldn't be sorry for it. She felt powerful in that dress.

Her once mousy hair had deepened lately into a beautiful dark chestnut that Kistralia had piled in intricate knots on her head, wispy tendrils poking out to frame her face. Her eyes were lined with a dark pigment that accentuated their almond shape, winging out to make her lashes appear longer. Her lips were covered in a soft pink that Kistralia had promised her would stay on all evening.

It was amazing, what a little hard work could do. When Avery had seen herself in the mirror, she had been practically speechless. Looking like this, she could even keep up with Megan.

Of course, she still had to wear her boots since there were no fancy shoes that even came close to fitting her in the camp. Beggars couldn't be choosers, anyway. Avery would take what she could get.

But even as she sat there, calmly watching over the crowd

beside Leviathan like some medieval princess, she wished that she had declined the request to attend. For all her yearning to learn about her people, she wanted to experience it as one of them. Not as some ruler that they revered. Leviathan was clear about setting proper boundaries, but Avery didn't agree.

And the fact that she hadn't visited Finn plagued her. Something had dislodged itself inside of her chest. Resolutely, she decided to check on him before heading to bed.

Still, she smiled and played the part Leviathan wanted her to embody. It was more important than ever to observe. Establishing irrevocable trust was the first step to stopping this insane mission of theirs. If not with Leviathan, then with the others.

Things were moving, and quickly. There was a little over a week left for her to develop some strategy that would placate them all. If it was her only option, Avery wasn't above using her powers to muscle her way into some compliance. She only hoped she was strong enough, if it came to that.

But if only for a few hours, she would take a breath. Just this once.

She sipped deeply from the fermented berry wine, letting the alcohol dull her senses and help her relax. Now when was the blazing ceremony supposed to begin?

Moons above, she was breathtaking.

Was that *Avery?*

Finn heard her laugh. The sound echoed melodically across the cavern of rocks behind him in the darkness, tickling his ears.

What the blazar had happened to her? Finn had expected to find her scared and alone, trapped in some tent on the edges of camp and heavily guarded. That is, if she was there at all. He never thought she would have blended in like this.

His eyes narrowed. Had her hair always been so dark? And her smile so infectiously bright? Her cheeks blushed perfectly as she laughed with the others.

And that dress. She stood to take another glass of wine offered to her, turning away from him. Her back was exposed, revealing her curves as the fabric hugged her in all the right places.

Or were they the wrong ones? Wrong. Definitely wrong. He shouldn't be looking at her like that.

Finn averted his gaze, taking a fortifying breath as he sunk farther into the darkness. He couldn't very well waltz in and blend with the crowd. Not dressed as he was. He had to find a way to talk to her. Maybe if he could get her alone, he could come up with some kind of plan to get them out.

With a quick glimpse at the assembly, he realized everyone was taking their places for the ceremony. A large holofire glowed brightly in the center of the revelries, intended to mimic the ancient bonfires that were used during the first rituals. It let off a warm light in the darkness of the cavern, emanating heat to ward off the wet chill beneath ground. And there were flowers everywhere, scenting the air with a heady sweetness that made his stomach roll. Although how they had gotten flowers down here, Finn could only guess.

The Federation was salivating to get information on the Origin. It was one of their top priorities, considering the real threat their extremist tactics presented to the tourists in Milderion. Any attempt to communicate aboveground had to be incredibly dangerous.

But Finn knew that firsthand. He had often traded information on behalf of the Rebellion with an Origin leader. Mylan had shared a great friendship with Finn's father, which is the only reason the man trusted Finn. Perhaps he could be an avenue for escape, if Finn played his cards right. At the very least, Mylan would know the status of the Rebellion forces. It was as good a place as any to start.

The mutters of the crowd quieted as the attendees took their places in two rows, one on either side of the holofire. The lines led a path directly to the platform where Avery sat regally beside an old woman.

Leviathan. It could only be her.

Although Mylan was open to Finn's suggestions of collaboration, the old crone controlling them down here was firmly set against any interaction with humans. Why she held so much sway when Reanges were supposed to be governed by a collective democratic body, he couldn't say. It was certainly not how Nos Valuta operated. But then again, these were extremists. They didn't often operate based on reason.

He prayed she hadn't sunk her claws into Avery. His eyes darted back to her. Please, let her still be the girl he knew.

He leaned against a wall of rock, the cool wetness of it pressing through the thin fabric of his shirt. If he could make it to the end of the ceremony, maybe he could catch her in the revelry afterward. If he couldn't get Avery alone before he passed out, he'd be no good to either of them.

Someone called for silence before the old woman began to speak.

"Our forefathers and those before them initiated this rite

a thousand years ago," she called out, her voice strained. "In those times we were no better than the humans, so disconnected and blind without our brothers' and sisters' minds and hearts to guide us. On this day, we celebrate our bond, as one people!" The crowd cheered. Finn was familiar with the words, having heard them every year for the past eighteen of his life.

But instead of continuing the ceremony aloud, they swiftly quieted. Everyone still focused on Leviathan, even Avery, who was staring at her astutely. They carried out the gestures that went along with the ceremonial rite, clasping hands with their friends and touching heads to their mates.

But there was no sound, save for the rustling of fabric. The crackling of the holofire before them.

It couldn't be. Finn looked sharply at the old woman standing beside Avery. She was a So'. Leviathan was a So'.

All this time, and they had kept it hidden, even from the Rebellion. Avery moved to Leviathan's side and took her right hand, grasping it at the wrist in the symbol of commitment. Of bonded friendship.

And just like that, it was over. The people were cheering and rejoicing as the new couples lined up to accept the goodwill of the overseer. Who was Leviathan. Their So'.

And Avery, too. Each Reange joined hands with her as they approached the raised platform. Even in his weakened state, Finn could see that she wasn't unaffected by it.

Petralias was a moving celebration, one that he had always longed to be a part of. Even if he lived among them and fought beside them, he would never truly be a Reange. But he would never be fully human, either. His family had left that life when he was too young to even know what it meant. He was a walking contradiction, stuck between both worlds. Between two parts of himself. Accepting one entirely would mean rejecting the other.

Finn pulled his thoughts away from such morose chatter in his brain. Now wasn't the time to be bemoaning his sorry situation.

He moved closer to the front of the celebration, keeping to the shadows. Hopefully everyone was pleasantly drunk enough to ignore the stumbling human lurking around the edges.

Finn's vision blurred as he desperately clung to consciousness. He couldn't go into the darkness again. He simply refused. He was so close to her now, he could hear her talking to someone. Her lilting voice carried across the air.

"I'm telling you I don't know how to dance this way." She giggled flirtatiously before adding, "I'm sorry if I step all over your toes. I swear I won't mean to." Even though he couldn't see her, it sounded as though she was batting her eyelashes to go with the effect.

She was flirting with someone. That blazing girl was flirting with some besotted extremist while he was literally dying trying to save her ass. Well, see if he ever bothered to try and save her again, the ungrateful, traitorous little—

"The human!" someone screeched, and Finn tensed, turning his attention in the direction of the voice. All at once, the crowd erupted into chaos. They surged around him quickly, blocking out any chance he had at catching sight of Avery.

So much for a plan.

He raised his laser shard, but it was promptly knocked from his hand. He had little strength to evade the others. Fingers dug tightly into his arms, pulling his body left and right. Trying to kill the So', they accused. As if he would ever harm a hair on Avery's head.

His mind floated in and out of consciousness as the crowd threw him from one person to the next. But he would stay awake this time if it killed him.

Then the hands dropped him. Everything fell silent as angry faces calmed. People stepped away as he fell backward, unable to support himself.

Yeah. He definitely should have just stayed in that bed.

But he never hit the ground. He was weightless, floating on a cloud. It was a peculiar sensation, and one he chalked up to delirium.

And then she was there. She leaned over him in her gown of pale green. Had her eyes always been so piercingly golden? He couldn't remember, and wasn't sure he even cared.

She was saying something to him. He could see her lips moving quickly, her forehead creased with deep lines of worry. He reached up and touched her cheek, smiling at the silkiness of the skin there. Maybe this wasn't Avery. Maybe it was some holovid version of her he dreamed up on his deathbed.

What did it matter if he died? Moons above, he'd be happy to go right now if it meant looking at her until the end took him. But who would protect her, if he was gone?

Good point. He still had things to do

CHAPTER TWENTY

"The human!" someone yelled.

Panic surged through Avery in a rush before all hell broke loose around her. Angry faces flashed as she was pushed behind a wall of bodies, hysteria spreading through the crowd like an exploding star.

What the blazar were they doing? The human? That could only mean . . . .

Choking on her own breath, Avery's heart nearly beat out of her chest with hope. She dove mind first into the mob, their anger swirling dangerously with fear. And then there he was. She saw Finn through the eyes of many, his body pulled back and forth by the infuriated Reanges.

They wanted to protect her. But that did nothing to quell the rage that blazed a trail through her system. They were hurting him.

Harnessing her fury, Avery grabbed the consciousness of the entire assembly. *Calm*, she commanded, the strength of her will arising from some place yet unknown. Leviathan's presence was there, too, in that strange world of thought and feeling. Thankfully there was no resistance on her part.

Gathering the power wound tightly in her chest, Avery lifted her hands, guiding the air from the inner circle of the mob and swiftly pressing outward. Bodies pushed back with the unseen force, stumbling dazedly away from Finn as her power moved them to the edges. Avery cleared a path for herself, keeping her tight hold on the crowd as she moved toward him.

He began to fall, his eyes closing as his body swayed backward, and she threw her power out quickly to catch him. He landed in the soft pillow of air a foot above the ground. She held him suspended, determined to keep him from further harm.

"Finn," she gasped, running to his side, her hands searching for injury over his arms. His hooded eyes met hers. Something electric hit her deep and deliciously in her belly.

"Are you all right?" she asked, her eyes roving over him for any obvious signs of injury. "Can you hear me?"

She looked up around her, realizing she had forgotten the others. It took too much effort to keep him afloat and hold onto their minds to maintain it simultaneously for long. But thank the galaxy, their frenzy had passed.

Avery gathered her wits. "Nevril! Someone get me Nevril!" she called. After a dazed moment, they moved to do her bidding, searching for the healer in the crowd. If she hadn't been so focused on Finn, she could have called out to the woman's mind herself.

"You're gonna be okay," she said to him, her throat thick with emotion. He was, she knew. If he came out of his coma and was conscious enough to try and get to her, then he hadn't been damaged beyond healing.

He still watched her face, his eyes searching before he dazedly reached up to lightly graze her cheek. He grinned, heavy stubble gathering in a dark shadow at the dimple in his right cheek. Her heart flipped.

"You're gonna be okay," she said again, leaning down to touch her forehead to his as she sent up a prayer of thanks to whomever was listening. A murmur of surprise moved throughout the crowd around her, but she was too preoccupied to care.

As her emotions calmed, so did her ability to hold him afloat. Her control was slipping. Frantically, she slipped his arm up and over her shoulder as she used her abilities to position him on his feet.

"Enough gawking," Leviathan's voice rang out clear across the crowd. Avery was glad she had been able to bring them to reason, even if by force. "Let's return to the celebration," the older So' continued, motioning to the musicians to start up a livelier tune to dance to. "The night is still young, and it is Petralias!"

A cheer resounded, and Avery could feel the unease of the crowd float away into the eaves of the cavern above, replaced once more with the revelry of earlier. Leviathan had used her influence to encourage everyone to return to the party. Avery shot her a glance, nodding her thanks.

The last of her power slipped through her grasp as Finn fell on her. Looking wildly about, no one seemed inclined nor willing to come close to them. They were too consumed by the celebration.

But then someone was there, grabbing Finn's left arm and taking half of the weight to share between them. Petra's gaze met Avery's from across Finn's broad chest. Avery's mouth fell slightly open.

"Well, let's go," Petra said calmly, jerking her head toward the path ahead. "He needs to get back to the clinic, right?"

Avery nodded, returning her focus to Finn and pushing forward, trying to coax him to take steps. He wasn't carrying a great deal of weight himself, but at least he was still semi-functional. Together, Avery and Petra made their way toward the heart of the camp.

"How did he get here?" Avery looked up at Nevril's question as she jogged to meet them, bedecked in a fine dress of deep crimson for the evening. Avery wished she didn't have to ruin the evening for them like this. It was one of the only times they could forget about what was happening around them. Forget what they had lost. What they were going to lose.

"I don't know," Avery replied with heavy breaths, focusing her remaining strength on putting one foot in front of the other. "He just showed up. He seems ready to pass out, but he's definitely conscious."

Nevril pulled out a small device and ran a quick body scan as she walked backward in front of them, taking stock of his vitals. "Everything looks normal," she said, reading through the results. "His heart rate is elevated, but blood sugar is quite low. He needs to rest and get some food into his system. Blazing idiot, getting out of bed like that," she added with a few grumbles.

Avery let out a steadying breath, thankful again for their good luck. She shared a smile with Nevril, both of them relieved that he had finally awoken. The healer was one of the only people in the Origin that Avery knew harbored no ill will for humans. She was there out of the necessity of her people. Nothing more, nothing less.

Avery tried to subtly observe Petra as they walked. Why was she helping at all? Why would she come forward, of all people?

Petra had hated humans with a fervor that Avery would never be able to understand. And yet she had still come to help Finn. As much as she wanted to pry into her complicated mind, Avery simply didn't have the strength.

In fact, just focusing on walking was taking a great deal of exertion. Never had she used her power on such a broad scale before, and all at once. Leviathan would certainly be happy to see such progress, but it would take a toll on her body. Using her gift in such extremes still taxed her.

But Avery had never felt anything like it. The sheer power of harnessing that many minds in unison was intoxicating. It had filled her with a high unlike any she had ever experienced. It could be dangerous, having such complete control over so many.

Leviathan would have her believe it was her right. If that was true, then Avery's word could be law.

They tripped, jostling Finn between them, and he let out a small grunt of pain, air whooshing past his lips. For the first time that night, Avery was grateful for her sturdy boots beneath her skirts.

He looked down at Avery, then Petra. "A girl on each arm?" he slurred out with a lopsided grin. "Seems like my night's improving."

Petra's sound of disgust filled the silence as the weight of Finn's head leaned against Avery's neck. She smiled, probably for the first real time since coming to this place.

And just like that, she no longer felt so incredibly alone.

He was a complete and utter ass. Avery couldn't remember why she ever wanted him to wake up in the first place.

It had been a full day since he showed up and effectively collapsed in her arms, but he was already pretty much back to his former self. After a few meals of broth and plain bread, Finn was apparently feeling good enough to flirt with every living thing within a hundred yards.

Nevril was an easy target, being as beautiful as she was. And it turned out that Kistralia had somehow wrangled her way into nurse duties. She was probably the only one who had offered to look after the human.

Avery was surly and out of sorts, glowering at everyone who came into his cell. She couldn't figure out what was plaguing her.

Despite lavishing attention on everyone else, Finn had yet to speak more than three words together to Avery. It was almost like he was deliberately trying to ignore her. Every time they had more than five minutes alone, he shut his eyes and pretended to rest. Avery had spent more hours than she could count listening to the way his breath sounded when he slept. She could tell when he was faking it.

Not that Avery could trust her instincts, anyway. She was on the verge of collapsing from exhaustion herself. Resting on the floor beside his bed all night, she refused to leave his side. She feared another scene like the night before.

In the Origin, she was literally the only one who would—

or even could—protect him. Perhaps Nevril would speak up, but she would be powerless against Leviathan. Avery wondered how long before her powers could eclipse the old So's.

Even as Avery considered what would happen to him, her lids began to droop heavily over her eyes. Petra had brought her a change of clothes, so at least she wasn't attired in her gown anymore. But her hair was still done up, and she had yet to wash the makeup off her face. She looked horrible.

Letting her head droop, Finn and Nevril's voices melded together in a soothing lullaby of sound. She let her lids close for a moment. Just a moment wouldn't hurt. . . .

"You should go get some sleep, Avery," Finn's voice was calm and firm, more collected than she had heard since he had awoken.

She forced her eyes open, rubbing a hand over her face to wake herself up. Finn was now situated comfortably with a few pillows tucked behind him so he could sit up. Nevril was nowhere in sight.

"I'm fine," she responded. Had she dozed off? That couldn't happen again. She couldn't trust anyone. She had to stay near him.

"You're not fine," he scoffed. "You've been sitting there drooling on your own shirt for the past two hours."

"Two hours?" Avery was shocked. How could she have let her guard down for so long?

"Listen, I'll be fine, all right?" he told her. "I'm sure I've got diplomatic immunity or something."

"Or something?" She raised a brow.

He stared at her intently before his eyes jerked to a sound beyond the tent entrance. Now that he was awake, there were two guards at the post. "We can't talk yet. Not here. What have you gotten us into, anyway?"

"Me?" she said, rising to her feet in an uncoordinated combination of movement. "I saved your ass, Lunitia, more than once."

"Don't be naive," he chastised. "We can't trust these people. You don't know what—"

"Naive?" she huffed. "I've done fine without you so far. And I can guarantee we're safer here than in your precious Nos Valuta where your brother sold us out."

He stiffened. "What do you know about Valuta? Nobody will tell me anything."

Avery looked away, shuddering a sigh. "They don't have any intel. No info from the surface. In or out," she added. "Apparently the So' is too valuable to risk discovery." She glanced back at him, a peculiar sensation clenching her chest as she saw fear in his eyes. "But I would know. I would feel it if something . . . ." She wasn't certain how to explain it.

"You'd *feel* it?"

"If . . . if they were gone." She met his eyes. "I'd know."

Finn laughed bitterly. "I don't know what they've filled your head with, sweetheart, but that sounds like a load of—"

"I don't have the strength for this right now," she said firmly, surprising him enough to actually shut him up. "I'm the only thing standing between you and a public execution, so you're just gonna have to trust me."

After a few moments, he replied, "I can take care of myself." His hands were fists at his sides, the muscles ticking in his jaw.

"Are you insane?" she scoffed, her voice rising. "Do you have any idea what they wanted to do to you? What I had to—"

"You're not responsible for me, all right?" his near shout interrupted her. Then, quieter: "So don't factor me into the equation. Now go get some sleep before you pass out standing up."

They stared at each other, Avery not knowing what to say in the face of his sudden stubbornness. So he thought he could take care of himself? Even there?

He was an ignorant asshole.

"Fine," she said tightly. "You want to be alone? Good luck, Ambassador," she added, striding toward the entrance.

"Avery, I—" he started, but she was already ducking under the flap. If he didn't want her around, then there was nothing she could do about it.

Besides, her head was spinning. Her fight with Petra the previous morning followed by the ceremony and the scene with Finn had utterly depleted her energy sources.

She made her way down the path to her tent, not more than a few minutes' walk from his. At least she wouldn't be far away if anything should happen.

Not that she cared. He was an ungrateful lout that probably deserved whatever the Reanges wanted to do to him. Why did it matter if she let them have him?

Avery kept one ear open. Just in case.

"What do you plan to do with me?" Finn asked, keeping his back as straight as possible as he faced Mylan. He may be bedridden, but he could at least conduct himself with the dignity of his position.

"That depends on you, I'm afraid," the older man responded, his chin rising. Assessing. "You seem to hold a peculiar sway over her."

Finn kept his features blank. "She can barely stand to be around me."

"Hmm," was all Mylan replied, crossing his arms over his chest as he regarded Finn. "I've been given leave to do with you as I see fit. And it seems to me that the best way to get Avery to cooperate with us is to let you stay here until you regain your health, although it goes expressly against our laws here."

Finn sneered. "You mean Leviathan's edicts?"

Mylan let out a low laugh. "I'm surprised it took you this long to figure it out."

"That you've had a So' down here all along?" Finn asked incredulously. "How could you not have told the council at Nos Valuta?"

"Who says they didn't know?" Mylan countered.

Finn's mind reeled. There were more things at play here. More than he clearly realized. He knew the council had been hiding things, but cooperation with the Origin? It went against everything the Rebellion stood for.

"I know we haven't always cooperated with the Rebellion," Mylan said with sincerity, "but we are on the same side. We all want to be free to live our lives without fear of the Federation."

"Even me? A human?" Finn said, disdainful sarcasm dripping from his words. Mylan said nothing, forcing Finn to look away. "The Federation is going to attack Nos Valuta."

"We know," Mylan responded calmly. Finn started, sharply meeting the man's gaze. "Did you think Avery would not tell us? Perhaps you underestimate her."

"Don't tell me what I think of her," Finn snapped.

Mylan snorted, continuing, "Our scouts delivered intel last week. They're planning to make a move after Petralias. Federation forces are even now gathering in the city."

Panic flared. "But wasn't that yesterday? You can't just—"

"We celebrated early. The sacred day isn't for a week and a half," Mylan clarified with a shake of his head, neglecting to elaborate further.

"Then you have to let me go." Finn leaned forward, gripping the bedside. "You know the only chance they have is if I can alert them of the attack. There are nearly a thousand lives— *Reange lives*—under that mountain. Every one of them will be slaughtered if we don't warn them."

"You would leave her here with us? Alone?" Mylan asked, surprise in his words.

Finn clenched his jaw in frustration. The last thing he wanted to do was leave Avery. But every move he made now was critical. His mind conjured up images of Grigg and Nova, along with a dozen other faces that could even now be dead because of his inactivity. He had lost too much time already.

"I have a responsibility to them. They are my family," Finn said earnestly, passion coloring his voice. "I can't just let them die. Not when I could do something to stop it."

"And what is that?" Mylan wondered. "At most, you'll get there in time to die alongside them." Finn was silent. "The best chance they have, that any of us have, is for that girl out there to lead us."

Mylan was right. But Finn's heart fought against the idea of wasting time here waiting for her to master her gift. Of letting her shoulder the burden of this monumental task alone. He would not be another weight around her neck.

"We don't have time," Finn ground out fiercely. If only he had been stronger.

"She's already further along than you think," Mylan said

with a small smile of awe. "She's further along than any of us could have hoped. Even Leviathan believes she is nearly ready."

Finn frowned, trying to understand what Mylan was saying. Avery was ready? For what? The girl had no training whatsoever. She had yet to lead so much as a conga line, let alone a band of Reanges into battle.

"And right now," Mylan added, "she needs you to support her. Regardless of what the others think, or the connections she has made here, your presence will make the difference for her. It already has."

Finn shook his head with a snort. "Avery couldn't care less if I was sucked into the nearest black hole. In fact, she'd probably push me in."

"What is it like to be a human, unable to feel the truth of things within another?" Mylan asked quietly. "You can say what you will, but I saw how she refused to leave you when you were injured. How she hovered over you as the fever threatened to take you, barely sleeping from the fear of your loss. You would have died if she hadn't forced us to aid you. You nearly did, anyway."

Something in his chest lurched and he broke eye contact, looking toward his feet. Avery's worried face rose, unbidden, to his mind. She shouldn't have bothered. He had a way of pulling through tough situations. He always had before.

"No, you will not go yet," Mylan said, turning away. "Rest and recover. She will need your help in the days ahead, though the council would not like to admit it."

"But Nos Valuta"—Finn could hear the torment in his own voice—"they have to be warned."

Mylan frowned, almost apologetically. "The council has decided that any outside contact is too risky. Not with Avery finally here among us. External communication is forbidden until she has mastered her skills. Our intel last week was the last one we will receive."

Finn's heart dropped, disappointment and dread blending into an unbearable tangle in his chest.

"Remember that they are our people, not yours," Mylan added gravely. "This choice was not made easily."

When Finn was finally alone, he let out a growl, balling his hands in the sheets. He grabbed the cup of water at his bedside and threw it across the cell. There was no relief as it clattered uselessly to the floor, its contents leaving a trail of darker brown down the side of the tent.

He was stuck.

CHAPTER
TWENTY-ONE

"Faster," Fiora yelled at Avery as she ran through moves on the mat. Another day had passed while Avery slept, longer than she would have liked, but it took that long to gather her strength again.

Once she had finally woken up, the thought of facing Finn was nearly unbearable. She could feel his presence through the minds in the clinic, so she dove into her normal routine to regain some semblance of control. As long as she kept tabs on him, he'd be all right.

She jabbed the air, sending kicks and punches into an imaginary opponent as she honed her technique. Her frustration was a tangible knot, twisting around in her chest like some ball of wire that threatened to choke her from within. She let out a grunt of frustration as she pushed herself harder, sweat pouring from her temples.

"Good," Fiora said, circling Avery as she practiced. "Focus on your form. Pick up that elbow."

Things were different now, although she couldn't say how. Finn was finally awake, and that was all she had hoped for since the day they arrived. But now he was one more person for her to worry about. Her need to protect him contrasted heavily with her desire to help her people.

She had given up on the hope that she would save Gran. Now she was faced with the possibility that she might have to give up Finn, too.

Leviathan would never let him remain here. It was impossible. That meant they would either send him away or abandon him aboveground to the mercy of the Federation. She couldn't let that happen.

With a cry, Avery grabbed the air around her, using the invisible tendrils to wrap her limbs as she whipped around for a gravity-defying roundhouse kick. She landed on the ground, kneeling as she fought to steady her breathing.

"A little irritated today, are we?" Fiora asked. Avery could hear the satisfied smile in her voice. She longed to wipe it from her face.

Avery stood, wiping her forehead. "Not at all," she said between breaths, "just focusing on getting everything right."

"Your jabs could use a little more force," Petra's voice sounded from behind. Avery fought the urge not to roll her eyes at the intrusion.

"Petra!" Fiora shouted suddenly, drawing Avery's attention to the entrance of the gym. "Just the girl we needed this morning."

"Another sparring match?" Avery said sardonically. "Didn't

we cover this a few days ago?"

"Yes," Fiora agreed as she backed away from the mat, "but this time we're going to have a little help from our elder So'."

"What exactly does that mean?" Avery asked, but before she could get an answer, Petra was on the mat, throwing a quick jab to her face. Avery's eyes widened, dodging it with a deft drop. Not fast enough. Petra countered with a left uppercut, catching Avery across the chin. Pain speared her jaw, and she saw stars just long enough to stagger backward.

"Sorry," Petra said with a small grimace.

Avery tasted coppery blood in her mouth. She scowled at Petra.

"Do you need a minute?" Petra asked, and Avery growled, calling on her gift and propelling herself forward with the momentum to catch Petra in the stomach. But the move didn't have the added impact that should have come from her powers. What the blazar happened?

Before she could dwell on it, Petra used a complex move to twist her feet with Avery's, swinging her entire bodyweight around until Avery was flying through the air. She had a half second to anticipate before her body slammed into the mat, knocking the air from her lungs.

Avery rolled to her hands and knees, gasping as her lungs struggled to regain control of the air intake.

"Leviathan is blocking your gifts for this particular match," Fiora explained as Petra let Avery regain her composure. "We thought it would be good for you to spar on even ground for once."

Was there no end to what her mind could ultimately do? Leviathan probably derived immense satisfaction keeping secrets from her. The old woman liked to lord over anyone and everyone.

But how strong was Leviathan, really? Could Avery counter her? This whole plan for the Petralias mission was a waste of life, on both sides. She didn't understand why no one could see that. But perhaps they could be made to see.

What she had been thinking of as a curse could actually be their salvation. She was the one Reange who truly knew what it meant to be human. To live in both worlds.

Maybe with a new leader, they could save Nos Valuta and unite their forces. Have a real chance against the Federation. The high-profile Petralias celebration offered a unique opportunity to bridge the impassible gap between Reanges and humans. If only Avery's powers impacted humans.

But they had Finn.

Finn, who was some big shot in Milderion. A public figure, a celebrity. He basically had public immunity, at least as far as the Federation was concerned. He could get into any party he wanted in either galaxy, no matter the host, as long as it was covered by a media stream.

A plan came together in a wild array of thoughts, one she couldn't dismiss. Avery rose to her feet, dissecting the possibilities.

But Petra was on her in a second, bringing her once more into the fight that wasn't finished. But she was on a completely different level. Without her gifts, Avery was a child trying to best a full-grown adult. Petra put her on the ground again and again, although Avery refused to concede. She'd rather be sucked out a vac seal before she'd submit.

On the fifth occasion of being knocked flat on her back, Petra followed through, pressing against Avery's shoulder with her hand as she leaned down to bark at her, "Stay down, damn it."

Avery narrowed her eyes at the command, wanting nothing more than to wipe that ridiculous air of superiority off Petra's face. Knocking her arm away, she pushed herself to her feet once more.

"If you don't stay down, I'm going to have to really hurt you," Petra said cautiously, flicking a glance toward Fiora, who only looked amused.

Avery resumed her position on the mat, ready to begin again despite the earnest protests of her weary muscles.

"Then don't blame me for this," Petra warned before she started in on the attack. Avery blocked the first blows before Petra got a few good jabs in on her face. Seeing stars, Avery raised her arms to prevent any more damage. Petra took the opportunity to grab her shoulders, bringing her knee into direct contact with Avery's ribs.

Letting out a whoosh of air, Avery managed to control the pain enough to grab onto the knee, knocking it away. Petra, unfazed, came back around for another attack. It was all Avery could do to block her face and retreat, taking the hits as they came.

"What the hell is wrong with you people?" a voice yelled, scant seconds before Petra's assault stopped. Avery was too dazed to do more than back away, dizziness forcing her to plop down on the mat's edge.

"You don't belong here," Petra growled.

"You're beating her senseless, you idiot!" was the response. She finally recognized Finn's voice. What was he doing here? If he was wandering around camp, he needed an escort. She needed to keep watch over him.

Looking up at the two arguing on the mat, she vaguely registered that they had begun fighting in her stead. Even several of the Reanges who had been training had stopped their own tasks to watch the fight.

Petra advanced slowly on Finn, reminding Avery of the time back at Valuta when she had witnessed a similar scene. Only Finn had been shirtless then. Blushing, she gave her head a slight shake, pushing herself to her feet.

Finn was still fatigued, Avery could tell, but the weeks of rest hadn't diminished his talent. Having a better understanding of the skill it took to fight at their level, Avery was in awe of the dexterity they both displayed. They were so completely in their element when committed to the act of physical combat.

She watched for a few seconds, her breath leaving her as she admired Finn's skill and use of force. He could have overpowered Petra several times with brute strength, but he chose to meet her blow for blow in a fair fight. In that regard, they were quite evenly matched.

But a fine sweat had broken out on his brow, his color beginning to fade. He was tiring quickly. Perhaps he had less strength than she realized.

"Enough!" she yelled, coming between them as they both lost their focus, concentrating on her. Avery pushed Petra away and placed a hand on Finn's chest, facing him. "We were training, that's all."

Finn's eyes flickered down to her hand, their blue depths alight with something she didn't recognize. He glanced quickly at Petra, his breath coming in loud pants. "I don't know what they've been teaching you, sweetheart, but that wasn't training." He pressed against her, his chest an immovable wall against her palm, seemingly intent on going after Petra once more.

"Stop," she said, bringing his stormy eyes back to meet her

own. "Please, I know what I'm doing." She could feel the moment he gave in, his shoulders relaxing ever so slightly. "What are you doing here?" she asked. "Why are you out of bed?"

"Nevril gave me the all-clear last night," he replied. "You're the one who's been out of it for a day. How are you feeling?" His voice dropped to a level only the two of them could hear. Her heart picked up its pace.

"I'm fine," she said in the same volume, hoping to reassure him. Avery realized her hand was still on his chest, and she cleared her throat, snatching it away quickly.

Petra stewed with anger behind them, all of it aimed at Finn. It set Avery on edge.

"Shouldn't you be in your cage?" Petra sneered at him.

"You tell me. My babysitters are the ones who brought me here," he replied, gesturing toward the two guards that stood near Fiora. "It's not like anyone bothers explaining things to me."

"Way to keep it together, So'," Fiora praised, drawing Avery's attention as she walked toward them. "I expected you to tap out as soon as you felt that first hit, but you took it like a pro."

"Are you insane?" Finn started up from beside her, his deep voice indignant. "I knew you were extremists, but I never thought you'd be stupid enough to—"

"Finn." Avery held up a hand to stop him, grateful that for once he obeyed. Using the back of her hand, she wiped at the moisture on the corner of her chin and wasn't surprised to find that it came away smeared with blood.

"I'm not kidding," Fiora continued with a proud smile. "We'll make a Reange out of you yet."

"Hmph," Finn grunted, adding under his breath, "if you

mean you'll make her a suicidal maniac, then yeah."

Avery's mouth twisted. If only he knew how close he was to the truth. "We're gonna have to cut today short, anyway," Avery said with quiet authority. "I need to speak with the council. I have a plan that may work."

"Absolutely not," Leviathan said resolutely. Finn wasn't exactly surprised. "And we particularly aren't going to discuss this with the human in the room."

"That *human* is my friend," Avery bit out with equal determination, planting her feet firmly. "And he is welcome in this discussion, because we need his cooperation."

He wasn't a Reange, but even Finn could feel the surprise of those around them. Particularly when Leviathan made no move to counter. The old crone merely shared a look with Mylan, seated to her left, before offering Avery a reluctant nod to continue.

Finn, for his part, was honestly speechless. Who was this girl who commanded the attention of such a powerful audience? How had she changed so much in such a short amount of time? It was incredible.

"This plan—this mission you've concocted will result in needless loss of life. Our people deserve more than that," Avery began, inspecting each council member seated in the circle in which she now stood, Finn at her side. "You know as well as I do that this is the desperate act of a dying hope. But hope isn't lost yet."

"So your solution is to let Lunitia secure us entry into the event in Milderion," Mylan replied. "I have a suspicion that is not your only request."

Avery looked toward him as she spoke. "I propose we take them hostage."

"Who?"

"The Minister and Nick," she replied quickly.

"Ha!" Leviathan let out a bark of laughter, the room erupting into murmurs of disbelief. This wasn't going to work.

Avery had filled him in on enough details on the way for him to know the Origin already had a mission in place. And it was one blazing destructive plan. Whatever Avery was hoping she could accomplish with this new scheme of hers, the Origin wouldn't cooperate. They were unreachable.

"Listen to me!" Avery commanded, the room falling silent as she cut the air with her hand. Finn tensed. "If we take them under our control, we can force them to confess to the duplicity of the Federation. It could plant the seed of doubt in the minds of the people—undo the Federation's power at its center." There was an intoxicating passion in her voice. An acute awareness formed in the center of his chest as he listened to her speak. "I know how much the history of our people pains each of you. But the injustice of the Federation has clouded your vision."

Mylan spoke, curiosity written plainly on his face. "What do you mean?"

"The people on Earth don't know the truth," she explained, holding her hands out in an open plea. "Media coverage around everything tied to the history of the war is completely false. If we could expose what happened here, it would lead to a Federation shutdown. They'd be forced to overturn the government. It would give us the chance we needed to enter peace talks and—"

"And why would humans care?" a council member asked with disgust.

She laughed. Avery actually stood there and laughed at the question.

Spinning around to peer at the man, she placed a hand on Finn's shoulder. His skin tingled under her touch, the peculiar sensation running up his arm like fire.

"Is Finn not proof enough?" she asked. "He has saved me time and again to secure hope for our people. Saved me so that I might have the chance to save you all, often at the immediate threat to his own life. Do not make such ignorant comments again," she commanded, and the man lowered his eyes.

Finn looked down at her, his brows knitting together at her description of his actions. She made him sound heroic. Like a martyr, even. Did she really think he had saved her for the sole reason of the cause? Protecting her had been much more selfish than that.

"At its core, the Federation is controlled by a democratic people," Avery continued. "There are those on Earth who fight for peace. Many humans disagree with what is happening here, but they've never had proof to refute the Federation's claims. Fracturing the very foundation of the minister's leadership would cause it to crumble. That's more powerful than any sign, I don't care how devastating."

There was silence as they deliberated, and although Finn could hear nothing, he knew that they held council within their minds. Avery's concentration was palpable, her features coming together in a frown that did little to detract from her natural beauty. Her freckles scrunched together in that familiar way, making his gut twist.

Was this really the girl he had saved once? She needed little of his help now. Something unfurled deep in his chest, and he had the ridiculous urge to take her hand in his own. To share in the intoxicating power she exuded. But he didn't.

The tent was full of Origin leaders, filling nearly all the available space. Petra drew his attention from the other side of the room, her gaze flickering to meet his. She set her jaw, raising her chin in question before he looked away.

He had been furious when he saw Petra kicking Avery's ass in their sparring match earlier. Already Avery's left eye was beginning to swell. Blazing fools. If they had more time, he would gladly train her himself. And he could avoid beating her senseless to do it.

"I request that we speak openly"—Avery's voice penetrated his thoughts, and he returned his focus to the council before him—"so that Finn may hear my proposition."

"By all means," Leviathan said with a wave of her hand, although she sounded none too pleased to agree to it. "Let's hear how you plan to expose the Federation to the intelligent humans on Earth."

"Fiora," Avery called forward the trainer who had been overseeing the fight earlier. "You know the building's schematics. If we have Finn's help, create a diversion, can we get them out of there?"

"Possibly," the woman nodded. "But the sheer number of Federation soldiers guarding the event will be a challenge. Once Klein is out of sight for more than five minutes, they'll lock it down."

"Then you should keep your original plan in place," Finn spoke this time, drawing Avery's attention. She glowered at him. He ignored it. "In case things go sideways, you'll have a backup."

"There won't be a need for one," Avery countered. "If things go wrong, I'll be—"

"You are not coming," he said firmly, shaking his head as he realized where her mind was going. The thought of her being captured again made his blood run cold.

"It's not your decision, really," Avery pointed out, returning her attention to the council in a short dismissal.

"The hell it isn't!" he said forcefully, stepping forward and meeting Leviathan's gaze himself. "You can't honestly mean to let her go through with this. She'll be putting herself right back into the hands of the Federation. Do you even know what they'll do to her if they catch her again?"

"Do not preach to me of the risks, human," Leviathan spat. Her gaze swept the room, resting on Fiora. "Is she ready?"

The woman exchanged a glimpse with Avery. "Possibly, but... I'm not certain this is the time to test her."

Leviathan nodded. "While your bravery is commendable, Avery, you will be staying in the Origin."

Avery's fist clenched at her side as she opened her mouth to speak.

"I think you've said quite enough today, girl." Leviathan stopped any objections. "We have agreed to your scheme. Be thankful we are giving you that much."

Avery didn't speak, but Finn could see something in her eyes. Something she was holding back. She lifted her chin defiantly. She was incredible.

Stupid. But incredible.

At least she'd be safe. This time she'd be safe through all of it.

"Then it's settled. Fiora, begin preparations with the human," Leviathan clipped.

"Sure," Finn murmured under his breath. "It's not like I have a name." Avery elbowed him in the side.

"I expect a new proposal for the council to approve by the end of tomorrow." Leviathan pushed up from her chair to lean heavily on her cane as she moved to stand before Avery. "You had better hope your precious humans can live up to your expectations, my dear. We'll find out soon enough, in either case."

"All right, what aren't you saying?" Finn asked as soon as they reached her tent.

"I can't believe you did that!" she yelled in response, fury at his earlier outburst coursing through her veins.

"You didn't answer my question."

"It's just like you to open your big mouth and ruin everything." She shook her head. "I would have been able to convince them to let me go if you had let me handle it, damn it."

"Are you serious?" he said with half a laugh. "There's no way in—"

"How did you know I was holding something back?" she interrupted. Avery had enough of him thinking he could dictate to her. For him to try it in front of the others . . . . She didn't like it.

"You know as well as I do that if you let them bring Nick and Klein back here, they're as good as dead. Or worse," he pointed out. "And I know you better than that, Avie."

Avery flushed at the nickname. No one had called her that since she left Earth. Clearing her throat, she replied, "Let's wait until the others get here."

"Others?"

"Avery." Fiora ducked her head under the doorway, Petra close on her heels. "We heard your call. What's this about? What do you need to discuss that couldn't be said in front of the council?"

"Thank you for coming," Avery said. "Both of you."

Petra lowered her eyes. "I will always come when you need me," she responded awkwardly.

"As interesting as this all is," Finn interrupted, gesturing to the women, "what the blazar is going on? What's your real plan?"

Avery was genuinely surprised he had guessed she had something up her sleeve. Then again, Finn had always been able to see through her.

Fiora looked at her sharply. "You have a plan that deviates from what you told the council?"

Avery slapped Finn on the shoulder, frowning. He seemed determined to make this more difficult.

"Ow," he said flatly.

"Avery, you know I can't—"

"Please, Fiora, just listen," Avery pleaded. *You can say no. Just please listen*, she added for Fiora alone. Hesitating a few moments more, Fiora crossed her arms over her chest, not objecting.

"I do want to take the hostages, but not to bring them back here," Avery began delicately. "By the time we got anything out of them, if we could at all, it would be too late. The Federation would come up with a new tactic or use Nos Valuta as a bargaining chip. We can't afford the risk, with so many lives in the balance."

"So what are you suggesting?" Finn asked.

She paused, controlling her voice before explaining. "I want to broadcast their confession to Earth. A live feed direct from the Petralias celebration that night."

Finn snorted. "Okay, now I know you really have been brainwashed," he mumbled. "You've got a better chance trying to refreeze the ice caps than getting my brother to confess to anything. He's a master at manipulation. He's been doing it his whole life."

"So have you," she countered, and for once he didn't have a reply. Turning back to the others, she continued, "I have a friend in the capital. Her father is a huge media host, and I'm sure we can get access to his feed if I ask her. If I tell her what's at stake. It would be the story of the century—they'd be crazy not to help."

Fiora shook her head. "Even if you could get this to work, the Federation controls all official streams directly from the Port Station on the other side of the Gate. You couldn't broadcast to Earth unless you were physically in the control room on the Station."

Avery shook her head. "Not for major political events. They open the channel for the main feeds, specifically so they can offer live coverage. There'll be no barriers if we have the right access code to get through." Thank the galaxy for Megan's dad. Avery never thought that information would come in handy.

Of course, this whole plan was contingent upon Megan. Avery was depending on the idea that she could convince Megan to help them. If the Petralias celebration was as big as the council said, then Megan's family would absolutely be there. Getting to her was one thing, but convincing her to vouch for them might prove complicated.

No one spoke, and Avery looked back and forth between the three before her. Fiora's feelings were on a precipice; she was unable to choose one way or the other. But she was considering it. That was good. More than Avery had hoped for. And Petra wanted to please her more than anything, even if it meant going against direct orders. Who knew what Finn was thinking. His face was granite. Unreadable.

"If we damage their confidence in the leadership," Avery continued, "the Federation will have its hands tied by its own bureaucracy. The Rebellion forces can take advantage of the confusion and push back. We can force them off Echo, reestablishing sanctions at the Gate." She met Fiora's gaze, opening her mind. *We can have peace again. I know you want that, too.*

"It has disaster written all over it," Finn fumed through clenched teeth.

"And when has that ever stopped you before? Aren't you the master of ill-planned ideas?" Petra barked from her side of the tent. She took a step closer to Avery. "I'm all in, my So'. I will follow where you lead."

Avery nodded at her, turning her gaze back to Fiora.

"If we do this," her trainer said firmly, "you are not coming with us."

Avery tilted her head before replying. She'd have to be delicate about convincing them. "You'll need me to—" she got out before Fiora cut her off.

"No."

"Be reasonable about thi—"

"No, Avery," Finn said this time, drawing her eye to him. He reached out, holding her shoulders in a warm grip. "You want us to do this? Then you're not going to be a part of it."

She glared at him. Why, after all this time and training, did people still treat her as though she was so fragile? The reverence was uncalled for and irrational. She was the strongest, of everyone in the Origin. Perhaps on the planet. Not bringing her along was a decision based on fear, and nothing else.

None of them supported her being a part of the mission. Not the council and not her closest friends. Not even Finn.

Especially not Finn.

Well. She'd just see about that. They couldn't do this without her, and she didn't intend to let them.

CHAPTER
TWENTY-TWO

The next week was a mass of preparation and breathless anticipation. The entire camp moved forward to ready themselves for the mission ahead. More than anything, they were ecstatic to finally see their So' in action.

Avery committed herself tirelessly as the date approached. She spent her mornings honing fighting techniques and practicing formations with the team. They still refused to allow her to go with them, but she insisted on training. Should anything go truly wrong, they would have no choice but to let her leave and help.

They had spent the better part of twenty-four hours developing an impenetrable plan, woven with Finn's knowledge and what they'd need to do to kidnap Klein and Nick.

But the four of them—plus Krez to make five since Fiora

refused to keep him in the dark—had worked together in secret to come up with a separate plan. Even though they recorded a vid plea from Avery that Finn would show to Megan, she had no intention of them truly having to use it. She was going with them, whether they wanted her there or not.

They decided to keep their intentions from the other three on the team until they reached the surface. Fiora would then reveal their new objectives and catch them up to speed on what they needed to know.

Linderly was their tech expert. A young girl, no more than sixteen, who was bright and bubbly with black tattoos of all different kinds covering every available space on her arms. She told Avery proudly when they first met that she was one of the only people in the past five years to actually hack the Fed servers. And Linderly's older brother, Markes, who had neon-yellow hair and a hilarious personality to match, was their weapons expert.

Drantz was the third, an older man with a quietness to him that hinted at the horrors he had experienced. His gentleness belied his immense fighting skill. He could hold his own against Krez, who was at least twice his size.

With Avery's help, their group learned to read each other effortlessly, working together as a perfectly calibrated system. Motley as they were, Avery knew she would have little trouble convincing them to follow her when the time came. She just hoped that once she was on the surface, there wouldn't be any issue convincing Fiora.

Her gift flowed more strongly than ever, as though finally having a purpose was all she had needed. Sneaking out of the Origin certainly wouldn't be an issue.

Finn trained right alongside them. He focused on Avery,

upbraiding her nearly as ferociously as Fiora. He was a perfectionist when it came to technique. Clearly his own skill had not come from lack of discipline.

Whatever else he was, Finn was a phenomenal fighter.

He seemed surprised to see her ability, though. The first time she had laid him flat on his back, with the use of her powers, his astonished face had been priceless. It had taken her a full five minutes to stop laughing.

From then on, he had known better than to underestimate her. It was truly exhilarating when they fought together. He was so controlled that even when he bested her, Finn was able to keep from truly injuring anything. He was gentler than she had anticipated. More patient.

But he refused to leave her side. Not that Avery minded. She wanted to keep an eye on him as much as he did with her. Mylan had been able to convince the council to let him roam the camp without a guard, taking responsibility for him. However, Avery still didn't trust anyone in the Origin not to hurt him. He was vulnerable there, in a way that she wasn't even certain he realized.

She heard the whispers that followed them . . . the outrageous thoughts that opened to her as they walked together. Cristane had shown her one evening, after Petralias, the image of Avery touching her forehead against Finn's. It had been a question, Avery knew, but she had been too embarrassed to answer.

Touching heads was a sign of love between the Reanges. It was an action reserved for only the closest of bonds. Avery only vaguely remembered it.

Everyone assumed they were together, and she did nothing to correct the idea. If they thought he was hers, then it could only serve to keep him safe.

She was cautious around him, for appearances. But she couldn't deny that something had changed.

There was a heavy awareness between them now. Something vibrant and real connecting them, pulsing with life. They did their best to ignore it, but it was like trying to ignore an exploding star. The radiation was beginning to singe them both.

There was too much at stake for her to be distracted, so Avery pushed it to the back of her mind. The closer she got to anyone, the more at risk they became.

Avery froze, certain she heard footsteps. For the fifteenth time, she reminded herself that if someone tried to sneak up on her, she would feel them well before they approached. Hugging the shadows, she kept to the edges of the camp, headed for the main entrance.

The team, led by Fiora, had left a little over two hours before. Avery waited until she knew Leviathan was distracted before moving forward with her plan. But she had to work swiftly and silently if she was to avoid discovery. And more importantly, catch up with the team that had a good head start.

Finn had tried to speak with her earlier, but Avery had made sure they weren't alone together. Despite the fact that he obviously wanted privacy, she couldn't take the risk. If anyone could see through her facade, it would be him. And he would ferret the truth right out of her.

The wounded look he had given her when she dismissed him had been like a knife to her gut. But she couldn't deviate from her plan. He'd get over it soon enough.

Crouching by a tent near the stairs that led up to the Origin's entrance, Avery thought how best to approach. There were two guards, kids who had been too young to go with the team. They should be somewhat easy to control.

Avery, wait, a voice called out from the darkness beyond. Nevril, confident and calm as always. The healer had stayed behind as well, as the Origin was unable to spare her to help with the mission ahead.

Avery immediately locked into her mind, stopping the woman in her tracks even as she had been leaving Avery's tent. Nevril was searching for her. She had known when her tent was empty what she was planning to do. This wasn't good.

It's not what you think, Nevril pleaded. *Petra sent me.*

Petra? Avery responded. Why would she have sent any help? Avery had barely spoken more than two words alone with her over the past few days.

She knew you were planning to follow them. That you wouldn't let them go alone. Nevril made sure Avery could feel her pride. Her support. *She wanted me to tell you that she'll be waiting for you. When you reach them, she'll be ready.*

Avery sat back on her heels, unsure how to feel about it.

You know you will need a guide. You can't expect to navigate the city without one, Nevril reasoned. *Now go—I'll create a distraction, so you only have the two up there to deal with.*

As if they'll be a challenge, Avery responded, releasing Nevril's body into her own governance. *Thank you.*

Moons be with you, my So', she added solemnly before heading off to generate whatever kind of diversion she had in mind.

Avery didn't waste it, moving forward as she reached out to grasp the minds of the two young guards at the stairs. As she approached, both girls stepped to the side, their eyes blank and unseeing as Avery quietly passed them, making her way toward the entrance. With any luck, she had successfully wiped their minds. Leviathan wouldn't even be able to tell she had left until it was too late.

Scrambling up the steps carved into the rock, Avery reached the small doorway she had passed through over a month ago. She climbed the metal staircase beyond, continuing up until her breath was heavily labored. She was immensely thankful for the tough training she'd endured these past weeks. It was only that and the subtle use of her power that helped her go faster than the others as she ascended. Hopefully it would be enough to catch up to them.

Once she hit the main tunnels, Avery broke into an evenly paced run. Although she had brought one, she didn't actually need a light in the darkness. Her powers gave her a wider awareness of the physical. It was like seeing with a different sense.

She could feel the others ahead of her, though the distance was too wide to make contact. But they weren't moving as fast as her.

After an hour or so, sweat making the pack she carried stick unpleasantly to her back, she felt the flicker of awareness. She was close. They were ahead, and within reach. Flying out across the space between them, Avery touched the life forces of those ahead of her. Settling on Petra, she reached into her consciousness.

That took you longer than I thought, Petra said as soon as Avery was in her mind.

You knew I would come, Avery responded. She wasn't sure if it was a question at all.

I knew you were too strong to stay.

Devotion rolled over Avery, emanating from Petra in waves. There was loyalty there that Avery had never felt before. It had been a long time since she had connected with Petra in this way. She had been too frightened before. Too angry, still, over what she had done.

But Petra had been the only one to understand. The only one to know that Avery couldn't stay behind. That she deserved to do her part in all this as well. That she needed to.

I'm going to hang back, Avery told her, slowing her pace to a light jog. She didn't want to get too close. It wouldn't help if they discovered her when they were still near enough to send her back. *But I'll be within reach*, she added.

So she followed them, alone in the darkness. For hours she moved silently, nothing but the steady rhythm of her breathing to break the silence. She prayed Leviathan wouldn't be stupid enough to come after her. She was grateful she had the team to focus on.

When finally they reached the surface, Avery nearly fell over with her first breath of the fresh air outside. It was crisp and cool, blissfully lacking the moisture of the caverns below in the Origin. The smell of salt on the breeze was sweetly familiar.

Thank the moon it was night, and they had the cover of darkness. Avery didn't know if her eyes would have been able to take full sunlight yet.

But following them became more difficult. They broke into separate groups of two, heading for the rendezvous point of Finn's apartment. Avery chose to follow Petra and Krez, although watching Finn leave the sanctuary of the tunnels with Fiora nearly had her revealing herself to go after him.

The smarter choice was to tail Petra, who was wise to her

presence already. She would go out of her way to make it easier for Avery to pursue them through the city.

They reached the large building where Finn and the others waited. Petra intentionally slowed as they moved around back to the service entrance, leaving the door ajar for Avery. She slipped inside after them, glancing at the rows of terrain vehicles lining the cavernous space.

This should be interesting, Petra drawled, and Avery realized they were still connected. She closed off the channel to her mind immediately, stopping any bond between them. Silently, she hid behind one of the large columns that supported the building, watching.

Finn left the group to gather the uniforms they would need to sneak in as maintenance crew. Now would be as good a time as any. She hoped to get them on her side before he returned.

Avery gathered the tethers of the group, bringing their minds together as one as she stepped out of her hiding spot. *Calm*, she willed, controlling their response as they registered that she had followed them.

"What are you doing here?" Fiora was the first to speak, her voice shrill.

"I think you know the answer to that," Avery responded, moving toward them. "I couldn't stay back there and let you do this alone."

"Y—You had specific orders . . ." Fiora began, stumbling over her words. "You went against the council—"

"Come now, love," Krez's deep voice interrupted her. "You aren't really surprised, are you?"

Avery met his gaze, returning his conspiratorial smile. She was pleasantly shocked to receive his instant support.

"She knows her value—" Fiora began, but was interrupted

once more.

"Her value is here," Petra said passionately, gesturing to them all. "With us, fighting alongside us. We all knew this wasn't going to work without her."

The other three remained silent.

Markes finally stepped forward, reaching out to clasp Avery's wrist. He grinned as he said, "Thank the moons. We'd have been space dust for sure if you hadn't shown up."

Linderly bounced forward to hover beside her brother, nervous eyes shifting to Fiora. "I'm glad, too. This way I won't even have to shadow our comms since you can connect us with the merge. It's a much more logical plan of action."

Drantz was quiet but relieved. Their spirits had lifted just by having her there. Her gift was one thing, but to inspire hope? That was the true wealth of her power. Avery was only just beginning to realize that.

You know I have to be here, Avery spoke to Fiora, opening the entire team together as one. *This is how we will win*, Avery urged. *My place is here.*

Fiora's will shifted. She would agree to bring Avery along, if for nothing else than that they had come too far to turn back now. Avery smiled, letting her pleasure run over and through them all, relishing in the excitement of the mission ahead. She had been worried she would have to control Fiora completely. It had gone better than anticipated.

"Avery!" The angry shout came from behind her. She was slow to turn, knowing what she would find.

Finn's arms were full of uniforms in the same fashion he now wore. White overalls that featured a pair of green stripes running down the outer legs and arms. He threw the heap of clothing to the ground as he strode toward her, his expression causing Avery to take a step back. But Petra moved between them, shoving him as he approached with a snarled, "Back off."

Finn turned away abruptly, physically shaking. Avery was frozen. She'd never seen him so angry. Never imagined he'd have it in him. He turned back to face her, his features hardened in an immovable frown. His chest rose and fell in rough motions.

She met his eyes, their blue depths darkening to the color of a dusky sky. Her own breath was ragged. "You can't stop me, Finn." Her voice sounded strange to her ears. Unsteady.

With a growl, he turned, leaving them in the darkness of the garage without looking back.

She couldn't be that stupid.

She couldn't have actually snuck out of the safety of the Origin to try to make this hairbrained scheme of hers actually work.

Finn had never been so overcome with fear and anger in his entire life. When he saw her standing there, that smug look on her face . . . If Petra hadn't stopped him, who knows what he would have done?

Cursing, Finn slammed his fist against the shower wall, relishing in the pain of the hard marble surface. Water ran down his back as he struggled to strategize. He had hoped he could convince Fiora to return to their original plan. To just kill Klein outright.

He was willing to do it. Even if it meant killing Nick and themselves in the process.

As long as Finn had the satisfaction of seeing his brother's face as he realized what was happening, it would be more than worth it. They'd all go out in a blaze of glory. Slice the head right off the snake.

But that was all different now. He couldn't do anything with Avery there. Moons above, he could barely concentrate on anything other than her. How was he supposed to do his part in all of this knowing she was in harm's way?

He hadn't spoken to her since they made their way up to his apartment. He could barely even look at her. Not that he would have been able to get a word in, anyway, with Markes and Linderly making such a big fuss over the place as they entered. But at least there were some professionals in their group. Fiora merely raised an eyebrow as she moved through the penthouse with the others, methodically clearing the area.

They had chosen to set up their operation there because of the privatized security Finn had installed to avoid the media. Not even Nick had access to it, which meant it was safe from the Federation, too. Or at least he hoped that was still true.

Turning the water off, Finn dried himself and donned fresh clothes. He'd have to speak to her. Try and convince her to stay here while they continued on without her. Thank the moons he was immune to her powers, unlike the others.

He had until tomorrow night. He had to convince her, if nobody else would. She was too important to Echo.

She was too important to him.

CHAPTER TWENTY-THREE

A very meandered around the apartment for a while after showering and grabbing some food Drantz prepared. It was surprisingly delicious, despite the shocking lack of ingredients in Finn's kitchen. But she doubted he was the kind of guy who cooked often.

Finn had kept to his room, refusing to speak to her since they arrived. Although Fiora was similarly frustrated, at least she accepted that this was Avery's decision. He was merely acting like a child.

Wanting space to think, she retreated outside to the terrace that overlooked the city. She moved to the far edge, sitting down against one of the concrete columns that bordered either side of the glass windows.

Finn's apartment was more spectacular than she could have

anticipated. It was just the sort of place Avery had imagined living in on the upper levels back home. When she had normal dreams for her future. It was wide and open, with broad windows lining every outer wall. Clean designs and modern furniture, the best tech that money could buy. She wondered how loaded his family actually was.

She should have paid more attention to the gossip feeds back on Earth. If she had her blazing wristport, she could look him up herself. There was no way she was going to ask Petra or the others.

The terrace was a large space, all concrete and lined with glass railings. There was even a small fountain surrounded by a few benches. Avery leaned her head against the wall behind her, gazing up at the night sky above. The last time she had seen the stars, it had been with Finn on that mountainside.

She couldn't understand his anger. Maybe he thought she would be a liability to the team. Avery had hoped he would have seen by now. That he would understand, the way the others did. The purpose of a So' was to bring people together.

Having him back, even if he was blazing mad at her and things were strangely awkward between them, was like having a part of herself back. When he was standing beside her... it made her stronger, somehow.

Not that she needed him. She had proved beyond a doubt that she could handle herself on her own. But he challenged her and complemented her to become the best version of herself. She was starting to realize just how important he had become.

"Want some company?"

Avery jumped at the sound of Finn's voice coming out of the darkness, slamming her head on the pillar behind her. "Ouch," she cried, rubbing her head. "Moon above, why are you sneaking up on me?"

"Hey," he snapped. "You want me to leave, just say the word, my So'."

"Don't, Finn. Please." Her voice was soft in the silence surrounding them. She turned forward again, staring blankly at the lights of the city.

He rubbed the back of his neck, moving to take a seat beside her. Her pulse quickened. His hair was wet, darker than usual, and brushed back. He must have just showered.

"And in answer to your question," he said, "did you think I would let you out of my sight now?"

"Oh, so now you're stalking me?" she asked, threading sarcasm into her voice. "That's a really attractive quality."

"Since when do you care about my attractive qualities?" he replied. She heard the smile in his voice, sending her heart into rapid stutters. Were things okay between them again? She couldn't bring herself to ask.

"I don't," she finally managed to say, shaking her head. When did she start taking his stupid comments seriously? Probably about the same time she started thinking of him as some kind of unconscious role model for honorable actions.

Silence fell, making the air heavy and thick against her skin. Her mouth felt dry.

"I thought you were angry with me," she said, her voice hoarse and quiet.

"I was. I am," he added with a dark laugh. "You're the most stubborn—" But he cut himself off, jerking his head to study the view before them. He pulled up a knee, propping his arm against it with a sigh. "But I know why you're doing it. Why you think they need you," he acknowledged.

She couldn't respond, her face heating in the darkness. She

struggled to find something to say. It felt good to have him there beside her. To have him on her side again. Finn's support made her feel powerful. Like she could do anything. Without holding back.

His heat filled the empty space between them, warming her side with his proximity. They sat there, staring out at glimmering lights of the city beyond. The faint sound of passing cruisers drifted up from the levels below.

"You can't honestly mean to go through with this," he said, his voice rough.

Avery didn't know how to handle this version of him. Wise-cracking, hot-headed Finn, she could deal with. But this guy? When he was around, she could barely form coherent words. Her breathing turned shallow.

"You know it's a suicide mission, right?" he continued.

"Not if I'm here," she countered, turning to meet his eyes. The brightness of the moons illuminated his face in pale light. Her heart ached.

"I'm serious, sweetheart, this isn't—"

"What, you don't think I can handle it?" It was her turn to joke, trying to alleviate the throbbing in her chest as she let out a little nervous laugh. "Have you forgotten that I can kick some serious ass these days?" She leaned over, playfully nudging him with her shoulder. "I know you've been asleep for a long—"

His hands were on her face before she even realized what he was doing. He laced his fingers into her hair, forcing her to look at him.

"This isn't a joke, Avery," he whispered, his eyes moving over her. Her own gaze fell to his lips as he spoke. "You can't put yourself at risk like this. I don't care how powerful you are. Let the team go on without you."

"You don't have to save me, anymore, Finn," she said quietly. Her pulse throbbed in her veins, each breath coming in shallow bursts. "This is what I was meant for." His face contorted into confusion, and she continued in a painful whisper, "You don't owe your honor anything. I—I'm doing what you wanted me to do all along."

"Moons above," he whispered. "Do you actually think . . . ." He trailed off, and there were only moments before his mouth came down, claiming her own.

Avery couldn't think, didn't dare to even try in that moment. His skin was smooth against hers, and she realized he must have shaved after his shower. The smell of him infiltrated her senses in a delicious rush of clean heat. She reached up, clasping his wrists beneath her fingers in an attempt to steady herself.

His lips moved across hers, searching for something she didn't quite know how to give. His fingers tightened in her hair, rubbing deliciously along her scalp. He tasted warm and strong against her lips, commanding hers with quiet sincerity. Speaking without words.

As soon as it had started, Finn pulled away. He rested his forehead against hers, their breath mingling together.

In the weighted moments following that monumental change of pace, mortification began to rise. It swirled within Avery, combining strangely with the odd elation that had blossomed there.

She pulled away, the air becoming difficult to breathe as neither of them said a word. His hands fell away, leaving her skin chilled and barren. The silence was painful. Her heart was heavy in her chest.

Avery blushed, unable to meet his eyes. Moving quietly to

her feet, she stepped over him to hurry back inside.

"Avery," he said her name slowly and deliberately, as though coming out of a fog. By the time he was moving, she was already through the door and out of reach.

Fiora looked up as she came inside, and Avery's face ignited once more with heat. Her trainer's eyes widened as Finn followed immediately behind. Avery stifled a groan. She ignored both of them, heading to the guest room to get some sleep.

But even after she laid down, snuggled in the cozy sheets of the bed, she could still taste him on her lips. Feel his fingers tangled in her hair. She smothered her face in the pillow. What a disaster this had turned into.

Sunrise came quickly, and Avery got hardly any rest at all. Drantz had whipped up some breakfast, and they ate standing in the kitchen, discussing the preparations needed for the day ahead. There were roles to be reviewed. Floor plans to go over.

Petra and Finn would head out to collect the uniforms and IDs they'd need for the night ahead. Avery was thankful for the separation. She needed more time to think.

Avery collected dishes, volunteering to clean up the mess, if for nothing more than to keep her hands busy. As everyone moved to the living room, and Petra started to leave, Finn lingered in the kitchen, willing Avery to meet his gaze as she stacked plates.

She raised her eyes to his, feeling the routine betrayal of her heart as it flipped over in her chest. His eyes pierced her, asking her a silent question that she wasn't ready to answer. Not yet.

"Finn," Petra barked from the entryway, "sometime this century."

He ignored her, opening his mouth to say something.

"Finn!" Petra's voice stopped whatever he was going to say.

"Listen, Blueberry." He jerked his face to look at her as he pointed a finger. "I don't take orders from you."

Petra curled her lip, but stayed put. She folded her arms across her chest and waited, watching them as though she had all the time in the world.

Finn growled angrily, turning back to Avery. "Later," he warned, and she felt the pit of her stomach fall somewhere below her feet.

Avery watched him turn without a word, her eyes flickering to Petra's as he headed for the front door. She clenched her jaw before turning to follow him, disappearing through the entryway. This was going to be more difficult than she'd thought.

Finn tried not to let Petra get under his skin, but the girl completely had it out for him. She had since the first moment he met her. Sure, it made sense now considering she had been working for the Origin this entire time, but it didn't really help. For Avery's sake, he tried to play nice—he really did.

Avery, that confusing and ridiculous girl who was leading this insane plan to overthrow the Federation. Why had he kissed her last night? He couldn't figure it out himself.

Well, that wasn't exactly true. Somewhere along the way, he'd fallen for her.

She'd been smart and beautiful since the day she stormed into his cell on the Port Station, bare feet poking out of that ridiculous jumpsuit. But Avery was more than that.

She was intelligent and self-sufficient. She had blossomed on her own in an environment that was against her very nature.

The Origin was not an easy place to thrive, and yet she had flourished. Her gifts had grown exponentially, and it gave him a glimpse of the leader she would be one day.

It was intoxicating.

So yeah, he knew blazing well why he had kissed her. But he couldn't figure out what made him do it the night before they were going into a mission that would challenge them all. What a stupid move on his part.

Now they had to deal with this thing between them, or risk it getting in the way of her concentration. And if she faltered, in any way, it would be entirely his fault.

Way to go, genius.

Finn let out an exhausted breath, running a hand through his hair. He leaned forward on the console of the little cruiser they had hacked to get them around the city. As he tried to gain some composure, Petra's death glare was burning a hole straight in the side of his face.

Finn leaned back, swiveling to face her. "Okay, what is your problem?"

"My problem?" Petra had the indignation to look surprised.

"Yes," he said tersely. "You are taking this whole 'humans are evil' thing a little too far, don't you think? We have bigger things to concentrate on right now."

"Excuse me?" She narrowed her eyes, top lip curling up over her teeth.

"You heard me," he said viciously. "I don't know what the blazar's wrong with you, but you've gotta get your shit together."

"You want to know what's wrong with me?" Petra leaned forward, tilting her head.

"Did I glitch? I'm pretty sure that's what I just said."

After a moment, Petra reigned in her anger, turning away as she said calmly, "I don't have to tell you anything."

"Maybe not, but I'd legitimately like to know," Finn said honestly, returning his attention to the controls as he brought the craft into the loading dock of the catering service hosting the party. He had a connection who would give them all the supplies they needed.

"You should leave her alone," Petra ground out between her teeth.

"What was that?" he asked, looking at her again.

"I said leave Avery alone," Petra spat. "She doesn't need a sycophant like you drooling all over her."

"Whoa, whoa, whoa." Finn held his hands up. "Keep using big words like that, and you're gonna lose me."

"This isn't a joke. Everyone has seen the way you look at her."

"Who said I was joking?" he quipped. "And that's the pot calling the kettle black if I ever heard it."

Her face twisted in confusion. "You humans and your inane references—"

"I just mean that you follow her around like a blazing lap dog. You have since the first moment I met you. What's the problem? Your So' won't give you enough attention or—" He stopped himself, realization dawning. "Moons above, that's it, isn't it?"

"I don't know what you're talking about," Petra replied too quickly. She turned away, busily checking the logs on her monitor.

"You're in love with her," he stated, coming to his feet as the pieces clicked into place.

"You're ridiculous," she croaked, her voice breaking with

emotion.

"You've been in love with her since the start of this thing, and she hasn't shown you a lick of interest, so you're taking it out on me?" He barked with laughter. "Now, that's not just unfair, it's unsportsmanlike."

"Shut up," she warned, gripping the controls. She hung her head, as though defeated. Finn felt a pang in his stomach. He guessed it was sympathy.

"Listen," he began awkwardly, "I didn't mean to—"

"Yes, you did," she cut him off bitterly.

"No. I didn't." Silence stretched between them, but it was more comfortable now. As though they had finally reached the crux of this anger between them. "But I won't apologize for what I feel for her."

"What you *feel* for her?" That had Petra pulling herself up to face him, her mod green eyes flashing. "What exactly *do* you feel for her, Lunitia?"

He didn't respond right away, wondering if he should voice the words, even to himself. He wasn't used to caring so deeply about anything. Moons above, if they were going to die anyway, maybe he *should* just say it.

"Well?" Petra asked, her voice unsteady.

"I love her."

Avery's breath stopped as she heard Finn's response.

Unable to prevent herself, she had kept a line on Petra as they left. It wasn't that she didn't trust them, but Avery refused to allow for any surprises. They weren't going far, so her link remained strong even while they cruised the city.

She had kept a low profile, telling herself she would only dive into Petra's consciousness if something was wrong. When she felt her anxiety skyrocket, she had no choice but to check in on them.

That they were fighting was no surprise, really, but when she realized it was over her? Avery excused herself to the bedroom, terrified Fiora would notice her distraction and ask about it.

Hearing Finn say those words . . . Avery had been shocked out of the connection. She ripped herself away from the conversation, back into her own head.

Pressing the heels of her hands into her eyes, she tried to block the raw emotion warring within Petra. She was anguished. Heartbroken. Furious with Finn. And it was all Avery's fault.

How had she not realized . . . but it all made a certain kind of sense now. The way Petra had acted since arriving in the Origin. Her despondent need for forgiveness. And even before that, back at Nos Valuta. Avery didn't know how to feel. How to react. What was she supposed to do now? Pretend she had no idea? It would change everything.

And then there was Finn.

Her heart somersaulted, forcing her to close her eyes against the sensation. Wrapping tightly around the exhilaration, she fought for control before she rattled the furniture in the room. Without an outlet, the energy sparkled in her blood, leaving her borderline euphoric. Her veins oscillated beneath her skin.

Was that what he had been trying to tell her last night?

But she didn't have the luxury to worry over it. Regardless of what she had heard, there was too much at stake to become distracted.

She moved to the bathroom adjoining the guest room, touching the faucet disc to fill the sink. She splashed cool water on her face. Looking up from the white granite, Avery stared at herself in the mirror. Her eyes had taken on a new depth recently, changing to a rich golden hue as her powers developed. A side effect of her gift. They appeared strange to her, nearly glowing.

Her face was harder, somehow. Older. But she was still there. Her features were still the same. She was just . . . evolved.

"This is going to work," she whispered, gripping the edge of the counter and nodding to herself.

She turned away, grabbing a towel to dry her face. Pushing out a short breath, she headed back to the others.

The plan had to work. It was their only shot.

CHAPTER TWENTY-FOUR

"So you remember what to do from here, right?"

"Fiora, we've gone over it enough," Avery said, grasping her wrist firmly from the open hatch of the black cruiser. "Don't worry." She tried to grin past the nervous anxiety racing through her system. *We've got this, right?* she asked the team, looking to the others gathered on the sidewalk.

Linderly grinned broadly, and Markes shot her a big thumbs-up. Krez and Drantz nodded. They were connected by Avery's gift. Seeing and moving as one controlled unit, able to call to one another as needed. Just as they had trained.

Fiora gave Avery's wrist a squeeze before moving away from the vehicle to join the others. Avery watched her as Finn pulled up into the moving traffic above. They moved on, dressed in black catering uniforms, disappearing into the pedestrian traffic of the city.

Avery still found it shocking that Echo actively used its ground level. It was not unusual to see terrain vehicles driving around on the surface roads, either. There was a thriving surface life here in a way that had been lost to Earth. That died years ago along with the air quality, sending humans searching upwards for luxury and clean oxygen.

Finn planned to saunter in the front door with Petra and Avery on either arm. They'd be forced to admit him, considering that he was already on the guest list. The Federation clearly hadn't wanted to sully the Lunitia name, as the media was reporting that Finn's absence over the past weeks was due to sickness.

Finn had changed over to an elegant blue suit with a high neck, the black lapel cutting diagonally from shoulder to waist. And he'd put some product in his hair, slicking it over to the side in the latest fashion. It would be a miracle if he kept from mussing it through with his fingers.

Avery had brought along her Petralias dress in her pack and readied herself in the same fashion as that night. Petra had borrowed Nevril's dress. It was sleek and red, held up by thin bands of silver over her shoulders. But she had added a slit, traveling all the way up the leg to her upper thigh.

Linderly hacked their wristports earlier that day, reprogramming the data so that their identities would clear for the task ahead. She hadn't been able to revive Avery's, and instead had to inject a false reader beneath her skin. Avery looked down at her wrist, fingering the small bump.

They drove the rest of the way in silence. Whether from nerves of their impending mission or the awkward situation between the three of them, Avery couldn't tell. She was just glad the trip was short, and they were soon pulling up to the theater where the party was being held.

Built in the style of early human government buildings, the theater was a large structure of stone. A wide set of stairs led to tall white columns lining the entire front face. Carved into the top facade was an intricate depiction of the first human explorers meeting the Natives on Echo. It had become more ironic than artistic.

Finn typed commands into the system as a comm came up on the screen asking for ID verification. Following protocol, he touched his wristport to the reader. They got the all-clear and pulled into the line of cruisers leading to the main staircase.

And then they were walking up the stairs, the pathway sectioned off with the soft blue glow of barrier ropes. Bright lights from media vid cams lit up the area in the night. Reporters yelled at Finn, hoping to get a direct shot. The three of them followed the procession making their way to the entrance, forced to advance at a stagnant pace as those in front of them stopped for interviews and holovids.

They reached the main landing, continuing through the large columns lining the building's front. The entrance, two tall doors nearly a full level in height, were propped open to offer a peek at the lights within.

As they entered, Avery's breath lodged in her throat. There were so many people attending, the marbled floor of the lobby was barely visible. Sparkling balls of light hovered in the air above, casting a flickering romantic glow over the crowd beneath. How would she ever be able to find Megan in all this?

"Here we go," Finn said, his voice level and low as he slid an arm around their backs, guiding them into the room. Petra tensed, her discomfort bleeding into Avery. "And remember to smile," he added, plastering a charming grin on his own face that showcased his dimple.

Before Avery could remind him that they weren't idiots, a short man with a familiar face, dressed in an outrageously bright-yellow suit, began striding purposefully toward them from across the room. A woman trailed behind with quick steps, carrying a holovid cam.

"Shit," Finn bit out beneath his breath. "Just let me do all the talking, okay? That goes for you, too, Blue."

"*Don't* call me that," Petra warned, her smile a thick layer of artifice.

"Damn, and here I thought we were gonna be friends," he drawled, his hand pressing against Avery's back in reassurance. The man was a few yards away, waving his hand at Finn with a familiar flamboyance. "We've got to keep the vids on us. This will be good. As long as there's a feed, the Feds can't touch us, so don't be surprised if I . . . improvise."

"Improvise?" Avery felt her brows pulling together, forgetting where she knew the reporter from. "Finn, I don't think that's such a good—"

His kiss cut her off, his mouth soft and warm against her own, and Avery was too shocked to do anything but stand there for the first few seconds. He took advantage of her disorientation, splaying his fingers across her back and pulling her closer as he deepened the embrace, her eyes closing. Avery pressed her hand against his chest, responding to him for a split second before Petra's anguish tore through her.

Pushing against him, she pulled back, scanning his ocean eyes like he had suddenly lost his mind. "What are you—"

"Finn Lunitia, you dirty, dirty boy." The yellow-suited man was practically salivating, his assistant shoving the holovid cam in their faces as he grinned. "Where in the galaxies have you been?"

Finn stared at Avery for a moment longer before tearing his eyes away to greet him with a lazy smile. "Oh, you know… here and there, Mixtie."

Avery's mouth fell open before she caught herself. Of course! No wonder she recognized him. Mixtie was the most popular media host on both worlds. Megan's dad hated him.

"And who are these charming ladies?" Mixtie asked, a bright twinkle in his eye as he followed them. "You've always had varying tastes, but two flavors at once?" He waggled a finger at them, making a *tsk* sound with his tongue.

Petra was fuming, anger bubbling off her like boiling water, scalding Avery's mind.

What the blazar is going on? Fiora's presence was worried and insistent in both their heads. The stress had alerted the others. Great.

Calm down, Avery pleaded to Petra. *It's just to draw attention to us. Stay focused.*

"Making up for lost time," Finn answered Mixtie with a grin. "Now, if you'll excuse us, we really ought to find the bar. The night is young, and Petralias waits for no one."

"Of course, of course!" Mixtie said, shooing them along. "But I'll expect an exclusive later, Finn darling. You know you're one of my best trending topics!"

"Absolutely," Finn agreed over his shoulder, pulling them along with him.

"What the blazar was—" Petra began, but Finn cut her off.

"We gave them a little viral content," he explained under his breath. "Now we can focus, and he won't pester me for the rest of the night."

"Fine," Petra spat. "Now get your hand off my ass before I break it." He pulled his hands away from both of them.

"Any update on the others?" Finn tried to change the subject. Not that Avery minded. Her stomach was a tangle of anxiety on a variety of levels.

Avery reached out to the team, focusing on Fiora. They were in the kitchens, familiarizing themselves with the layout and hiding weapons along their path of exit.

"All good," Avery replied to Finn as they moved deeper into the crowd.

"Do you see her?" Petra asked, her green eyes flashing over the guests. Avery had shared a memory of Megan, so they all knew who they were hunting for. If she was here, they'd find her.

"Not yet." Avery's eyes sliced through the people around her, scouting for a glimpse of platinum hair or the sound of her familiar laughter.

"Keep looking," Finn said, reaching for tall glasses from a passing waiter. Taking a sip of the beverage, Avery relished in the sweet bubbly flavors on her tongue, trying to seem like she belonged.

"How are we going to find one girl in all of this?" Petra said darkly. She was right. Even with the six of them looking simultaneously, it was going to take all evening. If only they had . . .

"Wait a second," Avery said, perking up with an idea. Many of the wait staff, and even the attendees, were Reanges. "Maybe I can . . . ." She closed her eyes, gingerly reaching out with her gift around her.

There! She found one, two . . . five . . . ten minds near her, grasping onto their tethers with a firm grip. Careful to keep them separate from the collective consciousness of the six, Avery probed into their memories, searching for a face she knew nearly as well as her own.

"Avery?" Finn asked, touching her elbow.

"Hush," Petra snapped, smiling at someone who nodded at them as they passed. "Let her concentrate."

Avery ignored them, expanding her gift farther, searching through each new Reange she came across. Surely one of them would—

"There!" Petra gasped, pulling Avery out of her search and back into her own head. "Isn't that her?"

Avery followed her line of vision across the room, her heart lurching in her chest. Megan was right there, not a hundred feet away from them. Unsurprisingly, she had a horde of people swarming around her. She was dressed beautifully in a gown of deep purple, her hair flowing in curls over her exposed shoulders.

"This is it," Finn whispered in her ear. "You're on, sweetheart."

Go on, Petra encouraged her. *We'll be right here.*

With a last glance at them, Avery made her way across the room, anticipation quickening her steps. Chatting animatedly with the people around her, Megan's gaze brushed briefly over Avery as she neared, doing a double take as recognition registered. Her blue eyes seemed to grow twice their size, a smile cracking across her face. She pushed out from the group, breaking into a little run.

"Avie!" Megan cried. Catching her in a hug, Avery wrapped her arms around Megan. Curls brushed against her face, a familiar heady perfume wafting into her nose, nearly making her cry out with longing.

For what she had lost. For how far she had come. For how

much she had changed.

"What the blazar are you doing here?" Megan exclaimed, pulling back to stare at her. "You've been totally off grid for months! I thought you were mad at me or something, when I couldn't get ahold of you— Why would you worry me like that? It's so unlike you, and where did you even get the credits to buy a ticket? How did you convince your Gran to let you—"

"Megan, slow down." Avery stopped her, holding her hands up in a plea. She ignored the stab of guilt as Megan mentioned Gran. "I need to talk to you."

"Uh, of course we're going to talk. You've got to catch me up on where the blazar you've been." She laughed, grabbing Avery's hand and pulling her back to her group. "Where are you staying? Say you'll come with us! The apartment here is amazing, and just *wait* 'til you see our options for a summer fling. We're talking prime choices here—"

"Megan, stop." Avery dug in her heels, glimpsing back toward Finn and Petra who watched them closely. Finn was frowning.

"What?" Megan asked, following her gaze to look back. She gasped, turning fully to face Avery again. "Is that— Are you here with *Finn Lunitia*? And what's up with your eyes? Avie, you didn't get *gen mods*?"

"We don't really have time to—"

"Oh, no, you don't. I get the full download," Megan interrupted her, eyes shifting to Finn and back. She looked Avery up and down, as though seeing her for the first time. Her eyes narrowed, finally realizing something was different. "What have you gotten yourself into?"

"You can't be serious." Megan laughed softly.

Avery had pulled her into one of the smaller auditoriums for privacy. They sat in the rows of green upholstered chairs lining the theater. Petra and Finn entered after them, standing near the exits as Avery explained their situation. What they intended to do.

"You're saying you're some kind of . . . Native royalty? And the Federation is out to get you?" Megan shook her head with another laugh. "You do realize you sound like a complete loon, right? Avery, the minister would never—"

"The minister is behind it all," Avery said hastily, trying to remain calm enough to convince her. "Don't you see? Everything they've told us, everything we've been led to believe, is a lie. It's all so they could have this world. So they could control Echo themselves."

Megan moved slowly, taking Avery's hands in a gentle squeeze. "Avery, I think we should go get my parents. They have a good healer here and—"

"Moons above, why won't you listen to her?" Petra snapped, striding up to them. "Avery doesn't lie. Aren't there any brains in that pretty head of yours?"

"What did you just say?" Megan sputtered, peering up from her seat and giving Petra the once over.

"Or maybe she made a mistake in trusting you, after all," Petra added disdainfully.

"Who even *is* this person?" Megan threw the question to Avery.

Petra's anger flared, taking a step forward. "I'll show you

who I—"

"Petra," Avery warned, holding up her hand. *You're not helping.*

Finn chimed in from where he watched the crowd through the partially opened door, "I have to agree with Blueberry. We're wasting time we don't have. Maybe we should go to plan B."

"Plan B?" Petra glared at him. "You don't even know what plan B entails."

"Well, I know it's gotta be better than sitting here waiting for my brother and the Feds to show up and screw us all over." Throwing a look over his shoulder, he added, "And about that. I really think I should know what we are—"

"Enough!" Avery couldn't prevent her voice from rising as she came to her feet. With a swift wave of her arm from across the room, she slammed the door shut in front of Finn, turning the lock. "You two,"—she pointed at Petra and Finn—"shut up."

When she turned back to Megan, the girl was on her feet, head tilted in question. "What the blazar was that?"

"I told you," Avery tried to speak delicately. "All the stories are true. Those vids we used to watch about Natives and what they could do . . . it's real. All of it. And more. They took Gran," she added, her voice cracking. "I don't know if she's still alive, but . . . ." Avery trailed off before grief overpowered her.

Megan was silent, moving to walk past Avery and down the aisle as she rubbed her fingers over her forehead. The movement was so familiar to Avery that she nearly laughed. They were finally getting somewhere. Megan was starting to think.

"Megan, you are smart," Avery reasoned. "Smarter than you ever want anyone to know. But I do." She paused before adding darkly, "What do you think the Federation would do for that kind of power? What do you think they've already done?"

Megan turned away, looking toward the stage ahead. Petra was frustrated, anxiety rolling off her in the thick mess. The others could feel it, too, but Avery made sure they knew there was no danger. Not yet, anyway.

Be patient, she told Petra, ignoring the skepticism that greeted her thoughts. *She's beginning to waver.*

"Okay," Megan said, turning back to them, tossing her hair over her shoulder. "Let's say I did believe you. My father would never agree to help. The Federation would ruin us if they found out he used his feed to broadcast something like that."

"If we do this right, the Federation won't be able to do anything to anyone," Avery replied.

Megan shook her head. "So you have a few parlor tricks. But Avie, we can't go up against them. They're . . . ." She paused, searching for words. "They control everything."

Avery frowned. How could she convince Megan of this when it had been so difficult even for herself? Megan had always been moved more by proof than words, anyway. Avery would have to do something to shock her. Something to make her realize how important this was. How much was at stake.

Avery reached out, turning both her hands over as she manipulated the air surrounding Megan. Concentrating, she grabbed hold of the molecules hugging her form, urging them to rise. Megan let out a screech as her purple-heeled shoes left the ground, her body lifting into the air at Avery's command.

"What the blazar is going on?!" Megan's hands splayed out around her, trying to control the wavering of her body in mid-air. "Let me down! Let me down!" Her voice trembled, on the verge of tears.

"I'm sorry," Avery apologized, bringing her swiftly to the floor. As soon as her feet were beneath her again, Megan looked up, eyes full of something close to fear. "I . . . you have to understand, Megan. It's me," Avery added softly, stepping forward. "It's still me."

There was silence. Nothing but the murmur of the crowd beyond the doors and the heaviness of Megan's frightened breathing. Avery knew they were running short on time. This had already taken longer than she anticipated. They'd have to hurry if they wanted everything in place by the time Nick and Klein were scheduled to appear.

Petra broke the quiet forcefully. "We don't have time for this bullshit." Megan flinched. "I told you that you shouldn't waste your energy on her. She's just like all the others. She'll never—"

"Excuse me," Megan said, her eyes sharpening to spear Petra clear through, "but *nobody* tells me what I am to my best friend."

"Oh, I like her," Finn said from his place at the door.

Avery felt a grin tug at the corner of her mouth. *Told you,* she said to Petra smugly.

Megan walked the few steps to Avery, bringing their hands together as she stared into her eyes. It was the same look she had given her before hacking their IDs and sneaking into a shady club on Level 1. The same one from that time they snuck a space rat into Saedi Mescuva's lock bin. It was the one they always shared before doing something completely crazy together.

"My father will never go for it," Megan said, her voice shaking. Avery's heart lurched before Megan broke into a sly grin, adding, "So I guess that means we'll have to swipe his cam."

Avery let out breathless laughter, bringing Megan in for a

tight hug. "I knew I could count on you," she whispered, tears stinging the corners of her eyes.

"What do you need me to do?"

CHAPTER
TWENTY-FIVE

Finn was on the edge of his toes, unable to relax for even a moment. And perhaps that was a good thing, given the circumstances. He needed every available bit of adrenaline if he was going to outwit Nick.

"Stop fidgeting," Avery said from beside him, drawing his eyes to her. She stared back, calmer than she had any right to be.

"Easy for you to say," he replied dryly, trying to infuse a humor into his tone that he didn't feel. "You've got powers to stop blasters before they reach you. Some of us are a little more vulnerable."

"Don't worry." She grinned up at him, her golden eyes reflecting brightly against the light of the hover chandeliers. "I'll protect you, sweetheart."

A smile tugged at his lips, his gut twisting as she teased him with his own words. She had no right to look so magnificent. Weren't people supposed to harden as they got stronger? Then why did she only become more radiant?

His hand had nearly burned as he touched the skin of her back on their way inside. He flexed his fingers, the memory tingling, even now.

Kissing her had been a moment of insanity on his part. It was an effective tactic to distract the media—he hadn't lied about that. But Finn knew his real reasons. The minute she appeared in that dress, with an air of owned dignity that came so naturally to her now . . . kissing her had been all he'd wanted to do.

Which complicated things. Particularly since they needed to focus on anything but. She had other things to worry about. And he needed to concentrate on protecting her. On making sure she made it through this stupid idea of hers alive.

Yeah. So maybe he shouldn't have done it.

"Avery, I—" he began, but she tensed. She turned away, the crowd starting to buzz with excitement.

He followed her gaze, his jaw tightening as Nick came into view. His brother looked the same as always as he entered, composed as ever and not a hair out of place. His wide smile captivated the room, while he shook hands and greeted attendees as he circulated.

"Are you ready?" Avery asked, visibly rigid.

"No," he replied, mouth twisting. He scanned the crowd around Nick. "There's no sign of Klein."

Her eyes followed his, her fierce concentration telling him she was speaking to the others. Alarms were blaring in his head. Something wasn't entirely right.

"We should stick to the plan," she said, drawing his attention back to her. "When Klein shows up, Nick will bring her to us," she reasoned.

"No," he said flatly, his nerves rejecting the idea. "It's too much of a risk."

"What other choice do we have?" she asked, focusing on him. Something unsaid passed between them. "Everyone's already seen you. They'll know that we're here soon, if they don't already." She offered her arm to him. "The others are in place. Let's go." It wasn't a suggestion.

He stared at her, hesitating a split second before grabbing her arm and dragging her forward, straight into Nick's line of sight. There was no turning back. He had never had a problem jumping in head first before, and he wouldn't falter now. Not when she needed him.

If she was diving off this cliff, then he would follow her.

The moment Nick saw them, Finn's insides turned. His brother's chin came up the fraction of an inch that only Finn would read as a question. Putting on a show, Finn jerked Avery's arm, lurching her body as he threw a glance toward the back of the room. Turning, they made their way to the auditorium, knowing Nick would follow.

As they entered, Finn scanned for any sign of Petra and Megan hidden in the rows of green seats leading up to the stage. Nothing. He hoped they were ready.

They had a few seconds before Nick arrived, coming into the auditorium as confidently as he had the event itself. He was trailed by two large Federation soldiers in blue dress uniforms.

"Bodyguards?" Finn let out a short laugh. "Nervous, Nick? Or are you just surprised I'm alive?"

"Finnegan," Nick said darkly, using the condescending

tone normally reserved for his lectures. "You know by now that I only stunned you. Do you think I'd kill my own brother?"

Finn's grip tightened on Avery's arm for a moment before he gained control of himself and loosened it. "I really don't know anymore," Finn replied, not having to act. "Which is why I came here with a bit of security," he added, nodding his head toward Avery.

"Finn, don't do this," Avery said, her voice cracking as she played her part. "There's still time to change your mind. Minister Klein isn't even here—"

"Shut up," he snapped at her, shaking her roughly. "I brought her here for you. A peace offering."

"Peace?" Nick asked, his eyes narrowing.

"I've given it some thought," Finn nodded. "You're right. We are family, and I can't turn away from that."

"Well, Finn, I'm not sure what to say," Nick replied, rubbing a hand thoughtfully over his chin as he took a few steps. "This is quite the reverse of our last conversation."

"A few weeks being held by the Origin has a way of changing one's mind," Finn said grimly.

"The Origin?" Nick laughed loudly, eyeing Finn pointedly. "And yet, you look no worse for wear."

"It's been a few days since I escaped," he explained. "It wasn't easy, getting out of there with her in tow."

"I can imagine." Nick nodded his head. He took a few steps down the aisle toward them. "I can take her off your hands, Finnegan. Once we have her detained properly, you and I can talk. It's been a while since the Lunitias were together in public. I have to say, it will be an excellent touch, that we came together for Petralias."

"Absolutely." Finn grinned, hoping it appeared nonchalant.

"But before I do," he said, taking a small step backward. "Hand her over to you, that is. I need to know what your deal is with the Federation. What has Klein promised you?"

It was time to make this plan of Avery's really work.

Avery analyzed the two brothers, amazed that two people could look so alike and yet be so different. Finn was doing an excellent job leading into this. Better than even she had imagined. She was fairly certain she wouldn't be able to lie so seamlessly. Even to a man like Nick.

Petra and Megan hid behind a column on the opposite side of the auditorium, a holovid cam in Megan's hands recording the conversation. The others waited for them in the halls beyond, ready to usher them out as soon as they had what they came for.

"The Federation has promised a great many things to us, Finn," Nick replied to his question. "The Lunitias can reclaim our position of true power on the council after this. We can reestablish what our father threw away all those years ago."

Finn's grip on her tightened. Her heart ached for him.

"If we go along with their genocide?" Finn asked, leading Nick into the answers they needed.

"The Federation has only done what was needed to keep the future of humanity safe. To give our own species a way to survive."

"So the Natives are a necessary casualty? Is that what you mean?" Finn sounded flippant, barely invested in the conversation. If Avery didn't know him better, she would believe he didn't care one way or the other.

"There are things you don't know, Finn," Nick responded. "The Federation, and Minister Klein for that matter, do what is necessary."

"Meaning what?" Finn laughed, a grin settling on his face. "I just have to get used to killing innocent people?"

"We all do things in war that we may find . . . unpleasant. Including Minister Klein."

There. Not a full confession, but it should be enough, Avery told the group as they were waiting for her command. They were there with her, open to her experiences through her mind. Finn kept Nick talking.

Are you sure? Fiora asked, indecision clouding her thoughts. *Klein isn't here. Perhaps we should take him with us. Return to our plan to bring him to the Origin.*

Avery, we have a problem, Petra interrupted, drawing their attention to her where she hunched beside Megan on the floor of the auditorium. *The feeds are blocked—her father's codes aren't getting us through.*

Avery struggled to maintain her focus, anxiety unfurling in her belly. *Linderly—patch in and see what you can do*, she ordered. *We have to keep trying. We have enough to start an—*

"What?" Finn's voice was sharp and tinged with alarm, dragging her mind back to the reality in front of her.

"You thought these were the only soldiers?" Nick replied languidly.

Avery threw a worried glance at Finn, fear piercing her as she saw the muscle in his jaw begin to tick.

"Finnegan." Nick's tone was almost patient. "Did you really think we didn't know you'd be coming?"

Finn pulled Avery's arm once more, this time maneuvering

her behind him. Something was wrong. The soldiers started toward them.

"If you knew all along, then why meet us here? Why let me talk at all?" Finn sneered, stepping forward.

Nick shrugged. "I wanted to see what you'd say."

Krez is coming, Fiora said in her mind. *Stay there,* she implored, trying to keep panic from infiltrating the collective consciousness of the group. Avery controlled her breathing, willing a calm concentration to influence the minds of the others.

Petra, Avery called to her. *Stay down. Get Megan out of here and keep working on that code. Now!*

There was a moment's hesitation before Petra followed the orders. They worked their way silently across the darkened area of the auditorium to the cleared exit. Avery was vaguely aware of Megan resisting Petra, and Petra's ensuing anger, but she was too distracted to note it.

Blastfire sounded from the stage behind, and Avery flinched as the two soldiers went down before they could even draw their weapons. Krez had made it to them, his presence sure and confident from where he stood on the stage. He kept his blaster aimed firmly at Nick.

The others were moving, making preparations for them to get out of there. Linderly had discovered a veil protocol on the security feed. The Federation had merely been biding its time. Toying with them until they were ready to make a move. Now that she bypassed the code, they were able to view the real-time feeds.

Avery faltered, seeing the screen on Linderly's tablet as clear as if it had been in her own hands. Harding was there. Leading a group of Feds as they marched along the edges of the crowded room, pushing past the elegant attendees in an agitated hurry.

No. Avery fought to retain her control, blocking the terror that clawed up her throat. He was coming for them.

"What have you done, Nick?" Finn asked, striding toward his brother. Krez jumped down, moving into position beside Avery.

"Only what needed to be—"

He was cut off as Finn's fist connected with his face, causing Nick to stagger backward to the floor with a grunt, clutching his nose.

"You are no brother of mine," Finn spat, continuing forward to straddle him on the ground. He grabbed the collar of Nick's fine suit, slamming another blow to his face. And once he started, it was like he couldn't stop. He kept punching him, driving Nick's head into the ground with sickening cracks.

"Finn!" Avery cried, running to him as he continued his assault. The others waited on them. They had to get out of there.

"We have to leave," Krez insisted firmly behind her.

Avery grabbed Finn's arm but nearly pulled away when he looked at her. His eyes were feral. His emotions shuttered quickly as he recognized her, coming to his feet. His fists were red with blood, Nick's body lying motionless on the floor beneath him.

"What are you waiting for?" Petra shouted, bursting into the room at a full run, her thigh flashing through her high slit with each stride. Anger flared as Avery realized she hadn't stayed with Megan.

"We have to move," Krez said again, his voice edging on frantic.

Leave now! Fiora yelled. Avery saw Harding advancing toward the others through her eyes. So many Federation soldiers were heading straight for them. They were compromised.

Completely.

"We can't leave them!" Avery choked out, hearing blastfire in their minds. Fed soldiers had them cornered. The other team was completely trapped.

"There's no time!" Krez countered forcefully, dragging Avery behind him as they made their way to the second avenue of escape. Crawling up onto the stage, they ran toward the service elevator that led to the roof.

Krez threw Avery at Finn as they entered the elevator, the four of them breathing heavily. Petra pulled out the tablet she had been using earlier.

Finn pushed Avery behind them into the corner, pressing some buttons on the doorway's control panel to activate the override.

"What are you doing here?" Avery yelled, ignoring the way Petra flinched. "I told you not to leave her!"

"It was her idea!" Petra frowned, tapping furiously into the tablet. "Weren't you following us?"

"I've been a little distracted," Avery bit out, jumping as Finn slammed his elbow against the control panel, the touch pad exploding in a burst of flame and sparks. "Any luck with the codes? Can we get through the block?"

"She's going to keep trying." Petra's voice was low. "It's not looking good."

"What's going on?" Finn asked, moving to peer over Petra's shoulder. She had pulled up the security feed, connecting with Linderly's hack so they could monitor what was happening to the others in real time.

Avery didn't need to watch the vid to see what her mind could portray so clearly. She was in that hallway with them. The Federation rounded the four up, forcing them to their knees in a circle facing one another.

Linderly and Markes grasped each other's hands. Drantz was stoic, a hardness settling into his features. And Fiora was confident and determined as ever, despite what was happening. She wouldn't let the others see her hesitate.

Despite their appearances, fear had begun to cloud their minds. Avery could feel it seeping into every quickened breath. And she couldn't control it. She couldn't stop it from taking over. It wasn't supposed to happen like this. Her plan was crumbling. Perhaps the fear was her own.

They had known. The Federation had known they were coming all along.

A man dressed in the finer uniforms of an officer approached, making his way to the center of the circle. Avery saw him through the eyes of the four different souls, all aware of the death they knew would come at his hands. All ready.

"Where is she?" the man asked in a lightly inquisitive voice.

"Harding," Finn growled in the elevator beside her.

"I won't ask you again," Harding said, pulling out a small pistol and pointing it at the body closest to him. *Fiora.* Avery concentrated on her trainer, forcing her panic down, wracking her brain for a way out. She couldn't let terror take over the others. There had to be a way to stop this.

It's all right, my So', Fiora said, speaking directly to her.

No! Avery cried, a choked sob escaping her body. Fiora was giving up. Pain and horror swirled within Avery, reaching its fingers up to pierce her chest as she realized Fiora had already accepted it. Was already prepared for this.

No. This wasn't supposed to happen. This couldn't be happening.

I promise you, it's all right, Fiora told her again, her warmth reaching across their minds and caressing Avery's very soul. *Just get out of here. I am not afraid.*

"No!" Avery cried, taking a step forward. She reached her hand out, grasping air.

A shot rang out, deafening her with a stabbing buzz inside her brain.

Recoiling from her own mind, Avery severed the merge of the group. Fiora's life began to slip away from her grasp, bit by aching bit. The pain was excruciating, robbing her of all thought. Tears streamed freely down her cheeks, torment blossoming within her chest and taking firm root within her soul. She choked on a ragged whimper, falling to her knees in agony.

And then Fiora was gone, where Avery couldn't find her. She reached out desperately, searching for someone who wasn't there. Her light had been extinguished.

Solid arms wrapped around her. A voice told Avery it was going to be all right. Finn.

But it wasn't. It never would again. In that moment, something had shifted. There was a sorrow in her soul that was permanent. It had struck deep and true, claiming a spot in the depths of her heart. A merge ripped from her, in the worst way imaginable.

In that instant, Avery knew she would never be rid of this searing loss.

"Did you see that?" Harding called up to the security vids. He knew they were watching. "Now, who's next?" He stepped over Fiora's limp body, moving around the circle.

Avery clenched her jaw, emotions running wild. There was nothing she could do. Nothing any of them could do. They had been caught. She had led them into this, and they were all going to die.

Krez's sorrow brushed against her, the full magnitude of what he had lost wracking through Avery as she opened her mind. He tried to contain his emotions, was actively shielding her from them, but he couldn't quell a pain so all-consuming. Avery lost her breath, an anguish so pure stabbing her chest that she wanted to rip out her own heart.

She let out a loud sob, turning over in Finn's arms as she realized Krez was broken. Fiora was dead. His wife was dead, and it was going to kill him, too.

It was her fault. This was all her fault. She couldn't bear it.

Her mind exploded, reaching in a thousand different directions until she found herself flying throughout the barriers of the building around them. She soared, moving swiftly through walls and hallways until she woke to find herself staring at Drantz.

Her eyes jerked to the area beside her, Fiora's body silent and unmoving. Her red hair spread out around her, darkened beyond recognition in a tangle of blood on the floor. She pulled her eyes away, meeting Markes's gaze as he gave her hand a squeeze. She was in Linderly's body.

This was not the merge. It was something entirely different. Avery hadn't just transferred her desires into Linderly's mind. She was *inside* of her body. And yet, she was still in her own. She could see Finn, still. Process that she was lying in his arms.

She was in both places at once. Controlling two bodies with one consciousness. Avery stepped into the sensation boldly.

She might have lost Fiora, but she could still save the others.

CHAPTER TWENTY-SIX

"What is she doing?" Finn asked, coming unhinged as he held Avery in his arms.

"I would highly suggest you do not kill any more of my people," Avery said flatly. At the same time, he heard the words echo from the surveillance vids on the tablet in Petra's hands.

"If you want me alive," Avery said, Linderly mimicking her in perfect unison, "then you will not harm another soul."

"And why would I care about having *you* alive?" Harding sneered, seeing only the tattooed girl on her knees before him.

"You are searching for the So', aren't you? Are you so ignorant to believe I can only be in one place at a time?"

Finn's heart lurched. Avery was down there? In Linderly's body? Then who the hell was up here? Was she in both places?

Frightened, he asked Krez and Petra, "What happens if

Harding shoots Linderly while she's controlling her like that?" They didn't respond. "What happens?!" he yelled.

The others shared a glance. "I don't know," Krez admitted, torment fracturing his voice. "What she's doing. It's not the merge. She's fully taken control of Linderly's body. I've never seen this before."

Adrenaline rushed through Finn's veins as he struggled to maintain his composure. If that bastard Harding was there, then it meant they had anticipated this move.

He hadn't wanted to believe Nick. But he was right. They had walked straight into a trap.

"I'll make a trade," Avery said firmly. Finn's heart stopped.

"Avery, no!" He shook her body, but she was focused on her Linderly-self. It was as though she didn't feel him at all. "He won't stick to any deal. Don't. Please," he begged, knowing that Harding would kill them all if he got the chance. Even Avery.

"My life for the rest of my team," she said. He heard the words come from Linderly's voice on the tablet. He squeezed her arms tightly.

"I must admit, I'm intrigued," Harding replied, squatting to look at Linderly directly. "Is that really you in there, Avery?" He reached out and tapped Linderly's forehead with a little smile. "This one isn't dead too, is she?" Krez flinched at the words, the only outward sign Finn had seen that his wife's death had fazed him.

"You must promise me to let them go," she demanded. "I won't harm anyone, and I'll do as you say. But I want everyone in this building released with their freedom."

Harding stood to pace, as though debating his options. But Finn knew. Harding would never let them go.

"And what about your grandmother, little girl?" he asked

maniacally. "Don't care about her anymore, do we?"

Finn felt Avery stiffen in his arms as she let out a little gasp of surprise.

"Yes," Harding drawled out the word. "She's still kicking, although barely. Honestly, I didn't think you'd give up on her so soon. But then," he said with a flip of his hand, "I'm not one to reject a perfectly good offer. I think I'll accept. Although we'll have to wait until after the event is over. We can't interrupt the minister's entrance. Surely, you understand."

Avery nodded, the gesture coming through in Linderly's body.

Harding smiled, making a small sound of satisfaction, before adding gleefully, "Now be a good girl and come out of there. My men would love to have a word with you and whomever else you've got hidden in that elevator with you."

And then she was back in Finn's arms. Her eyes opened, and she stared up at him.

"No," Petra said, shaking her head back and forth as though to deny the deal Avery had made. "We won't allow this." She glimpsed urgently at Krez, seeking confirmation. "We won't let this happen."

Avery smiled gently at Finn, touching his cheek. There was something in her eyes. Something more than what was going on around them. Something she wanted to say.

But then it was gone, and she was pushing away, getting to her feet to stand before Krez and Petra.

"Open the doors," she told Petra, peering at the tablet that controlled the elevator since Finn had fried the panel.

"No," Petra said immediately, taking a step back.

"Open them." Avery looked up, her voice liquid steel as she commanded, "Or I'll force you to."

Petra turned away, unable to follow Avery's suicidal command.

Krez grabbed the tablet from her. He typed in the override commands, activating the emergency release sequence. They began to move back down toward ground level.

"What have you done?" Finn asked, bewildered. There was no way any of them was making it out of this alive. Avery had just made sure the Federation had all the ammunition they would ever need.

Megan pressed against a wall as the Federation soldiers marched past her, clutching the second tablet she had stolen from her father's bags to her chest. Her feet ached in her tall heels, and she cursed herself for the thousandth time for wearing the impractical things.

Then again, it wasn't like she knew her best friend was going to show up and ask her to help in a mission to overturn the Federation.

She watched as the soldiers made their way purposefully toward the auditorium where Petra had returned to help Avery. This whole idea was insane, from start to finish. Was she really going along with it?

Of course she was. This was Avery, not some stranger. And Megan was smart enough to understand what the ambassador had been saying. He *was* in league with Minister Klein, and they were hiding something. Something big. Something that even Avery hadn't told her yet.

Avery was the kind of person who was quiet, always letting

Megan lead. It had only been a few months since they were last together, and yet she was entirely changed. Avery commanded these people like it came naturally to her. What had she been through in so short a time? How could so much have changed?

Megan berated herself for shrugging off Avery's absence. Comms were usually spotty when they visited Echo, but she should have known something was wrong when Avery went silent. She had let herself get swept up into the excitement of her own drama, as per usual, and Avery had been out there suffering.

But Avery was there now, and she needed her help. Megan wouldn't let her down this time.

Alone again, Megan moved farther down the dimly lit corridor, keeping against the wall. She pulled the tablet out and spent a few minutes trying to run more code.

No use. The blazing thing was too secure for her to even think about cracking. She may have been first in their class, but Megan had no idea how to get past it. The likelihood of them being able to bypass it remotely was slim, if they could do it at all. It would need to be done manually, and on the Station itself. Although how they'd be able to get there was a mystery.

But she'd made a promise. Petra refused to go back and help the others until Megan swore to do everything in her power to get the message out. Avery needed this to work. She was the one counting on them. On her.

Megan wondered frantically if she should go to her father. Surely, he'd be able to help them. He'd want to do the right thing. But if Avery could barely convince her, what hope did Megan have in persuading him? They weren't exactly on good terms lately. He'd brush it off as another one of her attempts to get attention. If she wanted to help, she'd have to do it alone.

Trying a new idea, she got to work on the tablet in her hands. She had linked it with Petra's wristport before they separated. Maybe she could still get a message to her.

"Keep moving!" a voice barked from the direction the soldiers had gone, pulling her gaze up. "We've got to get them to the Station before any of these damned civilians catch wind of it." She flushed, realizing the group was heading back. Directly toward her.

Megan clutched the tablet in one hand, moving it behind her body, away from the approaching Feds. She started walking toward them, stumbling ever so slightly in her best attempt at appearing drunk.

She snuck a look at the formation as they passed, seeing a soldier carrying a heap of pale green over one shoulder. She gasped, truly losing her step. She recognized Avery's pale face as her head was jostled by the soldier's movements. She was unconscious, a bloody gash oozing from the side of her head.

"Can I help you, ma'am?"

Megan flinched, jerking her eyes to the man standing before her as she noticed she had stopped to stare. He was older, gray hair sneaking up his temples, and he wore the insignia she recognized as a captain in the Federation forces.

Plastering a mischievous smile on her face, Megan ignored the furious tempo of her heartbeat. "I can't seem to find the restroom." She giggled, gesturing wildly around her, praying it resembled intoxication. "And now I can't find my way back to the party," she said with a pout. "Could you help me?"

He stared at her for a moment with an assessing frown. After what felt like an eon, he replied coolly, "You're going the right way now to the gathering. Just keep following this hallway back to the main doors." He gestured that way, putting his hand on her back to push her in the direction he indicated.

Megan walked on, trying to erase the feel of his touch. An uncomfortable layer of sweat formed at the base of her hairline, beneath her curls.

She hurried her steps, looking away as more Feds filed out of the auditorium doors. She caught a flash of red silk held up between two soldiers, and she nearly dropped the tablet. Things had not gone well in there.

She rapidly entered in commands as she walked back toward the crowded main room. She had to get the information encrypted before they left atmosphere. There'd be no way to reach Petra's wristport via a direct comm if the Feds took them through the Gate. Megan could at least make sure they had what they needed to finish the job from there.

There was a commotion from the main hall, drawing her attention. She peeked around the corner to see Minister Klein making her way through the crowd, a wide smile on her face as she greeted those around her.

Megan tensed, adrenaline flooding her system. The minister wasn't far away, and seemingly headed in her direction.

Making a split-second decision, she backed around a corner and waited. She didn't think the minister would be blatant enough to directly address the captain after what had just happened, but if there was a chance . . .

Megan hesitated. This comm would be traceable. She didn't have the time needed to properly encrypt the data. Once it went live, they'd come after her, too. She couldn't hide from this choice, or brush it off as a joke.

Avery's lifeless face flashed through her mind, her forehead smeared in blood as they took her away. Did she believe in Avery? Enough to risk her life?

Megan released a short puff of breath. She'd have to work fast.

CHAPTER TWENTY-SEVEN

Avery awoke in a white room, identical to the one where the Federation had held her when they took her from Earth. It seemed ages ago. Had it only been a few short months? She was restrained on a metal table, still in her dress of pale green.

Once Petra had opened the elevator doors, soldiers had swarmed and taken them all out with stun blasters. She hadn't even been able to use her powers to defend them, after Fiora's death had drained her. Krez, Petra, and Finn tried to fight, but even they weren't any match for heavily armed Feds.

And now she was back in the Federation's hands. Held captive in the Station where they did unspeakable things to Reanges. During her time in the Origin, Avery had heard rumors. Had glimpsed the memories of those who'd had family taken. When people were brought there, they didn't return.

Avery was unable to do anything but wait for the fate she had sealed for herself. For all of them. Tears pooled in the corners of her eyes, making the ceiling blur.

She had failed.

They played right into the hands of the Federation. She had led a group of people who believed in her, in her idea and her hope, straight into a trap. They would use them all as lab rats and then toss them away, just like those who had come before. Like her own family.

"We meet again, Miss Vey." Harding's voice sounded loudly over the speakers. Avery bit her cheek to keep from reacting. "I must say, I was quite impressed with what you did with your friends back there. That little trick was . . . illuminating. The minister will be pleased."

Avery didn't respond, refusing to give him the satisfaction.

"Oh, she's dying to meet you," Harding assured her, a smile in his tone. "But all in good time."

"And my friends?" Avery asked with a wavering voice, hoping that Finn had been wrong. That this man had some semblance of respect for the sacrifice she had tried to make. "Did you keep your part of the bargain?"

"Oh, I don't think so." His words shattered her, a soft sob erupting from her chest as she heard what she feared most. "No, we need them for our little Native collection. Would you like to see?"

A vid appeared on the ceiling above her. It was a room filled with people. Petra drew her eyes immediately, standing on the edge of the crowd with Krez and the others, still in her red dress. And there were more—people she recognized from Nos Valuta. At least some of them were still alive. Her eyes tore through the crowd, searching for any sign of Finn.

Moon above, please let him be—

"Looking for this one?" Another video stream popped up beside the first. Finn's slumped body sitting in the corner of a solitary cell, his face a ragged mess of bruises and dried blood. "Or maybe this one?" Harding taunted. Avery choked back a loud cry at the sight of her grandmother strapped to a table. Wearing a sleeveless med-gown, open wounds covered nearly every inch of her skin, as though she had been slashed hundreds of times. What had they done to her?

"Oh, she's alive, just like I said," Harding confirmed calmly. "Wouldn't want you thinking I'm a complete liar, now would we?"

Gathering her composure, Avery closed her eyes against the images before her. Through clenched teeth, she asked with as much self-control as she could manage, "What do you want from me?"

"Dear girl," he cooed, ending on a lilting bout of laughter. "Nothing but what you've already offered. Your life."

Finn jerked up with a start, realizing from the strength of his headache that he had been unconscious for quite a while. He brought a hand to his jaw, rubbing it as he popped his neck. Without much memory beyond being stunned unconscious, he could assume that someone had beaten him while he was out cold. How hospitable of them.

Avery. His heart lurched as the full memory of what had happened came flooding back to him. Blazing loon of a girl. Why had she trusted that this would work? Why hadn't he prepared better? He never should have let her come with them. He should have forced her to stay at his apartment. Or better yet, sent her back to the Origin entirely. It was the only place she could truly be safe.

Finn let out a shout, slamming his head against the wall behind him. Maybe they wouldn't all make it out of there. But he would be damned if he wasn't going to try.

He banged his feet against the floor, making as big a ruckus as he could manage with his hands tied behind his back. Predictably, a Federation guard opened the cell door, investigating the noise.

Great. The guy was larger than your average Fed. That would make things a little more difficult.

Finn used the corner to shimmy his way up into a standing position as the guard moved inside, his blaster aimed at Finn's chest.

"Hey there," Finn said, forcing a grin. "Couldn't help but notice there's no bathroom in here. Think you could help me out?"

The soldier gave him a look of disgust, his attention shifting ever so briefly in surprise. The moment gave him the opportunity he needed. Finn shot out a leg to catch the blaster in a swift kick, knocking it away to rattle harmlessly to the floor. Continuing the movement, Finn whirled around and ran full speed to slam his body into the guard. They flew together across the small room, crashing into the wall.

Pushing Finn away with a grunt, the guard gained his footing, eyes flashing to the blaster across the floor. Finn was up in an instant, leaping from one foot in a spin, bringing his extended leg down on the guard's neck. The man crumpled into a heap on the floor, with no signs that he'd be waking up anytime soon.

Finn laid on the floor next to him, pressing his bound hands against the key card attached to the guard's belt. He let out a satisfied "ha" as he felt the restraints unfold, freeing his hands. Rubbing his wrists, Finn scrambled across the floor to grab the discarded blaster, swiping the guard's pass on his way out.

He moved silently through the halls, a single purpose in his mind. He had to get Avery the blazar out of there.

Avery moaned in agony as she watched the screen above her, her cries mingling with Gran's. On screen, Harding held a knife, carving slow lines into her grandmother's flesh as she screamed. It was for her, Avery knew. They were trying to break her.

And it was working. At least, Avery's heart was broken, shattered into a million pieces, like grains of cosmic dust. Her soul was exhausted. Even if she had the will to use her gift, there simply was no strength left in her to do so. She couldn't even connect with the others, if they were near enough.

Fiora was dead.

She had been killed, merely by following Avery's orders. And now the rest of them would die as well. Even Finn. She had been so confident . . . so sure that her plan would work. That they had the team and the will to see it through.

She had been so utterly naive. What a pathetic excuse for a So' she had turned out to be.

Gran's screams shifted into some semblance of raw agony,

the sounds sending chills down her spine as she struggled to free her own arms from restraints. She had even made things worse for her grandmother.

"Stop!" Avery shouted, ignoring the tears that escaped down the sides of her temples. "Please! Don't hurt her anymore! I'll do anything you want!"

But Harding didn't stop. He continued, glee on his face as he inflicted cut after meaningless cut. He wasn't doing it for any purpose. There was nothing she could do or say to stop him. It was merely the surest form of torture for Avery. To bring further unimaginable grief, pushing her to the edge of her own sanity.

None of it mattered, anyway. Her life was over. And she had dragged the lives of countless others down with her.

"It doesn't matter," she whispered to herself, pressing against the cold metal of the table beneath her cheek. She warily retreated into her mind, trying to block out the sounds. *Just let it be over soon.*

CHAPTER
TWENTY-EIGHT

Finn counted three guards in front of the room where the rest of the team was being held. Having the key pass was good for more than opening doors. It gave him access to the main security feeds, allowing him to see where the hostages were being held.

He was moving on autopilot, stopping to take two swift breaths before rounding the corner and shooting twice, each blast finding its target. Before the third guard could raise his blaster, Finn was running full force at him and smashing them both into the cell door.

With a few well-placed punches, Finn was able to get him to the ground. Lifting the man by his collar, he slammed his skull into the floor with a loud crunch. The guard fell limp. Finn breathed heavily as he climbed to his feet and passed the key card across the door lock. It slid open.

"Finn?" a familiar voice called out. Grigg ran forward from the crowd of Reanges, Nova hot on his trail.

Relief struck clear through to his heart. They were still alive. Finn smiled wide, clasping Grigg's arm as he approached, bringing him in for a quick embrace. Nova was close behind, laughing as she wrapped her arms around him in turn.

"How many do we have?" Finn asked, his gaze roaming the room.

Petra's astonished eyes met his as she left her place by Krez's side, where he sat catatonic on the floor beside Drantz. Her red evening gown stood out sorely against the white jumpsuits of the others. Of course, Finn didn't look much better in his dirty blue suit. Markes and Linderly came out from the crowd to follow her.

"Thirty total, although not all of them are going to be useful in a fight," Grigg responded tightly. "What's your plan?"

"Finn." Petra's voice was tight as she approached. "How did you get here? Where's Avery?"

"Don't you know?" he asked, gesturing to the side of his head.

She shook her head slowly before answering, "No. I haven't felt her since . . . since they took us. None of us have."

"That's not good," he murmured, looking away. "She's being held in a different wing of the Station. Presumably they don't want you guys too close to her."

"There's more," Petra added. "When I woke up, there was a message waiting for me." She tapped in commands to her wristport, bringing up a holovid. "It's from Megan."

"Who's Megan?" Grigg asked, getting an elbow to his ribs from Nova.

Petra ignored him. "She encrypted the data, but Linderly was able to get into it."

"How do you even have access to your port?" Finn asked. "Didn't they disable them when they brought you in?"

"I developed a protocol to prevent it," Linderly answered, her eyes bright. "They ran the code to shut it down, but the system restarts after one hour."

Finn nodded, catching on. "And you installed it when you doctored up their port IDs before we left my place."

"Finn, she sent us more," Petra said, shoving her arm toward him as the vid began to play. His brows jerked up. He saw their team being carried, unconscious, by the Federation soldiers away from the event. As the vid continued to play, it moved to focus on Harding in the background, speaking with a woman who looked blazing similar to . . . .

"Klein," Finn said in disbelief. "Megan got a holovid of this?" He looked up at Petra.

Petra nodded, and Linderly interjected with, "You can't hear much of their conversation, but put it together with the coverage of your conversation with your brother . . . ."

"There's only one problem." Markes took a place beside his sister. "We can't get the vid out, even from here."

Linderly nodded. "It's going to have to be from the main control room."

Finn laughed sharply. "Of course, it is."

"Finn," Petra bit out, "we don't have time for your—"

"You're right," he interrupted her, his mind working double time to catch up with the plan taking shape. "I'm assuming you have a way to get past their system. Or do we need access?"

"I put a bug on this," Linderly replied, pulling a small data chip from somewhere in her black braid around her head. "If we get it into one of the main ports in the control room . . . it should do its thing. We already loaded it with the message—all that needs to be done is connecting it."

Finn was already running rapid calculations. If he sent them on to get out of there, he should be able to get to the bridge without being detected. He could still make Avery's plan work.

"Oh, no, you don't." Petra fumed, shaking her head and grabbing the chip. "It's going to be me."

"Petra,"—his eyes jerked to her as he responded—"you have to lead the others out of here. You're the only one who knows the layout of this place."

She frowned, looking away as his words sunk in.

"It's where you are most valuable," he reasoned, gesturing to the others in the room. "I need you to get them out of here. Prep an escape, so that when I find Avery, you can lead her out quickly. Nobody else knows the Station the way you do. They'd be running blind."

She averted her gaze, resisting for another moment before conceding with a nod. She extended the chip to him, and he wrapped his fingers around the small bit of data.

"Good," he said, returning his attention to the others. "Now, get going. Grigg and Nova, you're coming with me. Grab some weapons off the guards in the hallway," he added, jerking his head toward the exit.

With one last shared look, Petra, Linderly, and Markes moved to start gathering people together. Finn knew she could get them to a ship and get the hell out of there. He eyed Krez, sitting empty-eyed on the floor. He wouldn't be of any use to anyone, but at least they had Markes and Drantz for some defense.

"Let's get going," Finn said, resolved.

"Finn," Petra called out to him, and he looked over his shoulder. "Don't let her do anything stupid."

A grin tugged at his lips as he replied, "I thought that was my job." He turned to jog away, Grigg and Nova following behind.

The three of them worked well together, clearing the hallways as the team they had trained for years to become. Finn would have had a much harder time moving through the heavily guarded Station without them.

"Are you going to let us in on what's going on?" Nova asked as they rounded their fifth corner, taking out three guards that stood at a large white door. "I mean, I'm all for following you blindly into battle, but knowing the plan could be helpful."

"Do we even have one?" Grigg added sarcastically.

"Sorry, I thought it was obvious," Finn replied, taking out the next Fed hiding behind a pillar with a single blast. "Save the girl. Send the message. Free the world."

"Oh," Grigg said, shooting a guard who had been trying to sneak up on them from behind. "Just that, huh?"

"Listen," Finn said, his eyes shifting between them, "when we find her, I'm gonna ask you to do something that you're probably not gonna like."

Grigg and Nova both frowned, glancing at each other uncertainly.

"But if you've ever called yourselves my friends," he continued gravely, "you'll do it for me. Fair warning—she's not gonna like it, either."

Grigg shared another look with Nova, and she nodded softly. He turned back to Finn. "What do we need to do?"

CHAPTER
TWENTY-NINE

Avery wrenched against the restraints, relishing in the pain as her skin tore. Anything to take her away from the horrific sounds above her. She would go mad long before Harding ever came to finish her off.

There was a struggle beyond her cell, and Avery jerked her head up in alarm. With a loud blast, the door slid open to reveal Finn. Her heart lodged in her throat. His face was a mask of concentration, leveling his gun around the room before moving his attention to her.

Relief filled his eyes as he ran to her side, the tears pouring from hers in earnest. She bit her lips, squeezing her eyes shut to keep from crying out. He was all right. Thank the galaxy, he was still alive. Pulling a knife from somewhere, Finn cut her feet free, followed swiftly by her hands.

Avery threw her arms around him as she sat up, threading her fingers through his dark hair, tucking her face into the heat of his neck. Finn seemed frozen for half a second before returning the embrace.

For those few breaths, not even a supernova could have separated them.

"Finn, we need to move," a voice warned from the doorway, and Avery looked up. Grigg had his blaster trained on the hallway to the right. Nova was beside him, covering the left.

Finn pulled back, holding Avery's face in his hands, his blue eyes searching. "Are you okay?"

Avery nodded, flinching as Gran's cries resonated around them. Finn threw his eyes up at the ceiling where it was broadcasting from. The video of her grandmother filled his vision. His face hardened.

Grabbing her hand, Finn pulled Avery off the table, making sure she could still walk.

"I'm fine." She brushed his hands away, aware that her appearance suggested otherwise. The dress she wore was half-covered in grime and dried blood. Her wrists were a mangled mess of flesh as she hastily wiped the wetness from her cheeks. "Where are the others?" she asked, ready to follow him.

"On their way out. Along with a few extras the Feds have been keeping up here. Now, let's get going—"

"Then you should go, too." She stopped him, drawing his eyes back to her. "If I go with you, I'll only put everyone in more danger, and I can't . . . ." She gasped, her breath constricting into uneven bursts.

"Avery, we can still finish this thing." Finn reached into his breast pocket. He pulled out a small data chip, handing it to her. "Megan came through, in a big way," he explained. She took it, staring at the small silver square resting in the palm of her hand. "This has everything we need on it. All we have to do is upload it to the control room server and—"

"Time to go!" Grigg yelled, blastfire nearly drowning out the end of his words. Finn jerked around, raising his own weapon and moving forward with Avery at his back.

She grasped the chip tightly in her palm. The metal dug into her skin. She could barely wrap her mind around what Megan had done for them. What this small piece of tech truly meant. She could still complete the mission.

But it would have to be alone.

Avery wouldn't lose any more lives. It might be too late for her, but it wasn't for Finn. She would get him out alive. She would get all of them out. And Gran, too, if she could swing it.

Not that Finn would agree. But she had Grigg and Nova, who could certainly overpower him long enough to accomplish it. If she used her gift to influence them, they would have to obey her orders. That is, if she could muster the strength to use it at all. He wouldn't be happy, but since when had she cared about pissing Finn off, anyway?

They had come this far together. It was her responsibility to take it the rest of the way.

"Come on," Finn urged, dragging her as the four of them made their way through the Station halls. Avery saw at least nine soldiers lying on the ground as they left, realizing how heavily she had been guarded. And these three alone had taken them down.

Good. At least Grigg and Nova knew how to handle themselves. Finn may be a good fighter, but he surely couldn't take on the both of them at once. She would definitely have the upper hand.

Futilely, she tried to piece together something to say to him. Some way to say goodbye. He would be furious. If only there was more time.

Their group halted when they reached an end to the hallway, the path diverging in two opposite directions. Finn pushed his blaster behind his back, turning to grasp her shoulders beneath his hands. His eyes shifted over her face, as intense a blue as she had ever seen them. She should make her move now, while she still had the courage to do so.

Slowly, he lifted one hand up, threading his fingers through her disheveled hair. He stared at her, the muscle in his jaw moving erratically. She knew that look. Had seen it on him a dozen times before. Her gaze shifted in question to Grigg and Nova who stood a few steps down the left corridor.

What was he thinking? They didn't have time for this. Now was as good a time as any to say goodbye. Probably her only chance to—

Finn's mouth was on hers before she could gather her thoughts at all.

Avery lost all sense of awareness in that moment, overcome instead with the sensation that a fragment of him was shifting into her. She could feel, in that one kiss, a part of his soul passing through her lips.

It was both wonderful and terrible, knowing that this would be the last time she would see him. His mouth lingered against hers. Their breath entwined exquisitely as his hands moved down to grasp her own. It was almost like he was . . . like it was *him* who was saying goodbye.

He pulled away, his features set in stone. "You"—his voice was quiet and firm as he spoke—"are the single most spectacular person I have ever known." He leaned forward to rest his forehead against hers, adding in a whisper, "I know what you're thinking, sweetheart. But I started this mess. It's only right I should get to finish it."

And then he pushed her to stumble down the hallway. Grigg and Nova grabbed onto her arms in fierce holds. Avery jerked her gaze from them back to Finn, trying to catch up with what was happening. He jogged backward, away from them, the dimple in his right cheek deepening as he flashed her that mischievous grin. He raised his arm, holding something up in his fingers with an apologetic shrug. Avery gasped.

He had swiped the data chip from her hand.

Finn could see the realization hit her like a sunset dropping hastily into water, the shock spreading across her features in small degrees, and then all at once. Her golden eyes widened as she started to jerk against Grigg and Nova. He didn't have the luxury to watch further, turning to run before it was too late.

He could only hope they could resist her powers long enough for him to lock her out. Finn wouldn't let her sacrifice herself for this, not when he could do it for her. Avery deserved to live. She deserved the chance to help the thousands of others who would be changed by her. As he had been.

Finn fired his blaster at the control panel on the wall ahead without breaking pace. In response, the blast door to the hallway in front began to close. Using his momentum, he dove to the floor, sliding across the smooth white surface with inches to spare before it shut behind him. The loud reverberation of his choice echoed in the hallway, closing him off for good from

Avery and her chance at following.

He could hear her screaming, her protests muffled from the other side of the door. It shook impressively with loud thuds, and he guessed she was using Grigg to his full potential. He let out a huff of laughter, glad at least that she still had some fight left.

Finn turned, taking off into a run as he made his way toward the control room. He knew from the schematics he pulled earlier that this hallway would lead him there directly. Pulling a smaller blaster from his waistband, he rounded the final corner that opened to the main bridge of the station, expecting to find it fully staffed.

Except there was no one there. The entire place was empty. Finn stepped forward with caution. His eyes moved to the curved wall of windows that looked out across the vast expanse of space. The Gate orbited beside the station in plain view, the blue-and-white marble of Earth not far beyond. It was eerily quiet.

Finn didn't waste the opportunity, running immediately to one of the vid desks and using the key card he had stolen to log in with the authorized credentials.

Pulling the chip from his jacket pocket, he set it on the upload pad. All he had to do now was activate the transfer, scan his key pass, and it would be over.

CHAPTER THIRTY

"No!" Avery screamed again, using every ounce of her strength to push Grigg to the breaking point, trying to force the blazing door open with brute strength.

She was seething with rage. Rage at herself. At Finn for tricking her. At the fates for conspiring against her and ruining every plan she had ever hoped to see through. Kneeling to the floor, Avery grabbed her head, rocking back and forth in despair as emotions overloaded her system.

This was her responsibility. *Hers*. Not Finn's. That blazing idiot had gone and ruined her perfectly good plan with his stupidly misplaced sense of duty. He was going to die. There was no way out of this, now that he had gone off to play hero. Her throat tightened, dread filling her lungs until she could barely breathe.

They weren't even his people. Why did he care so much about them?

"He's not doing it for us," Nova said, her voice pained. She looked up at her, trying to silence the rushing panic as she fought to understand. "He's doing it for you."

Avery's heart constricted in her chest, and she closed her eyes tightly in a grimace, releasing Grigg of the tether that connected her mind to his. He came back to himself with forceful intakes of breath, leaning heavily against the wall as he regained his composure. Avery was ashamed she had used him so, against his own will.

Falling to her knees, she buried her face in her hands and wept. Finn would never survive this. Did he expect her to be able to leave him?

"We can still save your grandmother." The comment came from Grigg. He leaned heavily against the wall, trying to support himself. "Finn wanted us to save her. It was his only order, beyond getting you out of here."

She looked away, powerful sobs wracking her body. Damn that idiot. This was her choice to make. How dare he take that away from her?

"Do you give up so easily, my So'?" Nova asked quietly.

Maybe she did. Maybe it just wasn't in her to win this fight. Maybe she wasn't the leader they had been waiting for. There were others out there. Other So's. She was sure of it. The worlds were too big not to house more secrets. There would be others to rise up and take her place.

She could give up. There was no shame in that.

Fiora's face came to her mind unbidden, proud and laughing as Avery had refused to give up back in the Origin. Her voice floated through Avery's memories. *We'll make a Reange out of you, yet . . . I am not afraid . . . .*

Wiping her face with the back of her hand, Avery pushed herself up, coming to her feet. She could do this. She just had to keep going. She had the powers of the So' surging through every atom of her body. A gift that had led her people for thousands of years. And that was worth more than all the feelings of despair that this world—or even two—could throw at her.

The Federation wanted to control her? She would show them what real control looked like.

Avery's face turned to stone. Building from the small spark in her chest, power blossomed to a raging fire coursing through her veins. Energy bubbled up, lightening her head with sharp tingles and igniting her blood in a euphoria she had never before felt.

Reaching out with her very soul, Avery expanded her awareness outward, feeling Grigg's and Nova's essences, connecting with them and to one another. She flew through the Station much as she had back on Echo, moving throughout its hallways in a race until she found the others.

Petra was barking orders, filing the survivors into a large ship in the hangar. She jerked her head up, staring back in the direction they had come. *Avery?*

Wrapping her control around each of them, Avery joined them all together in the merge. She felt their elation, realizing she was still alive. The hope it sparked. She willed their hearts to be strong, and to fight.

Leave, now, Avery commanded Petra, and for once, she did not argue. Unable to disobey the So's pure command, Petra followed the others onto the ship. She would get them out of there, and as quickly as possible.

Avery left them, returning her attention to Grigg and Nova

before her. *Find my grandmother, if she's still alive. Get out of here. Wait if you can, but leave if you must.* They nodded, jaws slack with awe. Neither hesitated as they turned away from her and ran down the hallway. Avery could even feel Gran—still alive, but barely. They would make it out, and take her with them. For that she was glad.

Avery could sense more than just the Reanges now. It was as though her body was in tune with the very essence of the air. She could feel the molecules buzzing around her, oscillating with every millisecond of time that passed. It was a peculiar awareness, but intoxicating in a way that robbed her of thought.

Turning to the sealed door in front of her, Avery reached out beyond it to search for Finn. She saw him in the control room ahead. And behind him, another presence approaching. Captain Harding.

Avery let the anger and rage build within her until it was a painful ache burning through every vessel in her body. Overwhelming emotion was fuel to her gift, and she finally understood how to harness it. She had always been the key to unlocking this incredible power within herself. If only she had realized it sooner.

Her eyes bursting with ravenous flames, Avery gathered the untapped power that surged around and through her, compressing it into an undiluted sphere of raw energy. In one smooth motion, narrowing her eyes, she propelled it violently toward the door in her path.

CHAPTER THIRTY-ONE

"Ambassador Lunitia." Finn didn't have to guess who was behind him. He'd recognize that sadistically amused voice anywhere. He quickly finished entering in the commands to initiate the transfer. Spinning away from the console, Finn raised his weapon to shoot first and ask questions later.

But Harding's guards were quicker, knocking Finn's blaster out of his hand as soon as he tried. He fumbled for the key pass, the final step to release Linderly's bug, but he was too slow. They twisted one of his arms behind his back, pressing a blaster to the back of his skull.

Shit. This wasn't going so well.

"I didn't expect to find you here," Harding drawled, rubbing his hands together as he roved his gaze across the room.

"Afraid I can't say the same for you," Finn countered with

a soft laugh. "This is just the sort of place you'd expect to find evil masterminds."

"Ah, there's that sharp wit of yours," Harding replied, tapping his temple. "You know, your father was much the same way." He walked toward Finn, a bounce in his step. "He wasn't laughing when he died, though. Just like you won't be, either."

"How do you know anything about my father?" Finn spat, all trace of humor gone as rage surged in his belly. He was one step away from getting that chip to upload. He was so close. So damned close.

"Oh, I know more than you think," Harding promised. "Perhaps I was even there when it happened. But it's really neither here nor there at this point. You won't be alive much longer. I just want you to see us catch your little Elite before I—"

A loud boom sounded from the hallway, the screams of soldiers following quickly behind. Finn frowned, his gaze flickering to the white hall that led directly to the bridge. Whatever was happening was beyond the bend in the hall, hidden from view. Harding looked over his shoulder, a similar baffled expression on his face.

If Grigg and Nova hadn't followed his orders . . . if they had let that stubborn good-for-nothing girl talk them into trying to save him . . . . Finn's imagination ran wild in the fifteen seconds it took.

And then she was there, rounding the corner and stalking toward them like some avenging angel. The air around her vibrated, her loose hair floating out from her shoulders. The folds of her green dress billowed around her legs.

Finn's heart sank into his gut. She should be gone, far away from there by now. On a ship with her grandmother halfway to the next star system.

"Don't just stand there. Go after her!" Harding yelled at the few soldiers left that stood in the room with them. The one holding Finn remained, keeping him restrained.

Four of them filed into the hallway, making it halfway to Avery before she stopped in her tracks. Finn's pulse raced, and he strained against his captors with a growl of frustration. She was good, sure, but she could never take on that many at once.

One moved forward, not even bothering to lift his weapon, and Avery broke into a run straight toward him. In one smooth motion, she leapt from the ground and propelled her body toward him, slicing feet first through the air over his shoulder. She locked her arms around his neck in the process, using her exaggerated momentum to swing him with her as she went. A sickening crack wrenched the air. She released his body, twisting to the floor and kneeling in front of the remaining three.

They all attacked together, and Finn's heart stopped in the three seconds before he saw their bodies explode away from her. One crashed against the wall, crumbling in a motionless heap to the floor, as the other two were pushed back nearly all the way to the control room.

Finn was frozen, genuine awe removing his ability to react.

The two remaining soldiers came to their feet, but Avery advanced on them quickly. Running toward the one closest to her, Avery used the man's own leg to climb up his body, swinging her knee up as she did to catch him in the face. Now above his head, she turned to deliver a crushing blow with her right fist straight into his temple.

"Watch out!" Finn yelled as the last soldier pulled out a small pistol. There was no way she could get close enough to disarm the woman in time.

The soldier pulled it around, aiming it straight at Avery,

but it didn't faze her. With a wave of her hand, the pistol flew straight out of her grip and clunked harmlessly against the wall.

Avery grinned. She ran straight ahead, coming unnaturally off the ground at the last moment, her fist raised to plant a blow in the soldier's face. Finn heard bone crunch as she went down, a useless pile at Avery's feet.

"Stop right there!" Harding yelled at Avery, Finn only now remembering he was still in the room. Avery stopped in her tracks. Harding pointed a blaster straight at Finn.

Screw that. He'd be damned if he'd let Harding use him as some kind of bargaining chip.

He slammed his head backward, catching his distracted guard square in the nose. The man released him, and Finn swiftly turned, landing a solid uppercut to his jaw. Unconscious, the Fed fell back against the vid screens behind him, sliding unceremoniously to the floor.

Finn didn't waste his chance with second thoughts. He leapt toward the control panel, extending his body as he reached out to aim for the reader, the key pass tightly clutched between his fingers.

The images before Avery unfolded in slow motion, but even with her gifts she was not fast enough to stop them.

Finn stretched in midair, something between his fingers brushing the vid screen of a console. Harding angrily fired his blaster, a live beam aimed straight at Finn's exposed side. Avery's arms reached out as she screamed.

The room erupted quickly, the scene playing out as Finn

slammed his hand down on the screen and fell to the ground, curling in a ball around his wound. Avery let the fresh surge of fury propel her, grabbing a handful of throbbing energy and thrusting it at Harding with all her strength.

It hit him like a ton of bricks, visibly knocking the wind from him as his body was hurtled violently across the room. The captain slammed against the far wall, the force shattering the vid screens with a loud crunch. He fell to the ground, blood trickling from his nose, his head bent unnaturally. She had killed him.

Avery ran to Finn, falling to the floor beside him. She gently pulled his hand away from his wound to look at the damage herself.

"No," she muttered, the frustration of her timing hitting her with its irony. Seconds. That's all she would have needed. Idiot. She could have handled this alone.

He was losing blood too fast, with no sign of clotting. Tears spilled from her eyes as she fought to control the hysteria that bubbled up within her. Avery pressed her hands against the wound, blood rapidly soaking her fingers. It was warm against her skin, staining a deep and glistening red.

She knew she was watching his life force drain away. There was already a steady pool of crimson spreading out around her knees from beneath him.

Distantly, she heard the holovid they had recorded playing on the monitors in the room. She glanced up. It filled every available screen. Finn had gotten the message out. Thanks to the Federation's own system, it was making its way into every home and cruiser, every wristport and tablet, across the earth below.

"You did it," she told him, dry sobs wracking her body as

she leaned over him. She released one hand to maneuver his head into her lap.

"Avery." He barely got out her name before wincing with a ragged cough. She blanched as blood coated his mouth, leaking out and down his cheek.

"Shhh," she whispered to him, smoothing the dark hair away from his forehead. "It will be all right. Don't speak."

"How did you do that," he wheezed, ignoring her, "in a dress?"

Avery let out a horrible laugh through her tears, shaking her head. "Don't waste your energy," she choked out. "If you talk, you'll make the bleeding worse."

"Well, we both know that's a lost cause then," he joked, trying to laugh.

"Shut up," she commanded, pressing her hand more firmly to his side. He gasped in pain, the grin wiping from his face. She felt his struggle not to cry out, as he endured the worst of it.

"Avery, I have to tell you . . . have to tell you that I . . . ." His eyes were glassy as he looked up at her, a piercing and sincere blue. "I love you."

She released a harsh sob of laughter, before leaning down to press a fierce kiss to his lips. "I know, you idiot."

He smiled at her, his eyes wetting as the light began to fade from their blue depths.

"No," she cried, rocking on her knees. "No, Finn." A long breath slipped from his lips, his eyes losing focus. "Finn!" she yelled. "Fight, damn you!" Panic surged within her. She wouldn't let this happen. She couldn't.

Avery felt her power condense into a tight ball within her chest, alighting with a new flame. She held onto it with every fiber of her being, seeking to control this new sensation. It was so much different than before. She could feel *Finn*. Sense his existence. His pain.

She saw the wound in his side, and yet she did not. She felt him as a living thing, encompassed by malleable energy. She could perceive the very matter of his skin where it had ripped apart, the flesh burnt and torn into an ugly semblance of its natural state.

Avery called out to it, focusing on that wild and beautiful energy that circulated around and through them both. She gripped his life force, wrapping her power around the very cells that made up his body. Channeling everything she had left, Avery refused to let him go.

A pain erupted in her head, worse than any she had ever experienced, but she relished in the agony. With sheer desperation, she envisioned his cells mending in her mind. *Willed* them to come together. Pulling her hands away from his wound, she watched with staggering breaths as the flesh in his side began to repair itself, folding inward and fusing together in a slow and beautiful reformation.

Avery screamed, the pain searing her mind until she only saw white hot light. She felt the warm blood that spilled from her nose as she pushed through the blinding torture, but she would not yield. Not yet.

With exacting care, she forced his body to mend. Rejoining his organs together, Avery encouraged the blood flow to reestablish, bringing life back into him. Finally, with a gasp of pure anguish, she sealed the skin on the outside of his body as the pain overtook her. She collapsed forward, slumping uselessly across his body.

She registered the slow breaths coming in steady waves

from his chest. The soft beat of his heart thumping against her ear. Somehow, she had been able to keep Finn from dying. She had saved him.

It didn't matter what happened to her now.

CHAPTER THIRTY-TWO

"Why hasn't she woken up yet?" Finn stared hard at Avery through the glass of the infirmary window.

"We don't know for certain," Brinstal answered beside him. "All her vitals are reading fine. By all accounts, she should have regained consciousness by now. But what she did . . . ." She trailed off into thought. "It took a serious toll on her system. I've never seen that kind of damage before."

His fists clenched at his sides, unable to do anything for her as she lay unconscious on the hover bed. She was there because of him. Because she had pushed herself beyond everything for him.

It had been two weeks since he had nearly died on the Station. And maybe he had. He hadn't followed the light or anything, but he vaguely remembered her screaming at him to fight, and then . . . nothing.

He came to when Petra was dragging Avery off his body, screaming at her to wake up. He would never be able to wrench the image of her, covered in blood and limp in Petra's arms, from his mind. The sheer agony of thinking she was dead for those few minutes until they confirmed she had a pulse was something Finn never wanted to repeat. Ever.

When the Feds hadn't pursued them off the Station, Petra and the others had decided to come back. Once it was known that Avery was loose and attacking the Station, the whole place had gone into lockdown. Standard procedure, considering the sensitive intel taking place there. Luckily, it gave them the clean break they needed.

He still wasn't sure what Avery had actually done to him. There wasn't a single scratch left on his body. He woke up feeling better than he had going into the fight to begin with.

But it had cost her.

"Any change?" Petra entered the observation room. He glanced over his shoulder with a short shake of his head. She stood beside him and looked at Avery.

They had returned to Echo after collecting what information they could from the Station. In the lockdown, the Gate had been left unregulated, allowing them to pass through without issue.

Avery's idea had worked. Finn still couldn't believe it. In the scandal of the holovid release, the council had been forced to call an emergency investigation into the minister's position. The Federation had halted all movement on Echo, allowing for the remaining Reange leaders and sympathizers to band together and establish some semblance of control. Passage through the Gate was suspended, meaning no one could get through, except by official petition to Armistice officials.

Nick had disappeared. Finn wasn't sure if he had killed him when they fought in the auditorium. If Avery hadn't pulled him off Nick, he didn't know if he would have been able to stop. And what was worse, Finn wasn't sure what would have been better. If Nick survived, they certainly hadn't seen the last of him.

The Rebellion leaders had begun the process of moving their base into Milderion, reclaiming the huge building that had served as the government capital for hundreds of years. The tall silver structure rose above the skyline, sweeping in a wide arc as it curved into the sky. As Echo rebuilt its government, it would serve as a central location for anything the leaders and workers could ever need.

It's where they currently were keeping Avery, in the medical facilities located on the lower levels. Brinstal was ecstatic to be back in her old labs, as the tech was far superior to even what they had in Nos Valuta.

"Megan's been asking if she can visit," Petra said quietly, pulling Finn from his thoughts. He raised a brow, not replying. Petra actually tolerating a human? The strange friendship that had formed between those two still didn't make sense to him.

"You know that's not possible," Brinstal replied succinctly.

Tensions between humans and the Reange were at an all-time high. Strict regulations had been put into place preventing any human from entering the capital building until official terms of the new Armistice could be negotiated. Ones that would actually be followed this time. Beside himself, of course, as he had official business as a representative. That, and the fact that he threatened to crash his cruiser into the lobby if they didn't let him see her. But who counted that little detail, anyway?

"This is a secure facility," Brinstal continued. "Perhaps in a few days after we move her—"

"She's being moved?" Finn peered sharply at the healer.

Brinstal nodded. "There's no need to keep her in observation. Her body just needs time to heal. There's a suite of rooms being prepared for her and her grandmother on the upper level living quarters."

"So you're keeping her here," Finn said, more to himself than the others. Although they tolerated his presence, Finn wasn't allowed to live there, as Petra and the others did. He didn't realize until that moment that he had hoped she would . . . . What? Come and stay with him in his apartment, grandmother in tow? Yeah, that wouldn't be awkward at all.

Avery's grandmother was being kept in a medically induced coma as they healed her wounds. Brinstal suspected the Federation had been performing some kind of experimentation on her as well. She seemed to know more, but clearly wasn't revealing anything to Finn.

They were bringing her out of it in a few more days, anyway, expecting a full recovery. At least Finn could give Avery that. They had rescued her grandmother after all.

"Is there anything we can do?" Petra asked. "There has to be some way to bring her around . . . ."

Brinstal placed a consoling hand on her shoulder, giving them both a resigned smile. "Wait. Just be patient. She'll come back to us when she's ready."

Finn turned back to the glass. *Wait?* That was all she could give them? Well, that was just great. The one thing he could do was the one thing he was the worst at.

At least he knew Petra would be utter shit at it, too.

CHAPTER THIRTY-THREE

Avery opened her eyes to the brightness of natural sunlight. Wincing, she raised her hand to try to bat the annoyance away. But she moved slowly, her limbs clumsy and unnaturally heavy.

Someone gasped in the quiet of the room, footsteps tearing away in a rush before Avery could even tell who had been there.

Struggling, she rubbed her eyes, leaning up in the soft bed to look around. She was in a beautiful room, decorated in soft creams and blues. A balcony opened from the wall of windows beside her bed, revealing mountains and an azure sky.

Echo. She was back on Echo.

"Avery." A painfully familiar voice filled the silence, jerking Avery's eyes to the doorway.

"Gran?" Tears immediately burst from Avery as she

hunched over herself, unable to contain the intense wave of relief that surfaced.

Her grandmother bolted from the door to throw herself onto the bed, taking Avery into her arms. She gave into the sobs as Gran held her, gently stroking her hair.

"Shhh," Gran said, quieting her. "Shhh, it's all right now. It's over."

They rocked back and forth for awhile before Avery regained her composure, pulling back to look into Gran's eyes. Grigg and Nova had done as she'd asked. They had saved her. She smiled, throwing her arms around her grandmother, hugging as tightly as her exhausted muscles would allow.

Someone else entered, hovering at the doorway. Avery felt her presence even before she looked up from her embrace. Petra's green eyes shifted away, not wanting to intrude on such a private moment. Closing her eyes, Avery realized there were more. Reanges all around her and throughout the building below. Her connection was stronger than she had ever felt before, her perception of the others a seamless extension of herself. As though she was partially in the merge itself. Without even trying.

"What happened?" she asked, pulling back from Gran to wipe some of the remaining wetness away from her face. "The last thing I remember . . . ." With a start, her eyes jerked to Petra. "Where's Finn?"

Gran caressed Avery's cheek and smiled softly. "I think we'd better leave you to rest up a little. There'll be time for more questions later, Avie."

She was tired, she would admit. It seemed as though even this short exchange had drained her. But she couldn't sleep yet.

Where is he? she asked Petra, ignoring Gran, who tried to

tuck her back into the sheets. But sleep was already pulling her under.

The next time she awoke, someone was pressing a scanner to her wrist, the cold metal of the tablet chilling her skin. Avery blinked, confused. The sun was higher, making the room brighter than before. It was earlier in the morning. . . . Had she slept through the night?

"Welcome back." A voice drew her eyes to the person holding the device, seated beside her bed.

"Lissande?" Avery's throat was dry, her voice cracking.

"Here." Lissande reached for a glass of water by the bed and helped Avery sit up to take a few thirsty swallows.

"What are you doing here?" Avery was scared to even ask where she was. Or what had happened. "Where is everyone? Is Gran—"

"She's fine," Lissande assured her, a secretive smile spreading across her face. "And so are you," she added, studying the chart. "It's been a couple days since you last woke up."

"A few days?" Avery gasped, gripping the sheets.

"Yes, well," Lissande said delicately, clearing her throat. "It's been a little over three weeks since your escapade on the Station."

"Moons above," Avery whispered, dropping her head into her hands. So much time had passed. So many things could have gone wrong. Surely, she had been needed in that time.

"I sent Linderly to let the others know you were coming around," she said, gathering her instruments and returning them to her bag.

"Linderly was here?" Avery asked, suddenly ravenous for information.

"Mhmm," she answered. "They've all been taking turns

watching over you. It seems you've gathered quite the group of companions. Finn, in particular, was not happy that he missed you the last time you—"

"Finn's all right?" Her eyes jerked up, a thrill surging through her chest.

Avery's consciousness suddenly ripped away from her. She shifted through every Reange she could sense, moving throughout the building as she had on the Station with alarming speed. Each and every person's awareness opened to her, allowing her to see through their eyes. She gasped, the feeling both effortless and strangely new.

And then she saw him, or someone did. He was running.

Bolting through the hallways, he knocked into people as he went, careless in his haste. Somehow, she knew he was close. Knew the layout of the building without having explored it herself. She followed him in the minds of the others he passed. He didn't slow his pace, bypassing the elevators and taking the stairs up a side hallway, ascending two at a time. She lost sight of him as he barreled around a corner to the path that led to her room, away from any Reanges who could provide her a view of him.

And then he was there. Panting with heavy breaths and mussed hair, staring at her from the doorway. Lissande smiled knowingly at him as she passed. She threw a last look at Avery before leaving the two of them alone.

Finn's eyes were fixed on her, never faltering even as Lissande left, his chest rising and falling as he struggled to catch his breath. Silence stretched between them, thickening the air with an exhilarating electricity.

"You're awake," he said stupidly, a small grin pulling at his mouth.

"You noticed." More silence.

Avery had never wished more that she could read his thoughts. She had never known him to be so quiet. Even when he had been dying, Finn hadn't been able to shut up.

He walked slowly to her side, his eyes sliding to her hands where they rested in her lap. The bed gave slightly beneath his weight as he sat down, taking her hand in his own. His warm skin brushed over hers, their fingers entwining. Avery's throat felt dry again.

"You . . . ." He trailed off quietly, ducking his head before meeting her eyes. Taking a slow breath, he tried again. "You healed me."

Her face grew hot, the memory of the experience searing her from the inside out. She *had* healed him. How had she done that? She could barely remember what had come over her in that moment. What she had done . . . he was human. There was no reason it should have worked. Remembering it now, what had passed between them seemed incredibly intimate. She had reached into him. She had brought him back from the brink of death. Perhaps death itself.

She couldn't hold his gaze, looking down at their hands joined on her lap. Using her free hand, she ran her thumb over his, tracing small anxious circles on his skin. She swallowed around the lump that formed in her throat.

"Avery!" Grigg stormed into the room, a huge smile on his face. He didn't slow down, pushing Finn out of the way to bring Avery halfway off the bed into a warm embrace. Nova entered not far behind, along with Markes and Linderly, wide smiles on all their faces.

"All right, all right," Finn said, pushing Grigg back. "We get it. You're happy she's awake." Grigg let Finn pull him, grabbing his head in a lock as they dissolved into a heap of playful grappling.

"We can't believe you actually did it," Linderly squealed, bouncing on her toes as she came to Avery's side.

"Do they always do that?" Markes asked, eyeing Finn and Grigg as he followed his sister.

"You have no idea," Nova replied, placing a hand on her hip.

Avery laughed, the sound lighter than she had heard from her own lips in the past few months. Finn finally shrugged Grigg off, locking eyes with Avery. It sent a pang straight through her heart. She looked away nervously, returning her attention to the others.

"You didn't think I would?" she finally responded to Linderly, a hand going to her chest in mock offense. "I'm hurt."

"Nah, we knew you had it in you," Grigg said cheerfully, slapping Finn on the back. Hard. "*This* was the one who thought you couldn't handle it."

"Yeah," Avery said, turning a sharp eye to Finn, "about that—"

"Grigg, have I ever told you how much I just love having you around?" Finn interrupted, smiling broadly at his friend before immediately darkening to a glare. "Now leave," he said flatly.

"As much as we'd love to let you and Finn get back to . . . ." Nova trailed off with a suggestive wave of her hand. "Whatever was going on in here before we showed up, the council is already asking for you."

Avery's throat grew tight. Her gaze flickered briefly to Finn before she replied, "Already? They can't let me, I dunno, wake up first?"

Nova shrugged apologetically. "I don't give the orders. They wanted to speak with you as soon as Brinstal gave you the all-clear."

Finn helped Avery from bed, and she was surprised that she actually didn't feel too incredibly drained. Granted, she had been asleep for nearly a month. But all considered, things could have been worse.

When she asked about Petra, Avery was shocked to hear she was with Megan, outside of the capital building. Finn and the others caught her up to speed on the state of Echo as they made their way to the council rooms.

Her plan had ultimately worked, but things were still delicate. The next few months would be critical to establishing regulations between Echo and Earth. That Megan, a human, wasn't able to even set foot in this building wasn't a great start. It didn't sit well, knowing that the council was already gravitating toward another extreme.

Finn refused to leave her side, standing behind her seat instead of taking his own when they reached the council's grand hall. The Elders praised her, giving her pats on the back and a few hugs as she entered. Her eyes widened when she saw Mylan sitting among the faces there, though Leviathan was nowhere to be seen. She tested his mind but was met with a steel wall that she frankly didn't have the strength to challenge at the moment. Perhaps the old woman was closer than she thought. . . .

Avery let it go, focusing on the meeting itself as the council debriefed her on the situation. The gratitude and reverence that buffeted her during those first meetings was overwhelming.

The Federation was still present on Echo, but the tumultuous situation of Earth's government had them at a standstill. The Rebellion forces had risen up, taking back the cities at the first sign of trouble some weeks ago. With the Gate closed and Federation interaction effectively stalled, they were even able to reclaim Milderion.

Avery was in awe that so much could happen in the span of a few weeks. It seemed incredible, that the tides had turned so dramatically for them. But nothing was solid until the investigation into Klein's leadership could be concluded. The holovid Megan had been able to capture wasn't exactly solid evidence of criminal activity. It was merely enough to spark an inquiry, garnering the outrage of human sympathizers.

The journey toward peace was far from over. But her people finally had a chance.

The rest of the day passed in a blur as Avery rotated among dignitaries, officials, and others who wanted to meet with her. Her celebrity in the capital wasn't an ideal situation. She hoped it would soon die down as they became more comfortable with the idea of a So' in their midst.

Finn was always there, watching her patiently from the sidelines. They hadn't been alone together since that morning, and Avery was glad that the demands on her time gave her an excuse to avoid it. She could barely even meet his eyes.

Why was it so difficult to think of what he meant to her? When he was dying, Avery had known without a doubt what she felt for him. But she had been asleep for a long time. And things were different now.

Already, they were preparing her for a role she didn't quite understand. Her position in the new government would be integral, despite her age. And, more than anything, Avery wanted to have a say in the decisions being made from there. If her role as a So' gave her a powerful voice, then she would never take that opportunity for granted.

But it meant her life would change. In more ways than one.

CHAPTER
THIRTY-FOUR

"Something on your mind, my So'?" Finn's voice brushed against her ears as Avery looked out from the balcony of her suites.

Twenty levels up, the view was absolutely spectacular. Avery supposed she didn't mind the extra responsibilities, if she got to live in a place like this. She watched the sun sink into the mountains, the sky turning deep shades of orange and pink as the clouds melted into the rays of light.

"Just thinking," she said, keeping her eyes focused away from him. His hand rested next to hers on the railing, his fingers not an inch away. Her chest tightened.

As she expected, Finn had been reluctant to leave her side at all over the past week since she awoke. He lingered in the evenings, only leaving the capital building to go home and sleep, and he was always there by the time she woke up in the mornings. He came with her to meetings, to her medical checkups . . . . He even made a habit of dining with her and Gran in their quarters.

She smiled, loving that Finn had been able to charm her grandmother. It seemed they had become close while Avery had been asleep. And Gran actually liked him. Would wonders never cease?

Not that she minded him refusing to leave her side. His presence was a boon to her strength. A constant reminder of the power she had within herself. But she was reluctant to give in to her feelings. They hadn't spoken of it, or been anything other than friendly since she awoke. There hadn't been an opportunity.

If she was honest with herself, Avery was frightened. Of what it would mean to open herself to that kind of vulnerability. What she had felt on the Station . . . what she had done for him. . . . She wasn't sure she could choose anything over Finn. And that was dangerous, for more people than just herself.

Avery turned her face to the breeze, relishing the warm, salty air as it swept against her face. Her loose hair whipped about her shoulders. Finn shifted, the side of his arm brushing against hers.

"Avery." His warm voice caressed her. Her stomach flipped. "I've been wanting to . . . ." He paused, turning fully toward her.

"Yeah?" she asked, gripping the railing as she looked at him in the orange light of the fading sun. His eyes were nearly gray as they moved across her face. Her breath caught.

"It's just that . . . ." His voice faded as she leaned toward him, pulled in by some invisible lure. "Moons above, you're beautiful," he whispered, tugging her the rest of the way to him.

And he was kissing her again, and it was marvelous and terrifying, and she never wanted it to end.

He moved them, pressing her against the glass railing, threading his fingers through her hair. Leaning into her, they explored one another over and over, until she felt ready to crawl out of her own skin.

He tasted of sweet wine and pletch pudding. And something else. Something entirely Finn. She stifled a laugh against his mouth.

"Call me crazy,"—Finn pulled away briefly to say against her lips—"but I think it's generally acknowledged that women aren't supposed to laugh when you're trying to seduce them."

"Oh, is that what you're doing?" she asked playfully. Finn moved his lips to her exposed neck. Desire curled low in her belly, and she had a hard time adding, "I hadn't noticed."

He nipped at her, and she giggled before pulling back to study his face. There was a smile in his eyes. A lightness that she had never seen before in him. It was breathtaking.

"Finn, I . . . ." Her eyes riveted on the base of his neck. She had to explain to him why she had been so distant. Why she couldn't say the words to him. She owed him at least that. "I just wanted to—"

He stopped her with another kiss, his lips pressing against hers with more urgency. And she gave into it, returning his embrace with as much passion, if not more. Could she deny this? The love she felt for him was consuming and frightening. It was, perhaps, the only thing she couldn't control in this new world that was building up around her.

She pulled away from him, placing her hands on his chest.

The sounds of their heavy breathing mingled with the wind surging around them. She stared into his eyes, speaking to him without words. And without her gift. There had always been this strange connection between them, even from the beginning. Acknowledging it felt as natural as breathing.

He made her stronger. More aware of the power within herself. She wouldn't fight that.

"I love you," she blurted out, too loudly.

A grin spread slowly across his face. He pressed his forehead against hers. "I know, you idiot."

She laughed as he threw her words back in her face. Wrapping her arms around his waist, Avery tucked her head against his chest. His own arms wove around her, his chin rubbing the top of her head softly.

"What now?" His voice drifted down to her, rumbling through his chest beneath her cheek.

"We keep moving forward," she replied, looking out at the twinkling lights of the city coming alive in the dwindling light. Her people weren't out of the dark yet, but they had a much better chance at a future.

She would continue down this path she had chosen, confident in her vision for the future. For where she wanted to lead them.

"There's still a lot of work to do," she added, thinking of the things she wanted to change. The things she hoped to accomplish with her influence in the days ahead.

She knew they had gathered data from the Station. It could be essential to understanding what the Federation had truly been doing over the past decade. And Gran and Lissande were an integral part to that puzzle. There were more of them out there, Avery was sure.

The Federation had tried to weed out the So's as best they could, but there were countless refugees hidden on Earth. She had already spoken with Gran about the possibility. Finding more people like her would give Echo the chance it needed to stand up against the Federation as a true power. This time, they would be ready.

She smiled, tightening her arms around Finn's waist. Whatever happened, he would support her. And the others, too. They were stronger together.

"And I know just where to start."

AVERY'S STORY WILL CONTINUE...

ACKNOWLEDGEMENTS

When you set out to write a book, you don't always think of all the people it will ultimately take to get it to publication. But it really does take a village to help your story see its way through to reality.

I can't thank my editor, Marinda Valenti, enough for her infallible wisdom and attention to detail. She did not, however, edit this acknowledgment, so I apologize to her if she's cringing somewhere in the world.

And to Ashley Sharpe, for catching all those lingering bits that needed attention when I thought I was already at the end. You are not only an amazing editor, but a phenomenal friend. I can't ever say that often enough, nor deeply enough.

My gorgeous cover design was only possible with the brilliant talents of my illustrator, Allie Preswick. Thank you so much for listening to my vision and capturing the essence of Avery in your unique and beautiful style.

To my family, who have endured a lifetime of insane dream retellings and fostered this slightly strange imagination of mine. My brother for space consultations, my dad for constant support, and my mom for all the teamwork and feedback and rereads.

And to my partner and best friend in life and love, Leo. You kept me going with your unstoppable optimism and constant support. I'm just glad you didn't have to lock me in an old castle and throw away the key until it was finished.

J ESSICA LYNN MEDINA has spent the better part of her life sacrificing sleep to devour good stories in one form or another. When she's not writing or reading, she is watching the newest anime or digesting extrapolated theories from her latest fandom. Jessica lives in St. Louis, Missouri with her husband, a lazy black lab, and one quirky hound mix.

CATCH UP WITH JESSICA ONLINE

www.JessicaLynnMedina.com

@medinajlynn

CPSIA information can be obtained
at www.ICGtesting.com
Printed in the USA
LVHW090822120219
607105LV00031B/368/P